即選即用

第二版

銀行英語會話

THE CONVERSATION IN BANKING ENGLISH

楊曜檜 著

五南圖書出版公司 印行

序 言

　　本書是依照筆者在金控、銀行工作的實務經驗而寫成的銀行英文攻略寶典，為筆者另兩本《超實用銀行英語單字》和《即選即用銀行郵局金融英文單字》的姊妹篇著作。《超實用銀行英語單字》和《即選即用銀行郵局金融英文單字》目前為國內最具權威的銀行英文單字學習書籍，前者為方便攜帶的銀行英文單字口袋本，後者為附有音標、例句、搭配用語、銀行日語單字、郵局英文及補充說明的完整版。筆者在此特別感謝臺灣銀行、土地銀行、第一銀行、國泰世華、台新銀行、彰化銀行、臺灣企銀、日盛銀行、台中銀行等銀行的捧場和支持，甚至有整個分行的行員一起團購《超實用銀行英語單字》和《即選即用銀行郵局金融英文單字》這兩本書，讓筆者非常感動。這也顯示出國內銀行行員對銀行工作實務上所用到的英文學習書的熱烈呼求。因此在完成「銀行英文單字」方面的兩本著作後，因應廣大行員和有心學金融英文人士的需求，本人完成了另一本金融／財金英文權威級著作：《即選即用銀行英語會話》，以銀行工作實務上會用到的情境會話為主軸，搭配重要銀行英文實用金句和重要單字補充，是國內最創新、專業的金融英文書籍。特別針對以下對象加以設計編寫：

　　一、在銀行、郵局、信用合作社、農會、漁會等金融機構上班的行員。因工作所需必須掌握實務中常用到的金融英語常用會話及單字，故本書適用作為各大金控、銀行、郵局員工教育訓練的基本教材。

　　二、本書適合作為專科、大學財金、國貿、會計、銀行保險等科系課程的正規教科書或參考書。本書以實務經驗寫成，有助於學生了解行員在銀行工作實務中常用的金融英文情境會話。

三、準備商業／金融英檢或多益的考生。財團法人語言訓練測驗中心（LTTC）於101年推出商業／金融英檢的考試，並預定近期正式舉辦商業／金融英檢供金控、銀行、大學商學院作爲專業金融英文的認證證照，故此書教材內容可供準備金融英檢之用。另多益考試在聽力常聽到的英文對話上，也多採用金融辦公情境，故對有志於商業／金融英檢或多益得高分的考生來說，此書爲極爲可貴的考試準備用書。

四、準備銀行招考的考生。眾所皆知，公股銀行的英文科試題都不容易，除了考一般生活單字外，也往往考一些金融英文單字和閱讀測驗。本書收錄了相當完整的金融英文情境會話，考生可以由看情境會話的方式來學金融英文單字，讓背單字變得更輕鬆。

五、出國旅遊或留學民眾。在國外旅遊或觀光，常需到當地的銀行辦理兌換外幣或是兌現旅支；而留學生更是常需跟國外當地的銀行往來，如辦理開戶或是換匯等。但金融英語是屬較專業英語，一般人也不知道如何用日常生活的英文表達專業的金融英文會話，因此如能掌握本書所介紹的金融英文會話，到了國外就再也不用擔心和當地銀行打交道。

筆者一開始從未想過寫一本銀行英文方面的書籍，但自從筆者去銀行工作後，發現在銀行工作的實務上，用以前在學校所學的一般英文並不夠用，而坊間充斥著過多的升學考試或英檢書籍，卻缺乏由臺灣人自己爲臺灣本國銀行的行員所寫的專業銀行英文學習書。即或是有，也往往缺乏專業和創新，或是不符合臺灣各家銀行的行員需求。因爲即使坊間有少數金融英文的書，卻都是向國外，如歐美或是日本買財經英文的版權，但卻因國情不同以及這些外國人寫的金融英文與國內銀行業和金融機構的法規、風俗和習慣都不相同，對國內金融從事人員來說，這些外國人寫的金融英文並沒有幫助。因此國內金融機構的行員非常缺乏一本由了解臺灣金融業的自己人寫的金融財經英文專書。

　　有在銀行上班的朋友跟我抱怨說：「怎麼臺灣的出版社都沒有出版一本眞正道地的金融英文學習書呢？」因爲他發現有些出版社所出版的商用英文書籍當中，把bank teller誤譯成「銀行出納員」，其實行員在實務工作上的道地講法應該是「銀行櫃員」才對。坊間另有書籍把password envelop翻譯爲聽起來很奇怪的「密碼信封」，但行員在實務工作上的講法應爲「密碼函」才對。更離譜的是，友人還發現，這些坊間粗製濫造的商用英文在裡面說明內容也錯誤百出，例如在介紹「支票帳戶」時，說支票存款帳戶的利息較低，但實際上臺灣的本國銀行所開立的支存戶都是「不計息」的。這項資料在網路上或是各家銀行營業廳讓民眾領取的開戶約定書都有白紙黑字地註明，是臺灣各家銀行的公開揭露資訊，該書的作者和編輯都未花時間來查證資料而導致寫出的說明錯誤百出，因而出現這種不專業、誤導讀者的說明，令人遺憾。正因爲「銀行英文」是「專業英文」，沒有其金融專業背景或是沒有銀行實務工作經驗的人士來編寫的話，　其寫出來的產品在一般行員眼中根本不能閱讀，因爲缺乏專業性和實用性，就像一個從來沒有下水游泳的人所寫出的純理論來教授如何游泳的書一樣。

　　筆者再舉一例，坊間這種外行充內行人所寫的商用英文書籍當中，不少書都大量濫用一句話，就是有客人來銀行開戶時，行員都會問：「Do you want to open a current account or a checking account？（您要開活存戶或是支票帳戶？）」這句話錯在哪裡？

　　首先，current account就是checking account的同義詞，意思完全一樣，都是「支票存款帳戶」之意，只是current account是英式英語，而checking account是美式英語。坊間商用英文書籍把current account誤譯爲「活存戶」是因爲不了解國外和國內銀行服務的差異。其實在歐美國家，支存戶和活儲戶的功能一樣，都可以使用金融卡、臨櫃辦理現金存、提款，只是附加了開支票的功能。因爲歐美支存戶的定義、功能和臺灣的並不相同，因此

有些翻譯人士誤會，往往將current account也譯作「活存戶」。筆者爲什麼知道？因爲有天在銀行上班時，看到一位美國人來我們銀行的ATM取款，但他不太確定ATM螢幕上顯示的選項，就問我應該要選哪一個？我看到ATM螢幕上有「支存帳戶」（checking account）和「活儲帳戶」（savings account）、「信用卡帳戶」（credit card account）讓客戶選擇。我直覺應該就要選「活儲帳戶」（savings account）。但當那位外國人按下ATM上的savings account的選項時，螢幕卻出現「交易失敗」。後來那位外國人說可能選錯了，因爲他在美國的那家銀行根本沒有開「活儲戶」（savings account），而只有開「支存戶」(checking account)，後來改按checking account的選項，ATM就吐鈔了！

筆者覺得很奇怪，他怎麼可以從「支存戶」直接提出現金來？因爲臺灣的支存戶是無法提現的，也沒有發給客戶支存戶專用的金融卡。回家後查閱相關資料，才發現原來美國或歐洲銀行的支存戶和臺灣不一樣，大部分的外國人去銀行開戶都有開立「支存戶」（checking account），卻沒有開「活儲帳戶」（savings account），因爲歐美銀行所開立的「支存戶」就包含了「活儲戶」的功能，像是領錢、提款等，又可以開支票，難怪不需再加開「活儲帳戶」（savings account）了。在臺灣，支存戶是附屬在活儲戶的一個帳戶，你不能只開支存戶而不開活儲戶。這就是接下來要指出：「Do you want to open a current account or a checking account?」的第二個重大錯誤。不少眼尖的行員驚訝地發現，坊間的商用英文書籍或是中國大陸所出版的銀行英文書籍當中，大量出現這種跟現實脫節又悖離國內銀行相關法規的句子來。因爲依據中華民國法令及各家銀行的規定，一般來說，要開支存戶之前，一定要先開活儲戶後，並和銀行往來一段時間，銀行才再視往來狀況後，考慮讓客戶是否可以加開支存戶。舉國泰世華爲例，要開「支存戶」時，除了不能信用不良或是有退票紀錄之外，還必須和銀行有良好的往來，活期存款的三個月以來的平均每日餘額需超過新臺幣金額三十萬元以上才能

申請開立支存戶。而玉山銀行是活存戶的平均六個月內的每日往來餘額需達到三十萬以上才能申請。以下是筆者實際到各家銀行訪查的支票存款帳戶開立的基本條件：

銀行	與銀行活存往來的最低時間	平均每日餘額超過新臺幣金額
中國信託	六個月	三十萬
兆豐商銀	六個月	十　萬
永豐銀行	六個月	十五萬
渣打銀行	六個月	五十萬
玉山銀行	六個月	三十萬
台新銀行	六個月	三十萬
國泰世華	三個月	三十萬

當然，達到支存戶的申請資格並不代表銀行一定會接受開立支存戶。銀行還會先去徵信，去票據交換所等機構查詢公司負責人的信用狀況，並由作業主管視該客戶與銀行往來狀況來決定之。絕非如坊間這些不專業人士所寫出來的情境，「個人戶一開始就可以申請開立支存戶」，行員也絕對不會這樣問。筆者在銀行工作這麼久，還沒有聽過服務臺的行員在自然人一開始進門表明要開戶時，會問客人：「您要開活存戶或是支存戶？」況且，臺灣的本國銀行通常只讓企金戶，也就是公司戶可以申請開立支存戶，除非在特殊條件下，才可能讓一般自然人開支存戶。因此從坊間這些粗製濫造的情境會話就可以看出，這些寫金融英文的編輯或是作者根本沒有在金融業工作的實務經驗才會寫出如此荒誕又悖離現實的內容。另一個坊間商用英文所犯的

共同錯誤，就是編造出不正確的信用卡英文情境。這些錯誤的情境往往是一位外國人來辦信用卡，結果行員問他要辦哪種信用卡。這在有實務工作經驗的行員眼中，是非常地偏離事實和違反銀行內規的。因爲外國人在臺本國銀行辦卡的條件很高。舉某民營銀行爲例，外國人辦理信用卡之規定，要滿足下列的條件：

　　一、需爲非高風險行業之從業人士及年薪達新臺幣一百五十萬元以上。

　　二、並應有本國籍人士爲連帶保證人，而且幫忙作保的中華民國本國人士的年薪也需要高達新臺幣一百五十萬元以上。

　　因此哪有可能非中華民國本國人士的外國人一進入銀行大廳，行員就隨便讓他辦卡，完全不顧授信風險？坊間其他的財經英文書籍所介紹到外國人來臺灣銀行辦卡的設計對話內容往往是與事實不符的。這樣的內容不但有誤導讀者之嫌更是非常不專業。友人再接著向我抱怨，坊間有些書籍打著最新「財經英文」或「金融英文」的名義，雖然出版日期是印著近幾年出版，但翻開內容卻是老舊過時，與目前狀況脫節。例如說，裡面談外匯的部分還是在講法國法郎、德國馬克等不流通貨幣，這就當場被抓包了！因爲早在西元2002年，歐元就已正式成爲歐盟國家的法幣，怎麼可能到現在法國還在用法國法郎呢？更離譜的是，坊間有些過時的金融英文書籍裡面還在談什麼「信匯」！現在有哪家國內銀行在匯出匯款時還讓客人可以辦「信匯」的？信匯早就過時了！國內銀行業務目前只剩票匯和電匯（或SWIFT），另有西聯匯款和VISA Money Transfer（易匯通）等，早已沒有信匯的業務了。反而最近在銀行業很夯的「悠遊聯名卡」、「悠遊debit卡」、「行動銀行」或「行動支付」的介紹和說明在這些號稱最新版的財經英文書籍當中卻隻字未提。聽完友人對市面上金融英文書籍內容的抱怨，筆者深感國內極需一本眞正有銀行實務工作經驗的人所寫、具有「專業」和「創新」這兩個重要元

素、眞正能滿足國內行員需求所寫的銀行英文學習書。

　　本書另一個優點是採用實用又道地口語，讓行員跟外國人溝通無障礙，例如說行員常碰到外國觀光客來銀行換匯，通常行員都會問客人一句話，就是「您要哪種面額的呢？」一般商用英文書籍可能會寫道，可以說：「In what denominations would you like?」但其實在道地的美語會話中，「你要哪種面額的？」不會用到這麼難的句子和單字，道地的美國人講的其實很簡單，就是「How do you want it?」上面句子的it 就是指「money」之意。或更禮貌一點的：「How would you like your money?」再來，公司的「大小章」怎麼翻譯？開戶時，如果剛好是一個外國人要開公司戶，而你要跟他說要帶公司的大小章，要怎麼用英語表達？在本書的情境對話中，就會介紹到「公司大小章」的英文就是the company seal and the company's licensing representative's Chinese seal, both of which are authorized by the Ministry of Economic Affairs. 筆者會這樣翻是先把「公司大小章」給拆開來翻的。法人（也就是公司）的「名稱章」，稱爲「大章」，而公司負責人名字的印章稱爲「小章」。所以我先翻「公司大章」：the company seal 就是公司大章，也可以譯作the corporate seal。當然seal也可以用stamp代替，所以也可以講the company stamp。然後，公司的小章譯爲the company's licensing representative's Chinese seal，因爲「公司的負責人」譯作the company's licensing representative 。再來個人「印章」的英文是personal Chinese seal。所以公司的小章就是the company's licensing representative's (Chinese) seal。如果要強調公司要用在經濟部已登記的大小章才行的話，可以說「公司大小章」are authorized by the Ministry of Economic Affairs。也因此，《即選即用銀行英語會話》從情境會話中教導讀者很多實用的銀行英文單字，幫助讀者克服語言障礙，讓行員碰到外國人時也能輕鬆應對。

坊間一般的金融英文以「經濟學理論」爲主，並沒有介紹到銀行實務工作會用到的英文，而本書正以實務銀行爲主要內容。舉例來說，《即選即用銀行英語會話》在裡面就有教行員怎麼說「如果您把定存解約，您在利息上會有所損失。存期未滿一個月，將不計息。超過一個月的，利息將以實際存期打八折計算。」這句在銀行工作上常用到的話。筆者將它翻成道地的英文，可以說成If you cancel the time deposit before the maturity date, you will suffer a loss in interest. For deposits cancelled within one month, the bank will not pay any interest. For those cancelled after one month, the interest payable on such deposit shall be calculated at a rate of 80% of the actual deposit tenors. 以上舉的一些道地的美語講法，正是本書講究「專業」的「創新」特色之一。「專業」和「創新」正是本書的兩大特色。是繼筆者的上一本書《即選即用銀行郵局金融英文單字》之後，另一本極具「創新」的著作。

當《即選即用銀行郵局金融英文單字》上市時，有行員看到這本書的內容後說：「我在銀行工作了二十年，終於見到一本我要的銀行英文學習書了！」對這位行員的反應，筆者不意外，因爲《即選即用銀行郵局金融英文單字》這本書是一本由正港臺灣人寫的眞正創新之作，非坊間一般財經英文書籍可以比擬。這就像蘋果前執行長賈伯斯領導下的團隊成功研發出iPhone，搭配iTune和Apple app，成功整合出吸引人的軟硬體，而改變了世界使用手機的生態和習慣，超越了傳統只有一般功能的手機。賈伯斯之所以能夠成功，親近蘋果人士分析說，原因在於賈伯斯是爲自己設計出迷人又創新的產品，只製造自己也願意親自使用的產品，並且許多分析師都認爲iPhone的成功就是靠「創新」來幫助客戶達成夢想。因爲賈伯斯相信，賣夢想比賣產品更加地重要！這也正是筆者開創出這套銀行英文教材的信念：「幫助行員實現學好在銀行工作上所用到的實務英文的夢想！」。因此很多行員都認爲，《即選即用銀行郵局金融英文單字》正是臺灣出版界的iPhone！是具有改變既有市場的創新產品！因爲這本書同樣融入了當年賈伯

斯「創新」的精神和元素，顛覆了傳統單字書僅附上單字詞條、例句的內容，本書採用了銀行combo卡的概念，正如combo卡同時融合了提款卡、轉帳卡和信用卡的功能一樣，融入多項創新元素。

《即選即用銀行郵局金融英文單字》不單單只附上英文單字的詞條、音標、例句、英文同義字、英文搭配用語等，更大的特點是網羅了筆者多年來對於臺灣各家銀行研究的心得和報告以及對於各家銀行所推出的金融服務和產品的介紹。也就是說，《即選即用銀行郵局金融英文單字》不只是一本英文單字學習書，實質上也是一本介紹臺灣各家銀行服務發展概況的「財經專書」。例如在paperless account（無摺戶）這個詞條底下，就介紹了目前有推出無摺戶，也就是自動戶帳戶的各家銀行的產品內容，包括國泰世華、永豐銀行、渣打銀行和台北富邦銀行的無摺戶都有做詳實、客觀的介紹和說明，並以圖表的方式呈現，讓讀者一目瞭然。另外在介紹joint account（聯名戶）時，也有特別指出國內有哪些銀行允許客戶開立聯名戶，如聯邦銀行和新光銀行等目前就有「聯名戶」業務。

再來，雖然名為「單字」書，但筆者參照第一線工作的行員意見，在單字書中加入「每日一句」，共三百六十五句行員常用的必背銀行英文實用金句，並獨家收錄臺灣各家銀行的免付費電話，方便民眾查詢，重新定義和顛覆了民眾對於傳統英文單字學習書的認知。更貼心的是，筆者因為有實際在銀行工作的經驗，知道不少日本人來銀行辦事時，由於語言的差異，往往用英文溝通也很難讓日本人理解，因此在《即選即用銀行郵局金融英文單字》還收錄不少「銀行日語」重點單字，當碰到日本人時，可以用筆談寫漢字的方式讓行員和日本客人都能彼此了解。舉一個例子，之前在某銀行工作，有位日本人來換外幣現鈔，筆者任職的銀行換外幣現鈔一定會收「手續費」。「手續費」的英文是service charge或是handling fee都可以，也可以用bank commission。問題是，那位日本人聽不懂什麼是service charge或

是handling fee，但行員光是講money又沒有辦法表達「手續費」之意，這時候就不斷跟日本人比手畫腳個老半天，後來連作業主管都出動了，結果仍是一樣。日本人還是不懂為什麼銀行要跟他額外收一筆錢。筆者在旁邊看了很久，最後親自出馬，直接寫漢字給那位日本人看「手數料：100元」。他看了筆者寫的紙條就懂了！所以筆者才會在《即選即用銀行郵局金融英文單字》裡面收錄許多重要的銀行日語漢字，就是要應付行員在實務中碰到的各式各樣問題。

因此，《即選即用銀行郵局金融英文單字》將專業的財經英文單字、實用銀行句型和金融實務說明融合為一。既是金融英文單字和句型學習書，也是介紹臺灣各家銀行業務的財經書籍，是臺灣出版界最具創新力的產品之一，也難怪一上市就獲得臺灣各家銀行行員一致的好評。正如賈伯斯相信「產品創新是差異性上的競爭」，《即選即用銀行郵局金融英文單字》也因「創新」而改變了英文學習書籍的市場。這讓筆者想到之前在《商業周刊》介紹的一篇文章，說國外有一個年輕人，叫作伍德曼（Nick Woodman），他製作了一種在運動時也能穿戴的相機和攝影機，其他的相機大廠雖然財大氣粗，卻都沒有想到這個獨特的創新點子，結果伍德曼發揮「創新」做出了在衝浪也能拍照攝影的相機，最後成功搶占運動人士的相機市場，甚至連臺灣巨富郭台銘都拿出數十億元投資他的公司GoPro。筆者之前所發想的《超實用銀行英語單字》和《即選即用銀行郵局金融英文單字》也是和伍德曼所打造的運動專用相機一樣，其實很多大出版社以前都有機會發想出專門介紹銀行英文的專業書籍，可惜沒有出版社願意像筆者一樣不計算個人報酬、親身投入四、五年的時間實際查訪和研究臺灣二十多家銀行，並以自身具有在金控工作的實務經驗而得以發想出真正專業又創新的銀行英文學習書。正如同蘋果前執行長賈伯斯說過的一句話：「創新往往是過去經驗締結的結果，但假如你自身的經驗和大家都沒有什麼兩樣，就不可能朝向不同的方向邁進。」筆者對賈伯斯的這句智慧語錄相當認同，正因為筆者不同

於一般英文語言書作家編輯，有實際在金控和銀行工作的實務經驗，才能發想出《超實用銀行英語單字》和《即選即用銀行郵局金融英文單字》這兩本made in Taiwan的創新產品出來。

不過，在這兩本銀行英語單字書出版後，有不少行員向筆者反應，看了我寫的銀行英文單字之後，雖然可以和外國人溝通，但有時對於表達出句意完整的英文句子還是有困難。也因此，筆者再度費心費力成功地編寫出專為行員寫的《即選即用銀行英語會話》這本以「情境會話」和「重要句型」為主軸的創新著作出來。不同於坊間閉門造車的商用英文會話，往往只空有理論、卻不實際；本書的情境會話是依照筆者實務的銀行工作經驗和四、五年的二十幾家銀行真實走訪的調查所編寫而成，把實際在銀行所聽到的、看到的、行員說過的真實對話搜集、組織、整理並加以編寫成道地的銀行英文情境會話。就像筆者前面提過的，一般坊間的金融英文書籍，竟然亂寫行員一開戶就問客戶要不要開checking account（支存戶）這種悖離常情的句子，非常不道地也不專業。本書的情境會話以在臺灣各家銀行的法規和真實情況為依歸，這就是本書的創新和專業所在。

除了內容創新，《即選即用銀行英語會話》在主題選材上也創新。坊間的金融英文大都只著重在提款、存款、支票、信用卡、貸款和外匯等主題而已，接下來就拿不出新梗了。筆者依照自身在銀行工作實務經驗，特別收錄了「反詐騙」這創新主題，裡面並收錄行員在「關懷提問」常用到的英文對話和實用金句。另外，為滿足臺灣本國銀行的業務需要，本書在主題上，還收錄了最夯的「無摺戶」、「警示戶」、「靜止戶」、「祕密戶」、「黃金存摺」等主題，尤其最近不少銀行都跟進臺灣銀行開辦「黃金存摺」的業務，為行員在實務上常常會接觸到的工作內容。也因此，本書也將此重要主題收錄於內。再來隨著科技的進步，臺灣各家銀行也相繼推出感應式信用卡、網路銀行、行動銀行和OTP等銀行最新的業務或產品。本書將這些業務

內容一併收錄，全部都網羅在本書中。故在主題上，本書不但發揮了「創新力」更遙遙領先市場，而能滿足國內銀行行員對學習實務上會用到的銀行英文的需求。正如臉書創辦人馬克・佐伯格（Mark Zuckerberg）的理念，他曾說創辦Facebook的原因之一是為了「解決最重要的問題，大部分的企業這點都做得不成功而浪費了不少時間。」本人所著作的銀行英文三部曲《超實用銀行英語單字》、《即選即用銀行郵局金融英文單字》和這本《即選即用銀行英語會話》正是為了幫助行員解決在工作上所碰到的溝通問題，進而滿足行員的需求創造雙贏的局面。國內早期出版的財經英文著作大都乏人問津，最主要的原因，就是忽視「消費者只會為自己的需求買單」這事實，如果一本金融英文書的內容只著重理論，卻無法解決銀行行員在實務工作上所碰到的工作問題的話，是沒有半點用處的，對消費者沒有好處的產品，當然乏人問津。

　　《即選即用銀行英語會話》主打的正是「實務工作會用到的銀行英文」。舉例來說，筆者在銀行服務期間，常有行員問筆者，如果辦完交易，要跟外國人說「您的這筆交易已登摺好了」怎麼用英語講？其實行員主要想問的是「這筆交易」的「這筆」怎麼說？其實，「這筆」不用翻出來。「您的這筆交易已登摺在您的本子裡了。」可以簡單說成This transaction is recorded in your passbook. 如果是多筆的交易，就可以說：The transactions are recorded in your passbook.如果要指出是什麼交易，如存款或提款或轉帳，則可以說：The withdrawal is recorded in your passbook.（這筆提款已登摺在您的本子裡了。）如果是存款交易的話，可以說：The deposit is recorded in your passbook.（這筆存款已登摺在您的本子裡了。）如果是匯款交易的話，則可以講：The transfer is recorded in your passbook.（這筆轉帳已登摺在您的本子裡了。）另外，行員在開戶時常需要順便幫客戶開通網銀，但在介紹網銀時，有些簡單的中文卻不知道英文該怎麼說？像是網銀的密碼有「區別英文字母的大小寫」怎麼用英語說？像是密碼我們設定為dog的話，

實際輸入時，就不能輸入Dog，因為密碼有分大小寫。因此，英文的「大寫」、「小寫」字母怎麼說呢？看似簡單的中文，但如果沒有特別學習，也不知道。其實，「大寫字母」就說 uppercase 或拼作upper-case。而小寫字母就是 lowercase 或 lower-case。因此行員如果要對客戶說「請注意要區別大小寫」，可以說：Please carefully distinguish uppercase from lowercase, please. 上面的動詞distinguish是「區別」之意。如果覺得上面那句話太難，也可以說：Please remember the password is case-sensitive.（記得密碼有分大小寫。）上面的case-sensitive就是「有區別大小寫字母」的意思。用一個字就可以表達清楚。如果要跟對方講網銀密碼至少六位數，但不超過十二位數，也可以補充這麼說：Your password must be at least six but not more than twelve characters. Your password is case-sensitive.（您的密碼必須至少六位數，但不超過十二位數。您的密碼有分大小寫。）上面這句話也可以換句話說成：Your password is case-sensitive and must be a minimum of eight to twelve (8-12) characters或是這樣講：Your password must be between six and twelve characters long. 行員也可以補充說，銀行建議的密碼可以包含字母和數字這樣比較不容易被猜到密碼，而這句話的英文可以這樣表達：We recommend that your password consist of both letters and numbers so that other users cannot easily guess it.（我們建議您的密碼要包含字母和數字這樣別人就無法輕易猜到它。）如果是網銀規定一定要包含至少一個英文字母或一個數字時，則可以這樣說：Your password must contain at least one alphabetical character or one number. 以上是筆者在銀行服務期間，教導同仁辦理網路銀行業務會用到的英文的一、兩個實例。

從以上例子就可以看出，筆者是以實際在銀行協助同仁的銀行英文經驗來編寫《即選即用銀行英語會話》此書，並在介紹銀行內容的專業知識上，花了約四年左右實際走訪各家銀行來了解最新最真的業務和產品。把銀行相關的細節知識也掌握得一清二楚，舉例來說，跟實體ATM相比，網路

ATM的限制有什麼？筆者立刻就能回答因為沒有金庫，所以不能領錢外，也無法用網路ATM變更密碼，另外也無法在國外使用網路ATM。另外，很多人搞不多銀行的ATM到底一天最多可以領多少錢，筆者依照實際調查發現，並沒有一個通用的固定金額，整理如下：

每日限額	銀行名稱
15-30萬	HSBC 卓越理財VISA卡：30萬 HSBC 運籌理財VISA卡：20萬 HSBC 一般客戶VISA卡／金融卡：15萬
30萬	花旗銀行、澳盛銀行（澳盛跨行只有10萬）
20萬	凱基銀行、渣打商銀
15萬	臺灣銀行、玉山銀、台新銀、台北富邦、彰銀、合作金庫、大眾銀、台中銀、京城銀、華泰銀、元大銀行
12萬	兆豐銀行、永豐銀、中信銀、土地銀行、新光銀、陽信銀、安泰銀、三信商銀
10萬	台企銀、第一銀、華南銀、國泰世華、聯邦銀、星展銀、高雄銀、國泰世華銀行、板信銀、農業金庫、上海銀、日盛銀行、郵局
9萬	瑞興銀行（原大台北銀行）

在本書中，筆者將很多銀行知識融入情境會話中，以道地的英文來介紹臺灣各家銀行的服務概況。舉各家銀行的ATM通路為例，中國信託在統一超商有四千多臺的ATM，並且其中的八百臺左右是可以存款的二合一存

提款機。目前臺灣本島的統一超商是中國信託的ATM，但離島的金門、馬祖、澎湖的統一超商裡面的ATM是和玉山銀行、土地銀行和當地的信用合作社或農會合作。全家便利超商的ATM則主要以台新銀行為主。另一超商萊爾富的ATM則跟永豐銀行、聯邦銀行、國泰世華銀行、郵局、上海商業銀行和公股老行庫華南銀行合作，其中永豐銀和聯邦銀行的ATM在萊爾富占了最多分店。有設ATM的OK便利商店比較少，大部分都是新光銀行為主，再來就是台新銀行的ATM。捷運的部分，國泰世華占了臺北捷運的ATM通路，而聯邦銀行占了高雄捷運的ATM通路。但在超商ATM已飽和的狀況下，很多銀行轉往速食店設ATM，例如台北富邦曾經與麥當勞合作過，後來因為經濟效應不大已撤掉。最近筆者去摩斯漢堡時，也驚訝地發現渣打銀行的ATM設置在裡面。經過調查，才得知目前大臺北地區十七家的摩斯漢堡分店都已和渣打銀行合作。但渣打在中南部則還沒有設點。不止如此，之前筆者去美麗華看電影，結果發現美麗華裡面也有渣打銀行的ATM。可見渣打也開始搶ATM的通路，甚至連松山機場也成功設了自家的ATM。筆者將一些銀行知識的小細節都摸得一清二楚，就是要追求第一，成就卓越，寫出最好最實用最頂尖的金融財經英語專書，以滿足國內行員的迫切需求。

最後，因各金控、銀行等金融機構的相關法令、規定或相關活動經常變更、修改，故本書介紹的各銀行以及產品內容如與各銀行、金融機構的公開揭露資訊有不一致之處，請依各銀行、金融機構的公布資料為準。本書雖經多次編輯校對，但仍恐有疏失之處，尚祈各界前輩先進不吝指正。本人除了要感謝神和家人以及五南文化的支持之外，也特別要感謝游學弟的幫助。在搜集資料上，本人也很感謝臺灣銀行和國泰世華所提供的協助，才得以讓本書完成。

目　錄

開戶（開個人戶）
Opening A Personal Account

Bank teller : Hello, may I help you?

行　　　員：嗨，我可以幫您嗎？

Customer : I would like to open an account with your bank.

客　　　戶：我想要在您們銀行開戶。

Bank teller : Do you live nearby?

行　　　員：您住附近嗎？

Customer : Yes, I live nearby. Why do you ask this question?

客　　　戶：對，我住附近。為什麼問這個問題？

Bank teller : To fight against fraud, the bank has the responsibility to prevent accounts from being used as dummy accounts. Therefore, **according to the regulations, if you want to open an account, you must go to the bank where your household registration is located**. Don't tell me that because you admire our bank, you have to come a long way to our bank to open an account. We won't buy it.

行　　　員：為了防詐騙，銀行有責任防止帳戶被用作人頭戶。因此，**根據規定，如您想要開戶，您必須去您戶籍地所在的銀行**。不要說因為您仰慕我們的銀行，所以大老遠跑來開戶。我們不會相信的。

Customer : So what you mean is if I live in Shilin District, I cannot go to the banks in Beitou district to open an account.

1

客　　戶：所以您指的是，如果我住在士林區，我就不能到北投區的銀行開
　　　　　戶囉。

Bank teller：Yes, exactly. Now all the banks follow this rule. So if you do not
　　　　　live nearby, we must decline your request of opening an account
　　　　　with our bank.

行　　員：沒錯。所有的銀行都遵守此規定。所以您要是不住這附近，我們
　　　　　必須拒絕您在本行開戶的要求。

Customer：I see.

客　　戶：我明白了。

Bank teller：Have you opened other bank accounts within three months?

行　　員：您在三個月之內有在其他銀行開戶嗎？

Customer：No. Why did you ask?

客　　戶：沒有，為什麼問這個？

Bank teller：**Our bank won't allow you to open an account here if you have
　　　　　opened other accounts with other banks within three months**
　　　　　because we will be justified to suspect you may be a dummy ac-
　　　　　count holder; otherwise, generally speaking, you won't need to
　　　　　open so many accounts in such a short time. Now please take a
　　　　　number ticket and wait until your number is called by the service
　　　　　counter.

行　　員：**如果您在三個月內有到其他銀行開戶的話，我們銀行就不讓您開
　　　　　戶。**因為我們將合理懷疑您可能是人頭戶。不然一般來說，您沒
　　　　　有短時間大量開戶的需求。現在，請您抽一張號碼牌並等服務臺
　　　　　叫您的號。

(After a few minutes, the customer's number is called.)

（過了幾分鐘，客戶的號碼被叫號。）

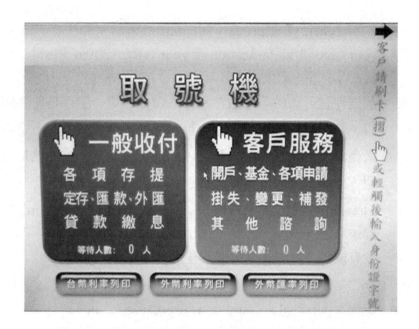

Bank teller : Please go to the service counter NO. 6.

行　　　員：請到六號服務臺。

Bank teller : Hello, what kind of transactions would you like to conduct?

行　　　員：嗨，您想辦什麼？

Customer : I would like to open an account.

客　　　戶：我想要開戶。

Bank teller : No problem. **Please give me your two forms of ID.**

行　　　員：沒問題。**請給我您的雙證件。**

Customer : What do you mean by "two forms of ID"?

客　　　戶：您說的「雙證件」是什麼意思？

Bank teller : Two forms of ID involve your primary identification and secondary identification. The primary identification is your national ID card. The secondary identification can be your health IC card or driver's license. If you are not a citizen of Republic of China, Taiwan, but a foreigner, your primary identification is your valid passport and your second identification is your **ARC (Alien Resident Certificate)** or your APRC.

行　　員：雙證件包含您的第一證件和第二證件。第一證件是您的國民身分證。第二證件可以是您的健保卡或是駕照。如果您不是中華民國（臺灣）的國民而是外籍人士的話，您的第一證件就是有效的護照，而第二證件是居留證或是永久居留證。

Customer : I have my national ID card as well as my health IC card. Here you are.

客　　戶：我有國民身分證和健保卡。在這裡。

Bank teller : OK. What kind of account do you want to open? Do you want to open a personal account or a corporate account?

行　　員：好。您想要開什麼戶頭？您要開個人戶還是公司戶？

Customer : I would like to open a personal account. Can I choose a checking account?

客　　戶：我想要開個人戶。我可以選擇支存戶嗎？

Bank teller : In Taiwan, you cannot just open a **checking account** in the beginning if you have not had any relationship with our bank before. You must open a **personal demand savings account** first. And if your average balance is over three hundred thousand NT dollars in your demand savings account for six months in a row, then you may apply for a checking account. Besides, Taiwanese banks usually only allow corporate account holders to apply for checking accounts. I know in the US or Europe you don't have to open a demand savings account first. You can directly open a checking account from the start because a checking account in the US already contains the features of a savings account. In Taiwan, on the contrary, a checking account is just affiliated with a savings account. You cannot open a checking account without opening a savings account first. I think this is one difference between the banks of Taiwan and those of other countries.

行　　員 ：在臺灣，如您之前從來沒有和我們銀行往來的話，您無法一開始就開支存戶。您必須先開活儲戶。如果您的活儲戶連續六個月的平均餘額都超過三十萬的話，您才可以申請開支存戶。況且，臺灣的銀行通常只允許公司戶申辦支存戶。我知道在美國或歐洲您不必先開一個活儲戶，您可以一開始就直接開支存戶，因為在美國的支票存款帳戶已經內含了活儲戶的功能。在臺灣則相反，支存戶是附屬在活儲戶底下的。您無法只開支存戶而沒有先開活儲戶。我認為這是臺灣的銀行和其他國家銀行之間的差異。

Customer ： All right. Then I choose to just open a personal demand savings account.

客　　戶 ：好吧，那我要選擇開活儲戶。

Bank teller ： OK. Do you want to apply for a **general service account**?

行　　員 ：好的，您想要申辦「綜合存款帳戶」嗎？

Customer ： What is a general service account? I have never heard of that before.

客　　戶 ：什麼是「綜合存款帳戶」？我從沒聽過耶。

Bank teller ： A general service account is also known as an all-in-one account or a composite deposit account. This type of account combines a demand savings account and a time deposit account. It also carries the function of time deposit pledge. If you choose a composite deposit account, you don't have to open a physical CD with our bank. We can help you open a CD just inside your passbook. Does it sound great?

行　　員：綜合存款帳戶也叫作綜存戶。這種戶頭包含了活儲戶和定存戶。它也有定存質借功能。如果您要開綜存戶，您不必開實體的定存單。我們可以把定存做在您的存薄裡。聽起來有沒有很棒啊？

Customer : Yes. It sounds really convenient. I've decided to open the general service account.

客　　戶：有啊。聽起來很方便耶。我決定開綜存戶好了。

Bank teller : Do you want to open a **foreign exchange account** as well? Our bank's foreign exchange account is a **multi-currency passbook**, which gives you the option of having a single or combination of foreign currency accounts under a single account number. I know that Chang Hwa Commercial Bank's foreign exchange account is not a multi-currency account. If their customers want to buy a new foreign currency, they need to go to Chang Hwa Commercial Bank to open a new currency account. On the other hand, our bank's foreign exchange account is a multi-currency general service account. If you want to buy a new foreign currency, you don't have to go to the bank. You can directly buy the new foreign currency via online banking or over the bank counter.

行　　員：您想加開外幣戶嗎？我們銀行的外幣戶是多幣別存摺，提供您在單一帳號下可以買單一或是多種組合的外幣。我知道彰化銀行的外幣戶不是多幣別的外幣戶。如果他們的客戶想要買新的外幣的話，還需要跑到彰銀去加開新的外幣帳戶。另一方面，我們的外幣戶是多幣別綜合外幣戶。如果您想要買進新的外幣，您不必跑到銀行，您可以直接透過網銀或是臨櫃買進新的外幣。

Customer : That's good. I know what you are talking about. I have a Chang

Hwa Commercial Bank's foreign exchange account. Last time I wanted to buy Renminbi, the bank teller told me that I had to go to the bank in person to open a Renminbi account because my foreign exchange account did not have that foreign currency yet. Therefore, I had to give the teller my two forms of ID and my original personal Chinese seal to open a new currency account. It is so inconvenient for customers. I also hear that First Bank has offered a compound savings account, which is in New Tawan dollars and Forex. In other words, First Bank's compound savings account combines a personal demand savings account with a foreign exchange account together in a single passbook.

客　　戶：這真好。我了解您所說的。我有彰銀的外幣戶。上次我想要買人民幣時，行員跟我說要我親自跑到銀行來加開人民幣帳戶，因為我的外幣戶還沒有加開過這個幣別。所以，我還要再給行員我的雙證件和印章才能加開新的幣別。這對客戶來說真不方便！我也聽說過第一銀行提供一個臺外幣綜合帳戶。換句話說，第一銀行的綜合帳戶在單一的存摺上結合了個人活儲戶和外幣帳戶。

Bank teller ： I see. Different banks have different types of bank accounts. I also know Bank of Taiwan have an "I-Smart money manangement account", which allows BOT's customers to buy mutual funds or stocks because this "I-Smart money manangement account" includes a trust account. Now please fill out these forms. You must provide the following information, such as your name, your ID number, your birthday, your nationality, your marital status, your telephone number, your cell phone number, your fax number, your registered address, your correspondence address, your educational background, your annual salary, and the name of a person to contact. **In a word, be sure to complete all the fields marked with a check mark.**

行　　　員： 我知道。不同銀行有不同的銀行帳戶。我還知道臺灣銀行有推出「I-Smart綜合理財帳戶」，可以讓臺銀的客戶買基金或是股票，因爲這個「I-Smart綜合理財帳戶」包含了信託基金戶。現在請填寫這些申請書。您必須提供下列資料，像是您的姓名、身分證字號、您的出生日期、您的國籍、您的婚姻狀況、您的電話號碼、手機號碼、傳眞機號碼、戶籍地址、通訊地址、教育程度、年收入和聯絡人姓名。**簡單說，就是把所有打勾的地方都填好。**

Customer： OK.

客　　　戶： 好的。

Bank teller： How would you want your original specimen signature and seal in the bank? Signature or Chinese seal?

行　　　員： 您想要怎麼設原留印鑑？簽名或是蓋章？

Customer： I would choose both the signature and Chinese seal together as my original specimen signature and seal.

客　　　戶： 我想要簽名加蓋章作爲我的原留印鑑。

Bank teller： Why? This way, if you are confined to bed or busy, your family members will not be able to conduct transactions for you because they cannot sign your name on your behalf.

行　　　員： 爲什麼？如果您臥病在床或是很忙的時候，您的家人就不能替您來銀行辦事，因爲他無法代替您簽名。

Customer： I know. But I have heard many family members stole their parents' Chinese seal to withdraw all their money from their account. That is too terrible. You can never be too careful. After all, I know the bank only acknowledges a depositor's specimen seal instead of acknowledging the depositor. If my passbook and my personal Chinese seal are lost and a bad guy gets them, he can use my passbook as well as my personal seal to withdraw all my money.

客　　　戶：我知道啊。但我聽過許多家人偷了他們父母的印章把他們的戶頭提領一空。這太可怕了！您必須小心。畢竟，我知道銀行只認章不認人。如果我的存摺和印章丟了而被壞人撿到，他可以用我的存摺和印章把我的戶頭提領一空。

Bank teller : I see your point. Yes, you are right. If someone bears your personal seal and it matches the original specimen signature and seal in the bank's files, he can use it to withdraw your money. That is why when you find your bank book or your personal seal is lost, you should immediately report it lost to the bank to protect your rights. OK. The next time you go to bank to withdraw your money, you must put your signature and your personal Chinese seal on the withdrawal slip to conduct the transaction. **By the way, our bank requires our customers to make a first deposit of at least 1,000 NT dollars into the account when opening an account.** Do you have at least 1,000 NT dollars with you?

行　　　員：我了解了。對，您說得沒錯。如果有人持有您的私章，和在銀行的原留印鑑相符的話，他可以用來提領您戶頭的錢。這就是為什麼當您的存摺或私章不見時，您要立刻向銀行掛失以保障您的權益。好，下次您去銀行提領錢時，您必須在提款條上用簽名加蓋章來辦交易。**順便一提，我們銀行要求客戶首次開戶至少要存一千元。**您有帶一千元嗎？

Customer : Here you are. I heard that Chinatrust requires their customers to make an initial deposit of at least 10,000 NT dollars to open an account, and E. Sun Bank requires at least 5,000 NT dollars to open an account.

客　　戶：給您。我聽說中國信託要求客人第一次開戶時至少要存一萬元，而玉山銀行要求開戶時至少存五千元。

Bank teller : Yes, I also know that. Different banks have different rules. Most local banks in Taiwan require their customers to make a minimum deposit of 1,000 NT dollars when opening a demand savings account currently although Cosmos Bank only requires an initial deposit of 500 NT dollars to open a bank account now. But in the old times, most banks only required their customers to make a minimum deposit of 100 NT dollars to open a demand savings account. The reason the banks have raised the amount to open an account from a minimum deposit of 100 NT dollars to 1,000 NT dollars is that many people open an account and then sell their bank accounts to scam gangs. To prevent dummy accounts and to fight against fraud, the local banks raised the amount to open an account. From then on, most local banks started to require their customers to make an initial deposit of at least 1000 NT dollars to open a savings account. Some banks, such as Sinopac, might require their customers to make an initial deposit of at least 5,000 NT dollars to open a savings account if they suspect you might be a dummy account holder. Some local branches of foreign banks and Mainland Chinese banks even require at least three million NT dollars to open an account. They only provide services for the wealthy.

行　　員：是的。我也聽說了。不同的銀行有不同的規定。近期在臺灣大部分的銀行要求他們客戶在開活儲戶時至少存一千元，雖然萬泰銀行要求存五百元就可開戶。但在以前，大部分的銀行只要求開活

儲戶至少存一百元就好。銀行從一百到要一千元拉高開戶門檻的原因是很多人開戶就把他們的戶頭賣給詐騙集團。爲了防止人頭戶和防詐騙，本地銀行就把開戶門檻拉高。從那時起，大部分的本地銀行就開始要求客人開戶時至少要存一千元。有些銀行，像是永豐銀行，如果他們懷疑您可能是人頭戶的話，或許會要求客人開戶至少要存五千元。有些外商銀或是中國在臺的分行甚至要求至少要三百萬才能開戶。他們只對有錢人提供服務。

Customer : Wow! Three million NT dollars! I wish I had so much money. By the way, does your bank's time deposit offer a pledge?

客　　　戶：哇！三百萬！我希望我有這麼多錢。順便一提，您們提供定存質借嗎？

Bank teller : Yes, you can choose to activate the time deposit pledge function. In addition, you must sign your name on the authorization agreement of the Personal Information Protection Law. You have to put your signature on the letter of authorization to agree that the Bank may from time to time, for the purposes of its operation, management, business development, credit checking, providing and marketing of financial products and services, data processing, preventing money laundering or fraud, collect, process, use and transmit any of the Customer's Information to the Joint Credit Information Center, Small and Medium Enterprise Credit Guarantee Fund, Financial Information Service Corporation, Taiwan Clearing House, National Credit Card Center and other corresponding financial institutions, credit agencies, or government agencies to store and process your personal information.

行　　　員：有啊。您可以選擇啓用定存質借功能。此外，您必須在個資法授

權書上簽名。您必須在授權書上簽名來同意銀行得隨時基於營運、管理、擴展業務、徵信、提供及行銷金融商品及服務、資料處理、防制洗錢或詐騙，於必要範圍內蒐集、處理、利用及傳遞任何關於客戶的資料給財團法人聯合徵信中心、財團法人中小企業信用保證基金、財金資訊股份有限公司、臺灣票據交換所、財團法人聯合信用卡中心以及其他相關金融機構、徵信部門或政府機關，以便儲存及處理您的個資。

Customer : OK.

客　　戶：好的。

Bank teller : Do you agree that our bank can use your basic information, including your name, birthday, ID number, phone number, address as well as your account information for the purpose of **cross-selling**?

行　　員：您同意我們銀行使用您的基本資料，包括姓名、出生日期、身分證字號、電話號碼、地址和帳戶資料作為共同行銷之用嗎？

Customer : No. I don't want to be bothered by sales calls.

客　　戶：不行。我不想要被推銷電話打擾。

Bank teller : OK. Would you like to apply for an ATM card?

行　　員：好的。您想要辦提款卡嗎？

Customer : Sure.

客　　戶：當然。

Bank teller : **Would you want your ATM card to have the functionality of international withdrawal?**

行　　員：**您想要您的提款卡有國際提領的功能嗎？**

Customer : Do you mean if I activate the functionality of international withdrawal, I can withdraw money at local ATMs in foreign countries?

客　　戶：您是說，如果我啟用國際提領的功能，我就可以在國外的自動櫃

　　　　　　　員機提款了嗎？

Bank teller : That's right. And **would you like to activate the functionality of transferring funds to a non-designated account number for your ATM card?**

行　　　員：沒錯。**您想要您的金融卡啓用非約轉功能嗎？**

Customer : What do you mean by that?

客　　　戶：您說的是什麼意思？

Bank teller : That means, if you activate the functionality of transferring funds to a non-designated account number for your ATM card, you can use your ATM card to transfer up to 30,000 NT dollars via an ATM per day. If you do not want this function, your ATM card will not be able to make any transfer.

行　　　員：我是說，如果您的金融卡啓用非約轉功能，您就可以在ATM（自動櫃員機）用金融卡一天最多轉三萬元。如果您不想要此功能，您的金融卡就沒辦法轉帳。

Customer : Well, I see. I want my ATM card to have the functionality of transferring funds to a non-designated account number.

客　　　戶：嗯。我了解了。我想要我的金融卡有非約轉功能。

Bank teller : OK. And we must take a photograph of you. Please look at the camera.

行　　　員：好的。我們必須幫您照相。請看鏡頭。

Customer : All right.

客　　　戶：好。

Bank teller : Here is your ATM card and the password envelope. Please keep it safe.

行　　　員：這是您的金融卡和密碼函。請妥善保管。

Customer : Wow. That soon? I thought you might tell me to come back five working days later to pick up my ATM card.

客　　戶：哇！這麼快啊？我以為您會跟我說要五個工作天後才能來領我的金融卡。

Bank teller : Our bank's ATM cards are pre-made, so we can issue them to our customers immediately. However, some banks' ATM cards are not pre-made. That is why they will request their customers to come five working days later to pick up their ATM card.

行　　員：我們銀行的金融卡是預製的，所以我們可以立即發卡給客人。然而，有些銀行的金融卡不是預製的。這就是為什麼他們會要求客人在五個工作天後才能來領金融卡。

Customer : I see.

客　　戶：我明白了。

Bank teller : You also need to set a four-digit passbook password for cash withdrawal over the bank counter. When you need to withdraw money from your account over a teller counter, the bank teller will request you to enter your four-digit passbook password through the password processor on the counter. Please set up your passbook password now.

行　　員：您也需設四位數臨櫃取款存摺密碼。當您要臨櫃領錢時，銀行櫃員會要求您透過在櫃檯上的密碼處理器輸入您的四位數存摺密碼。請現在設定您的存摺密碼。

Customer : So do you mean only when I make a withdrawal over a bank counter, do I need to enter my four-digit passbook password?

客　　戶：所以您是說只有當我臨櫃提款時，我才需輸入我的四位數存摺密碼？

Bank teller ： Yes.

行　　　員：是的。

(The Customer finished entering his four-digit password)

（客戶完成輸入四位數密碼）

Bank teller ： Please enter your four-digit password again and push "Enter".

行　　　員：請再次輸入您的四位數密碼並按「確認」。

Customer ： OK. It is done.

客　　　戶：好的。我完成了。

Bank teller ： Here is your passbook. I already gave you your ATM card and your password envelope, right? Now please change your PIN number of your ATM card at our ATM. **Please set a four-digit password for your magnetic stripe card first and then set a six to twelve digit password for your chip ATM card at an ATM. Your default password is contained in the password envelope.** You should open it and key in the default password first at an ATM. Then you can change the default password into your own PIN number.

行　　　員：這是您的存摺。我已經給您金融卡和密碼函了吧？請在本行的 ATM上變更您的金融卡密碼。**請在ATM先設一組磁條卡的四位數 密碼，再設一組六至十二位數的晶片金融卡密碼。您的預設密碼 在密碼函中。**您應該打開它然後在ATM輸入預設密碼。然後，您 就能把預設密碼改成自己的密碼。

Customer ： Why do I need to set a four-digit password for my magnetic stripe card?

客　　　戶：為什麼我需要為我的磁條卡設一個四位數密碼？

Bank teller ： Well, in some foreign countries, such as America or China, they still use traditional magnetic stripe cards instead of chip ATM cards, so if you go to these countries, you need your four-digit password for your magnetic stripe card to conduct transactions at local ATMs.

行　　員：嗯，在國外，像是美國或中國，他們仍然使用傳統的磁條卡而非晶片金融卡，所以您若去這些國家，您需要爲磁條卡設四位數密碼才能在當地的自動櫃員機交易。

Customer : I see. What is the six to twelve digit password for?

客　　戶：我明白了，那六位數到十二位數的密碼是做什麼用的？

Bank teller : It is for your chip ATM card. A chip card is also called a smart card or IC card. This kind of ATM card contains a chip, which enables your transaction safer. In Taiwan, all the ATMs only accept chip and PIN ATM cards. If your ATM card is still a magnetic stripe card, you cannot make any transaction at ATMs. You must go to the bank to replace your magnetic stripe card with a chip ATM cards.

行　　員：這是爲了您的晶片金融卡。晶片卡也叫作智慧卡。這種金融卡包含了一個晶片，能夠讓您的交易更安全。在臺灣，所有的自動櫃員機只接受晶片金融卡。如果您的金融卡仍然是磁條卡的話，您無法在自動櫃員機做任何交易。您必須到銀行把磁條卡換成晶片金融卡。

Customer : OK.

客　　戶：好。

Bank teller : In the future, all transactions you make will be recorded on a monthly statement and the bank will send a monthly paper statement to you. Of course, you can ask to stop receiving paper statements and ask for an **e-statement** instead. Once you apply for an e-statement, we won't send you a paper copy. The benefits of receiving e-statements include reducing paper cost, increasing your account security, and reducing your negative impact on the environment.

行　　員：在未來，您的所有交易紀錄都會記錄在每月的對帳單上，並且銀行會寄發紙本月對帳單給您。當然，您可以要求停止收取紙本對帳單而改要電子對帳單。一旦您申辦電子對帳單，我們就不會給您紙本的對帳單。收電子對帳單的好處有減少紙張的成本、提高您帳戶的安全性和減少您對環境的負面影響。

Customer : OK. I will register for an e-statement instead.

客　　戶：好，我就改申請電子對帳單好了。

Bank teller : I also have to tell you that the passbook cannot be transferred or pledged without the bank's written consent. And if the account balance is inconsistent with the bank's internal records, you shall agree that the bank's internal records should be considered correct.

行　　員：我也必須跟您說，未經銀行書面同意，存摺禁止轉帳或是質借，而且如果帳戶餘額和銀行的內部紀錄不一致的話，您當同意以銀行的內部紀錄為主。

Customer : I agree.

客　　戶：我同意。

Bank teller : You should also know that if the daily average balance of your savings account is less than the minimum balance of 5,000 NT dollars, interest will not accrue for that day. In other words, if your daily balance is less than five thousand NT dollars, the demand savings account will not bear any interest at all. When there is a change of the minimum balance amount for interest, the bank may announce such change on the business premises or on its website sixty days in advance.

行　　員：您也必須知道如果您的活儲戶的每日平均餘額不到新臺幣五千元的話，將不會計息。換句話說，如果您的每日餘額少於五千元，您的活儲戶將不會產生任何利息。當最低計息餘額改變的話，銀行會於六十天前在大廳或是在網站上公告。

Customer : I see. I also want to register for your online banking.

客　　戶：我明白了。我還想要申請網路銀行。

Bank teller : No problem. We also suggest our customer sign up for online banking when they open an account. After all, online banking is really convenient for our customers. It is done. Here is your password envelope for your online banking. Your default password is contained in the password envelope. You should open it and key in the default password when you enter into your online banking account for the first time. Then you change the default password into your own password. Remember to change the default password within one week; otherwise, the default password will become invalid and you must come to our bank to apply for a new password envelope again.

行　　員：沒問題。我們也是建議客戶在開戶時就申辦網銀。畢竟，網銀對客戶來說真的很便利。辦好了。這是您的網銀密碼函，函內是您的預設密碼。當您第一次登入網銀帳戶時，您應該打開密碼函並輸入預設密碼。然後把預設的密碼改成您自己的密碼。記得要在一星期之內變更預設密碼，不然預設密碼就會失效，然後您還要再來銀行重新申請新的密碼函。

Customer : Thanks. And I would like to know some benefits your bank provides for your customers.

客　　戶：謝謝。我還想知道您們銀行為客戶提供的福利。

Bank teller : Well, if you are our bank's depositor, you can come to our bank to get a calendar at the end of year. But the number of calendars is limited, so if all the calendars are passed out, you will not get one. Also, our bank gives our customers red envelopes at the beginning of the year and you can come to our bank and ask for our red envelopes. But the number of red envelopes is also limited. If you are too late, you will miss it.

行　　員：嗯。如果您是我們銀行的存戶，您可以在年底來我們銀行領一份月曆。但是月曆的數量有限，所以如果月曆都發完的話就沒有了。而且，我們還會在每年的年初發給客戶紅包袋，您可以來銀行拿紅包袋。但是紅包袋的數量也有限。如果您太晚來了，您就錯過了。

Customer : Thank you very much. Bye.

客　　戶：太感謝了。再見。

Bank teller : Wait. Here is our bank's "General Agreement for Accounts". Please take it home and make sure that you read everything, especially the provisions carefully.

行　　員：等一下。這是我們銀行的「開戶總約定書」。請帶回家並仔細地閱讀裡面內容，特別是那些約定條款。

補充單字

♦ household registration [`haus͵hold ͵rɛdʒ`streʃən] ***n.*** 戶籍

♦ ARC (Alien Resident Certificate) [`elɪən `rɛzədənt sə`tɪfəkɪt] ***n.*** 居留證

♦ checking account [`tʃɛkɪŋ ə`kaunt] ***n.*** 支存戶（支票存款帳戶）；甲存戶

♦ personal demand savings account [`pɝsn̩ dɪ`mænd `sevɪŋz ə`kaunt] ***n.*** 活期儲蓄帳戶

♦ general service account [`dʒɛnərəl `sɝvɪs ə`kaunt] ***n.*** 綜合存款帳戶

♦ foreign exchange account [`fɔrɪn ɪks`tʃendʒ ə`kaunt] ***n.*** 外幣戶

♦ multi-currency passbook [`mʌltɪ `kɝənsɪ ə`kaunt] ***n.*** 多幣別存摺

♦ cross-selling [`krɔs `sɛlɪŋ] ***n.*** 跨售；共同行銷

♦ e-statement [`i`stetmənt] ***n.*** 電子對帳單

實用金句

♦ According to the regulations, if you want to open an account, you must go to the bank where your household registration is located.

根據規定，如您想要開戶，您必須去您戶籍地所在的銀行。

♦ Our bank won't allow you to open an account here if you have opened other accounts with other banks within three months.

如果您在三個月內有到其他銀行開戶的話，本行就不讓您開戶。

♦ Please give me your two forms of ID.

請給我您的雙證件。

♦ In a word, be sure to complete all fields marked with a check mark.

簡單說，就是把所有打勾的地方都填好。

◆ By the way, our bank requires our customers to make a first deposit of at least 1,000 NT dollars into the account when opening an account.

順便一提，我們銀行要求客戶首次開戶至少要存一千元。

◆ Would you want your ATM card to have the functionality of international withdrawal?

您想要您的提款卡有國際提領的功能嗎？

◆ Would you like to activate the functionality of transferring funds to a non-designated account number for your ATM card?

您想要您的金融卡啓用非約轉功能嗎？

◆ Please set a four-digit password for your magnetic stripe card first and then set a six to twelve digit password for your chip ATM card at an ATM. Your default password is contained in the password envelope.

請在自動櫃員機先設一組磁條卡的四位數密碼，再設一組六至十二位數的晶片金融卡密碼。您的預設密碼在密碼函中。

開戶（開公司戶）
Opening A Company Account

Bank teller at the service counter：Hello, **what kind of transactions would you like to conduct?**

在 服 務 臺 的 行 員：嗨，**請問您要辦什麼交易？**

Customer：**I would like to open a corporate account with your bank.**

客 戶：**我想在您們銀行開個公司戶。**

Bank teller：You want to open a company account? Is your company located in the neighborhood?

行 員：您想開公司戶啊？您的公司在這附近嗎？

Customer：Yes, my company is just across the street.

客 戶：對啊，我公司就在對街。

Bank teller：Are you the **proprietor** of the business?

行 員：您是公司的所有權人嗎？

Customer：What do you mean by "proprietor of the business"?

客 戶：您說的「公司所有權人」是什麼意思？

Bank teller：I am asking you whether you are the responsible person of the company or not. In other words, are you the person in charge?

行 員：我是在問說您是否是這間公司的負責人？換句話說，您管理這間公司嗎？

Customer ： Yes, I am the owner of the company.

客　　戶：對，我是這間公司的老闆。

Bank teller ： I must ask you the question because only the company's licensing representative can apply for a company account.

行　　員：我必須問這個問題因為只有公司的負責人可以開公司戶。

Customer ： I see.

客　　戶：我明白了。

Bank teller ： **Please give me your two forms of ID, the business license, the business registration certificate, the company stamp plus the company's licensing representative's Chinese seal, both of which are authorized by the Ministry of Economic Affairs.**

行　　員：**請給我您的雙證件、公司營業執照和公司登記證明書和在經濟部登記的公司大章以及公司負責人的小章。**

Customer ： Here you are.

客　　戶：給您。

Bank teller ： Please fill out these forms. You must provide the following information, such as the company name, the registration certification number of company, the company address, your name, your ID number, the company telephone number as well as fax number, and the person to contact.

行　　員：請填寫這些申請書。您必須提供下列資訊，像是公司名稱，公司登記號碼、公司地址、您的名字、您的身分證字號、公司的電話號碼和傳真號碼，還有聯絡人。

Customer ： OK.

客　　戶：好的。

Bank teller ： Do you want to apply for an ATM card?

行　　　員：您要辦金融卡嗎？

Customer : Sure.

客　　　戶：當然。

Bank teller : Would you like your ATM card to have the functionality of international withdrawal?

行　　　員：您要金融卡有國際提領功能嗎？

Customer : Sure.

客　　　戶：當然。

Bank teller : Would you want your ATM card to have the functionality of transferring funds to a non-designated account number?

行　　　員：您要金融卡有非約轉功能嗎？

Customer : What do you mean by that?

客　　　戶：您指的是什麼？

Bank teller : That means, **if you activate your ATM card to have the functionality of transferring funds to a non-designated account number, you can use your ATM card to transfer up to 30,000 NT dollars via an ATM per day.** If you do not want to activate this function, your ATM card will not be able to make any transfer.

行　　　員：我是說，**如果您的金融卡啓用非約轉功能，您就可以在ATM用金融卡一天最多轉三萬元。** 如果您不想啓用此功能，您的金融卡就沒辦法轉帳。

Customer : Well, I want my ATM card to have the functionality of transferring funds to a non-designated account number.

客　　　戶：好，我要我的金融卡具有非約轉功能。

Bank teller : OK. And we must take a photograph of you. Please look at the camera. In addition, you must sign your name on the authorization agreement of **Personal Information Protection Law**.

行　　員：好的。我們必須幫您照張相。請看鏡頭。此外，您必須在個資法授權書上簽名。

Customer : All right.

客　　戶：好的。

Bank teller : **You also need to set a four-digit withdrawal password for your account.** When you need to withdraw money from your account over a teller counter, the bank teller will request you to enter your four-digit passbook password through the password processor on the counter. Please set your passbook password right now.

行　　員：**您還必須設四位數臨櫃取款密碼**。當您要臨櫃領錢時，銀行櫃員會要求您透過在櫃檯上的密碼處理器輸入您的四位數存摺密碼。請現在設定您的存摺密碼。

Customer : OK.

客　　戶：好的。

(The Customer finished entering his four-digit password)

（客戶完成輸入四位數密碼）

Bank teller : Please enter your four-digit password again and push "Enter".

行　　員：請再次輸入您的四位數密碼並按「確認」。

Customer : OK. It is done.

客　　戶：好的。我完成了。

Bank teller : Here is your passbook, your ATM card and the password envelope. Please set a four-digit password for your magnetic stripe card first and then set a six to twelve digit password for your chip ATM card at an ATM. Your default password is contained in the password envelope. You should open it and key in the default password first at an ATM. Then you change the default password into your PIN number.

行　　員：這是您的存摺、金融卡和密碼函。請在自動櫃員機先設一組磁條卡的四位數密碼，再設一組六至十二位數的晶片金融密碼。您的預設密碼在密碼函中。您應該打開它然後在ATM輸入預設密碼。然後，您再把預設密碼改成自己的密碼。

Customer : Why do I need to set a four-digit password for my magnetic stripe card?

客　　戶：爲什麼我需要爲我的磁條卡設一組四位數密碼？

Bank teller : Well, in some foreign countries such as America or China, they still use traditional magnetic stripe cards instead of chip ATM cards, so if you go to these countries, you need your four-digit password for your magnetic stripe card to conduct transactions at local ATMs.

行　　員：嗯，在國外，像是美國或中國，他們仍然使用傳統的磁條卡而非晶片金融卡，所以若您去這些國家，您需要爲磁條卡設四位數密碼才能在當地的自動提款機交易。

Customer : I see. What is a six to twelve digit password for?

客　　戶：我明白了，那六位數到十二位數的密碼是做什麼用的？

Bank teller : It is for your chip and PIN ATM card. A chip card is also called a smart card or IC card. This kind of ATM card contains a chip, which enables your transaction safer. In Taiwan, all the ATMs only accept chip and PIN ATM cards. **If your ATM card is still a magnetic stripe card, you cannot make any transaction at ATMs. You must go to the bank to replace your magnetic stripe card with a chip ATM card.**

行　　員：這是爲了您的晶片金融卡。晶片卡也叫作智慧卡。這種金融卡包

含了一個晶片，能夠讓您的交易更安全。在臺灣，所有的自動櫃員機只接受晶片金融卡。**如果您的金融卡仍然是磁條卡的話，您無法在自動櫃員機做任何交易。您必須到銀行把磁條卡換成晶片金融卡。**

Customer : Ok. Now I understand. Thank you very much.

客　　戶：好的。現在我了解了。非常謝謝您。

補充單字

♦ corporate account [`kɔrpərɪt ə`kaunt] *n.* 公司戶

♦ proprietor [prə`praɪətə] *n.* 所有權人

♦ activate [`æktə,vet] *v.* 啓用；開啓

♦ Personal Information Protection Law [`pɝsn̩l ,ɪnfə`meʃən prə`tɛkʃən lɔ] *n.* 個資法

實用金句

♦ What kind of transactions would you like to conduct?

請問您要辦什麼交易？

♦ I would like to open a corporate account with your bank.

我想在你們銀行開個公司戶。

♦ Please give me your two forms of ID, the business license, the business registration certificate, the company stamp plus the company's licensing representative's Chinese seal, both of which are authorized by the Ministry of Economic Affairs.

請給我您的雙證件、公司營業執照和公司登記證明書和在經濟部登記的公

司大章以及公司負責人的小章。

◆ If you activate your ATM card to have the functionality of transferring funds to a non-designated account number, you can use your ATM card to transfer up to 30,000 NT dollars via an ATM per day.

如果你的金融卡啓用非約轉功能，你就可以在ATM用金融卡一天最多轉三萬元。

◆ You also need to set a four-digit withdrawal password for your account.

你還必須設四位數臨櫃取款密碼。

◆ If your ATM card is still a magnetic stripe card, you cannot make any transaction at ATMs. You must go to the bank to replace your magnetic stripe card with a chip ATM card.

如果你的金融卡仍然是磁條卡的話，你無法在自動櫃員機做任何交易。你必須到銀行把磁條卡換成晶片金融卡。

開戶（開聯名戶）
Opening a Joint Account

Bank teller : Hello, may I help you?

行　　員：我可以幫您嗎？

Customer : **I would like to open a joint account with my girlfriend.** Does your bank provide this service? Because my girlfriend and I have asked many banks this question but they all said their bank did not have join accounts for their clients.

客　　戶：**我的女友和我想開個**聯名戶。您們銀行有提供這樣的服務嗎？因為我和我女友已問了很多家銀行這問題，但他們都說他們沒有給客戶提供聯名戶。

Bank teller : Our bank does have joint accounts for our customers. I know that Union Bank of Taiwan, Taiwan Cooperative Bank and Taiwan Shin Kong Commercial Bank also offer a joint account. But you must know some regulations and rules before you open this type of account because opening a joint account with your partner is a big commitment and one of the biggest decisions you will make in your personal relationship with someone you love and trust. Thus, it is a bad idea to open a joint account with someone you don't have a personal, intimate relationship with.

行　　員：我們銀行的確有給客戶提供聯名戶。我知道聯邦銀行、合作金庫

29

和新光銀行也有聯名戶。但您必須知道其規定和規範再開這種帳戶。因爲與您的伴侶開聯名戶是個很大的承諾，是您與您來往的人中所愛所信的人一起做的最大的決定之一。因此，和一位您沒有私人親密關係的某人開聯名戶是不智的主意。

Customer : Please tell me more.

客　　戶：請多告訴我一些。

Bank teller : **When two people decide to open a joint bank account, our bank will require you to sign an application form called a** man-date. The mandate sets out what the joint account holders can do. You need to know the bank will require two people's both original specimen signature and seal to make any vital transaction, such as cash withdrawal or funds transfer. And **you cannot make an** inter-branch withdrawal **or transfer at other branches**; you must return to your original account opening branch to make a withdrawal or transfer. But you can make a deposit in any branch. Some banks don't allow their customers to apply for an ATM card. Our bank, however, allows our clients to apply for an ATM card but our bank only issues one card to one person. So you two must decide who will have the ATM card. And if the ATM card is reported lost, both will lose access to their funds until a new card is issued. Besides, there are some law issues. For example, if either one of you died, who would inherit the funds in your joint account? Worse yet, if one person withdrew all the money from your joint account, the other would definitely blame our bank. You must take these issues into consideration.

行　　員：**當兩人決定要開聯名戶。我們銀行會要求您們簽一份申請書，叫作**授權書。在授權書規範了聯名戶的存戶什麼可以做。您要了解

銀行會要求兩人共同的印鑑才能辦重要的交易，像是提款或是轉帳。而且**您不能在其他分行做通提**或是**轉帳**，您必須回到原開戶行去做提款或是匯款。但您可以在任何分行做通存。有些銀行不允許客戶申辦金融卡。然而，我們銀行允許客戶辦金融卡但只發一張給一人。所以您們兩人必須決定誰持有金融卡。而且如果金融卡遺失了，兩人都沒有辦法領錢直到新卡發下。況且，這裡還有些法律問題。例如說，如果您們兩人其中一人過世，誰可以繼承聯名戶裡的錢？更糟的是，如果有一人把帳戶的錢全領光，另一人一定會責怪我們銀行。您們必須把這些問題考慮進去。

Customer : OK. So far I understand. my partner and I still want to open a joint account.

客　　戶：到目前為此我了解了。我和我的伴侶還是想要開聯名戶。

Bank teller : If it is the case, do you two live nearby?

行　　員：這樣的話，您們兩個都住這附近嗎？

Customer : Yes, we live nearby.

客　　戶：是的，我們住附近。

Bank teller : Now please give me your two forms of ID. I mean both of you.

行　　員：現在請給我您們的雙證件，兩人都要。

Customer : Here you are.

客　　戶：在這邊，給您。

Bank teller : **Please fill out these application forms for opening a joint account.**

行　　員：**請填這些聯名戶的申請書。**

Customer : OK.

客　　戶：好的。

Bank teller : **Would you like to apply for an ATM card?**

行　　　員：**您要申請金融卡嗎？**

Customer：Sure.

客　　　戶：當然。

Bank teller：OK. It is done. Thank you very much.

行　　　員：好，都辦好了，謝謝您。

補充單字

◆ joint account [ˋdʒɔɪnt əˋkaunt] ***n.*** 聯名戶

◆ mandate [ˋmændet] ***n.*** 授權委託書

◆ inter-branch withdrawal [ɪntəˋbræntʃ wɪðˋdrɔəl] ***n.*** 聯行提款；通提

實用金句

◆ I would like to open a joint account with my girlfriend.

我和我的女友想開個聯名戶。

◆ When two people decide to open a joint bank account, our bank will require you to sign an application form called a mandate.

當兩人決定要開聯名戶。我們銀行會要求您們簽一份申請書，叫作授權書。

◆ You cannot make an inter-branch withdrawal or transfer at other branches.

您不能在其他分行做通提或是轉帳。

◆ Please fill out these application forms for opening a joint account.

請填這些聯名戶的申請書。

◆ Would you like to apply for an ATM card?

您要申請金融卡嗎？

關　戶
Closing an Account

Bank teller : Hello, what kind of transactions would you like to conduct?

行　　　員：嗨，您想要辦什麼交易？

Customer : **I would like to clear up my account in your bank.**

客　　　戶：**我想要結清在貴行的戶頭。**

Bank teller : May I beg your pardon?

行　　　員：可以請您再說一次嗎？

Customer : What I mean is, I want to close my account in your bank.

客　　　戶：我是說，我想要關閉在貴行的戶頭。

Bank teller : I see. May I ask you the reason why you want to cancel your account in our bank?

行　　　員：我明白了。我可以問您關戶的原因嗎？

Customer : I want to terminate my account with your bank because my account in your bank used to be my **payroll account**. However, I changed my job last week, so there is no need for me to use this account in your bank.

客　　　戶：我想要關戶因為之前我是您們銀行的薪轉戶。不過，我上星期換工作了，所以沒有必要繼續使用您們銀行的帳戶。

Bank teller : Sir, **I suggest you not** cancel **this account, just in case you should use the account in our bank in the future.**

33

行　　　員：先生，**我建議您不要關戶，以便您未來還有可能用到我們銀行的帳戶。**

Customer : I have made my mind to close this account in your bank.

客　　　戶：我已下定決心要關掉在您們銀行的戶頭了。

Bank teller : I understand. Do you bring your passbook and your original **personal Chinese seal**?

行　　　員：我了解了。您有帶存摺和原留印鑑嗎？

Customer : Yes.

客　　　戶：是的。

Bank teller : **Have you filled out the withdrawal slip?**

行　　　員：**您已填好提款單了嗎？**

Customer : Yes, I already filled out the withdrawal slip.

客　　　戶：是的，我已填好提款單了。

Bank teller : OK, **please pass me your passbook, the withdrawal slip and your personal Chinese seal.**

行　　　員：好的。**請給我您的存摺、提款條和您的印章。**

Customer : Here you are.

客　　　戶：給您。

Bank teller : Please wait for a minute. It is done. Here is your cash. **Do you want to keep the cancelled passbook or do you want me to destroy it for you?**

行　　　員：請稍等一下。辦好了。這是您的現金。**您想要保留您已銷戶的存摺，或是您想要我替您銷毀？**

Customer : Well, you can destroy it.

客　　　戶：您可以銷毀。

Bank teller : OK. No problem. It is my pleasure to provide service for you.

行　　　員：好的。沒問題。為您服務是我的榮幸。

補充單字

◆ payroll account [`peˌrol əˋkaunt] **n.** 薪資戶；薪轉戶

◆ cancel [ˋkænsḷ] **v.** （定存、保單、帳戶、信用卡的）解約；取消

◆ personal Chinese seal [ˋpɝsṇḷ tʃaɪˋniz sil] **n.** 私章

◆ withdrawal slip [wɪðˋdrɔəl slɪp] **n.** 提款條；取款單

◆ destroy [dɪˋstrɔɪ] **v.** 銷毀

實用金句

◆ I would like to clear up my account in your bank.

我想要結清在貴行的戶頭。

◆ I suggest you not cancel this account, just in case you should use the account in our bank in the future.

我建議您不要關戶，以便您未來還有可能用到我們銀行的帳戶。

◆ Have you filled out the withdrawal slip?

您已填好提款單了嗎？

◆ Please pass me your passbook, the withdrawal slip, and your personal Chinese seal.

請給我您的存摺、提款條和印章。

◆ Do you want to keep the cancelled passbook or do you want me to destroy it for you?

您想要保留您已銷戶的存摺，或是您想要我替您銷毀？

利 率
Interest Rate

Customer : Hello. **How much is your bank's current interest rate for a personal demand savings account?**

客　　戶：嗨，您們銀行的活儲戶的利率目前是多少？

Bank teller : It is zero point twenty nine percent (0.29 %).

行　　員：利率是百分之零點二九。

Customer : That is really low.

客　　戶：真低啊。

Bank teller : Yes. **If you put money into a demand savings account, the interest is not high. However, if you put your money into a time deposit, you can earn higher interest.**

行　　員：是的。**如果您把錢放在活儲戶的話，利率不會很高。不過，如果您把錢放在定存的話，您能得到的利息就比較高。**

Customer : OK. I see. I decide to put my money into a time deposit. How much is your bank's interest rate for a time deposit?

客　　戶：好的，我了解了。我決定把錢放在定存。您們銀行定存利率是多少？

Bank teller : How long do you want to keep the money in the time deposit? Our bank's deposit terms range from one month to three years. **The interest of a time deposit varies with the maturity period. The**

longer maturity you choose, the higher interest rate is. Concerning the deposit terms, you can choose one-month, two-month, three-month, four-month, five-month, six-month, seven-month, eight-month, nine-month, ten-month, eleven-month, thirteen-month maturities, and one-year, two-year, as well as three-year maturities. You should choose the term that is right for you.

行　　員：您想做多久的定存？我們銀行的存期有一個月到三年。**定存利息會因不同的**到期日**而不同。您選擇的到期日愈長，利率愈高。**存期的話，您可以選一個月、二個月、三個月、四個月、五個月、六個月、七個月、八個月、九個月、十個月、十一個月、十三個月，還有一年、兩年、三年期。您應選擇適合您的存期。

Customer : I would like to choose the one-year term. How much is the interest rate for the one-year term?

客　　戶：我要選一年期。一年的定存利率是多少？

Bank teller : It depends. **We have a variable-rate time deposit and a fixed rate time deposit for you to choose.** Would you like to choose a variable-rate time deposit or a fixed rate time deposit?

行　　員：要看情況而定。**我們有機動利率和固定利率讓您來選。**您想選機動利率的定存還是固定利率的定存？

Customer : What is the difference? I really don't understand.

客　　戶：有什麼不同？我不懂。

Bank teller : **A variable-rate time deposit is a type of interest rate that fluctuates over time. If Central Bank raises the interest rate, the interest rate of a variable-rate time deposit will be up as well, and vice versa.** Therefore, if you expect Central bank to cut the interest rate in the future, I recommend you choose a fixed rate time deposit. On the contrary, if you expect Central Bank to raise the interest rate, I suggest you choose a variable-rate time deposit.

行　　員 : **機動利率是利率會隨著時間不斷浮動。如果央行升息，機動利率也會上調，反之亦然。**所以，如果您預測央行在未來會降息，我建議您選固定利率定存。相反地，如果您預期央行會升息，我建議您選擇機動利率定存。

Customer : I am not sure. Can you tell me your opinion? Maybe you know which one is better for me.

客　　戶 : 我不確定耶！您可以告訴我您的意見嗎？也許您懂哪個比較適合我。

Bank teller : Sorry. I cannot decide for you. I am not God. I don't know whether Central Bank will raise or lower the key interest rate. You must decide for yourself. That is your call.

行　　員 : 抱歉，我無法為您做主。我不是上帝。我不知道央行是否會升息或降息。您必須自己做主。這是您自己的抉擇。

Customer : OK. I would choose a variable-rate time deposit for one-year maturity. **How much is the interest rate for a one-year variable-rate time deposit?**

客　　戶 : 好的。我想要做一年的機動利率定存。**一年機動利率定存的利率是多少？**

Bank teller : It is one point thirty seven percent (1.37 %).

行　　員 : 是百分之一點三七。

Customer : OK. I will consider this plan. But I want to ask you a question. Are all the banks' interest rates the same? For example, Chintrust's one-year variable-rate time deposit interest rate is the same with your bank's interest rate?

客　　戶：好的。我會考慮這個方案。但我想問一個問題。所有銀行的利率都一樣嗎？例如說，中國信託的一年機動利率和您們銀行一樣嗎？

Bank teller : Not really. **Interest rates differ from bank to bank.** You may as well inquire other banks.

行　　員：不一定耶。**每家銀行的利率都有所不同。**您不妨問問其他銀行。

Customer : OK. I will inquire other banks to see which bank provides the most preferential interest rates. Thank you anyway.

客　　戶：好的。我會問其他銀行看哪家銀行提供的利率最優惠。還是謝謝您。

Bank teller : It is my pleasure. Oh, by the way, please give our bank branch ten points if you receive a survey call from our customer service center and ask you how many points you will give for our branch's customer service.

行　　員：不客氣。喔，對了，如果您從我們客服部接到調查電話，問您要給我們分行的客戶服務多少分時，請給我們十分。

Customer : OK. So it is a CS survey, right?

客　　戶：好啊。所以這是客戶滿意度調查，對吧？

Bank teller : Yes. It is very important for our branch. If we don't get a good score, our manager will be mad with us.

行　　員：對。這對我們分行非常重要。如果我們沒有得高分，我們經理會對我們生氣的。

Customer : No problem. Since you are so pretty and so kind, I will definitely help you.

客　　戶：沒問題。因為您是那麼美且人又好，我當然會幫您囉。

Bank teller : Thank you.

行　　員：謝謝。

補充單字

- ♦ maturity [məˋtjurətɪ] **n.** （定存、保單、支票的）到期
- ♦ deposit term [dɪˋpɑzɪt tɝm] **n.** 存期
- ♦ variable-rate time deposit [ˋvɛrɪəbḷ ret taɪm dɪˋpɑzɪt] **n.** 機動利率定存
- ♦ fixed rate time deposit [fɪkst ret taɪm dɪˋpɑzɪt] **n.** 固定利率定存

實用金句

- ♦ How much is your bank's current interest rate for a personal demand savings account?

  您們銀行的活儲戶的利率目前是多少？

- ♦ If you put money into a demand savings account, the interest is not high. However, if you put your money into a time deposit, you can earn higher interest.

  如果您把錢放在活儲戶的話，利率不會很高。不過，如果您把錢放在定存的話，您能得到的利息就比較高。

- ♦ The interest of a time deposit varies with the maturity period. The longer maturity you choose, the higher interest rate is.

  定存利息會因不同的到期日而不同。您選擇的到期日愈長，利率愈高。

- ♦ We have a variable-rate time deposit and a fixed rate time deposit for you to choose.

  我們有機動利率和固定利率讓您來選。

◆ A variable-rate time deposit is a type of interest rate that fluctuates over time. If Central Bank raises the interest rate, the interest rate of a variable-rate time deposit will be up as well, and vice versa.

機動利率是利率會隨著時間不斷浮動。如果央行升息，機動利率也會上調，反之亦然。

◆ How much is the interest rate for a one-year variable-rate time deposit?

一年機動利率定存的利率是多少？

◆ Interest rates differ from bank to bank.

每家銀行的利率都有所不同。

存　款
Making a Deposit

Bank teller : Hello, Sir, may I help you?

行　　　員 : 嗨，先生，我可以幫您嗎？

Customer : I would like to make a deposit.

客　　　戶 : 我想要存款。

Bank teller : Have you filled in the deposit slip?

行　　　員 : 您塡好存款條了嗎？

Customer : No. I haven't.

客　　　戶 : 沒有。我還沒。

Bank teller : **Do you bring your passbook with you? May I have your passbook?**

行　　　員 : **您有帶存摺嗎？可以給我您的存摺嗎？**

Customer : Oh, I forgot to bring my passbook. So can I still make a deposit?

客　　　戶 : 喔，我忘記帶我的存摺了。這樣我還可以存款嗎？

Bank teller : Yes, you can. **You can fill out a duplicate deposit slip. It carries a deposit receipt, so you still can keep your transaction record.** In fact, when customers make a deposit, the bank allows them to make a deposit without a passbook. However, **if customers want to make a withdrawal over the counter, the bank will require them to show the bank teller their passbook.** You cannot make a withdrawal without a passbook over the bank counter.

行　　員：是的，您可以。**您可以填二聯式存款單。它有一張**存款收據，**這樣您仍然能保有交易紀錄。**事實上，當客戶存款時，銀行都會允許他們不用本子就可以存款。不過，**如果客戶想要臨櫃提款，銀行就會要求一定要給行員存摺才可以。**您沒有本子就無法臨櫃提款。

Customer：Thank you for your explanation.

客　　戶：謝謝您的說明。

Bank teller：You are welcome. How much money would you like to deposit?

行　　員：不客氣。您想存多少？

Customer：I would like to deposit 600,000 NT dollars.

客　　戶：我想要存六十萬。

Bank teller：**Do you want to deposit the money into your own account or into someone else's account?**

行　　員：**您想存到自己的戶頭還是別人的？**

Customer：Into someone else's account.

客　　戶：存到別人的戶頭。

Bank teller：**Do you know the person whose account you are going to deposit money into?** Is it the first time for you to deposit money into his or her account?

行　　員：**您認識受款人嗎？**您是第一次存到對方的戶頭嗎？

Customer：Yes, I know the person. And it is not the first time for me to put money into her account.

客　　戶：是的。我認識這個人。這不是我第一次存到她的戶頭。

Bank teller：How are you related to the **beneficiary**?

行　　員：您跟收款人的關係是？

Customer : The beneficiary is my daughter.

客　　戶：受款人是我的女兒。

Bank teller : What is your purpose for making a deposit into her account?

行　　員：您存到她戶頭的目的是？

Customer : I plan to transfer money to her for her living expenses in college.

客　　戶：我打算匯錢給她作為大學的生活費。

Bank teller : OK, I see. I need to ask the above questions because our bank cares about our customers. There have been a lot of frauds, so please be careful.

行　　員：好的。我明白了。我必須問以上的問題是因為銀行要做客戶關懷。最近詐騙頻傳，請多加留意。

Customer : Thank you.

客　　戶：謝謝您。

Bank teller : Since you want to deposit more than 500,000 NT dollars, I must ask you to fill out the **declaration** form. And you have to give me your national ID card. Because according to Money Laundering Control Act, if you make a single cash transaction which is more than five hundred thousand dollars, you must fill out the declaration form to provide your personal information, including your name, national ID number, your birthday, your address, phone number and the amount of this transaction to **the authorities concerned.**

行　　員：既然您要存現金五十萬以上，我必須請您填申報書。您必須給我您的國民身分證。因為根據洗錢防制法，如果您單筆現金交易超過五十萬的話，您必須申報並提供您的個資，包括您的姓名、國民身分證字號、您的生日和您的地址、電話以及您交易的金額給

相關主管機關。

Customer　：Sure.
客　　　戶：沒問題。

Bank teller　：**Please take a look at the bill counter to confirm the amount while I am counting the banknotes.**
行　　　員：**當我數鈔時，請看著點鈔機來確認金額。**

Customer　：OK.
客　　　戶：好的。

Bank teller　：Oops! Some of your banknotes are mutilated, so they are rejected by the money counter. Mutilated banknotes are the notes that have been ripped, burned, or defaced. Our bank will not distribute or accept mutilated banknotes of any kind. But most of your banknotes are OK.
行　　　員：糟了！您有些現鈔已經毀損了，所以無法通過點鈔機。毀損的紙鈔就是那些有撕開、燒毀或是表面毀損的紙鈔。我們銀行不流通或是接受任何已毀損的鈔票。但您大部分的現鈔都沒問題。

Customer　：OK. I see.
客　　　戶：好，我了解了。

Bank teller　：**Here is your deposit receipt. Please keep it safe. Do you have any other transactions to conduct?**
行　　　員：**這是您存款的收據。請妥善保管。請問還有其他的交易要辦嗎？**

Customer　：No, thanks.
客　　　戶：沒有，謝啦。

Bank teller　：Have a nice day.
行　　　員：祝您有個美好的一天。

補充單字

- ◆ duplicate deposit slip [`djupləkɪt dɪ`pazɪt slɪp] *n.* 無摺存款單；二聯式存款單

- ◆ deposit receipt [dɪ`pazɪt rɪ`sit] *n.* 存款收據；存根聯

- ◆ beneficiary [ˏbɛnə`fɪʃərɪ] *n.* 受款人；收款人

- ◆ declaration [ˏdɛklə`reʃən] *n.* 申報

- ◆ the authorities concerned [ðɪ ɔ`θɔrətɪz kən`sɜnd] *n.* 相關主管機關

實用金句

- ◆ Do you bring your passbook with you? May I have your passbook?

    您有帶存摺嗎？可以給我您的存摺嗎？

- ◆ You can fill out the duplicate deposit slip. It carries a deposit receipt, so you still can keep your transaction record.

    您可以填二聯式存款單。它有一張存款收據，這樣您仍然能保有交易紀錄。

- ◆ If customers want to make a withdrawal over the counter, the bank will require them to show the bank teller their passbook.

    如果客戶想要臨櫃提款，銀行就會要求一定要給行員存摺才可以。

- ◆ Do you want to deposit the money into your own account or into someone else's account?

    您想存到自己的戶頭還是別人的？

- ◆ Do you know the person whose account you are going to deposit money into?

    您認識受款人嗎？

◆ Please take a look at the bill counter to confirm the amount while I am counting the banknotes.

當我數鈔時，請看著點鈔機來確認金額。

◆ Here is your deposit receipt. Please keep it safe. Do you have any other transactions to conduct?

這是您存款的收據。請妥善保管。請問還有其他的交易要辦嗎？

定 存
Time Deposit

Customer : I would like to make a time deposit. I know the meaning of a time deposit, so you don't have to explain to me. A **time deposit** is also known as a fixed deposit, right?

客　　戶：我想要辦定期存款。我知道定期存款的意思，所以您不必解釋給我聽。定期存款也叫定存，對吧？

Bank teller : Well, yes. But I want to tell you that now the interest rate is too low. Would you consider using the money to invest in mutual funds or buying an endowment insurance policy? You know, after all, the money you put in a time deposit is being eaten away by inflation. I will recommend that you consider other allotment of your assets instead of just putting money into a time deposit. If you don't care about financial planning, money won't care about you.

行　　員：是的。但我想告訴您說現在利率太低了。您有考慮把錢拿來投資共同基金或是買年金保險嗎？您曉得的。畢竟，您放在定存的錢都被通貨膨脹吃掉了。我會推薦您考慮其他的資產配置而不是把錢放在定存而已。如果您不理財，財不理您。

Customer : Well, thanks for your advice, but I already made my mind to make a time deposit.

客　　戶：這個嘛，謝謝您的建議，但我已經決心要辦定存了。

Bank teller : Anyway, it doesn't hurt to ask. How much money would like to put into a time deposit account?

行　　員：好吧，問一下比較保險。您定存要放多少錢？

Customer : Five thousand NT dollars.

客　　戶：新臺幣五千元。

Bank teller : No, you can't. **Our minimum deposit for a time deposit account is ten thousand NT dollars.**

行　　員：不可以，您不能這樣做。**我們的定存開戶最低存款金額是新臺幣一萬元。**

Customer : OK, then. I will put ten thousand NT dollars into the time deposit account. And I notice that your bank provides two types of CDs. One is the time savings deposit and the other is the time deposit. What is the difference?

客　　戶：好的。那麼，我就做一萬元的定存。我注意到您們銀行有兩種定存，一種是「定期儲蓄存款」，另一種是「定期存款」，有什麼不同？

Bank teller : Good question. **The interest rate of a time savings deposit is higher than that of a time deposit, but the time savings deposit only accepts natural persons to open this account.** That is to say, **the corporate account holder cannot apply for the time savings deposit. Moreover, the time savings deposit tenors only provide one-year, two-year, and three-year maturities for customers to choose.**

行　　員：好問題。**定儲的利率比定存高，但定儲只接受自然人開戶。**也就是說，公司戶的存戶無法適用定儲。**此外，定儲只提供一年、兩年、三年的存期讓客人選擇。**

Customer : I see.

客　　　戶：我明白了。

Bank teller : We have different ways of deposit and withdrawal for a time deposit. The time deposit can be divided into four categories:

(1) lump-sum deposit and withdrawal

(2) fixed deposit by installments

(3) principal-receiving and interest withdrawing time deposit

(4) lump-sum saving for small withdrawal

行　　　員：我們有好幾種定儲的存提方式。定儲可以分成四種：

(1) 整存整付

(2) 零存整付

(3) 存本取息

(4) 整存零付

Customer : Wow, so many choices. I don't understand these banking terms.

客　　　戶：哇！好多選擇。我不懂這些銀行術語。

Bank teller : **Simply put, you can choose the plan that your interest is credited into account every month or the plan that only when your time deposit matures, will your interest be credited into your account.**

行　　　員：**簡單說，您可以選擇您的利息每月入帳到您的戶頭，或是當您的定存到期時，您的利息才會入帳。**

Customer : OK, I will choose the latter plan that only when my time deposit matures, will the interest be credited into my account.

客　　　戶：好，我選第二個方案，只有當我的定存到期時，利息才會入帳。

Bank teller : How long do you want to keep the money in the time deposit? Our bank's **deposit tenors** range from one month to three years. The interest of a time deposit varies with the maturity period. The longer maturity you choose, the higher interest rate is. For example, if you choose a three-year maturity, the interest rate is 1.4 %. But if you choose a one-month maturity, the interest rate is only 0.88 %. As for the terms, you can choose one-month, two-month, three-month, four-month, five-month, six-month, seven-month, eight-month, nine-month, ten-month, eleven-month, thirteen-month maturities, and one-year, two year, as well as three year maturities. You should choose the term that is right for you.

行　　員：您定存想做多久？我們銀行的存期從一個月到三年都有。定存利息隨著存期而變化。您選的存期愈長，利息愈高。舉例來說，如果您選擇三年的存期，利率是百分之一點四。但如果您只選擇一個月的存期，利率就只有百分之零點八八了。至於存期的話，您可以選一個月、二個月、三個月、四個月、五個月、六個月、七個月、八個月、九個月、十個月、十一個月、十三個月，還有一年、兩年、三年期。您應選擇適合您的存期。

Customer : I would like to choose the one-year maturity.

客　　戶：我想選一年的存期。

Bank teller : Sir, we only accept less than six-month maturity currently; otherwise, you have to go to other banks to make a time deposit.

行　　員：先生，我們目前只接受六個月以下的存期，不然您就得到別家銀行去做定存。

Customer : Why? You just said your bank provides one-year, two year, as well as three year maturities.

客　　戶：為什麼？您剛才不是說您們銀行提供一年、二年，還有三年的存期嗎？

Bank teller : Yes. But the problem is, our bank has absorbed too many deposits, and we bear the huge burden of paying interests to our depositors. To cut down on the cost, we don't welcome those who come to our bank to open a long-term CD.

行　　　員：是的。但問題是，我們銀行吸收太多的存款，而我們要付給客人的利息負擔就很大。為了減少成本，我們不歡迎來我們銀行做長期定存的人。

Customer : OK. Then I choose the three month maturity.

客　　　戶：好吧。那我選擇做三個月的定存。

Bank teller : Would you like to choose a variable-rate time deposit or a fixed rate time deposit?

行　　　員：您要做機動利率定存還是固定利率定存？

Customer : What is the difference?

客　　　戶：有什麼差別？

Bank teller : A variable-rate time deposit is a type of interest rate that fluctuates over time. If Central Bank raises the interest rate, a variable-rate time deposit will also raise the interest rate, and vice versa. Therefore, if you expect a recession and Central Bank may lower the interest rate to boost economy, I recommend you to choose a fixed rate time deposit. On the contrary, if you to expect inflation to come and Central Bank may raise the interest rate to handle inflation, I suggest you choosing a variable-rate time deposit.

行　　　員：機動利率定存是利率會隨著時間而變化。如果央行升息，機動利率定存也會升息，反之亦然。因此，如果您預測經濟衰退而央行可能降息來刺激經濟，我建議您選擇固定利率定存。反之，如果您預測通膨會來臨而央行可能升息來對付通膨，我建議您選擇機

動利率定存。

Customer : I would choose a variable-rate time deposit.

客　　　戶：那我要選擇機動利率定存。

Bank teller : **Would you like this CD to be set for the** automatic renewal **at maturity or for the** automatic redemption **at maturity?**

行　　　員：您想要定存到期後自動展期嗎？還是到期後自動轉到活儲？

Customer : I would choose the automatic renewal at maturity.

客　　　戶：我想要到期後自動展期。

Bank teller : For how many times?

行　　　員：自動展期幾次？

Customer : For three times.

客　　　戶：展期三次。

Bank teller : Sure, let me check it again with you. You want a variable-rate time deposit with three-month maturity. The promised interest rate is 0.94 %. The amount you wish to put into the time deposit account is ten thousand NT dollars. This CD will be set for the automatic renewal at maturity for three times.

行　　　員：沒問題，讓我跟您再確認一次。您要做三個月的機動利率定存。到期利率是百分之零點九四。您要存的金額是一萬元。定存到期後會自動展期三次。

Customer : Yes, that is right.

客　　　戶：沒錯，就是這樣。

Bank teller : I might add that **our bank's interest of demand savings account shall be calculated on the basis of a year of 365 days for New Taiwan Dollar deposits. The interest is calculated on 20th of June and 20th of December respectively and is credited into**

your account on the following business day. For the time deposit, the interest shall be calculated on a monthly basis and paid at the maturity. If the actual deposit period is less than one month, the time deposit will bear no interest.

行　　員：我補充一下，我們銀行的新臺幣活儲利息以每年三百六十五日為計息基礎。利息於每年六月二十日及十二月二十日各結算乙次，並於次營業日存入存戶之帳戶內。定期存款的部分，足月部分按月計息，如果實際存期不滿一個月，將不計息。

Customer：OK. I get it.

客　　戶：好的，我了解了。

Bank teller：Sir, since your account is a "general service account", also called an intergrated account. Do you wish to make a time deposit inside your passbook? In other words, this transaction record of the time deposit will be printed inside your passbook. In this way, we don't have to issue a physical CD for you to keep. You have to know that if you lose your physical CD, the bank will charge you one hundred NT dollars to replace a new one for you.

行　　員：先生，既然您的帳戶是綜合存款帳戶，也叫綜存戶，您想要把定存放在存薄裡面嗎？換句話說，這筆定存交易將被印在您本子裡面。這樣一來，我們不必發實體的定存單讓您來保管。您必須了解，如果您遺失定存單，銀行會跟您收一百元的補發手續費。

Customer：That's OK. I prefer a physical CD. I like something I can touch.

客　　戶：沒關係。我比較喜歡實體的定存單。我喜歡摸得到的東西。

Bank teller：Well…But you only put ten thousand NT dollars into a time deposit. This cost the bank unnecessary expenses and a lot of time for bank clerks. **I will suggest you open a non-physical CD. Our**

bank provides three ways. The first way is making a time deposit inside your omnibus account. The second way is opening an electronic CD through Internet Banking. The last way is opening a non-physical CD at our ATM with your ATM card.

行　　員：可是您才做一萬元的定存。這樣會浪費銀行行員不必要的成本和時間。我建議您開電子存單。我們銀行提供三種方式。第一種是把定存做在您的綜存本子裡。第二種是透過網銀開電子定存單。最後一種是用金融卡透過ATM來開立電子存單。

Customer : No, I insist on opening a physical CD.

客　　戶：不要，我堅持要開實體定存單。

Bank teller : All right. If you insist…By the way, do you come from Australia?

行　　員：好吧，如果您堅持的話。順便一提，您是從澳洲來的嗎？

Customer : No. I live in Taiwan.

客　　戶：不是啊。我住在臺灣。

Bank teller : **Here is your CD. Please keep your CD well maintained. It is done. Can I help you with anything else?**

行　　員：這是您的定存單。請妥善保管好您的定存單。這樣就好了。請問您還有其他的業務要辦嗎？

Customer : Well. I have a question for you. I heard that the government started to collect the supplementary premium of National Health Insurance from the depositor's interest return. Can you tell me more concerning this matter?

客　　戶：嗯，我想問您一個問題。我聽說政府開始從存戶的利息所得徵收健保補充保費。您可以在這件事上跟我說明一下嗎？

Bank teller : Sure. If a single interest payment is less than five thousand NT dollars, your account will not be debited for the supplementary premium of National Health Insurance. If a single interest payment is between five thousand NT dollars and twenty thousand NT dollars, you should pay your supplementary premium of National Health Insurance with the bill issued by Bureau of National Health Insurance by yourself. If a one-time interest payment is up to twenty thousand NT dollars or more, the bank will directly debit the supplementary premium of National Health Insurance from your account. If a customer's time deposit is four million NT dollars and he chooses the plan that his interest shall be credited to his account every month, he will not need to pay the supplementary premium of National Health Insurance because his one-time interest payment is not more than five thousand NT dollars. Therefore, you don't need to worry unless your one-time interest payment earned on your deposit exceeds five thousand NT dollars. By the way, the amount of interest income tax exemption for your interest return on deposit is up to two hundred and seventy thousand NT dollars.

行　　員：好的。利息單次給付在新臺幣五千元以下不扣繳二代健保補充保費。利息單次給付在新臺幣五千到兩萬元以內由健保局寄發單據請客戶自行繳納健保補充保費。利息單次給付在新臺幣兩萬元（含）以上由銀行直接由您的帳戶扣繳健保補充保費。如果有一客戶定存四百萬元採每月付息，因每月利息不超過五千元，就不需扣繳健保補充保費。因此，別擔心，除非您帳戶所得的單次給付利息超過新臺幣五千元。順便一提，您存款利息所得稅的免稅額度為新臺幣二十七萬元。

Customer : Thanks.
客　　戶：謝謝。

補充單字

♦ time deposit [taɪm dɪ`pɑzɪt] *n.* 定期存款；定存

♦ time savings deposit [taɪm `sevɪŋz dɪ`pɑzɪt] *n.* 定期儲蓄存款；定儲

♦ credit [`krɛdɪt] *v.* 入帳 *n.* 信用

♦ deposit tenor [dɪ`pɑzɪt `tɛnɚ] *n.* 存期；存款期

♦ automatic renewal [ˌɔtə`mætɪk rɪ`njuəl] *n.* 自動展期

♦ automatic redemption [ˌɔtə`mætɪk rɪ`dɛmpʃən] *n.* （定存到期後）自動轉到活存

實用金句

♦ Our minimum deposit for a time deposit account is ten thousand NT dollars.
我們的定存開戶最低存款金額是新臺幣一萬元。

♦ The interest rate of a time savings deposit is higher than that of a time deposit, but the time savings deposit only accepts natural persons to open this account.
定儲的利率比定存高，但定儲只接受自然人開戶。

♦ The corporate account holder cannot apply for the time savings deposit. Moreover, the time savings deposit tenors only provide one-year, two-year, and three-year maturities for customers to choose.
公司戶的存戶無法適用定儲。此外，定儲只提供一年、兩年、三年的存期讓客人選擇。

♦ Simply put, you can choose the plan that your interest is credited into account every month or the plan that only when your time deposit matures, will your interest be credited into your account.

簡單說，您可以選擇您的利息每月入帳到您的戶頭，或是當您的定存到期時，您的利息才存到您的帳戶。

◆ Would you like this CD to be set for the automatic renewal at maturity or for the automatic redemption at maturity?

您想要定存到期後自動展期嗎？還是到期後轉到活儲？

◆ Our bank's interest of demand savings account shall be calculated on the basis of a year of 365 days for New Taiwan Dollar deposits. The interest is calculated on 20th of June and 20th of December respectively and is credited into your account on the following business day.

我們銀行的新臺幣活儲利息以每年三百六十五日為計息基礎。利息於每年六月二十日及十二月二十日各結算乙次，並於次營業日存入存戶之帳戶內。

◆ For the time deposit, the interest shall be calculated on a monthly basis and paid at the maturity. If the actual deposit period is less than one month, the time deposit will bear no interest.

定期存款是足月部分按月計息，如果實際存期不滿一個月，將不計息。

◆ I will suggest you open a non-physical CD. Our bank provides three ways. The first way is making a time deposit inside your omnibus account. The second way is opening an electronic CD through Internet Banking. The last way is opening a non-physical CD at our ATM with your ATM card.

我建議您開立電子存單。我們銀行提供三種方式。第一種是把定存做在您的綜存本子裡。第二種是透過網銀開電子定存單。最後一種是用金融卡透過ATM來開立電子存單。

♦ Here is your CD. Please keep your CD well maintained. It is done. Can I help you with anything else?

這是您的定存單。請妥善保管好您的定存單。這樣就好了。請問您還有其他的業務要辦嗎？

定存中途解約
Early Redemption

Bank teller : What can I do for you today?

行　　員：您今天要辦什麼？

Customer : **I would like to cancel my time deposit before maturity.**

客　　戶：**我要辦定存中途解約。**

Bank teller : May I ask why?

行　　員：我可以問為什麼嗎？

Customer : My church decided to build a church of our own, so I decide to contribute my money to the church to build a new church. That is why I want to cancel my time deposit before maturity.

客　　戶：我們教會決定建自己的教堂，所以我決定把我的錢捐給教會來建新教堂。這就是為什麼我要定存中途解約的原因。

Bank teller : Oh, that is touching. But I have to tell you this. **If you terminate your time deposit before maturity, you will forfeit the promised interest.** That is to say, if you cancel the time deposit before the maturity date, you will suffer a loss in interest. **For deposits cancelled within one month, the bank will not pay any interest. For those cancelled after one month, the interest payable on such deposit shall be calculated at a rate of 80% of the actual deposit tenors.**

行　　　員：真感人。但我必須跟您說，**如果您定存中途**解約，**您將會喪失約定好的利息。**也就是說，如果您把未到期定存解約，您在利息上會有所損失。**存期未滿一個月，將不計息。超過一個月的，利息將以實際存期的百分之八十計算。**

Customer：Well…That's OK. I decide to cancel my time deposit anyway.

客　　　戶：嗯…沒關係。反正我已決定把定存解約了。

Bank teller：OK. Don't blame me for not telling you in advance.

行　　　員：好吧。不要怪我沒有事先跟您說喔。

Customer：Oh, by the way, I have heard some banks announce that if you terminate a term deposit before maturity, you will not lose any promised interest at all. Have you heard of that?

客　　　戶：喔，對了，我聽一些銀行宣告說，如果您定存中途解約，您不會喪失任何約定好的利息。您有聽說過嗎？

Bank teller：Yes, I have heard of that. But the catch is, this type of time deposit is bound with some financial **commodities**, such as **deposit insurance**. In other words, you have to invest some of your money in those financial commodities sold by the bank. There is no free lunch in the world.

行　　　員：是的，我有聽說過。但是關鍵在於，這種定存都有綁一些理財商品，如儲蓄險。換句話說，您必須把部分的錢投資在這家銀行所販售的理財商品上。天下沒有白吃的午餐。

Customer：OK. I see.

客　　　戶：好的，我明白了。

Bank teller：**Do you have your national ID card as well as your original specimen seal with you?**

行　　　員：**您有帶您的國民身分證和您的原留印鑑嗎？**

Customer : Yes, here you are.

客　　戶：有啊，給您。

Bank teller : Thanks…Well, Sir, **according to our bank system, your original specimen seal is not this name chop.**

行　　員：謝謝。嗯，先生，**根據我們銀行的系統，您的原留印章不是這顆耶。**

Customer : Really? That's weird. But today I only brought this one.

客　　戶：真的嗎？奇怪了。但今天我只有帶這顆。

Bank teller : I am sorry. But if you don't have the right name chop, I can't let you cancel your CD before maturity. **If you really lost your name chop, I suggest you change your original specimen seal in the bank. But the bank will charge you one hundred NT dollars for the service fee.**

行　　員：很抱歉。但您如果沒有對的印章，我不能讓您定存中途解約。**如果您真的遺失您的印章，我建議您乾脆做印鑑變更。但銀行會跟您收一百塊的手續費。**

Customer : OK, I can accept that. I decided to change my original specimen seal.

客　　戶：可以啊，我接受。我決定做印鑑變更。

Bank teller : OK. I will process it for you right away…It is done. Your money in the time deposit has been transferred to your demand savings account. Do you want to wire the fund to the church now?

行　　員：好的。我立刻為您辦理……辦好了。您的定存錢已轉到活儲了。您要現在把錢匯給教會嗎？

Customer : Not now, but I will come back later to make the transfer. Thanks.

客　　戶：不是現在，但我等下會來辦轉帳。謝謝。

Bank teller ： You are welcome.

行　　員：不客氣。

補充單字

◆ terminate [`tɜ·məˌnet] *v.* 終止；（定存、保單的）解約

◆ commodity [kə`madətɪ] *n.* 商品

◆ deposit insurance [dɪ`pazɪt ɪn`ʃurəns] *n.* 儲蓄險

實用金句

◆ I would like to cancel my time deposit before maturity.

我要辦定存中途解約。

◆ If you terminate your time deposit before maturity, you will forfeit the promised interest.

如果您定存中途解約，您將會喪失約定好的利息。

◆ For deposits canceled within one month, the bank will not pay any interest. For those canceled after one month, the interest payable on such deposit shall be calculated at a rate of 80% of the actual deposit tenors.

存期未滿一個月，將不計息。超過一個月的，利息將以實際存期的百分之八十計息。

◆ Do you have your national ID card as well as your original specimen seal with you?

您有帶您的國民身分證和您的原留印鑑嗎？

◆ According to our bank system, your original specimen seal is not this name chop.

根據我們銀行的系統，您的原留印章不是這顆耶。

◆ If you really lost your name chop, I suggest you change your original specimen seal in the bank. But the bank will charge you one hundred NT dollars for the service fee.

如果您真的遺失您的印章，我建議您乾脆做印鑑變更。但銀行會跟您收一百元的手續費。

提　款
Making a Withdrawal

Bank teller : Hello, Mr. Yang. Long time no see. What kind of transactions would you like to conduct today?

行　　　員 : 嗨，楊先生，好久不見。您今天要辦什麼交易？

Customer : **I would like to withdraw money from my personal demand savings account.**

客　　　戶 : **我想要從我的個人活儲戶提款。**

Bank teller : What is your purpose for making a withdrawal? How much would you like to withdraw?

行　　　員 : 您提款的目地為何？您要領多少？

Customer : It is for buying a new car. And I would like to take out three hundred thousand NT dollars.

客　　　戶 : 是為了買新車。我想要提三十萬。

Bank teller : **Have you filled out the withdrawal slip?**

行　　　員 : **您填好取款條了嗎？**

Customer : Yes, I already filled out the withdrawal slip.

客　　　戶 : 是的。我已填好取款條了。

Bank teller : OK, please pass me your passbook as well as the withdrawal slip.

行　　　員 : 好的。請把您的存摺和提款條遞給我。

Customer : Here you are.

客　　　戶：給您。

Bank teller：Thank you. **Oh, you only put your** signature **on the withdrawal slip but the computer shows that your original specimen seal and signature is your signature plus your personal Chinese seal. Do you have your personal Chinese seal with you?**

行　　　員：謝謝。喔，您只有在取款條上簽名而已，但電腦上顯示您的原留印鑑是簽名加蓋章。您有帶印章嗎？

Customer：Yes, let me stamp my personal seal on the withdrawal slip. Here you are.

客　　　戶：有啊。讓我在取款條上蓋章。給您。

Bank teller：OK, let me verify your personal seal. Well, **your personal seal on the withdrawal slip is not consistent with the specimen signature and seal recorded in the bank.** Are you sure it is the right one? Do you want to check your backpack to look for the right one?

行　　　員：好的，讓我核章一下。嗯，您在取款條上蓋的章和銀行留存的原留印鑑不相符耶。您確定這是對的章嗎？您想要看一下您的背包找一下對的章嗎？

Customer：OK. Let me try checking my backpack to see whether I have another personal seal… I've got it. Here you are.

客　　　戶：好的，讓我檢查一下我的背包看看是否還有別的章……我找到了。給您。

Bank teller：Yes, it is the right one. **And how do you want it?**

行　　　員：是的，就是這顆。**您想要什麼面額的？**

Customer：Sorry, what did you say?

客　　　戶：抱歉，您說什麼？

Bank teller : **In other words, what kind of denomination do you want your money? All in thousand-yuan banknotes?**

行　　　員：換句話說，您要什麼樣的面額？都是一千元面額的紙鈔嗎？

Customer : Nope, please give me one hundred thousand in two thousand-yuan notes and one hundred thousand in thousand-yuan notes.

客　　　戶：不是。請給我二千元面額的十萬元和一千元面額的十萬元。

Bank teller : Certainly. Mr. Yang, I will process it for you in a moment.

行　　　員：沒問題。楊先生，我馬上就幫您辦好。

Customer : Thank you.

客　　　戶：謝謝。

Bank teller : You have set up a four-digit over-the-counter withdrawal password. Please enter your password. It is four-digit.

行　　　員：您有設一個四位數的臨櫃提款密碼。請輸入您的密碼。是四位數的。

Customer : Sure…It is done.

客　　　戶：好的。輸入完了。

Bank teller : The password you entered is correct. **Please take a look at the bill counter to confirm the amount while I am counting the banknotes.**

行　　　員：您按的密碼是對的。**當我數鈔時，請看著點鈔機來確認金額。**

Customer : OK.

客　　　戶：好的。

Bank teller : **It is done. The withdrawal is recorded in your passbook.** Here is your money. Please double check the amount before you leave the counter.

行　　　員：**辦好了。這筆提款已登摺在您的本子裡了。**這是您的錢。請在離

　　　　　　　開櫃檯前，再次確認您的金額無誤。

Customer　: Sure. It is very nice of you.

客　　　戶：好的。您人真好。

Bank teller : By the way, because our bank holds a CS survey that if you are sat-
　　　　　　　isfied with the teller' service, please cast a vote for me.

行　　　員：對了，我們銀行有舉辦一個客戶服務滿意度調查，如果您滿意我
　　　　　　　們的服務的話，請幫我投票。

Customer　: Oh, I understand. Many banks are now putting a great emphasis on
　　　　　　　Customer Satisfaction (CS), right?

客　　　戶：喔，我懂。很多銀行現在都很重視客戶滿意度，對吧？

Bank teller : Yes, it is our bank's way to make a customer satisfaction survey.

行　　　員：對，這是我們銀行用來調查客戶滿意度的方式。

Customer　: Sure. I will vote for you because you are so kind and nice.

客　　　戶：當然，我會投給您，因為您人很親切又很好。

Bank teller : Thank you very much.

行　　　員：非常謝謝您。

補充單字

♦ signature [ˋsɪɡnətʃɚ] *n.* 簽名

♦ denomination [dɪˏnɑməˋneʃən] *n.* 面額

♦ banknote [ˋbæŋkˋnot] *n.* 鈔票；紙鈔

♦ Customer Satisfaction (CS) [ˋkʌstəmɚ ˏsætɪsˋfækʃən] *n.* 顧客滿意度

實用金句

♦ I would like to withdraw money from my personal demand savings account.

我想要從我的個人活儲戶提款。

◆ Have you filled out the withdrawal slip?

您填好取款條了嗎？

◆ Oh, you only put your signature on the withdrawal slip but the computer shows that your original specimen seal and signature is your signature plus your personal Chinese seal. Do you have your personal Chinese seal with you?

喔，您只有在取款條上簽名而已，但電腦上顯示您的原留印鑑是簽名加蓋章。您有帶印章嗎？

◆ Your personal seal on the withdrawal slip is not consistent with the specimen signature and seal recorded in the bank.

您在取款條上蓋的章和銀行留存的原留印鑑不相符耶。

◆ How do you want it?

您想要什麼面額的？

◆ In other words, what kind of denomination do you want your money? All in thousand-yuan banknotes?

換句話說，您要什麼樣的面額？都是一千元面額的紙鈔嗎？

◆ Please take a look at the bill counter to confirm the amount while I am counting the banknotes.

當我數鈔時，請看著點鈔機來確認金額。

◆ It is done. The withdrawal is recorded in your passbook.

辦好了。這筆提款已登摺在您的本子裡了。

匯　款
Remittance

Bank teller : Hello, Sir, may I help you?

行　　　員：哈囉，先生，我可以幫您嗎？

Customer : I would like to make a remittance.

客　　　戶：我要匯款。

Bank teller : **Do you want to make an inter-bank funds transfer or make an inter-branch funds transfer?**

行　　　員：**您是要「跨行匯款」還是「聯行轉帳」？**

Customer : What did you mean?

客　　　戶：您指的是什麼？

Bank teller : An inter-bank funds transfer means, you transfer your money to another bank account. For example, you transfer money from your account in Bank of Taiwan to another account in First Commercial Bank. An inter-branch transfer, on the other hand, is a type of transfer between two different branches but still the same bank. For instance, if you transfer money from your account in Beitou Branch of Cathay United Bank to another account in Tianmu Branch of Cathay United Bank, it is called an inter-branch transfer.

行　　　員：跨行匯款是指，您把錢匯到另一家銀行的戶頭。舉例來說，您把錢從您臺灣銀行的帳戶匯到第一銀行的某帳戶。而聯行轉帳是在

相同銀行但不同分行之間的轉帳。例如說，您把錢從您國泰世華北投分行的帳戶轉到國泰世華天母分行某帳戶的轉帳，就叫聯行轉帳。

Customer : Thanks. Now I understand. I want to make an inter-bank transfer.

客　　戶：謝啦。現在我懂了。我想要辦跨行匯款。

Bank teller : OK. But you should know **if you make an inter-branch transfer, there is no service charge. And the request form you should fill out is a deposit slip instead of a remittance slip.** On the other hand, if you make an inter-bank transfer, you should fill out a remittance slip and there is a remittance charge.

行　　員：好的。但您要曉得，**如果您要聯行轉帳，則不收手續費。而您必須填存款單而非匯款單。**而如果您要辦跨行匯款，您要填匯款單而且有匯款手續費。

Customer : Wow! I didn't know that before.

客　　戶：哇！我以前都不曉得。

Bank teller : Do you want to transfer money from your passbook or by giving me cash directly? **If you have an account with our bank, I suggest you transfer money from your own account. This way, the remittance charge is lower. The bank only charges you thirty NT dollars for the remittance fee if the amount you want to transfer is within two million NT dollars. The bank will charge you additional ten NT dollars for every incremental one million NT dollars.** However, **if you plan to transfer money by directly giving me cash, the bank will charge one hundred NT dollars for the remittance fee within two million NT dollars and the bank will charge you additional thirty NT dollars for every in-**

cremental one million NT dollars.

行　　員：您要從您的戶頭直接匯還是直接給我現金？如果您在我們銀行有戶頭，我建議您直接從您的帳戶匯款。這樣手續費較低。如您要匯的金額在二百萬之內，銀行手續費只跟您收三十元，每增加一百萬元加收十元。不過，如果您想直接用現金匯，銀行的手續費是二百萬以內每筆一百元，每增加一百萬元加收三十元。

Customer : I see. Fortunately, I have a bank account with your bank and I have my passbook with me today.

客　　戶：我了解了。幸好我有在您們銀行有戶頭而我今天也有帶存摺。

Bank teller : Good for you. So, have you filled in the remittance slip?

行　　員：很好啊。所以說，您填好匯款條了嗎？

Customer : No, I haven't.

客　　戶：沒有，還沒填好。

Bank teller : **Please fill in the remittance slip. It is in duplicate.**

行　　員：**請填這張匯款單。這是兩聯一式的。**

Customer : Sure.

客　　戶：沒問題。

Bank teller : Do you know the beneficiary?

行　　員：您是否認識受款人？

Customer : Sorry, I am not following you.

客　　戶：抱歉，我不懂您的意思。

Bank teller : What I mean is, do you know the person that you want to transfer money to? I also want you to answer the following questions. **Is it the first time for you to transfer money to that person's account? How are you related to the beneficiary? What is your purpose for making a remittance?**

行　　　員：我是說，您認識您要匯款的那個人嗎？我也要請您回答下列問題。您是第一次匯款到對方的戶頭嗎？您與受款人之關係爲何？您辦理匯款的目的是？

Customer：Yes, I know the beneficiary. She is my landlord. I have to wire money to her to pay my rent every month. I have transferred money to her before.

客　　　戶：是的，我認識受款人。她是我的房東。我必須匯錢給她來付我的每月房租。我以前有轉帳給她過。

Bank teller：OK, I see. I need to ask the above questions because our bank cares about our customers. There have been a lot of frauds now, so please be careful.

行　　　員：好的，我明白了。我需要問以上的問題因爲銀行要做客戶關懷。現在詐騙頻傳，所以請小心。

Customer：That is OK.

客　　　戶：沒關係。

Bank teller：How much would you like to transfer to her?

行　　　員：您想要匯多少錢給她？

Customer：Thirty five thousand New Taiwan dollars.

客　　　戶：新臺幣三萬五千元整。

Bank teller：**Please also fill in the name of the beneficiary and the beneficiary's account number. Since you want to transfer more than thirty thousand NT dollars, according to the bank policy, you must fill in your own name, your ID number and your phone number. You also need to let me see your national ID card, please.**

行　　　員：**請您填上受款人的姓名和她的帳號。既然您要匯三萬元以上，根**

73

據銀行規定，您還要留下您自己的姓名、身分證字號和您的聯絡電話。也請您給我看一下您的身分證件。

Customer　：OK.

客　　　戶：好的。

Bank teller　：What is the name of the beneficiary bank and branch?

行　　　員：受款人的銀行名稱和分行名為何？

Customer　：First Bank, Tianmu Branch.

客　　　戶：第一銀行天母分行。

Bank teller　：**Would you like to have the remittance fee directly debited from your account or would you like to pay the remittance fee by cash?**

行　　　員：**匯款手續費要從您的帳戶直接扣除還是您要付現金給我？**

Customer　：Please debit my account directly. Thanks.

客　　　戶：請直接從我的帳戶扣除。謝謝。

Bank teller　：OK. It is done. The transfer is recorded in your passbook. Here is your passbook and receipt. Please keep your receipt safe. Is there anything else I can help you with?

行　　　員：好的。辦完了。這筆匯款已登摺在您的本子裡了。這裡是您的存摺和收據。請保管好您的收據。還有其他要辦理的業務嗎？

Customer　：No, thanks. But I want to ask you a question. My mother has accidentally transmitted a deposit to a wrong account, can she stop the transmission? What does she need to do to reverse the funds?

客　　　戶：沒有，謝謝。但我想要問您一個問題。我媽媽不小心轉了一筆錢到錯誤的帳戶去，她可以阻止這匯款嗎？她要做什麼才可以取消這筆匯款？

Bank teller　：No. Once the transmission has been made, the transmission cannot be reversed. It is important that all details should be verified before you make the transfer.

行　　　　員：沒辦法。一旦轉帳完成，就無法取消。所以在您轉帳前，確認好所有的細節是很重要的。

補充單字

◆ inter-bank funds transfer [ɪntə`bæŋk fʌndz træns`fɝ] *n.* 跨行匯款

◆ inter-branch funds transfer [ɪntrə`bræntʃ fʌndz træns`fɝ] *n.* 聯行轉帳

◆ remittance [rɪ`mɪtn̩s] *n.* 匯款；轉帳

◆ incremental [ɪnkrə`mɛntl̩] *adj.* 增加的

實用金句

◆ Do you want to make an inter-bank funds transfer or make an inter-branch transfer?

您是要「跨行匯款」還是「聯行轉帳」？

◆ If you make an inter-branch transfer, there is no service charge. And the request form you should fill out is a deposit slip instead of a remittance slip.

如果您是聯行匯款，則不收手續費。而您必須填存款單而非匯款單。

◆ If you have an account with our bank, I suggest you transfer money from your own account. This way, the remittance charge is lower.

如果您在我們銀行有戶頭，我建議您直接從您的帳戶匯款。這樣手續費較低。

◆ The bank only charges you thirty NT dollars for the remittance fee if the amount you want to transfer is within two million NT dollars. The bank will charge you additional ten NT dollars for every incremental one million NT dollars.

如您要匯的金額在二百萬之內，銀行手續費只跟您收三十元，每增加一百萬元加收十元。

◆ If you plan to transfer money by directly giving me cash, the bank will charge one hundred NT dollars for the remittance fee within two million NT dollars and the bank will charge you additional thirty NT dollars for every incremental one million NT dollars.

如果您想直接用現金匯，銀行的手續費是二百萬以內每筆一百元，每增加一百萬元加收三十元。

◆ Please fill in the remittance slip. It is in duplicate.

請填這張匯款單。這是兩聯一式的。

◆ Is it the first time for you to transfer money to that person's account? How are you related to the beneficiary? What is your purpose for making a remittance?

您是第一次匯款到對方的戶頭嗎？您與受款人之關係爲何？您辦理匯款的目的是？

◆ Please also fill in the name of the beneficiary and the beneficiary's account number. Since you want to transfer more than thirty thousand NT dollars, according to the bank policy, you must fill in your own name, your ID number and your phone number. You also need to let me see your national ID card, please.

請您填上受款人的姓名和她的帳號。既然您要匯三萬元以上，根據銀行規定，您還要留下您自己的姓名、身分證字號和您的聯絡電話。也請您給我

看一下您的身分證件。

◆ Would you like to have the remittance fee directly debited from your account or would you like to pay the remittance fee by cash?

匯款手續費從您的帳戶直接扣除還是您要付現金給我？

約定帳號
Registered Account Number

Customer : Hello, I have a question. I cannot transfer money between accounts through my ATM card at the ATM.

客　　戶：嗨，我有一個問題。我無法用金融卡從ATM轉帳。

Bank teller : How much did you just try to transfer?

行　　員：您剛試著轉了多少？

Customer : I tried to transfer fifty thousand NT dollars through the ATM, but the transaction was failed. I want to know why.

客　　戶：我試著透過ATM轉五萬元臺幣，但交易失敗。我想知道原因。

Bank teller : I see. In fact, **if customers do not set up any** registered account number **in advance, the bank will ban customers from transferring money more than thirty thousand NT dollars a day through ATMs or online banking.** Once you set up a registered account number with the bank, the bank will link your account with the registered account and you can transfer more than thirty thousand NT dollars to the registered account a day. Of course, this regulation is to protect your account.

行　　員：我明白了。**如果客人沒有事先設定好任何**約定帳號**的話，銀行會禁止客人用ATM或網銀每日轉出超過三萬元。**一旦您在銀行設定好了約定帳戶，銀行就會在您的帳戶和約定帳號做連結，您就可

以一天轉出超過三萬元到約定帳戶了。當然，這個規定是為了保護您的帳戶。

Customer : I see. Can I set up my registered account number through online banking?

客　　戶：我了解了。我可以用網銀來設約定帳號嗎？

Bank teller : No, you can't. **According to the bank's regulations, you should visit the bank in person with your ID card as well as your original specimen seal to set up the** designated account number.

行　　員：不可以。**根據銀行的內規，您必須本人親自到銀行，帶著您的身分證和原留印鑑來設定**約定帳號。

Customer : I see. It happens that I have my ID card as well as my original specimen seal with me. Should I take a number slip for General Transactions?

客　　戶：我明白了。我碰巧有帶我的身分證和原留印鑑。我應該抽一張「一般交易」的號碼牌嗎？

Bank teller : No, **you should take a number slip for the Service Counter.** Some banks allow you to add a designated account number over the bank counter. Our bank, however, needs you to perform this transaction at the service counter, which is also called the composite service area. Here is your number ticket. Please wait for a moment.

行　　員：不，**您應該抽一張「服務臺」的號碼牌。**有些銀行允許您到櫃檯設約定帳號。但我們銀行要您到服務臺辦此交易，而服務臺也稱作「綜合服務區」。這是您的號碼牌。請稍候一下。

Customer : Thanks.

客　　戶：謝謝。

(The customer's number is called. He went to the service counter.)
（客戶的號碼被叫號了。他去服務臺。）

Bank teller : Hello, what can I do for you?

行　　員：哈囉，您要辦什麼呢？

Customer : **I would like to set up the designated account number.**

客　　戶：**我要設定約定帳號。**

Bank teller : No problem. **Do you want to add the designated account number for the use of ATMs or Internet Banking?**

行　　員：沒問題。**您想要設定ATM還是網銀的約定帳號？**

Customer : I would like to add the designated account number for the use of ATMs.

客　　戶：我想要設定用在ATM的約定帳號。

Bank teller : Do you bring your ID card and your original specimen seal with you?

行　　員：您有帶身分證和原留印鑑嗎？

Customer : Yes, here you are. I want to add two designated account numbers. One account number belongs to Bank of Taiwan. The other belongs to Taishin International Commercial Bank.

客　　戶：有的，在這裡。我想要增加兩個約定帳號。一個是臺銀的，另一個是台新銀行的。

Bank teller : **Are these registered account numbers yours or someone else's?**

行　　員：**這些約定帳號都是您的還是別人的？**

Customer : Both are mine.

客　　戶：都是我的。

Bank teller : Then, please fill in this application form and sign your name on it.

行　　員：那麼，請填這張申請表並簽名。

Customer : OK. Do you know the bank code of Bank of Taiwan and the bank code of Taishin International Commercial Bank? Because I don't know.

客　　戶：好的。您知道臺銀和台新銀行的銀行代碼嗎？因為我不曉得耶。

Bank teller : The **bank code** of Bank of Taiwan is 004 and that of Taishin Bank is 812.

行　　員：臺銀的銀行代碼是004，而台新的是812。

Customer : Thanks. I have filled out the form. Here you are.

客　　戶：謝謝。我已填好這張申請表。給您。

Bank teller : **According to the Personal Data Protection Law, I must ask you to sign your name on the letter of authorization to authorize the bank to process your personal information.**

行　　員：**根據個資法，我必須請您在這張授權書上簽名來授權銀行處理您的個資。**

Customer : No problem. Here you are. I know the bank can add my linked account numbers into my chip and PIN ATM card. How many accounts can I link to my ATM card?

客　　戶：沒有問題。給您。我還知道銀行可以把我的約定帳號讀寫到我的晶片金融卡。我的金融卡可以寫多少個帳號？

Bank teller : You can link up to eight bank accounts to one card. The linked account numbers will appear on the ATM screen for you to select when you want to make a transfer. OK, it is done. Here is your ID card and your original specimen seal. **Please note that those linked account numbers will not be activated until the next working day.** The effective date is T plus one. Therefore, you cannot transfer more than thirty thousand NT dollars from your account to these linked account numbers now. Is there anything else I can help you with?

行　　　員：您最多可以讀寫八個銀行帳號到一張卡裡。當您要轉帳時，約定
帳號將會顯示在自動櫃員機的螢幕上讓您來選擇。好了，辦好
了。這是您的身分證和原留印章。**請注意這些約定帳號下個工作
天才會生效。**生效日是T加一。所以您現在還是無法從您的戶頭轉
超過三萬元到這些約定帳號。還有其他需要我服務的地方嗎？

Customer : No. Thanks.

客　　　戶：沒有了。謝謝。

補充單字

♦ registered account number [`rɛdʒɪstəd ə`kaunt `nʌmbə] ***n.*** 約定帳號（＝ linked account number）

♦ designated account number [`dɛzɪg,netɪd ə`kaunt `nʌmbə] ***n.*** 約定帳號

♦ bank code [`bæŋk kod] ***n.*** 銀行代碼；銀行代號

實用金句

♦ If customers do not set up any registered account number in advance, the bank will ban customers from transferring money more than thirty thousand NT dollars a day through ATMs or online banking.

如果客人沒有事先設定好任何約定帳號的話，銀行會禁止客人用ATM或網銀每日轉超過三萬元。

♦ According to the bank's regulations, you should visit the bank in person with your ID card as well as your original specimen seal to set up the designated account number.

根據銀行的內規，您必須本人親自到銀行，帶著您的身分證和原留印鑑來設定約定帳號。

◆ You should take a number for the Service Counter.

您應該抽一張「服務臺」的號碼牌。

◆ I would like to set up the designated account number.

我要設定約定帳號。

◆ Do you want to add the designated account number for the use of ATMs or Internet Banking?

您想要設定ATM還是網銀的約定帳號？

◆ Are these registered account numbers yours or someone else's?

這些約定帳號是您的還是別人的？

◆ According to the Personal Data Protection Law, I must ask you to sign your name on the letter of authorization to authorize the bank to process your personal information.

根據個資法，我必須請您在這張授權書上簽名來授權銀行處理您的個資。

◆ Please note that those linked account numbers will not be activated until the next working day.

請注意這些約定帳號下個工作天才會生效。

國外匯款
Foreign Remittance

Customer : I would like to transfer money to my friend in U.S. Can you help me?

客　　戶：我想要匯錢到美國給我朋友。您可以幫我嗎？

Bank teller : Of course. There are three ways for customers in Taiwan to transfer money to foreign countries. First and foremost, you can wire money through Telegraphic Transfer (T/T) or SWIFT. The second way is through Western Union. The third way is called VISA Money Transfer.

行　　員：當然。從臺灣匯錢到國外有三種方式。第一且最重要的，您可以透過「電匯」，或叫SWIFT。第二種方式是透過「西聯匯款」。第三種方式是透過「易匯通」。

Customer : So there are three ways. I've got it. Can you fill me with more details?

客　　戶：所以有三種方式。我知道了。您可以告訴我更多細節嗎？

Bank teller : Sure. Telegraphic Transfer Service is actually an outward electronic transfer of money wired by SWIFT to an overseas recipient's bank account. Payment is typically received within just a few days depending on the currency and country. In addition, SWIFT code is a standard format of bank identifier codes and it is a special and unique identification code for a certain bank. These codes are used when banks are wiring money and messages between banks. Each SWIFT message between two banks is authenticated with a secret key known only to the two banks involved, so it is safe and secure. The SWIFT code is made up of eight or eleven characters. An accurate SWIFT code is indispensable in ensuring the money successfully and promptly being credited to the beneficiary's bank account. Generally speaking, the beneficiary will receive the money within T plus three working days. However, sometimes wiring money through SWIFT to the beneficiary's account might be delayed because of all kinds of factors, including incomplete or incorrect payment details, capability of the beneficiary bank to process incoming funds in time, and local currency regulations. If you want to transfer money overseas through SWIFT or T/T, you must provide the bank with following information: (1) Beneficiary's account number (2) Country or Destination (3) Currency (4) Bank name (5) Bank city (6) Bank branch name (7) Receiver name (8) Receiver address (9) Receiver contact number (10) Purpose of remittance. **All in all, Telegraphic Transfer is a convenient and safe way to send money to your family members or friends overseas.**

行　　員：沒問題，電匯實際是透過SWIFT的向外電報匯款來匯到國外受款人的帳戶。匯款一般來說在幾天內就可以收到，要視外幣種類和國家。此外，SWIFT碼是一種標準格式的銀行認證碼，而它也是對某個銀行特別的辨識碼。當銀行之間匯款、交換訊息時，這些碼就會被用到。兩間銀行的每個SWIFT訊息是用只有這兩間銀行才會知道的密碼金鑰來加以驗證，所以很安全。SWIFT碼由八或

十一位數組成。正確的SWIFT碼在確保錢成功和快速地匯到受款人的銀行帳戶所不可或缺的。一般說來，受款人會在T加三個工作天收到款項。然而，有時透過SWIFT匯款給受款戶可能會因為各種因素而延遲，包含不完整或不正確匯款的細節、收款行未能及時處理匯入款和當地的外幣管制。如果您想要用電匯來匯到國外，您必須提供銀行下面資訊(1)受款人帳號(2)國家或目的地(3)幣別(4)銀行名稱(5)銀行所在城市(6)分行名稱(7)受款人姓名(8)受款人的住址(9)受款人的聯絡電話(10)匯款目地。總之，電匯是一種便利和安全的給您在國外的親朋好友的匯款方式。

Customer : What about the remittance commission?

客　　戶：那匯款費用怎麼算？

Bank teller : **As for the remittance fee, it usually involves the bank** service commission **and the** cable charge. However, some banks only charge their customers for the service commission whereas some banks only charge their customers for the cable charge. For example, Cathay United Bank only charges their customers for the cable charge of 400 NT dollars over the bank counter and if Cathay United Bank's customers wire money overseas via online banking, the cable charge is only 300 NT dollars. **In a word, there is no flat price for outward remittance to foreign countries.** In addition, **if you want the beneficiary to receive the remittance in full amount, the bank will charge you for additional cable charge.** For example, the bank may charge you 700 NT dollars for the service commission and 600 NT dollars for the cable charge. But if you want the beneficiary to receive the full payment, the bank will charge you additional NT 600 dollars for double cable charge.

行　　員：**關於匯款費用，通常包括了銀行的手續費和電報費。**然而，有些銀行只跟客戶收手續費，而有些銀行只跟客戶收電報費。舉例來說，國泰世華只跟臨櫃的客戶收電報費用四百元。如果國泰世華的客戶透過網銀來辦理電匯的話，電報費用只收三百元。**簡單說來，匯款到國外沒有一個統一價。另外，如果您要全額到匯的話，銀行會跟您收額外的電報費。**例如說，銀行可能跟您收七百元作為手續費和六百元作電報費。但您要全額到匯的話，銀行會另外再跟您收六百元作為雙電報的費用。

Customer：OK. Now I get a basic idea of T/T. Can you tell me about Western Union transfer?

客　　戶：好，我對電匯有基本概念了。您可以跟我講一下西聯匯款嗎？

Bank teller：Of course. **If you need to send the money right away, Western Union is probably a better option than transferring money to another account overseas through SWIFT since Western Union transfers are almost available immediately.** If you want to transfer money through Western Union, you need to provide the following information, inclusive of the sender's full name, the amount sent, the MTCN (transaction number), the city and country from which the money was sent. You also have to sign a receipt after you have verified all the details printed on the receipt are correct. After you complete the above-mentioned procedures, you can contact the intended receiver of your money, and pass the necessary information to the beneficiary such as the sender's name, the amount sent, the unique number of your transaction (MTCN), and so on, in order for him to get the remittance you sent.

行　　員：當然，**如果您想要立刻把錢匯過去，**西聯匯款**是比起電匯來說更好的選擇，因為西聯匯款幾乎是錢馬上就可以匯到。**如果您要透過西聯匯款來匯款，您要提供下列資訊，包含付款人的全名、匯款的金額、匯款控制號碼、匯款目的地所在的城市和國家名。在您確認好印在收據上的資訊無誤後，您也必須在收據上簽名。在您完成以上的程序後，您就可以聯絡您要匯款的對象並把必要的資訊告訴受款人，像是付款人的全名、匯款的金額、匯款控制號碼等等，這樣他才可以取得您匯出的款項。

Customer : So where can I use Western Union service in Taiwan?

客　　戶：我在臺灣哪裡可以辦西聯匯款呢？

Bank teller : Although in Taiwan Western Union is not allowed to set up their own service locations, Western Union is now cooperating with Ta Chong Bank and King's Town Bank, in enabling a convenient and quick fund transfer service. Of course, besides Ta Chong Bank and King's Town Bank, Cathay United Bank and Chang Hwa Commercial Bank used to provide Western Union service. However, Cathay United Bank and Chang Hwa Commercial Bank have ceased the Western Union service now. Therefore, you can go to the nearest Ta Chong Bank branch to transfer your money through Western Union.

行　　員：雖然在臺灣西聯匯款不被允許設自己的服務處。但西聯匯款現在與大眾銀行和京城銀行合作來推行便利和快速的匯款方式。當然，除了大眾銀行和京城銀行，國泰世華和彰化銀行以前也提供西聯匯款的服務。不過，國泰世華和彰化銀行現在已經終止了西聯匯款的服務了。因此，您可以去離您最近的大眾銀行分行來辦理西聯匯款。

Customer : Thanks. Can you tell me more benefits of Western Union?

客　　戶：謝謝。您可以跟我講更多西聯匯款的優點嗎？

Bank teller : Yes. Western Union transfer is very fast. The beneficiary doesn't have to wait for about one to four days for money to arrive. **Generally, once the sender completes the procedure of Western Union, the beneficiary will receive money in 15 minutes during business hours.** Therefore, it is very fast compared with traditional T/T. Another advantage is, you don't have to open a bank account to conduct Western Union transfer.

行　　員：可以。西聯匯款非常地快。受款人不必花一到四天等款項匯來。**一般來說，只要寄款人完成西聯匯款的手續，受款人在營業時間內大約十五分鐘以內就可以收到款項。**因此，它和傳統電匯比起來的話，它相當快。另一個優點是，您不必開一個銀行戶頭才能辦西聯匯款。

Customer : Thank you. If there are some advantages, there must be some disadvantages. Can you tell me any downside?

客　　戶：謝謝您。如果有優點，就必定有些缺點。您可以告訴我缺點嗎？

Bank teller : Well, **Western Union has a maximum of 15,000 US dollars for each transaction.** Telegraphic Transfer, on the other hand, has no limit. And the remittance fee of Western Union is higher. For example, if you transfer about 5,000 US dollars to China through Western Union, the bank will charge you about 22 US dollars for the remittance fee.

行　　員：好的，**西聯匯款有每筆交易最高美金一萬五千元的限制。**另一方面，電匯則沒有金額限制。而且西聯匯款的匯款手續費較高。例如說，您透過西聯匯大約五千美金到大陸的話，銀行會跟您收

二十二美金的匯款手續費。

Customer : OK, thanks.

客　　　戶：好，謝謝。

Bank teller : Last, let me introduce VISA Money Transfer. This service gives consumers a cost-effective way to transfer funds directly to recipients' VISA cards domestically and internationally. You can initiate a VISA Money Transfer to make person-to-person payments through Internet Banking or Automatic Teller Machines (ATM). VISA Money Transfer (VMT) offers you a new international remittance service. **VISA Money Transfer enables you to transfer money to the third party's VISA card account issued by another bank only at the charge of 200 NT dollars.** On top of this, there is no need for you to wait in line or complete complicated documents over a bank counter. The bank service commission for each VMT international remittance transaction only cost you 200 NT dollars. The fixed charge saves you the trouble of calculation. What's better, once you have sign up for VMT service, you can use Internet banking and ATMs to use VMT to transfer money. However, there are some downsides, too. VISA Money Transfer has a maximum of 25,000 US dollars for each transaction and it has to take about one to three working days for money to arrive.

行　　　員：最後，讓我介紹一下易匯通。這個服務使客戶以經濟效率的方式把錢直接匯到國內或國外的受款人的VISA金融卡帳戶裡。您可以透過網銀或自動櫃員機來開始用易匯通來進行個人匯款。易匯通提供您一個新的國際匯款服務。**易匯通能讓您匯款到另一家銀行發行的VISA金融卡帳戶裡，而手續費只要新臺幣二百元。**此外，您沒有必要排隊或是臨櫃填寫複雜的文件。每筆易匯通的跨國匯

款手續費只要花您二百元。這不二價省您很多計算的麻煩。更好的是，一旦您申請了易匯通的服務，您可以透過網銀或是ATM來使用易匯通匯款。然而，它也有些缺點。易匯通單筆交易限最高美金二萬五千元並且要花一到三個工作天錢才會匯到。

Customer : OK. I see. Where can I use Visa Money Transfer in Taiwan?

客　　戶：好的，我了解了。我在臺灣的哪裡可以辦易匯通呢？

Bank teller : VISA Money Transfer has teamed up with Taishin International Commercial Bank. If you want to use VISA Money Transfer, you can go to Taishin Bank to sign up for this service. But you have to notice, the **applicant** of Visa Money Transfer must be above-twenty-year-old citizens of Taiwan or foreign aliens who possess ARC that is valid for more than one year. If you have needs for regular micro remittance, I will recommend you sign up for VISA Money Transfer.

行　　員：易匯通已和台新國際商銀合作。如果您想辦易匯通，您可以去台新銀行申請此服務。但您必須注意，易匯通申請人的年紀必須滿二十歲以上的在臺國民或是持有一年以上有效期居留證的外國人。如果您有定期的小額匯款需求，我推薦您申辦易匯通。

Customer : Now I understand. Thank you very much.

客　　戶：現在我了解了。非常謝謝您。

補充單字

- ◆ Telegraphic Transfer (T/T) [ˌtɛləˋgræfɪk trænsˋfɝ] *n.* 電匯

- ◆ destination [ˌdɛstəˋneʃən] *n.* 目的地

- ◆ service commission [ˋsɝvɪs kəˋmɪʃən] *n.* 手續費

- ◆ cable charge [ˋkebḷ tʃɑrdʒ] *n.* 電報費；郵電費

- ◆ Western Union transfer [ˋwɛstɚn ˋjunɪən trænsˋfɝ] *n.* 西聯匯款

- ◆ applicant [ˋæpləkənt] *n.* 申請人；要保人

實用金句

- ◆ All in all, Telegraphic Transfer is a convenient and safe way to send money to your family members or friends overseas.

  總之，電匯是一種便利和安全的給您在國外的親朋好友的匯款方式。

- ◆ As for the remittance fee, it usually involves the bank service commission and the cable charge.

  關於匯款費用，通常包括了銀行的手續費和電報費。

- ◆ In a word, there is no flat price for outward remittance to foreign countries.

  簡單說來，匯款到國外沒有一個固定價。

- ◆ If you want the beneficiary to receive the remittance in full amount, the bank will charge you for additional cable charge.

  如果您要全額到匯的話，銀行會跟您收額外的電報費。

- ◆ If you need to send the money right away, Western Union is probably a better option than transferring money to another account overseas through SWIFT since Western Union transfers are almost available immediately.

如果您想要立刻把錢匯過去，西聯匯款是比起電匯來說一個更好的選擇，因為西聯匯款幾乎是錢馬上就可以匯到。

♦ Generally, once the sender completes the procedure of Western Union, the beneficiary will receive money in 15 minutes during business hours.

一般來說，只要寄款人完成西聯匯款的手續，受款人在營業時間內大約十五分鐘以內就可以收到款項。

♦ Western Union has a maximum of 15,000 US dollars for each transaction.

西聯匯款有每筆交易最高美金一萬五千元的限制。

♦ VISA Money Transfer enables you to transfer money to the third party's VISA card account issued by another bank only at the charge of 200 NT dollars.

易匯通能讓您匯款到另一家銀行發行的VISA金融卡帳戶裡，而手續費只要新臺幣二百元。

外 匯
Foreign Exchange

Customer : Hello, **can I exchange** foreign currency **here?**

客　　戶：嗨，我可以在這裡兌換外幣嗎？

Bank teller : This bank branch is an authorized money changer, so the answer is yes. But we only deal in a few foreign cash. **What kind of foreign currency do you want to change?**

行　　員：我們這間分行是外匯指定銀行。所以答案是肯定的。但我們只買賣幾種外幣現鈔。您要換什麼幣別的？

Customer : Can I exchange some US dollars into New Taiwan dollars here?

客　　戶：我可以在這裡把美金換成臺幣嗎？

Bank teller : Yes, you can. **How much would you like to exchange?**

行　　員：是的，您可以。您想要換多少？

Customer : **I want to convert one hundred US dollars into New Taiwan dollars.**

客　　戶：我想要把一百美金換成新臺幣。

Bank teller : No problem.

行　　員：沒問題。

Customer : **What is the current exchange rate for US dollars? Is the US dollar up or down now?**

客　　戶：美金現在的匯率是多少？美金現在是升了還是下跌了？

Bank teller : The US dollar is up now. **The exchange rate for US dollars into New Taiwan dollars is one US dollar to twenty eight point seven (28.7) New Taiwan dollars.** You can look at our exchange table.

行　　員：美金漲了。美金兌新臺幣的匯率是二十八點七。您可以看一下我們的外匯牌告。

US Dollar 美金	Buying Rate 買進匯率	Selling Rate 賣出匯率
Spot Rate 即期匯率	28.9	29.0
Cash Rate 現鈔匯率	28.7	29.2

Customer : I don't understand. I want to sell my US dollars to you. Why do you apply the buying rate to me?

客　　戶：我不明白。我要賣美金給您。但您爲什麼讓我用買進匯率？

Bank teller : Because the buying rate is not from the customer's perspective, but from the perspective of the bank. We, the bank, buy US dollars from you and give you New Taiwan dollars, so I apply the buying rate to you. Do you understand?

行　　員：因爲買進匯率不是從客戶的角度來看的，而是從銀行的角度。我們跟您買美金並給您新臺幣，所以您適用買進匯率。您了解了嗎？

Customer : OK. Why is there an exchange rate differential between thc buying rate and the selling rate?

客　　戶：好的。爲什麼買進匯率和賣出匯率有匯差呢？

Bank teller : There is an **exchange rate spread** because the bank needs to profit from the exchange rate differential.

行　　　員：有匯差是因為銀行要從外匯匯率的差價來賺錢啊。

Customer : What does the exchange rate spread mean?

客　　　戶：匯差是什麼意思？

Bank teller : **The exchange rate spread means, the difference in buying and selling price of foreign currencies.**

行　　　員：匯差是說，外幣的買進和賣出匯率的差價。

Customer : I see. Why is there a difference between spot rate and cash rate? Can you tell me?

客　　　戶：我明白了。為什麼即期匯率和現鈔匯率會不同呢？您可以告訴我嗎？

Bank teller : Simply put, foreign currency is not the legal tender, or legal currency in Taiwan.

行　　　員：簡單說，外幣在臺灣不是法幣。

Customer : I am confused. What do you mean by that? Can you explain to me?

客　　　戶：我搞迷糊了。您這話是什麼意思？您可以解釋給我聽嗎？

Bank teller : Well, what I mean is, **foreign cash** is actually a commodity in Taiwan. The bank deals in foreign currencies, just as a store owner buys and sells his goods. The bank has to buy foreign cash from other banks and has to bear the risk of transporting, storing, and protecting the foreign cash. On top of this, the bank also has to take the risk of accepting forged or altered foreign bills. There is also the cost of the bank insurance premium to protect those foreign banknotes. Therefore, **if you want to buy or sell your foreign cash, the cash rate is not as good as the spot rate.** The spot rate is better because the bank does not have to bear all the risks of transporting, storing or protecting the foreign cash. If you just buy or sell virtual foreign currencies from your passbook to make an investment, you don't really buy any physical cash that you can touch. There are just figure changes in your passbook. Thus, it will not cost the bank as much as when you buy or sell foreign cash. That is why the spot rate is better than the cash rate.

行　　員：好吧。我是說，外幣現鈔在臺灣實際上是商品。銀行買賣外幣就像商店老闆買賣他的貨品一樣。銀行必須從其他銀行買進這些外幣現鈔和必須承擔運輸、倉儲和保護外幣現鈔的風險。除此之外，銀行也必須承擔收到假鈔或變造鈔票的風險。而且也會讓銀行負擔幫外幣現鈔保險的費用。所以說，**如果您想買賣外幣現鈔，現鈔匯率沒有即期匯率那麼好**。即期匯率較好是因為銀行不必擔當運輸、倉儲或是保護外幣現鈔的風險。如果您只是在存摺上做虛擬的買賣外幣來投資的話，您不是真的買了任何摸得著的實體現鈔。只是在存摺上的數字變化而已。所以，銀行不會花到和您交易外幣現鈔時同樣的成本。這就是為什麼即期匯率比現鈔匯率還要好的緣故。

Customer：I see now.
客　　戶：我明白了。

Bank teller：So do you accept the exchange rate I just quoted to you? You may accept or decline our rate quotation. If you accept our bank's quotation, you have entered into a final and binding transaction and it cannot be reversed.

行　　員：所以您接受我剛才的匯率報價嗎？您可以接受或拒絕這個匯率報價。如果您接受我們銀行的報價，您這個交易就會進入最後的執行階段並且無法被取消。

Customer : Yes, I accept the quote.

客　　戶：是的，我接受這個報價。

Bank teller : Good. I'll set this rate quote. Please pass me your passport and your US dollars.

行　　員：很好，我就敲價了。請把您的護照和美金給我。

Customer : OK, here you are.

客　　戶：好的，給您。

Bank teller : Sorry. **Some US banknotes are not accepted by the currency detector** because some of your foreign cash is out of circulation.

行　　員：抱歉，**有些美鈔通不過**驗鈔機耶，因為您的有些外幣現鈔已經不流通了。

Customer : Really? Some of my US banknotes are rejected by the money detector?

客　　戶：真的嗎？我的美鈔有些通不過驗鈔機嗎？

Bank teller : Yes. So we can't accept the foreign cash. Do you have other US banknotes?

行　　員：是的。所以我們無法接受這些外幣現鈔。您還有其他的美鈔嗎？

Customer : Yes, here you are.

客　　戶：有的，給您。

Bank teller : OK. This time your banknotes are all accepted. You can get two thousand, eight hundred and seventy in New Taiwan dollars. And what denominations would you like the money in?

行　　員：好的。這次您的美鈔都通過驗鈔機了。您可以換到二千八百七十元的新臺幣。您要什麼面額的？

Customer : Actually, you can simply say, "How do you want it?" This is more like real English.

客　　戶：事實上，您可以直接說：「How do you want it?」這比較是道地的
英文。

Bank teller：Oh, I am sorry. My English is not so good. Thank you for telling
me.

行　　員：喔。抱歉。我的英文不是很好。謝謝您告訴我。

Customer：Give me two thousand yuan in one thousand-yuan notes and eight
hundred yuan in one hundred-yuan notes. And I want the seventy
yuan in ten-yuan coins.

客　　戶：給我一千元面額的兩千，一百元面額的八百元。然後我要十元面
額的七十元硬幣。

Bank teller：OK. No problem. I will process it for you right now.

行　　員：好的，沒有問題。我立刻為您辦理。

Customer：Thanks.

客　　戶：謝謝。

Bank teller：It's all done. Here is your **exchange memo** and your money. Please
keep them safe.

行　　員：辦好了。這是您的水單和錢。請妥善保管。

Customer：If I finish travelling around Taiwan and I have some unused New
Taiwan dollars, can I change them back into US dollars at your
bank?

客　　戶：如果我結束在臺灣的旅遊而我有未用掉的新臺幣的話，我可以在
您們銀行換回美金嗎？

Bank teller：Of course. But I would suggest **you should show us the exchange
memo we issued to you when you want to convert New Taiwan
dollars back into US dollars.**

行　　員：當然可以。但是我建議您當您要把新臺幣換回美金時，最好要出

示我們當初發給您的水單。

Customer : Thanks. By the way, I have some US coins. Can I also change these coins here?

客　　服 : 謝謝。對了，我有一些美元硬幣，我可以在這裡換硬幣嗎？

Bank teller : No, you can't. **Our bank does not deal in foreign coins. That is to say, we do not distribute or accept foreign coins.**

行　　員 : 不可以。**我們銀行不承兌外幣硬幣。也就是說，我們不散布或是接受外幣零錢。**

Customer : Oops, I just remembered. I also have one hundred thousand Australian dollars with me. Can I convert Australian dollars into New Taiwan dollars here? Does your bank exchange Australian dollars?

客　　戶 : 哎呀，我想起來了。我還有十萬元的澳幣，我可以在這裡把澳幣換成新臺幣嗎？您們銀行可以兌換澳幣嗎？

Bank teller : No, you can't convert your Australian dollars into New Taiwan dollars here because **our bank only deals in foreign cash for the US Dollar, Hong Kong Dollar, Japanese Yen, Euro, and Renminbi. If you want to change Australian dollars into New Taiwan dollars, I suggest you go to Bank of Taiwan or Mega International Commercial Bank to exchange your money there.** They deal in a lot of foreign cash such as the Australian Dollar, British Pound, New Zealand Dollar, Swedish Krona, Singapore Dollar, Swiss Franc, Korean Won, and Thai Baht. Also, you can find a branch of Bank of Taiwan just across the street, and it takes five minutes to get there.

行　　員 : 不可以。您無法在這裡把澳幣換成新臺幣，因爲**我們銀行只收美金、港幣、日圓、歐元和人民幣現鈔。如果您想把澳幣換成新臺**

幣，**我建議您到臺銀或是兆豐國際商銀換**。他們兌換很多種類的
外幣現鈔，像是澳幣、英磅、紐西蘭幣、瑞典克朗、新加坡幣、
瑞士法朗、韓圓和泰銖。您也可以在對街找到一家臺銀分行，大
約花五分鐘就到了。

Customer　：I see. Thank you.

客　　　戶：我明白了，謝謝。

Bank teller　：By the way, allow me to remind you one thing. Since you want to convert one hundred thousand Australian dollars into New Taiwan dollars at Bank of Taiwan, the transaction amount will definitely be more than five hundred thousand NT dollars. **According to Money Laundering Control Act, if you make a one-time cash transaction which is more than five hundred thousand NT dollars, you must fill out the declaration form to provide your personal and transaction information to the authorities concerned.**

行　　　員：對了，容我提醒您一件事。既然您想在臺銀換十萬澳幣，這交易的金額一定會超過五十萬臺幣。**根據洗錢防制法，如果您一次現金交易單筆就超過五十萬新臺幣的話，您必須填寫申報書和提供您的個人資料和交易資料給相關主管機構。**

Customer　：OK. By the way, I also heard that people can order foreign currency online if they are registered for your online banking. What are the daily limits for ordering online?

客　　　戶：好的。順便一提，我也聽說如果有申辦網銀的話，民眾可以線上訂購外幣。線上訂購外幣的每日限額是多少呢？

Bank teller　：Our bank's customers that sign in to online banking can order up to half a million NT dollars in foreign currency per day. Then, you can collect your foreign cash over the counter.

行　　　員：有申辦我們網銀的客戶可以一天訂購等值五十萬新臺幣的外幣。
　　　　　　然後，您可以來銀行櫃檯領取您的外幣。

Customer：Thank you for your explanation. It is really nice of you.

客　　　戶：謝謝您的說明。您人真好。

補充單字

◆ foreign currency [`fɔrɪn `kɝ·ənsɪ] *n.* 外幣

◆ exchange rate spread [ɪks`tʃendʒ ret sprɛd] *n.* 匯差

◆ foreign cash [`fɔrɪn kæʃ] *n.* 外幣現鈔

◆ currency detector [`kɝ·ənsɪ dɪ`tɛktɚ] *n.* 驗鈔機

◆ exchange memo [ɪks`tʃendʒ mɛmo] *n.* （兌換外幣的）水單

實用金句

◆ Can I exchange foreign currency here?

我可以在這裡兌換外幣嗎？

◆ What kind of foreign currency do you want to change?

您要換什麼幣別的？

◆ How much would you like to exchange?

您想要換多少？

◆ I want to convert one hundred US dollars into New Taiwan dollars.

我想要把一百美金換成新臺幣。

◆ What is the current exchange rate for US dollars? Is the US dollar up or down now?

美金現在的匯率是多少？美金現在是升了還是下跌了？

◆ The exchange rate for US dollars into New Taiwan dollars is one US dollar to twenty eight point seven (28.7) New Taiwan dollars.

美金兌新臺幣的匯率是二十八點七。

◆ The exchange rate spread means, the difference in buying and selling price of foreign currencies.

匯差是說，外幣的買入和賣出匯率的差價。

◆ If you want to buy or sell your foreign cash, the cash rate is not as good as the spot rate.

如果您想買賣外幣現鈔，現鈔匯率沒有即期匯率那麼好。

◆ Some US banknotes are not accepted by the currency detector.

有些美鈔通不過驗鈔機。

◆ You should show us the exchange memo we issued to you when you want to convert New Taiwan dollars back into US dollars.

當您要把新臺幣換回美金時，最好要出示我們當初給您的水單。

◆ Our bank does not deal in foreign coins. That is to say, we do not distribute or accept foreign coins.

我們銀行不承兌外幣硬幣。也就是說，我們不散布或是接受外幣零錢。

◆ Our bank only deals in foreign cash for the US Dollar, Hong Kong Dollar, Japanese Yen, Euro, and Renminbi. If you want to change Australian dollars, I will suggest you go to Bank of Taiwan or Mega International Commercial Bank to exchange your money there.

我們銀行只收美金、港幣、日圓、歐元和人民幣。如果您想換澳幣，我建議您到臺銀或是兆豐國際商銀換。

♦ According to Money Laundering Control Act, if you make a one-time cash transaction which is more than five hundred thousand NT dollars, you must fill out the declaration form to provide your personal and transaction information to the authorities concerned.

根據洗錢防制法，如果您一次現金交易單筆就超過五十萬新臺幣的話，您必須填寫申報書和提供您的個人資料和交易資料給相關主管機構。

旅行支票
Traveler's Check

Customer : Hello. May I buy **traveler's checks** here?

客　　戶：嗨，我可以在這邊買旅行支票嗎？

Bank teller : Yes. Our banks offer traveler's checks. Do you know how to use a traveler's check? Do you want me to introduce it for you?

行　　員：可以。我們銀行有提供旅行支票。您知道如何使用旅支嗎？您要我為您介紹嗎？

Customer : OK. I would like to know traveler's checks.

客　　戶：好啊。我想了解旅支。

Bank teller : Simply put, traveler's checks are pre-printed fixed amount checks that you can buy at banks. **Traveler's checks allow you to go to another country to make a purchase or cash them at local banks.** Most people buy traveler's checks to use as cash on vacation especially when they go to foreign countries. **American Express traveler's checks may be changed for cash in a lot of countries abroad. You can use them at shops, hotels, department stores, restaurants and so on.**

行　　員：簡單來說，旅支是您可以在銀行買到的事先印好固定金額的支票。**旅支允許您去其他國家消費或是在當地銀行兌現。**大部分人買旅支是作為旅遊中現金的替代品，特別是當他們去國外時。美

國運通的旅行支票可以在很多國家換成現金。您可以在商店、旅館、百貨公司、餐廳等地方使用旅支。

Customer : OK. What currency do traveler's checks have?

客　　戶：好，那旅支有什麼幣別？

Bank teller : A lot. For example, American Express provides traveler's checks in seven different currencies including U.S. currency, Canadian dollar, Pound Sterling, Japanese Yen, Chinese Yuan as well as Euro. **In Taiwan, the bulk of banks only offer U.S. currency and Euro denominated traveler's checks.** Our bank also only provides Euro and U.S. denominated traveler's checks. If you want to buy other currency denominated traveler's checks, please go to Bank of Taiwan or Mega Bank. As far as I know, both Bank of Taiwan and Mega bank allow people to apply for purchasing traveler's checks online.

行　　員：很多種。舉例來說，美國運通有提供七種不同幣別的旅支，包括美元、加拿大幣、英磅、日圓、人民幣和歐元。**在臺灣，大部分銀行只有美元和歐元計價的旅支。**我們銀行也只有提供歐元和美元的旅支。如果您想買其他幣別的旅支，請到臺銀或兆豐。就我所知，臺銀和兆豐都讓民眾線上買旅支。

Customer : OK. What denomination do your bank's traveler's checks have?

客　　戶：好。您們銀行的旅支有什麼面額？

Bank teller : You can take reference to the form below.

行　　員：您可以參考下面表格。

幣別 currency	面額 denomination
美金 USD	50、100、500
歐元 EUR	50、100、200、500

Customer : I see.

客　　戶：我明白了。

Bank teller : **When you buy a traveler's check, you should immediately put your signature on the check's upper portion in the presence of a bank teller.** The bank will give you a check purchasing agreement and an exchange memo.

行　　員：**當您買旅支時，您應在行員面前立刻在支票的上方簽名。**行員會給您旅支購買約定書和水單。

Customer : OK. If I want to **redeem** my traveler's check, what should I do?

客　　戶：好，如果我想把旅支兌現，我該怎麼做？

Bank teller : **You should date and countersign the check on the check's lower portion in the presence of the bank teller or a cashier when you want to cash your traveler's check.** The bank teller or the merchant will watch you sign and verify that your signature matches the original signature in the upper left corner of the check. The bank will request to see your passport. The bank teller will also photocopy all the traveler's checks you're going to cash, plus carefully jotting down each check's serial number. As you see, purchasing and redeeming traveler's checks at a bank can be time-consuming. It is one of the downsides for using a traveler's check.

行　　員：**當您想把旅支兌現時，您應該當著行員或是出納員面前，在旅支的下方簽上日期和複簽。**行員或是商家會看您簽名來確認您的簽名和左上方的原來簽名一致。行員會要求看您的護照。行員也會影印所有您要兌現的旅支並仔細記下每張旅支的序號。如您所見，在銀行買旅支和兌現旅支是非常耗時的。這是使用旅支的缺點之一。

Customer ： **Is there a handling fee for buying a traveler's check?**

客　　　戶：買旅支要收手續費嗎？

Bank teller ： Yes. The bank will charge you 200 NT dollars for the service fee.

行　　　員：是的。銀行會跟您收二百元手續費。

Customer ： Is there a daily transaction limit for purchasing a traveler's check?

客　　　戶：買旅支有每日交易上限嗎？

Bank teller ： Yes, there is. **The daily transaction limit for a person to buy a traveler's check is 25,000 US dollars.**

行　　　員：有的。**每個人每天最多只能買的旅支金額為美金二萬五千元。**

Customer ： I see. What if I lose my traveler's checks?

客　　　戶：我明白了。如果我的旅支不見了呢？

Bank teller ： Traveler's checks are easily replaced if they are lost or stolen. If you lose your traveler's checks, please contact your traveler's check issuer and contact the local police within 24 hours of losing your checks. So **please keep your proof of purchase and checks' serial numbers separate from your traveler's checks.** You need to provide the proof and information when the checks are lost or stolen.

行　　　員：當旅支不見或遭竊時，很容易補發。如果您的旅支不見了，請在遺失二十四小時內立即聯絡您的旅支發行者並報警。所以**請您將您的購買憑證以及旅支序號和您的旅支分開保管。**當您的旅支不見或是被偷時，您需要提供證據和資訊。

Customer ： OK. Will traveler's checks expire?

客　　　戶：好的。旅支會過期嗎？

Bank teller ： No, traveler's checks don't expire, so you can save your unused traveler's checks for your future trip. But of course, you also need to know traveler's checks do not bear any interest.

行　　員：不會。旅支不會過期，所以您可以把未用完的旅支存起來作爲未
來旅行之用。但是當然啦，您也要知道旅行支票本身不產生利
息。

Customer ： Thanks. **I would like to buy traveler's checks in dollar amounts
because they will be more widely accepted abroad.**

客　　戶：謝謝。**我想要買美元的旅支，因爲它在國外更廣泛地被接受。**

Bank teller ： How much do you want to buy?

行　　員：您要買多少？

Customer ： 1,000 US dollars in all.

客　　戶：共一千美元的旅支。

Bank teller ： How do you want it?

行　　員：您要什麼面額的？

Customer ： I want nine traveler's checks in one hundred-dollar denominated
check and two traveler's checks in fifty-dollar denominated check.

客　　戶：我要九張一百元面額的，和兩張五十元面額的旅支。

Bank teller ： No problem. Do you have your national ID card with you?

行　　員：沒問題。您有帶您的國民身分證嗎？

Customer ： Yes, here you are.

客　　戶：有，給您。

Bank teller ： OK, I will process it for you now.

行　　員：好的，我現在就幫您辦。

補充單字

♦ traveler's check [`trævləz tʃɛk] ***n.*** 旅行支票；旅支

♦ Euro denominated [`juro dɪ,namə`netɪd] ***adj.*** 歐元計價的

♦ redeem [rɪ`dim] ***v.*** 贖回；兌現；兌換（紅利點數）

♦ expire [ɪk`spaɪr] ***v.*** 過期；滿期

實用金句

♦ Traveler's checks allow you to go to another country to make a purchase or cash them at local banks.

旅支允許您去其他國家消費或是在當地銀行兌現。

♦ American Express traveler's checks may be changed for cash in a lot of countries abroad. You can use them at shops, hotels, department stores, restaurants and so on.

美國運通的旅行支票可以在很多國家換成現金。您可以在商店、旅館、百貨公司、餐廳等地方使用旅支。

♦ In Taiwan, the bulk of banks only offer U.S. currency and Euro denominated traveler's checks.

在臺灣，大部分銀行只有美元和歐元計價的旅支。

♦ When you buy a traveler's check, you should immediately put your signature on the check's upper portion in the presence of a bank teller.

當您買旅支時，您應在行員面前立刻在支票的上方簽名。

♦ You should date and countersign the check on the check's lower portion in the presence of the bank teller or a cashier when you want to cash your traveler's check.

當您想把旅支兌現時，您應該當行員或是出納員面前，在旅支的下方簽上日期和複簽。

♦ Is there a handling fee for buying a traveler's check?

買旅支要收手續費嗎？

♦ The daily transaction limit for a person to buy a traveler's check is 25,000 US dollars.

每個人每天最多只能買的旅支金額為美金二萬五千元。

♦ Please keep your proof of purchase and checks' serial numbers separate from your traveler's checks.

請您將您的購買憑證以及旅支序號和您的旅支分開保管。

♦ I would like to buy traveler's checks in dollar amounts because they will be more widely accepted abroad.

我想要買美元的旅支，因為它在國外更廣泛地被接受。

無摺戶
Paperless Account

Customer : I have heard your bank provides a kind of service known as "**paperless account**". What does a paperless account mean? Can you explain to me?

客　　戶：我聽說您們銀行有一種服務，叫作「無摺戶」。無摺戶是什麼意思？您可以解釋給我聽嗎？

Bank teller : **A paperless account is a type of account without a passbook. When a customer opens a paperless account, the bank only issues an ATM card to them. The customer will not receive a passbook. Therefore, the bank calls this type of account the "paperless account".** A paperless account is also known as a "non-physical account" or an "automated bank account."

行　　員：無摺戶是一種沒有存摺的帳戶。當客戶開無摺戶時，銀行只會發金融卡給他們。客戶不會拿到存摺。因此，銀行把這種帳戶叫作「無摺戶」。無摺戶也被稱作「非實體帳戶」或「自動化帳戶」。

Customer : I see. What benefits does a paperless account provide a customer with?

客　　戶：我了解了。無摺戶有提供客戶什麼優惠呢？

Bank teller : **A paperless account usually enables a customer to make an**

inter-bank transfer or withdrawal through ATMs without any service charge for a few times per month. Normally, if you want to make an inter-bank transfer through ATMs, the bank will charge you fifteen NT dollars. And if you make an inter-bank withdrawal through ATMs, the bank will charge you five NT dollars. However, **if your account is a paperless account, the bank will waive your bank service fee for using automated banking services.** For example, if you have a paperless account of Bank Sinopac, you can transfer money via ATMs with no charge up to four times per month.

行　　員：**無摺戶通常讓客戶每月享有數次的ATM跨行轉帳或提款免手續費**。正常來說，如果您要用ATM跨行轉帳的話，銀行會跟您收十五元手續費。如果您要用ATM來跨行提款的話，銀行會收五元手續費。然而，**如果您的戶頭是「無摺戶」的話，銀行會減免您用自動化交易的手續費**。例如說，如果您有永豐銀行的無摺戶的話，您可以每月ATM轉帳四次不收手續費。

Customer　：I see. If there are some benefits, I believe there are some downsides as well, right?

客　　戶：我明白了。如果有一些優惠。我相信也有些缺點對吧？

Bank teller：You got me. Actually, there are some downsides for a paperless account. For example, **a paperless account holder will be banned from making transactions over a bank counter or he will be charged for the service fee if this kind of transaction can be conducted through automated banking services.**

行　　員：被您發現了。事實上，無摺戶是有些缺點。例如說，**無摺戶的存戶禁止臨櫃交易**，或是如果要辦的交易可以透過自動化設施完成

的話，臨櫃就要收取手續費。

Customer : All right. Do all the banks in Taiwan provide paperless accounts?

客　　戶：好吧。所有在臺灣的銀行都有無摺戶嗎？

Bank teller : The answer is NO. As far as I know, only Bank Sinopac, Taipei Fubon Commercial Bank, Cathay United Bank, Chang Hwa Commercial Bank, HSBC, Chinatrust, Standard Chartered Bank, and Taishin International Bank have this type of account. **But the benefits and regulations of the paperless account vary from bank to bank.**

行　　員：答案是否定的。就我所知，只有永豐銀行、台北富邦、國泰世華、彰化銀行、匯豐銀行、中國信託、渣打銀行和台新銀行才有這種帳戶。**但是無摺戶的福利和限制每家銀行都不太相同。**

Customer : Can you tell me more?

客　　戶：您可以跟我多講一點嗎？

Bank teller : Yes. Take for example, Taipei Fubon Commercial Bank's V-banking. Its demand savings account interest rate is higher than the interest rate of Taipei Fubon Commercial Bank's demand savings account. What's more, when a V-banking account holder makes an inter-bank transfer or withdrawal through ATMs, their service charge will be waived by the bank for a couple of times per month. However, a V-banking account holder will be charged fifty NT dollars when he goes to use bank counter services.

行　　員：可以。舉台北富邦銀行的V-Banking為例，它的活儲利率比一般的有摺的活儲利率來得高。此外，當V-Banking的存戶用ATM做跨行轉帳或領錢時，銀行會每月減免幾次手續費。然而，當V-Banking的存戶臨櫃辦理交易時，會被收五十元手續費。

Customer : OK. Now I understand. I think the reason why the banks create this type of product, paperless accounts, is that the bank tries to encourage its customers to use automated services, thereby reducing the bank's manpower cost.

客　　戶：好，我現在知道了。我認為銀行創造無摺戶這產品的原因是因為銀行想要鼓勵客戶用自動化設施，以便減少櫃員人力成本。

Bank teller : Well. I think you are probably right. Maybe one day my job will be replaced by machines.

行　　員：嗯，我認為您可能是對的。也許有天我的工作會被機器給取代。

補充單字

♦ paperless account [`pepə-lɪs ə`kaunt] **n.** 無摺戶

♦ regulation [ˌrɛgjuˋleʃən] **n.** 規範；規定

♦ automated service [`ɔtəˌmetɪd `sɝvɪs] **n.** 自動化服務

實用金句

♦ A paperless account is a type of account without a passbook. When a customer opens a paperless account, the bank only issues an ATM card to them. The customer will not receive a passbook. Therefore, the bank calls this type of account the "paperless account".

無摺戶是一種沒有存摺的帳戶。當客戶開無摺戶時，銀行只會發金融卡給他們。客戶不會拿到存摺。

♦ A paperless account usually enables a customer to make an inter-bank transfer or withdrawal through ATMs without any service charge for a few times per month.

無摺戶通常讓客戶每月享有數次的ATM跨行轉帳或提款免手續費。

◆ If your account is a paperless account, the bank will waive your bank service fee for using automated banking services.

如果您的戶頭是「無摺戶」的話，銀行會減免您用自動化交易的手續費。

◆ A paperless account holder will be banned from making transactions over a bank counter or he will be charged for the service fee if this kind of transaction can be conducted through automated banking services.

無摺戶的存戶禁止臨櫃交易，或是如果要辦的交易可以透過自動化設施完成的話，臨櫃就要收取手續費。

◆ The benefits and regulations of the paperless account vary from bank to bank.

無摺戶的福利和限制每家銀行都不太相同。

警示戶
Watch-Listed Account

Customer : I have a problem with the ATMs of your bank.

客　　戶：我使用您們銀行的自動櫃員機有了問題。

Bank teller : What's the problem?

行　　員：您的問題是什麼？

Customer : I cannot withdraw my money with my ATM card from the ATMs. Therefore, I have to take a number ticket to withdraw my money over the counter.

客　　戶：我無法用金融卡從自動櫃員機提款。所以我必須抽號碼牌臨櫃提款。

Bank teller : I am sorry. Can you give me your ID card? Let me see what is wrong with your bank account.

行　　員：我很抱歉。您可以給我您的身分證嗎？讓我來看您的戶頭出了什麼問題。

Customer : Sure, here you are. Just be quick, I am in a hurry.

行　　員：當然，給您。只是要快一點，我在趕時間。

(The system shows that his account is marked as a watch-listed account.)

（系統顯示他的帳戶標記為警示戶）

Bank teller : Please wait for a moment, I will be right back.

行　　員：請稍等一下，我馬上回來。

(The bank teller ran to her supervisor for help.)

（行員跑向她的主管求助）

Bank teller : Sir, the computer showed that this man's account is a **watch-listed account**. What should I do?

行　　　員：副理，電腦系統顯示他的帳戶是警示戶。我該怎麼做？

Supervisor : Have you checked the system to see what the reason is.

主　　　管：您有查系統看警示戶是什麼原因嗎？

Bank teller : Yes. It shows that this man is a scam artist.

行　　　員：有啊。它顯示這個男人是個詐騙犯。

Supervisor : All right. We should report the case to the police. Just calm down and pretend that nothing weird happened. Don't let this man become suspicious.

主　　　管：好吧。我們應該報警。先冷靜下來假裝沒有什麼不尋常的事發生。不要讓這男人起疑。

Bank teller : I understand.

行　　　員：我了解了。

(The teller called the police. After a while, two police officers came and took the man to the police station.)

（行員打電話報警。過了一會，兩個警官來了並把這男人帶走了。）

Bank teller : Could you tell me more about the watch-listed account?

行　　　員：您可以告訴我更多警示戶的事嗎？

Supervisor : Of course. **A watch-listed account is a type of account which the police or the court has report to the original account opening bank because his account is used in a criminal activity.** After the original account opening bank receives the notice from the police or the court, the bank will report it to Joint Credit Information

Center. Joint Credit Information Center will disclose the information of the watch-listed account in the joint credit information for three years.

主　　管 ：當然可以。**警示戶是因這帳戶被用在犯罪用途而被警察或法院通報原開戶行而成爲警示戶**。在原開戶行接獲警方或法院的通知後，銀行就會把這帳戶通報到聯合徵信中心。聯合徵信中心會在聯徵上揭露警示戶長達三年。

Bank teller : I see. The reason that an account becomes a watch-listed account is, **the account holder probably sells his account to the scam gang and thus his account becomes a dummy account. When a dummy account is reported to the police, this account will be marked as a watch-listed account.**

行　　員 ：我明白了。一個戶頭會被列爲警示戶是因爲帳戶持有人極可能賣了他的帳戶給詐騙集團因此而使這帳戶變成人頭戶。當人頭戶被通報到警方時，這帳戶就會被列爲警示戶。

Supervisor : Yes, it is correct.

主　　管 ：是的，您說的沒錯。

Bank teller : Why did the customer say he could not use ATMs to withdraw money?

行　　員 ：爲什麼這名客戶說他無法使用自動櫃員機提款？

Supervisor : Good question. **When a man's account is marked as a watch-listed account, he cannot use any automated banking services, such as ATMs or online banking.** Therefore, the watch-listed account holder will have no choice but to go to a counter to deal with his problem. And when the watch-listed account holder wants to make a transaction over the counter, the bank system will tell the teller that his account is a watch-listed account. When that happens, we should report it to the police. In addition, **the watch-listed account holder's bank accounts with other banks will be marked as "derivative watch-listed accounts".** In like manner, a derivative watch-listed account holder will not be able to use any automated banking services. And the reason for marking other accounts as derivative watch-listed accounts is that in case the fraudster or the dummy account holder should go to other banks to open more accounts to use his account on frauds.

主　　管：好問題。**當一個人的帳戶被列爲警示戶時，他無法使用任何的自動化銀行設施，像是自動櫃員機或是網路銀行。**因此，警示戶沒有選擇而必須臨櫃來處理他的問題。而當警示戶持有人臨櫃交易時，銀行系統會通知櫃員這帳戶已被列爲警示戶。當發生這樣的狀況，我們必須報警處理。另外，**警示戶的持有人在其他銀行開的戶頭會被列爲「衍生管制帳戶」。**同樣地，衍生管制帳戶的持有人無法在自動化銀行做任何交易。而把其他帳戶列爲衍生管制帳戶的原因是怕詐欺犯或人頭戶持有人跑到其他銀行去開更多的戶頭來把帳戶用在詐騙上。

Bank teller : Now I understand. Thank you, Sir.

行　　員：現在我懂了。謝謝，副理。

Supervisor : It is my pleasure.

主　　管：不客氣。

補充單字

♦ watch-listed account [wɑtʃ `lɪstɪd ə`kaunt] **n.** 警示帳戶

♦ Joint Credit Information Center [dʒɔɪnt `krɛdɪt ˏɪnfə`meʃən `sɛntɚ] **n.** 聯合徵

信中心

♦ dummy account [`dʌmɪ ə`kaunt] **n.** 人頭戶

♦ derivative watch-listed account [də`rɪvətɪv wɑtʃ `lɪstɪd ə`kaunt] **n.** 衍生管制帳戶

實用金句

♦ A watch-listed account is a type of account which the police or the court has report to the original account opening bank because his account is used in a criminal activity.

警示戶是因這帳戶被用在犯罪用途而被警察或法院通報原開戶行而成爲警示戶。

♦ The account holder probably sells his account to the scam gang and thus his account becomes a dummy account. When a dummy account is reported to the police, this account will be marked as a watch-listed account.

帳戶持有人極可能賣了他的帳戶給詐騙集團因此而使這帳戶變成人頭戶。

當人頭戶被通報到警方時，這帳戶就會被列爲警示戶。

♦ When a man's account is marked as a watch-listed account, he cannot use any automated banking services, such as ATMs or online banking.

當一個人的帳戶被列爲警示戶時，他無法使用任何的自動化銀行設施，像是自動櫃員機或是網路銀行。

♦ The watch-listed account holder's bank accounts with other banks will be marked as "derivative watch-listed accounts".

警示戶的持有人在其他銀行開的戶頭會被列爲「衍生管制帳戶」。

靜止戶
Inactive Account

Customer : Hello, I would like to withdraw money today.

客　　戶：嗨，我今天想要提款。

Bank teller : OK. Please pass me your passbook and the withdrawal slip…Wait a minute, **your account is marked as an inactive account**.

行　　員：好的。請把存摺和提款條拿給我……等一下，**您的帳戶被標記為靜止戶**。

Customer : What do you mean by an inactive account?

客　　戶：您說的「靜止戶」是什麼意思？

Bank teller : Well, an inactive account is also called a dormant account. **When there has been no transaction in your account for an extended period of time, the bank will put your account in an inactive status.** For example, if for more than one year there has been no transaction in the demand savings account, most government-controled banks, such as First Bank, will deem such an account to be an inactive account. **No interest shall be payable on such inactive accounts.** On the other hand, Cathay United Bank will turn your savings account into an inoperative account if you have not made any transaction within two years and your balance is lower than 5,000 NT dollars, which does not reach the minimum standard of bearing interests in a personal demand savings account. However, Shanghai Commercial and Savings Bank doesn't have the mechanism of inactive accounts. Even if you have not made any transaction with the bank for ten years, your account will still be operative.

行　　員：嗯，靜止戶又稱爲休眠戶。**當您的帳戶在一段時間沒有做任何交易時，銀行會把您的帳戶設成靜止戶。**例如說，當您的活儲超過一年都沒有任何的交易時，大多官股銀行，像是第一銀行，會把這種帳戶視爲靜止戶。**靜止戶不會生息。**另一方面，如果您在兩年內都沒有辦任何交易而且您的餘額少於活儲最低起息標準新臺幣五千元的話，國泰世華會把您的帳戶轉爲靜止戶。然而，上海商銀則沒有靜止戶這個機制。即使您的帳戶十年沒有進出，您的帳戶仍然不會變成靜止戶。

Customer：I see. So can you tell me how to reactivate an inactive account?

客　　戶：我明白了。您可以告訴我如何重新啓用靜止戶嗎？

Bank teller：**To reactivate a dormant account, you must go to the bank in person with your ID card, your health IC card, as well as your original specimen seal and you have to fill out some application forms.**

行　　員：要重新啓用靜止戶，您必須帶身分證、健保卡和原留印鑑親自到銀行辦理，還要填申請書。

Customer：OK. I have my ID card, health IC card and the original specimen seal in the bank with me. Can I reactivate my dormant account now?

客　　戶：好的。我有帶身分證、健保卡和原留印鑑。我可以現在就重新啓用靜止戶嗎？

Bank teller : Yes, you can. But **I will have to pull your credit report from Joint Credit Information Center.**

行　　員：是的，您可以。但**我必須告訴您，我必須自聯合徵信中心調閱您的徵信資料。**

Customer : Why?

客　　戶：為什麼？

Bank teller : **Many inactive account holders reactivate their dormant accounts just in order to sell their bank accounts to a scam gang.** As soon as their accounts become active again, they will sell their accounts, thus making their accounts become dummy accounts. Therefore, the bank has to be careful.

行　　員：**因為很多靜止戶被重新啟用後，只是為了把他們的帳戶賣給詐騙集團。**一旦他們的帳戶重新被啟用後，他們就會賣掉他們的帳戶而變成人頭戶。因此，銀行必須小心謹慎。

Customer : That's OK. I understand.

客　　戶：沒關係，我了解了。

Bank teller : OK, it is done. But you have to make a transaction by depositing some money into your account to keep your account active.

客　　戶：好了，辦好了。但您必須存款到您的帳戶辦個交易使您的帳戶不變成靜止戶。

Customer : No problem. I will deposit 10,000 NT dollars into my account now.

客　　戶：沒有問題。我現在就存一萬元到我的帳戶。

Bank teller : Thanks. It is necessary for you to make a transaction to keep your account from becoming an inactive account.

行　　員：謝謝。您辦交易使帳戶不變成靜止戶是必要的。

補充單字

♦ inactive account [ɪn`æktɪv ə`kaʊnt] **n.** 靜止戶；久未往來戶

= dormant account [`dɔrmənt ə`kaʊnt]

♦ reactivate [rɪ`æktə,vet] **v.t.** 重新啟用；解除（靜止戶）

♦ scam gang [skæm `gæŋ] **n.** 詐騙集團（單數用scam gangster）

實用金句

♦ Your account is marked as an inactive account.

您的帳戶被標記為靜止戶。

♦ When there has been no transaction in your account for an extended period of time, the bank will put your account in an inactive status.

當您的帳戶在一段時間沒有做任何交易時，銀行會把您的帳戶設成靜止戶。

♦ No interest shall be payable on such inactive accounts.

靜止戶不會生息。

♦ To reactivate a dormant account, you must go to the bank in person with your ID card, your health IC card, as well as your original specimen seal in the bank and you have to fill out some application forms.

要重新啟用靜止戶，您必須帶身分證、健保卡和原留印鑑親自到銀行辦理，還要填申請書。

♦ I will have to pull your credit report from Joint Credit Information Center.

我必須自聯合徵信中心調閱您的徵信資料。

♦ Many inactive account holders reactivate their dormant accounts just in order to sell their bank accounts to scam gangs.

因為很多靜止戶被重新啟用後，只是為了把他們的帳戶賣給詐騙集團。

祕密戶
Confidential Account

Customer : Hello, **I would like to sign up for a** confidential account.

客　　　戶：嗨，**我想要申請**祕密戶。

Bank teller : Well, may I ask you the reason why you want to apply for a confidential account?

行　　　員：我可以問您辦祕密戶的原因嗎？

Customer : Actually, I just hit the jackpot in the lottery. I become a millionaire, but I don't want my family to know I have a lot of money now. You know, people are greedy and I must be careful. Therefore, I want my account to be more confidential. I don't want the bank to send the monthly statement to me because one of my family members may open my letter and find out how much money I have.

客　　　戶：事實上，我剛中樂透。我變成了百萬富翁，但我不想要我的家人知道我有很多錢。您曉得的，人都很貪婪所以我必須要小心為上。因此我想要我的帳戶更加地隱密，我不要銀行寄發每月對帳單給我，因為我的家人可能打開我的信件並發現我有多少錢。

Bank teller : Wow, first of all, congratulations. And you are really professional. As you said, **a confidential account is a type of non-statement account.** But you must be sure if you want to register for this type of account because **once your account turns into a confidential**

account, the bank will not inform you even if your CD matures. And even if you don't have enough funds in your checking account, which may cause your check to bounce, the bank will not volunteer to notify you.

行　　員：哇！第一，恭喜您了。您真的很專業。如您所說，**祕密戶是不寄發對帳單給客戶的一種帳戶。但您必須確認您要辦這種帳戶，因為一旦轉為祕密戶，即使您的定存到期，銀行也不會通知您。** 並且即使您的支存戶餘額不足而可能導致跳票，銀行也不會主動告知您。

Customer : I am sure. I also know that **a teller has no authority to read the information of a confidential account unless her supervisor authorizes her to do so.**

客　　戶：我很確信。我也知道除非**主管授權**，否則行員沒有**權限去看祕密戶的個人資料。**

Bank teller : That is correct. Have you worked at a bank before?

行　　員：您說得對。您以前有在銀行工作過嗎？

Customer : Well, that is a secret.

客　　戶：嗯，這是祕密。

Bank teller : OK, a secret it is. Do you have your ID card as well as your original specimen seal with you?

行　　員：好吧，祕密是吧。您有帶您的身分證和您的原留印鑑嗎？

Customer : Yes. I have. Here you are.

客　　戶：是的，我有，給您。

Bank teller : Please fill in this application form.

行　　員：請填這張申請書。

Customer : All right.

客　　　戶：好的。

Bank teller：Now it is done. **Your account has been turned into a confidential account.** Have a nice day.

行　　　員：現在辦完了，**您的帳戶已轉爲祕密戶。**祝您有美好的一天。

Customer：Thank you.

客　　　戶：謝謝您。

補充單字

◆ confidential account [ˌkɑnfəˋdɛnʃəl əˋkaunt] ***n.*** 祕密戶；保密戶

◆ authority [ɔˋθɔrətɪ] ***n.*** 權限；權威

◆ supervisor [ˌsupɚˋvaɪzɚ] ***n.*** 主管；上司

實用金句

◆ I would like to sign up for a confidential account.

我想要申請祕密戶。

◆ A confidential account is a type of non-statement account.

祕密戶是不寄發對帳單給客戶的一種帳戶。

◆ Once your account turns into a confidential account, the bank will not inform you even if your CD matures.

一旦轉爲祕密戶，即使您的定存到期，銀行也不會通知您。

◆ A teller has no authority to read the information of a confidential account unless her supervisor authorizes her to do so.

除非主管授權，否則行員沒有權限去看祕密戶的個人資料。

◆ Your account has been turned into a confidential account.

您的帳戶已轉爲祕密戶。

黃金存摺
Gold Passbook

Bank teller : Hello, what kind of transactions would you like to conduct?

行　　員：嗨，您想要辦什麼業務？

Customer : I would like to make a time deposit.

客　　戶：我想要辦定存。

Bank teller : OK. Before you make a time deposit, I would like to share a new product with you.

行　　員：好的。在您做定存之前，我想要跟您分享一個新產品。

Customer : What is it?

客　　戶：是什麼？

Bank teller : Well, now our bank initiates a new type of account, which is called the "**gold passbook**." Do you want to know more?

客　　戶：這個嘛，現在我們銀行推出一種新帳戶，叫作「黃金存摺」。您想知道更多嗎？

Customer : Yes, please tell me more.

客　　戶：好的，請跟我介紹多一點。

Bank teller : A lot of banks, like Bank of Taiwan (BOT), provide their customers with a new investment vehicle, called the gold passbook. Because Eurozone crisis hit the globally fragile economy, more and more people turn to purchase gold as a **hedge** against inflation and as a means of risk diversification. But it is inconvenient for most people to purchase physical gold because you have to rent or buy a safe-deposit box to store it. Therefore, our bank allows customers to make a virtual investment in gold by initiating the gold passbook to our customers. **All transactions of dealing in gold will be recorded in their gold passbook.**

行　　員：很多銀行像是臺銀有提供客戶一種新的投資工具，就是黃金存摺。因為歐債危機打擊全球本來就已衰弱的經濟，愈來愈多的人轉而擁抱黃金作為抗通膨的避險工具和分散風險的手段。但對大多數人來說購買實體黃金很不方便因為您還要租或買一個保險箱來存放。因此，我們銀行推出黃金存摺來讓客戶可以進行虛擬的黃金投資。**所有黃金交易都會被記錄在黃金存摺裡。**

Customer : Wow! That sounds good. I agree with you. More and more people prefer to hold gold as a safe-haven. According to recent news, the U.S. Federal Reserve has declared that it will not raise interest rates until 2015, which makes U.S. currency continue to be weak, so people are increasingly losing their confidence in paper money and turning to invest in gold.

客　　戶：哇！聽起來很棒！我同意您說的。愈來愈多的人抱黃金來作避險。根據最近的新聞，美國聯準會已宣布它直到2015年之前都不會升息，持續使美元疲軟，所以民眾才會愈來愈失去對紙幣的信心轉而投資黃金。

Bank teller : Yes. **A lot of investors want to buy gold as a hedge, so our bank has introduced gold passbooks to the customers.** As you said, gold is believed to be a safe haven for investors. Are you interested in opening a gold passbook account now?

行　　　員：是的，**很多投資客買黃金作爲避險，所以我們銀行推出黃金存摺給客戶。**如您所言，一般人相信黃金存摺是投資客的避險工具。您現在想開黃金存摺嗎？

Customer : Yes, but I also want you to tell me the downsides of the gold passbook.

客　　　戶：是的。但我想要您跟我講講黃金存摺的缺點。

Bank teller : OK. Like other investments, buying gold has its risks. The short-term risk of investing in precious metal has increased since no one is 100% sure whether the price of gold has already reached a ceiling or not. And **a gold passbook is a non-interest account. In other words, the gold passbook does not yield any interest at all.**

行　　　員：好的。就像其他的投資，買黃金也有它的風險。投資貴重金屬的短期風險不斷增加因爲沒有人可以百分之一百確定黃金的價格已漲到最高點了沒。並且黃金存摺是不計息的帳戶。也就是說，黃金存摺不會產生任何利息。

Customer : I see. A gold passbook is actually a non-interest-bearing account. That is why you are promoting the gold passbook to me. The bank has absorbed too much money and thus has to pay too many interests, so the bank tries to lure their depositors to transfer their money from time deposit account to gold passbook account. In this way, the bank can save the cost of paying interests to their depositors. I believe that is why so many domestic banks have rolled out gold passbook accounts.

客　　　戶：我明白了。黃金存摺是一種不計息帳戶。這就是爲什麼您向我推廣黃金存摺的原因。銀行已吸收太多存款並要付太多的利息，因

此銀行試著引導客戶把資金從定存轉移到黃金存摺上。這樣的話，銀行就可以省下很多付息給存戶的成本。我相信這就是為什麼很多本國銀行都推出黃金存摺的原因。

Bank teller : Maybe you are right. A lot of banks have launched this service of the gold passbook, such as Bank of Taiwan, Mega Bank, Taiwan Cooperative Bank, First Bank, Hua Nan Commercial Bank, Shanghai Commercial and Savings Bank, Yuanta Commercial Bank, Bank SinoPac, E. Sun Bank, Taishin International Bank and Taiwan Business Bank. Allow me to talk more about the advantages of the gold passbook. **You may want to know the amount of gold holdings in your gold passbook can be converted to physical gold.** That is, **you can not only make a virtual investment in gold through the gold passbook, but you can also convert your gold holdings in your gold passbook into physical gold in the form of gold bars and coins.** Furthermore, our bank allows you to deal in gold via Internet Banking. **With a gold passbook account, you can buy gold in one-gram increments. The gold passbook account also enables investors to use "dollar cost averaging" or "the Gold Piggy Bank", a monthly gold saving plan to invest in gold.** As for the program of "the Gold Piggy Bank", aka "the Gold Saving Plan", you can go to the official website of Bank of Taiwan to check it out. It has a comprehensive introduction.

行　　員： 也許您說的對。很多銀行都推出黃金存摺的服務，像是臺銀、兆豐銀、合作金庫、第一銀行、華南銀行、上海商銀、元大銀行、永豐銀行、玉山銀行、台新銀行和臺灣企銀。允許我介紹更多黃金存摺的優點。**您可能想知道您在黃金存摺持有的黃金數量可轉換成實體黃金。也就是說，您不但可以透過黃金存摺做虛擬的黃**

金買賣，也可以從黃金存摺提領出實體的黃金條塊和金幣。此外，我們銀行還讓您透過網路銀行來買賣黃金。有了黃金存摺帳戶，您可以以每公克來買黃金。黃金存摺帳戶也讓投資人可以用「定期定額」或「黃金撲滿」這個每月黃金投資方案來投資黃金。至於「黃金撲滿」這個方案（又稱「黃金儲蓄計畫」），您可以上臺銀的官方網站來查看。上面有完善的介紹。

Customer : So I can buy or sell gold through online banking, right?

客　　戶：所以我可以透過網銀來買賣黃金，對吧？

Bank teller : Yes, you can.

行　　員：是的，您可以。

Customer : I would like to open a gold passbook account.

客　　戶：我想要開黃金存摺。

Bank teller : No problem. Please give me your two forms of ID.

行　　員：沒問題。請給我您的雙證件。

Customer : Here you are.

客　　戶：在這裡。

Bank teller : Please fill out these forms. You must provide the following information, such as your name, your ID number, your birthday, your nationality, your marital status, your telephone number, your cell phone number, your fax number, your registered address, your correspondence address, your education attainment, your annual salary, and the person to contact.

行　　員：請填寫這些申請書。您必須提供下列資料，像是您的姓名、身分證字號、您的出生日期、您的國籍、您的婚姻狀況、您的電話號碼、手機號碼、傳真機號碼、戶籍地址、通訊地址、教育程度、年收入和聯絡人姓名。

Customer : OK.

客　　戶：好的。

Bank teller : Some banks, such as Mega Bank, require their customers to purchase gold at least in one-gram in opening a gold passbook, but our bank doesn't have this kind of rule.

行　　員：有些銀行，像是兆豐，會要求在開戶時至少購買一克的黃金，但本行沒有這樣的規定。

Customer : I see.

客　　戶：我知道了。

Bank teller : **There are a New Taiwan dollar-denominated gold passbook and a U.S. dollar-denominated gold passbook. The U.S. dollar-denominated gold passbook requires customers to buy gold in troy ounces while the New Taiwan dollar-denominated gold passbook requires customers to buy gold in grams.** Which one would you like to choose?

行　　員：有新臺幣計價和美元計價的黃金存摺。美元計價的黃金存摺要客人以每英兩來買進黃金，而新臺幣計價的黃金存摺則是要客人以每公克來買進黃金。您要選哪一種？

Customer : I would like to choose U.S. dollar-denominated gold passbook.

客　　戶：我想要美元計價的黃金存摺。

Bank teller : Good choice. Most domestic banks only have the New Taiwan dollar-denominated gold passbook, which allows the purchasing of gold in one-gram increments. However, Bank of Taiwan has rolled out the U.S. dollar-denominated gold passbook, which allows the purchasing of gold in one-tory ounce increments. The service of U.S. dollar-denominated gold passbook helps investors buy and sell gold without much impact of fluctuations in the exchange rate and helps them avoid the **fluctuations** of the New Taiwan Dollar against the U.S. dollar. But if you want to open a U.S. dollar-denominated gold passbook, you will need to open a foreign currency account first. And you may as well apply for linking your foreign exchange general service account with your U.S. dollar-denominated gold passbook. This way, you can transfer funds between your gold passbook account and your foreign exchange account.

行　　員：選得好。大部分本國銀行只有臺幣計價的黃金存摺，讓客戶可以用每公克來購買黃金。不過，臺灣銀行有推出美元計價的黃金存摺，讓客戶可以以每英兩來購買黃金。美元計價的黃金存摺幫助投資者買賣黃金不用擔心匯率波動的影響，也幫助他們避開臺幣兌美元的波動。但如您想開美元計價的黃金存摺，您需要先加開外幣戶才行。然後你不妨申請把您的外幣戶和美元計價的黃金存摺帳戶做相互連結的約定帳戶。這樣一來，您就可以在黃金存摺帳戶和您的外幣戶之間做資金轉移。

Customer：All right.

客　　戶：好的。

Bank teller：It is done. Here is your gold passbook. Please keep it safe. By the way, maybe one day our bank will also initiate a silver passbook. And maybe you will be interested in opening a silver passbook, too.

行　　員：辦完了。這是您的黃金存摺。請妥善保管。對了，也許有天我們銀行也會推出白銀存摺。而您也許也會有興趣開一個白銀存摺。

Customer：Wow. It seems to me that the bank is providing various services now.

客　　戶：哇，好像現在銀行一直都推出各種不同的服務啊。

補充單字

♦ gold passbook [gold `pæs͵buk] **n.** 黃金存摺

♦ hedge [hɛdʒ] **n.** 避險；避險工具；對沖

♦ dollar cost averaging [`dɑlɚ kɔst `ævərɪdʒɪŋ] (DCA) **n.** 定期定額

♦ fluctuation [͵flʌktʃʊ`eʃən] **n.** 波動；振盪

實用金句

♦ All transactions of dealing in gold will be recorded in their gold passbook.

所有黃金交易都會被記錄在黃金存摺裡。

♦ A lot of investors want to buy gold as a hedge, so our bank has introduced gold passbooks to the customers.

很多投資客買黃金作爲避險，所以我們銀行推出黃金存摺給客戶。

♦ A gold passbook is a non-interest account. In other words, the gold passbook does not yield any interest at all.

黃金存摺是不計息的帳戶。也就是說，黃金存摺不會產生任何利息。

♦ You may want to know the amount of gold holdings in your gold passbook can be converted to physical gold.

您可能想知道您在黃金存摺持有的黃金數量可轉換成實體黃金。

♦ You can not only make a virtual investment in gold through the gold passbook, but you can also convert your gold holdings in your gold passbook into physical gold in the form of gold bars and coins.

您不但可以透過黃金存摺做虛擬的黃金買賣，也可以從黃金存摺提領出實

體的黃金條塊和金幣。

♦ With a gold passbook account, you can buy gold in one-gram increment. The gold passbook account also enables investors to use "dollar cost averaging" or "the Gold Piggy Bank", a monthly gold saving plan to invest in gold.

有了黃金存摺帳戶，您可以以每公克來買黃金。黃金存摺帳戶也讓投資人可以用「定期定額」或「黃金撲滿」這每月黃金投資方案來投資黃金。

♦ There are a New Taiwan dollar-denominated gold passbook and a U.S. dollar-denominated gold passbook. The U.S. dollar-denominated gold passbook requires customers to buy gold in troy ounces while the New Taiwan dollar-denominated gold passbook requires customers to buy gold in grams.

有新臺幣計價和美元計價的黃金存摺。美元計價的黃金存摺要客人以每英兩來買進黃金，而新臺幣計價的黃金存摺則是要客人以每公克來買進黃金。

存款證明
Balance Certificate

Customer : **I would like to apply for a certificate of balance.**

客　　戶：**我想要申請存款證明。**

Bank teller : No problem. **First, you must take a number ticket and wait until your number is called by a bank teller.**

行　　員：沒問題。**首先，您必須抽一張號碼牌，然後等行員叫您的號碼。**

Customer : OK, thanks.

客　　戶：好的。謝謝。

(His number is called.)

（他被叫號了。）

Bank teller : Hello, what can I do for you today?

行　　員：嗨，您今天要辦什麼？

Customer : I want to apply for a certificate of balance. You know, **a certificate of balance is a certified notice of the balance of customers' bank account and accrued interest on a specific date.**

客　　戶：我想要申請存款證明。您知道的，**存款證明是客戶的銀行帳戶在特定日期的存款和所生利息的證明書。**

Bank teller : I know what a certificate of balance is. **Do you want to apply for a Chinese version or an English version?**

行　　員：我知道什麼是存款證明。**您想要申請中文版的還是英文版的？**

Customer : I want to apply for an English version.

客　　戶：我想要申請英文版的。

Bank teller : Do you have your ID card as well as your original specimen seal with you?

行　　員：您有帶您的身分證和原留印鑑嗎？

Customer : Yes, here you are.

客　　戶：有啊，給您。

Bank teller : And I must tell you that **the bank will charge you two hundred NT dollars for a service commission. The first copy is 200 NT dollars but the additional copy will be 100 NT dollars per copy.**

行　　員：我必須告訴您銀行會跟您收二百元的手續費，第一份是要收新臺幣二百元，但第一份之後的加印本是每本一百元。

Customer : Just two hundred NT dollars? That is **reasonable**. I have just been to another bank; however, the teller charged me three hundred NT dollars for issuing the first copy of a balance certificate.

客　　戶：只要二百元？價格還可以接受。而我剛去另一家銀行，發第一份存款證明，行員就要跟我收三百元手續費。

Bank teller : Really? Well, **different banks have different standards of service commissions.**

行　　員：真的嗎？**不同銀行有不同的手續費規範。**

Customer : I see. Thank you, bye.

客　　戶：我明白了。謝謝您，再見。

Bank teller : See you.

行　　員：再見。

補充單字

◆ certificate of balance [sə`tɪfəkɪt ɑv `bæləns] *n.* 銀行存款證明

◆ reasonable [`riznəb!] *adj.* 不貴的；合理的

實用金句

◆ I would like to apply for a certificate of balance.

我想要申請存款證明。

◆ First, you must take a number ticket and wait until your number is called by a bank teller.

首先，您必須抽一張號碼牌，然後等行員叫您的號碼。

◆ A certificate of balance is a certified notice of the balance of customers' bank account and accrued interest on a specific date.

存款證明是客戶的銀行帳戶在特定日期的存款和所生利息的證明書。

◆ Do you want to apply for a Chinese version or an English version?

您想要申請中文版的還是英文版的？

◆ The bank will charge you two hundred NT dollars for a service commission. The first copy is 200 NT dollars but the additional copy will be 100 NT dollars per copy.

銀行會跟您收二百元的手續費，第一份是要收新臺幣二百元，但第二份之後是每份一百元。

◆ Different banks have different standards of service commissions.

不同銀行有不同的手續費規範。

反詐騙
Anti-Fraud

Customer : I would like to transfer money.

客　　戶：我想要轉帳。

Bank teller : Have you filled in the remittance slip?

行　　員：您填好匯款單了嗎？

Customer : No, I haven't.

客　　戶：不，還沒。

Bank teller : **Please fill in the remittance slip. It is in duplicate.**

行　　員：**請填這張匯款單。這是兩聯一式。**

Customer : Sure.

客　　戶：沒問題。

Bank teller : Do you know the person that you want to transfer money to? I also want you to answer the following questions. How are you related to the beneficiary? What is your purpose for making a remittance?

行　　員：您是否認識受款人？我還要您回答下列的問題。您與受款人之關係為何？您辦理匯款的目的是？

Customer : No, I don't know the beneficiary. I would like to wire money from my account because something terrible happened.

客　　戶：我不認識受款人。我想要把錢從我的帳戶匯出因為有件可怕的事發生了！

Bank teller : What happened? Can you tell me? I really want to know.

行　　　員：怎麼了？您可以告訴我嗎？我真的很想知道。

Customer : The judge and the police officer just gave me a call and told me that my bank account was used by terrorists or syndicates and that I should transfer the funds in my account to a safer account for an investigation, or my assets would be seized by the police. You know, that is too horrible. At first, I didn't want to tell you because the judge told me not to tell anyone, but I couldn't help it.

客　　　戶：有法官和警官剛剛打電話給我說，我的銀行帳戶被恐怖份子或不法集團所用，而我應該把錢轉到一個較安全的帳戶以作為調查之用，否則我的資產就會被警察扣留。您懂嗎？這太可怕了！起初，我不想告訴您因為法官告訴我不要跟別人說，但我忍不住講了出來。

Bank teller : I suspect it might be a phone scam. The phone **scammers** were just lying to you and trying to gain your confidence. It is typical of their phone scam plan. **The phone scammers are trying to terrify you so much so that you may lose your head and will buy their lies. If you believe what they say to you, they will tell you to wire money to a dummy account which is controlled by the phone scammers.**

行　　　員：我懷疑這可能是一起電話詐騙。電話詐騙份子只是跟您說謊試圖取得您的信任。這是典型的詐騙手法。**電話詐騙集團試著恐嚇您讓您失去理智而相信他們的謊話。如果您相信他們所說的，他們就會告訴您把錢匯到被電話詐騙集團控制的人頭戶。**

Customer : Really? Are you telling me that they are not the real judge and the real police officer, but the phone scammers?

客　　戶：眞的嗎？您是說他們不是眞的法官和警官而是電話詐騙犯？

Bank teller：Yes. What those phone scammers tried to do for you is obvious. Sometimes, they try to intimidate you into obeying what they tell you. Sometimes, they may swindle their victims with lottery fraud. That is, they will tell you that you hit a jackpot in the lucky draw, so you have to transfer money to them as bogus administration fees. Usually, the victims are ordered to keep the details of the lottery win secret, so their family and friends won't know the phone scammers have called them.

行　　員：是的。這些電話詐騙犯試圖對你做的事眞的非常明顯。有時候，他們會試著恐嚇您去服從他們所言。有時候，他們會以中獎詐騙來誆騙他們的受害者。也就是說，他們會跟您說因爲您中了樂透，所以您必須把錢轉給他們作爲行政處理費用。通常受害者都會被命令要把中獎資訊保持機密，所以他們的親友也不知道詐騙集團已打電話給他們。

Customer：Yeah, **people should be suspicious of any texts, emails or paper mail claiming that they have really won a fortune.**

客　　戶：是的，**民衆應該小心任何告知他們眞的中了大獎的簡訊、電子郵件或紙本郵件。**

Bank teller：You are right. But sometimes people are just too overwhelmed with emotions to make right judgments. Do you still believe those phone scammers? They are not the real judge or police officer. This I can tell you.

行　　員：您說的不錯。但是有時候人們因爲情緒太過激動而無法下正確判斷。您還相信這些電話詐騙份子所說的嗎？他們不是眞的法官或警官啦。這個我倒是可以跟您保證。

Customer : But what if they told me the truth?

客　　戶：但是如果他們跟我講的是真的呢？

Bank teller : I will suggest you should dial anti-fraud hotline 165 to talk with some professionals. They will tell you it is a phone scam. Believe me, I have seen too many similar cases.

行　　員：我會建議您應撥打165反詐騙專線跟專業人士談一下。他們會告訴您這是電話詐騙。相信我，我看過太多類似的案例了。

Customer : Can you tell me what I should do right now?

客　　戶：您可以跟我講我現在該怎麼做嗎？

Bank teller : **You should dial anti-fraud hotline 165 first and report it to the police.**

行　　員：**您應該先撥打165反詐騙專線並報警。**

Customer : I see. Thank you. You saved my money. If you had not told me it was a phone scam, I would have wired my money to the phone scammers.

客　　戶：我明白了。謝謝您。您救了我的錢。如果您沒有告訴我這是電話詐騙的話，我可能已經把錢匯給詐騙集團了。

Bank teller : Thank you, but I am just doing my duty. **There have been a lot of telephone frauds, so please be careful.**

行　　員：謝謝，但我只是做我該做的而已。**最近電話詐騙事件頻傳，請多加小心。**

補充單字

◆ duplicate [`djupləkɪt] *n.* 副本；第二聯； *adj.* 副本的

◆ beneficiary [ˌbɛnəˋfɪʃərɪ] *n.* 收款人；受款人

◆ scammer [`skæmə] *n.* 詐欺犯；詐欺集團團員

實用金句

♦ Please fill in the remittance slip. It is in duplicate.

請填這張匯款單。這是兩聯一式。

♦ The phone scammers are trying to terrify you so much so that you may lose your head and will buy their lies. If you believe what they say to you, they will tell you to wire money to a dummy account which is controled by the phone scammers.

電話詐騙集團試著恐嚇您讓您失去理智而相信他們的謊話。如果您相信他們所說的,他們就會告訴您把錢匯到被電話詐騙集團控制的人頭戶。

♦ People should be suspicious of any texts, emails or paper mail claiming that they have really won a fortune.

民眾應該小心任何告知他們真的中了大獎的簡訊、電子郵件或紙本郵件。

♦ You should dial anti-fraud hotline 165 first and report it to the police.

您應該先撥打165反詐騙專線並報警。

♦ There have been a lot of telephone frauds, so please be careful.

最近電話詐騙事件頻傳,請多加小心。

塗 改
Alteration

Bank teller : What can I do for you today?

行　　員：我今天可以為您辦什麼？

Customer : I would like to withdraw money from my personal savings account.

客　　戶：我想要從我活儲戶提款出來。

Bank teller : **What is your purpose for making a withdrawal? How much would you like to withdraw?**

行　　員：**您辦理提款的目的為何？您要領多少？**

Customer : It is to buy a gift for my coworkers.

客　　戶：我想要給我的同事買個禮物。

Bank teller : Have you filled out the withdrawal slip?

行　　員：您填好提款單了嗎？

Customer : Yes, I already filled out the withdrawal slip.

客　　戶：是的，我已填好了。

Bank teller : OK. Please pass me your passbook as well as the filled-out withdrawal slip.

行　　員：好，請給我您的存摺和填好的取款條。

Customer : Here you are.

客　　戶：給您。

Bank teller : Thank you. Wait a minute, the amount in words you wrote down is **altered** by you.

行　　員：謝謝。等一下，您填的大寫金額有做塗改。

Customer : Yes. Because I just found out I wrote down the wrong words.

客　　戶：是啊。因為我發現我寫錯字了。

Bank teller : **Since you have altered the amount in words on the withdrawal slip, I have to make the withdrawal slip void. Please rewrite a new one.**

行　　員：因為您有在提款條上塗改大寫金額，我必須把這張提款條作廢。請重寫一張。

Customer : OK. But I want to tell you **some banks no longer require their customers to write down** the amount in words. **The customers only need to write down** the amount in figures.

客　　戶：好的。但我想跟您說，有些銀行已不要求客戶寫大寫金額了。客戶只需寫小寫金額就好了。

Bank teller : Oh…Yeah…Maybe it is the trend. I know Bank of Taiwan only requires their customers to write down the amount in words when they fill out the withdrawal slip. Their customers can write down the amount in figures if what they fill out is the deposit slip. After all, people seldom have chance to actually write down words with their hand because most people are used to using computers or smart phones to key in words. Many young people even cannot write Chinese characters without making a mistake.

行　　員：嗯……是啊……這可能是一種趨勢。我知道只剩臺灣銀行會要求他們的客戶在寫提款條時要寫大寫金額。他們的客戶在寫存款條時，可以寫小寫金額。畢竟，民眾很少有機會真的親手寫任何字

因為大部分人都習慣用電腦或是智慧型手機來輸入字詞。很多年
輕人甚至寫中文就一定會寫錯。

Customer : Yeah, it is a problem caused by computers and smart phones. OK, I
am done. Here you are.

客　　戶：是啊，這是電腦和智慧型手機導致的問題。好了，我填好了。在
這裡。

Bank teller : Thank you. Let me verify your signature. Well, **your personal signature on the withdrawal slip is not consistent with the original
specimen signature recorded in the bank. Could you sign your
name again?**

行　　員：謝謝。讓我檢驗您的簽名。嗯，您在取款單上的簽名和您在銀行
的原留印鑑卡上的簽名不一致。您可以再簽一次嗎？

Customer : OK. Let me try signing again.

客　　戶：好，我再重簽看看。

Bank teller : Yes, it is the right one. It is done. Here is your cash. Please check
the amount before you leave the counter.

行　　員：好，這次是對的。辦好了。這是您的現金。請在離開櫃檯前確認
金額無誤。

Customer : Sure. It is very nice of you. Thank you very much.

客　　戶：好的，您人非常好耶。非常謝謝您。

補充單字

◆ alter [`ɔltə] *v.* 塗改；變造；竄改

◆ the amount in words [ði ə`maunt ɪn wɝdz] *n.* 金額數字的大寫

◆ the amount in figures [ði ə`maunt ɪn `fɪgjəz] *n.* 金額數字的小寫

實用金句

♦ What is your purpose for making a withdrawal? How much would you like to withdraw?

您辦理提款的目的為何？您要領多少？

♦ Since you have altered the amount in words on the withdrawal slip, I have to make the withdrawal slip void. Please rewrite a new one.

因為您有在提款條上塗改大寫金額，我必須把這張提款條作廢。請重寫一張。

♦ Some banks no longer require their customers to write down the amount in words. The customers only need to write down the amount in figures.

有些銀行已不要求客戶寫大寫金額了。客戶只需寫小寫金額就好了。

♦ Your personal signature on the withdrawal slip is not consistent with the original specimen signature recorded in the bank. Could you sign your name again?

您在取款單上的簽名和您在銀行的原留印鑑卡上的簽名不一致。您可以再簽一次嗎？

存零錢
Depositing Coins

Bank teller : Hello, what can I do for you, Sir?

行　　員：先生您好，我能幫您辦什麼呢？

Customer : I would like to deposit a lot of **coins**.

客　　戶：我要存很多硬幣。

Bank teller : **Have you sorted coins first before you come here?** For example, you should put fifty-yuan coins together, then put ten-yuan coins together, then put five-yuan coins together and finally put one-yuan coins together.

行　　員：**在您來之前您已把硬幣分類好了嗎？**例如說，您應該把五十元硬幣整理在一起，然後把十元硬幣整理在一起，再把五元硬幣整理成一堆，最後把一元硬幣集中在一起。

Customer : No. But I think the bank has coin sorters. You know, you don't have to sort coins by tellers, but by this kind of machine.

客　　戶：還沒。但是銀行有硬幣分類機吧。您懂的，不必由行員來分類硬幣，可以由機器來做。

Bank teller : Well, I must tell you. **There is no such machine at the bank to sort coins out. But we do have coin-countering machines to count coins.**

行　　員：我必須告訴您。**在銀行沒有這種機器可以把硬幣分類。但是我們**

有數幣機來計算硬幣的數目。

Customer : Sorry, I don't know. Let me sort my coins by myself now…OK, it is done.

客　　　戶：抱歉，我不知道。現在讓我自己來把硬幣分類……好了，我做完了。

Bank teller : **Please give me those coins you have sorted out.**

行　　　員：**請把分類好的硬幣給我。**

Customer : Here you are.

客　　　戶：給您。

Bank teller : Sorry. Some of your fifty-yuan coins are out of **circulation**. Only Bank of Taiwan accepts the old coins. Our bank only accepts coins or banknotes that are in current circulation.

行　　　員：抱歉，有些您的五十元硬幣已經不**流通**了。只有臺灣銀行還接受這些舊版的硬幣。我們銀行只接受目前還在流通的硬幣或是現鈔。

Customer : I see.

客　　　戶：我明白了。

Bank teller : Please wait for a moment. Let me put those coins into coin rolling machine to count the amount…It is done. The amount of the coins is five thousand NT dollars in total. Please write down the amount on your deposit slip.

行　　　員：請稍待一會。讓我把這些硬幣放進數幣機裡來數算多少……算好了，硬幣的總金額是五千元。請在您的存款單上記下金額。

Customer : OK. Let me give you my passbook as well as the deposit slip.

客　　　戶：好的，我把存摺和存款條給您。

Bank teller : Let me process it for you right now. …OK, it is finished. **Here is**

your updated passbook. This transaction is recorded in your passbook, please double check it for me. Can I help you with anything else?

行　　員：我現在為您辦理。……好了，辦好了，這是您補好摺的存摺。這筆交易已登摺好了，請核對一下。還有其他我可以為您服務的地方嗎？

Customer：No, thanks. See you.

客　　戶：沒有，謝謝。再見。

補充單字

♦ coin [kɔɪn] *n.* 零錢；硬幣

♦ coin-countering machine [kɔɪn `kaʊntɚɪŋ məˋʃɪn] *n.* 數幣機

♦ circulation [ˏsɝkjəˋleʃən] *n.* 流通

實用金句

♦ Have you sorted coins first before you come here?

在您來之前您已把硬幣分類好了嗎？

♦ There is no such machine at the bank to sort coins out. But we do have coin-countering machines to count coins.

在銀行沒有這種機器可以把硬幣分類。但是我們有數幣機來計算硬幣的數目。

♦ Please give me those coins you have sorted out.

請把分類好的硬幣給我。

♦ Here is your updated passbook. This transaction is recorded in your pass-book, please double check it for me

這是您補好摺的存摺。這筆交易已登摺好了，請核對一下。

掛 失
Report It Lost

Bank teller : Hello, Sir. What can I do for you?
行　　　員：先生您好，我可以為您做什麼嗎？

Customer : A very bad thing happened. I don't know what to do.
客　　　戶：不好的事發生了。我不知道該怎麼辦？

Bank teller : Don't lose your cool. Tell me what happened.
行　　　員：不要失去理智。告訴我發生什麼事。

Customer : OK. I lost my ATM card. I am worried that some bad buys may use my ATM card to withdraw all my money from my account so that I will be broke and become a beggar in the street.
客　　　戶：好，我把我的金融卡搞丟了。我很擔心有壞人會盜用我的金融卡把我的錢從帳戶裡提領一空，然後我就會破產，變成街上的乞丐了。

Bank teller : Don't be worried. **You should report the loss of your ATM card immediately. I can process it for you right now.**
行　　　員：不要擔心。您應該立即掛失您的金融卡。我馬上就為您辦理。

Customer : OK, thank you. After I report it lost, what should I do next?
客　　　戶：好的，謝謝您。在我掛失後，我下一步該怎麼做？

Bank teller : **The bank will replace your ATM card but it will take five working days for your card to be ready.** Therefore, you should

come to the bank in person with your ID card to collect your new
ATM card five working days later.

行　　員：**銀行會**補發**金融卡給您，但要花五個工作天卡片才會弄好。因
此，您在五個工作天後，請本人持身分證來銀行領您的新金融
卡。**

Customer : OK, thank you. I also want to know if there is any other way for
me to report my ATM card or passbook lost.

客　　戶：好的，謝謝您。我也想知道有沒有別的方法讓我掛失金融卡或存
摺？

Bank teller : Yes. **You can also call our customer service call center to report
your ATM card lost if it is inconvenient for you to go to a bank
branch to report it lost over the counter.** Our customer service
representatives will ask you some personal questions to ensure you
are the right person and will process it for you immediately.

行　　員：有的。**如您不方便來銀行臨櫃辦理掛失的話，您也可以撥打我們
的客服中心來掛失金融卡。**我們的客服人員會詢問您私人問題來
確認您是本人並且會立即為您處理。

Customer : Well. **Does your bank have a** toll-free number **for your customers?**

客　　戶：好。**您們銀行有**0800免付費電話**嗎**？

Bank teller : Yes, there is. **The toll-free number is 0800-XXX-XXX. But I
have to tell you that you cannot use your cell phone to call the
toll-free number.**

行　　員：有的，**我們的免付費專線是**0800-XXX-XXX。**但我必須告訴您，
不能用手機來撥打免付費電話。**

Customer : OK, now I understand. Thank you very much.
客　　戶：好的，我了解了。非常謝謝您。

補充單字

◆ replace [rɪ`ples] *v.* 補發

◆ toll-free number [ˌtol`fri `nʌmbɚ] *n.* 免付費電話

實用金句

◆ You should report the loss of your ATM card immediately. I can process it for you right now.

您應該立即掛失您的金融卡。我馬上就為您辦理。

◆ The bank will replace your ATM card but it will take five working days for your card to be ready.

銀行會補發金融卡給您，但要花五個工作天卡片才會弄好。

◆ You can also call our customer service call center to report your ATM card lost if it is inconvenient for you to go to a bank branch to report it lost over the counter.

如您不方便來銀行臨櫃辦理掛失的話，您也可以撥打我們的客服中心來掛失金融卡。

◆ Does your bank have a toll-free number for your customers?

您們銀行有0800免付費電話嗎？

◆ The toll-free number is 0800-XXX-XXX. But I have to tell you that you cannot use your cell phone to call the toll-free number.

我們的免付費專線是0800-XXX-XXX。但我必須告訴您，不能用手機來撥打免付費電話。

保 全
Security Guard

Security guard：Hello, how can I help you?

保　　　全：您好。我可以為您做什麼？

Customer：Hello, where is the teller?

客　　　戶：嗨，行員在哪裡？

Security guard：Because too many customers suddenly came in, she just went back to the counter to support other tellers. Now I am on her behalf to serve customers.

保　　　全：因為剛才突然來了很多客人，所以她回到櫃檯來支援其他行員。現在我代替她來服務客戶。

Customer：I see. As a **security guard**, are you satisfied with your work? Could you talk more about the work as a security guard?

客　　　戶：我懂了。作為一個保全，您滿意您的工作嗎？您可以跟我談談保全的工作嗎？

Security guard：Yes, I would be happy to share with you. A bank security guard has to go to the bank branch before 8:00 a.m. every morning because a teller alone cannot enter into the bank to open the door. **Most banks require a bank teller to enter into the bank along with the security guard together in the morning. This is a kind of mechanism of check and balance.** This way, if one day a bank teller has evil thoughts and wants to rob the bank of money, it will become difficult for him to do so because the security guard will stop him.

保　　全：好的，我很高興跟您分享。銀行保全必須每天早上八點前就到分行，因為行員無法單獨開門進去銀行。**大多數銀行要求行員早上必須會同保全一同進入銀行。這是種制衡機制。**這樣一來，如果有天行員起了邪念想要監守自盜，由於保全會阻止他，而讓事情變得困難。

Customer : OK. So you have to arrive here at 8:00 a.m. And after you arrive, what do you do?

客　　戶：好。所以您必須每天早上八點就到。在您到了之後，您要做什麼？

Security guard : After I arrive at the bank, I have to stand at the entrance to open the door for the bank manager and other bank clerks to come in. So, I am kind of watcher. I also have to do some cleaning, throw away old newspaper and put today's newspaper on the right place. At 9:00 a.m., I have to open the gate for customers to come into the lobby to deal with their banking business.

保　　全：在我到達銀行後，我必須在入口處站著來幫銀行經理或是其他行員開門讓他們進來。所以，我有點像守門人。我也必須做些清掃、丟舊報紙還有置換當天新報紙的工作。在九點的時候，我必須打開大門讓客人進來大廳辦理他們的業務。

Customer : All right. Then during the banking hours, what will you do?

客　　戶：好，在營業時間，您又做什麼？

Security guard : **During the banking hours, I have to stand at the front door to watch the people. If I find anyone look suspicious, I must**

be more careful and report it to the bank manager right away in some cases. In case a bank robbery should occur, I have to fight against and subdue the robber. Of course, if the bank robber carries a gun, I will have to be cautious before I take any action. After all, you know, according to the law, a security guard in Taiwan is not allowed to carry a gun, so I can only hold a baton to protect the tellers in the bank.

保　　全：**在營業時間，我必須站在大門處來監看民眾。如果我發現任何可疑人物，我必須提高警覺，並在一些狀況下，馬上跟銀行經理報告。**萬一銀行搶案發生，我必須對抗和制伏搶匪。當然，如果銀行搶匪有拿槍的話，我也必須在採取任何行動之前小心為上。畢竟，根據法律，在臺灣的保全是不允許持有槍的，所以我必須拿保全棍在銀行保護行員。

Customer : All right. How do you judge whether a man is a potential threat to the bank?

客　　戶：好，您如何判斷一個人是否會對銀行造成潛在的威脅？

Security guard : There are many ways to judge. For example, if a man wears a helmet and a mask entering a bank branch, and won't put away his helmet and mask after I ask him to do so, he may well be a potential robber. Or when a man rides on a still scooter whose engine is still running, I will keep a close eye on him.

保　　全：有很多方式來判斷。例如說，如果有人戴安全帽和口罩進入銀行，在我要求之後，仍不肯脫下他的安全帽和口罩，他極有可能就是潛在搶匪。當有人坐在不動的機車上卻不熄火，我就會對他加以留意。

Customer : Oh. I see. Besides protecting the bank, what else do you need to do?

客　　戶：喔，我懂了。除了保護銀行，您還要做什麼？

Security guard : I also need to provide simple service for customers. For instance, **I have to lead customers to the right banking counter.** If they want to open an account, I will lead them to the service counter or so-called composite service counter. If they want to make a withdrawal, I will have to guide them to the teller counter. Sometimes, I have to answer some simple questions, such as "Has your bank started to pass out calendars?" or "When does your bank start to allow customers to exchange new banknotes?"

保　　全：我也需要服務客戶。例如說，**我必須引導客戶到正確的銀行櫃檯**。如果他們要開戶，我要引導他們到服務臺或是所謂的「綜合服務區」。如果他們想要提款，我要引導他們臨櫃。有時候，我要回答一些簡單的問題，如「您們開始發月曆了嗎？」或「您們什麼時候可以換新鈔？」

Customer : OK. But does not your bank also have a bank usher at the door?

客　　戶：好。但是您們銀行不也是有個引導員在門口嗎？

Security guard : Yes. **The bank usher's main duty is to receive customer and answer some more professional questions.** However, you know, sometimes when a bank usher is too busy, I also have to help receive customers. Some banks even don't place a bank usher at the door. The security guard has to do all the work, such as receiving customers or answering questions.

保　　全：是的。**引導員的主要工作就是接待客戶和回答更專業的問題。**不

過，您懂的，有時當引導員太忙了，我也必須幫忙接待客戶。有
些銀行甚至不會在門口設引導員。保全必須做全部工作，像是接
待客戶或是回答問題。

Customer ： I get it. Thank you.

客　　　戶：我了解了。謝謝。

Security guard ： It's my pleasure. Oh, it is almost 3:30 p.m. It is about time for
me to close the gate. Bye.

保　　　全：不客氣。喔，快三點半了，該是我關門的時刻了。再見。

Customer ： Bye.

客　　　戶：再見。

補充單字

◆ security guard [sɪ`kjurətɪ gɑrd] *n.* 保全

◆ bank usher [bæŋk `ʌʃɚ] *n.* 銀行引導員；白手套

實用金句

◆ Most banks require a bank teller to enter into the bank along with the security guard together in the morning. This is a kind of mechanism of check and
balance.

大多數銀行要求行員早上必須會同保全一同進入銀行。這是種制衡機制。

◆ During the banking hours, I have to stand at the front door to watch the
people. If I find anyone look suspicious, I must be more careful and report it
to the bank manager right away in some cases.

在營業時間，我必須站在大門處來監看民眾。如果我發現任何可疑人物，
我必須提高警覺，並在一些狀況下，馬上跟銀行經理報告。

♦ I have to lead customers to the right banking counter.

我必須引導客戶到正確的銀行櫃檯。

♦ The bank usher's main duty is to receive customer and answer some more professional questions.

引導員的主要工作就是接待客戶和回答更專業的問題。

沒收偽鈔
Confiscating Counterfeit Money

Bank teller : Hello, Sir, what can I do for you?

行　　員：嗨，先生，我可以爲您辦理什麼服務嗎？

Customer : I would like to make a deposit.

客　　戶：我想要存款。

Bank teller : Have you filled in the deposit slip?

行　　員：您塡好存款單了嗎？

Customer : Yes, I have filled in the deposit slip.

客　　戶：是的，我塡好存款單了。

Bank teller : Do you bring your passbook with you? Can I have your passbook?

行　　員：您有帶存摺來了？可以給我您的存摺嗎？

Customer : Yes, here you are.

客　　戶：是的，在這邊。

Bank teller : **How much money would you like to deposit?**

行　　員：**您要存多少？**

Customer : I would like to deposit 800,000 NT dollars.

客　　戶：我要存八十萬新臺幣。

Bank teller : Do you want to deposit the money into your own account or into someone else's account?

行　　員：您想把錢存入您自己的戶頭還是別人的？

Customer　: I want to deposit the money into someone else's account.

客　　戶：我想要把錢存入別人的戶頭。

Bank teller : Do you know the person whose account you are going to deposit money into? Is it the first time for you to deposit money into his or her account?

行　　員：您認識受款人嗎？這是您第一次把錢存到對方的戶頭嗎？

Customer　: Yes, I know the person. And it is not the first time for me to put money into her account.

客　　戶：是的，我認識對方。而且這不是我第一次把錢存到她的戶頭。

Bank teller : **Since you will deposit more than 500,000 NT dollars, I must ask you to fill out the declaration form.** And you have to give me your national ID card. Because according to Money Laundering Control Act, if you make a one-time cash transaction which is more than five hundred thousand dollars, you must fill out the declaration form to provide your personal information, including your name, national ID number, your birthday, your address, phone number and the amount of your transaction to the authorities concerned.

行　　員：**既然您要存超過新臺幣五十萬，我必須要求您填申報單。**您必須給我您的國民身分證。因為根據洗錢防制法，如果您單筆現金交易大於五十萬新臺幣的話，您必須填寫申報書，提供您的個資，如您的姓名、您的身分證字號、您的出生年月日、您的地址、電話號碼和您交易的金額給相關主管機關。

Customer　: Sure, it is done. Here you are.

客　　戶：好的，我填完了。給您。

Bank teller : Please take a look at the bill counter to confirm the amount while I am counting the banknotes.

行　　　員：在我點鈔時，請看著點鈔機來確認金額。

Customer : OK.

客　　　戶：好。

Bank teller : **I am sorry. Your money is not accepted by the money detector. I think these banknotes are counterfeit.**

行　　　員：**我很抱歉。您的錢沒有通過點鈔機。我認為這些紙鈔是偽鈔。**

Customer : Really?

客　　　戶：真的？

Bank teller : Yes. **Our bank policy is, if your money is rejected by the money detector, we will not accept this deposit and we have to confiscate the counterfeit banknotes.**

行　　　員：是的，**我們銀行的規定是，如果您的錢未能通過驗鈔機，我們就不收這筆存款，並且我們要沒收偽鈔。**

Customer : Wow. I don't know my banknotes are false money.

客　　　戶：哇。我不知道我的紙鈔是偽鈔。

Bank teller : That's OK. **I just want to tell you I cannot return your counterfeit money to you.**

行　　　員：沒關係，**我只是跟您說我無法把偽鈔還給您。**

Customer : Well, I understand. Thanks anyway.

客　　　戶：我了解了。還是謝謝您。

補充單字

♦ cash transaction [kæʃ træn`zækʃən] **n.** 現金交易

♦ confiscate [`kɑnfɪsˌket] **v.** 沒收

♦ counterfeit banknote [`kaʊntɚˌfɪt `bæŋknot] **n.** 假鈔

實用金句

♦ How much money would you like to deposit?

您要存多少？

♦ Since you will deposit more than 500,000 NT dollars, I must ask you to fill out the declaration form.

既然您要存超過新臺幣五十萬，我必須要求您填申報單。

♦ I am sorry. Your money is not accepted by the money detector. I think these banknotes are counterfeit.

我很抱歉。您的錢沒有通過點鈔機。我認為這些紙鈔是僞鈔。

♦ Our bank policy is, if your money is rejected by the money detector, we will not accept this deposit and we have to confiscate the counterfeit banknotes.

我們銀行的規定是，如果您的錢未能通過驗鈔機，我們就不收這筆存款，並且我們要沒收僞鈔。

♦ I just want to tell you I cannot return your counterfeit money to you.

我只是跟您說我無法把僞鈔還給您。

自動櫃員機
Automated Teller Machine (ATM)

Bank teller : Hello, what can I do for you, Sir?

行　　　員：先生您好，我有什麼可以幫您的呢？

Customer : I would like to make a deposit.

客　　　戶：我想要存款。

Bank teller : How much do you want to deposit?

行　　　員：您要存多少？

Customer : Just twenty thousand dollars.

客　　　戶：只存二萬元。

Bank teller : I see. I would suggest you should use our automated banking services because it is more convenient for you. First, **you don't have to take a number ticket and wait in line for a long time until your number is called. Next, once you are used to using an Automated Teller Machine（ATM）to make a deposit, you can deposit your money into your account through an ATM any time.** And **You don't have to rush to bank before 3:30 p.m.. You can make a deposit or make a withdrawal at an ATM anytime you like. In general, banks in Taiwan allow you to withdraw 20,000 to 30,000 NT dollars per transaction and up to 100,000 or 120,000 NT dollars per day.** To be more specific, if you use an

ATM to make an inter-bank withdrawal, you can withdraw up to 20,000 NT dollars per transaction. And if you use your own bank's ATM to make a withdrawal with the same bank's ATM card, you can withdraw up to 30,000 NT dollars per transaction. Does it sound great to you?

行　　員：我明白了。我會建議您去使用我們的自動化設備，因為對您來說比較方便。首先，**您不必抽號碼牌還要排很長的隊等叫號。再來，一旦您習慣使用「自動櫃員機」（簡稱為ATM）來存款的話，您可以在任何時間都能把錢存進您的帳戶。而且，您不必趕著在下午三點半前來銀行。您可以在您喜歡的時候來存錢或領錢就好。一般來說，在臺灣的銀行讓您每次交易可以提二萬到三萬，每日上限到十萬或十二萬。**更具體地說，如果您用ATM做跨行提款，您每次交易最多可以領到兩萬元。而如果您用自己銀行的ATM並用同家銀行的提款卡來做提款的話，您每次交易最多可以領到三萬元。聽起來很棒吧？

Customer : Well…I am not sure. All you just talked about is the benefits of using an ATM. What about the downsides of using ATMs? Can you tell me about the downsides?

客　　戶：嗯……我不確定耶。您剛才只有談到用ATM的好處。那用ATM的壞處呢？您可以講講壞處嗎？

Bank teller : Well, in some rare cases, the banknotes you try to deposit might be stuck in an ATM and you need to inform a bank teller to help you get out the stuck banknotes. Another shortcoming of ATM is, **most Taiwanese banks' ATMs only provide banknotes in denominations of 1,000 NT dollars. If you want to take out denominations of 100 NT dollars, I would suggest you use the ATMs of**

Bank of Taiwan or Cathay United Bank.

行　　員：嗯，在一些少數情況下，您要存的紙鈔可能會卡在ATM中，而您需要通知行員來幫您取出鈔票。另一個用ATM的缺點是，**大部分臺灣的銀行的ATM只提供一千元**面額。如果您想要領一百元面額，我會建議您用臺銀或國泰世華的ATM。

Customer : Well, I see. But I don't trust machines. What can an ATM actually do?

客　　戶：好，我了解了。但我不信任機器。自動櫃員機到底能做什麼？

Bank teller : The ATM, in fact, can do a lot of things. For example, **you can withdraw money or make a deposit or transfer money through the ATM. In addition, you can also pay your bills such as tuition, telephone bill, insurance premium, and credit card bill through the ATM.** Furthermore, you can also pay your tax, including Land Value Tax, House Tax, as well as Vehicle License Tax through the ATM.

行　　員：事實上，ATM可以做很多事。例如說，**您可以用ATM存提款、轉帳。而且，您可以用ATM來繳費，像是學費、電話費、保險費和信用卡費。**再來，您可以用ATM來繳稅，包括地價稅、房屋稅、和汽車牌照稅。

Customer : Wow, it sounds great. Can you tell me more?

客　　戶：哇，這聽來不錯。可以多告訴我一點嗎？

Bank teller : Of course. Generally speaking, most banks' banking hours are from 9:00 a.m. to 3:30 p.m.. On weekends and national holidays, banks are not open. Therefore, it is impossible to go to a bank to make a transaction on weekends or holidays. However, the ATM can help our customers get most transactions done. For instance,

you can check your balance or change your PIN number via the ATM. Most ATMs also allow their credit cardholders to take out a cash advance against the balance of a credit card. A cash advance is a short-term currency loan. The cardholder can get a cash advance at an ATM by using the PIN assigned by the bank. Anyway, an ATM can do a lot of things as a bank teller. After all, the purpose of ATMs is to replace flesh-and-blood bank tellers.

行　　員：當然可以。一般來說，大部分銀行的營業時間是早上九點到下午三點半。在週末和國定假日，銀行沒有營業。因此，週末或假日去銀行辦交易是不可能的。然而，ATM能幫客戶做大部分的交易。舉例來說，**您可以用ATM查餘額或是變更您的密碼。大部分的ATM都讓信用卡卡友預借現金。**預借現金是短期貸款。持卡者可以在ATM用銀行給的密碼來預借現金。總之，一臺自動櫃員機可以像櫃員一樣辦很多交易。畢竟，自動櫃員機的目的就是要取代有血有肉的銀行行員。

Customer : OK. I know ATMs provide New Taiwan dollars, but I want to ask you whether ATMs also provide foreign currencies or not.

客　　戶：好。我知道ATM有提供新臺幣，但我想問您ATM是否也提供外幣呢？

Bank teller : Yes. Our bank has set up a few **Foreign Exchange ATMs** at some branches. A Foreign Exchange ATM is an ATM in selected branches that dispenses foreign cash. Our bank's Foreign Exchange ATMs dispense foreign cash in US Dollars, Japanese Yen, Hong Kong Dollar and Renminbi only. But I have to remind you that not every branch has a Foreign Exchange ATM. To find out more about locations of Foreign Exchange ATMs, please visit our website.

行　　　員：有的。我們銀行有架設一些外幣提款機在一些分行。外幣提款機在一些選定的分行提供外幣現鈔。我們銀行的外幣提款機只提供美金、日幣、港幣和人民幣的現鈔。但我必須提醒您不是每家分行都有外幣提款機。要查詢外幣提款機的據點，請到我們的網站去查詢。

Customer　：What currencies and denominations can I withdraw from your bank's Foreign Exchange ATM?

客　　　戶：從您們銀行的外幣提款機我可以領到什麼幣別的外幣和面額？

Bank teller　：You can withdraw US Dollars (100), HKD (1,000), JPY (10,000) and Renminbi (100). Only these denominations are provided and cannot be exchanged for smaller denominations.

行　　　員：您可以提一百元面額的美金，一千元面額的港幣，一萬元面額的日幣和一百元面額的人民幣。只有提供這些面額的現鈔而且不能換成較小的面額。

Customer　：How much can I withdraw from your bank's Foreign Exchange ATM in each transaction?

客　　　戶：我從您們銀行的外幣提款機每次可以領多少元？

Bank teller　：You can withdraw up to 3000 US dollars or HKD 25,000 or JPY 300,000 per transaction.

行　　　員：您每次提領最多可到美金三千元或港幣二萬五千元或日幣三十萬元。

Customer　：How much can I withdraw from your bank's Foreign Exchange ATM each day?

客　　　戶：我每天可以從您們銀行的外幣提款機領多少錢？

Bank teller　：The total amount of cash withdrawal of both foreign currencies and New Taiwan Dollars shall not exceed the equivalent value of

100,000 NT dollars each day.

行　　　員：每日提領「外幣」及「新臺幣」現鈔合計不可以超過等值新臺幣
十萬元整。

Customer：What does it cost to withdraw foreign cash from your bank's Foreign Exchange ATM? How about the exchange rate?

客　　　戶：從您們銀行的外幣提款機提領要收多少手續費用？那匯率又如
何？

Bank teller：All the charges are already included in the foreign exchange
spread, so our bank will not charge any other direct fees for using
our bank's Foreign Exchange ATM to our customers. For withdrawals during the banking hours, the listed cash selling rate is applied. Withdrawals after the banking hours are considered to be the
transactions of the following business day, and the last cash selling
rate of the previous business day is applied. In addition, for now
our bank offers preferential exchange rates, which are three cents
less for US dollars.

客　　　戶：所有的手續費都包含在匯差裡頭了，所以我們銀行不會再跟您收
額外的使用外幣提款機的手續費。營業時間內提領外幣現鈔適用
本行牌告現鈔賣出匯率，營業時間外提領現鈔視為下個營業日的
交易，匯率適用本行前一營業日最後一次的牌告現鈔賣出匯率。
另外，目前本行美金匯率減讓三分優惠。

Customer：Where can I use your bank's Foreign Exchange ATM?

客　　　戶：我在哪裡可以使用您們銀行的外幣提款機呢？

Bank teller：Our bank has installed Foreign Exchange ATMs at its business
department, Keelung, Songshan, Hsinchu, Taichung, Changhua,
Tainan branches and so on to provide small foreign exchange with-

drawal services for our customers.

行　　員：我們銀行目前於營業部、基隆、松山、新竹、臺中、彰化、臺南
　　　　　等分行設置外幣提款機，提供本行客戶小額外幣提款之服務。

Customer：OK. Is there any service charge in using a common ATM?

客　　戶：好。那用一般的ATM要收手續費嗎？

Bank teller：Yes, there is a service charge. **The handling fee for an inter-bank transfer is fifteen NT dollars per transaction and the handling fee for an inter-bank withdrawal is five NT dollars per transaction.** Thus, I would suggest you find the ATM of your original account opening bank and use the same bank's ATM card to make a transaction. This way, when you withdraw money, you won't be charged for the handling fee.

行　　員：是，要收手續費。**每筆跨行轉帳的手續費是新臺幣十五元而跨行提款的手續費是每筆五元。**因此，我會建議您找原來自己開戶行的ATM並用同銀行的金融卡來辦交易。這樣的話，當您提款時，您就不會被收手續費。

Customer：Is there a daily transaction limit for withdrawing money from an ATM?

客　　戶：用ATM提款有每日限額嗎？

Bank teller：As I said earlier, most banks set the daily withdrawal limit between 100,000 NT dollars and 120,000 NT dollars. Our bank allows you to withdraw up to 100,000 NT dollars of your available account balance per day. For SmartPay purchases using your chip PIN, your daily limit is also 100,000 NT dollars of your available account balance.

行　　員：如同我早先所提過的，大部分銀行把每日提款限制在新臺幣十萬

到十二萬之間。我們銀行讓您每天可以領到十萬元新臺幣。用您的晶片密碼來做SmartPay消費扣款的話，您的每日限額也是每天可用餘額的十萬元新臺幣。

Customer : I see. What is the maximum amount I can transfer via an ATM a day?

客　　　戶：我明白了。透過ATM轉帳我每天最多可以轉出多少錢？

Bank teller : If you use our ATM to transfer money to a designated account or a registered account, every transfer amount limit is two million NT dollars per transaction and the daily transfer amount limit is up to a total of three million NT dollars. On the other hand, **if you use our ATM to transfer money to a non-designated account or a non-registered account, the daily transfer amount limit is only up to thirty thousand dollars a day.** But you have to notice that the daily transfer amount limit contains both physical ATMs as well as web ATMs. That is, if you have used the web ATM to transfer 30,000 NT dollars to a non-registered account, then you cannot transfer any money via a physical ATM again in the same day.

行　　　員：如果您用ATM轉帳到「約定帳戶」的話，每筆轉帳交易的限額是每筆二百萬，而每日轉帳的限額總共是新臺幣三百萬。另一方面，**如果您用ATM轉帳到「非約定帳戶」的話，每日最多只能轉三萬元。**但您必須注意這每日轉帳的限額包含實體ATM和網路ATM。也就是說，如果您已使用網路ATM轉三萬到非約轉帳號的話，您就無法在同一天再用實體的ATM轉任何錢出去了。

Customer : By the way, I also notice the slot of your trash cans your bank places beside ATMs is very narrow. Why is that?

客　　　戶：對了，我也注意到您們ATM旁邊銀行所置放的垃圾桶開口很窄。

為什麼啊？

Bank teller : The bank makes the slot of our trash cans narrow on purpose. The reason is simple. A few years ago, a man threw a still burning cigarette butt to the trash can beside an ATM and a fire broke out, so from then on, most banks decided to make the slot of trash can more narrow in case someone should throw garbage to the trash can. The trash cans beside ATMs are for customers to throw ATM receipts.

行　　員：我們銀行是故意把垃圾桶開口弄窄的。原因很簡單。幾年前，有人把未熄的菸蒂丟到ATM旁邊的垃圾桶裡而發生火災。從那時起，大部分的銀行決定把垃圾桶開口弄窄一點以免有人把垃圾丟到垃圾桶內。在ATM旁的垃圾桶是讓客人丟明細表的。

Customer : OK, I see. Thanks. Last time a bank teller told me their bank's ATMs can also help their customers to make a time deposit through an ATM. Is it true?

客　　戶：好的，我了解了。謝啦。上次有位行員跟我說銀行的ATM也可以幫客人做定存，是真的嗎？

Bank teller : Yes, it is true. But not every bank's ATM provides this service. Our bank's ATM does provide this service. **You can open an electronic certificate of deposit at an ATM.** It is simple and easy. By the way, you can also open an electronic certificate of deposit via online banking. Either way will do.

行　　員：沒錯，是真的。但不是每家銀行的ATM都有提供這服務。我們銀行的ATM是有這服務。**您可以在ATM開電子存單。**這很簡單又容易。順便一提，您也可以透過網銀開立電子存單。任一方法都行得通。

Customer : OK. But what if I want to cancel my electronic certificate of deposit? Can I cancel my electronic CD through an ATM?

客　　戶：好的。但如果我想要把電子存單解約怎麼辦？我可以透過ATM來解約嗎？

Bank teller : Yes, our bank can allow you to cancel electronic CD through an ATM. However, some banks, such as Chinatrust, does not allow their customers to cancel their electronic CD through ATMs. That is, you can only open an electronic CD at a Chinatrust ATM but you cannot cancel an electronic CD at an ATM. If you need to cancel your electronic CD, you must go to a Chinatrust branch to cancel it over the bank counter.

行　　員：是的，我們銀行允許您透過ATM來解約電子存單。但是有些銀行如中國信託不讓他們的客人透過ATM來解約。也就是說，您只可以在中國信託的ATM開電子存單但無法在ATM解約電子存單。如果您要解約您的電子存單，您必須去中國信託的分行臨櫃辦理解約。

Customer : Now I understand. It turns out that ATMs are really helpful and provide customers with a variety of services.

客　　戶：現在我懂了。原來ATM還真方便而且又提供客戶多樣的服務。

Bank teller : That's right. That's why more and more young people choose to use an ATM instead of performing their transactions over the counter. This way, you don't have to go to bank in person and wait for a long time. And if you know foreign friends, you can recommend them to use our ATMs as well. Customers will be able to select their preferred language when using our bank's ATM. All instructions concerning the ATM transactions will then be shown in the customer's desired language, such as English or Chinese.

行　　　員：對啊。所以愈來愈多的年輕人都選擇使用ATM而非臨櫃辦理交易。這樣一來，您不必親自到分行還要等很久。而且如果您有認識的外國友人，您也可以推薦他們用我們的ATM。使用我們銀行的ATM時，客戶可以選擇他們的偏好語言。所有的ATM交易指示都會以客人選擇的偏好語言來呈現，像是英文或是中文。

Customer ： Well, I think you miss one point to talk about. That is, banks want their customers to use automated banking services to cut down on their manpower cost. If all customers turn to ATMs to conduct their transactions, the bank will be able to lower a lot of costs and make more money. Am I right?

客　　　戶：嗯，我認為您有漏掉一點沒有提到。也就是說，銀行想要客人使用自動化銀行設施以便減省人力成本。如果所有的客戶都轉而使用ATM來辦交易的話，銀行將能夠降低很多成本而賺更多的錢。我說對了嗎？

Bank teller ： Yes. I think you are right. In Taiwan, automated banking and self-service are becoming the norm in banking. That is why so many banks encourage their customer to use ATMs instead of conducting their transactions over the counter. Some banks will even give their customers various coupons or benefits if they use ATMs to conduct their transactions.

行　　　員：是的。我認為您說得沒錯。在臺灣，自動化銀行及自助設施變得是常態了。這就是為什麼很多銀行鼓勵客戶使用ATM而非臨櫃辦理交易。如果客人用ATM來辦交易的話，有些銀行甚至會送客人各樣的禮券或優惠。

Customer ： I see. I think you should be worried that one day your job may be replaced by an ATM.

客　　戶：我明白了。我想您該擔心有天您的工作被自動櫃員機給取代。

補充單字

◆ Automated Teller Machine [`ɔtə͵metɪd `tɛlɚ mə`ʃin] *n.* 自動櫃員機；自動提款機

◆ denomination [dɪ͵nɑmə`neʃən] *n.* 面額

◆ Foreign Exchange ATM [`fɔrɪn ɪks`tʃendʒ e ti ɛm] *n.* 外匯提款機；外幣自動櫃員機

◆ electronic certificatee of deposit [ɪlɛk`trɑnɪk sɚ`tɪfəkɪt ɑv dɪ`pɑzɪt] *n.* 電子存單

實用金句

◆ You don't have to take a number ticket and wait in line for a long time until your number is called.

您不必抽號碼牌還要排很長的隊等叫號。

◆ Once you are used to using an Automated Teller Machine（ATM） to make a deposit, you can deposit your money into your account through an ATM any time.

一旦您習慣使用「自動櫃員機」（簡稱為ATM）來存款的話，您可以在任何時間都能把錢存進您的帳戶。

◆ You don't have to rush to bank before 3:30 p.m.. You can make a deposit or make a withdrawal at an ATM anytime you like.

您不必趕著在下午三點半前來銀行。您可以在您喜歡的時候來存錢或領錢就好。

♦ In general, banks in Taiwan allow you to withdraw 20,000 to 30,000 NT dollars per transaction and up to 100,000 or 120,000 NT dollars per day.

一般來說，在臺灣的銀行讓您每次交易可以提二萬到三萬，每日上限到十萬或十二萬。

♦ Most Taiwanese banks' ATMs only provide banknotes in denominations of 1,000 NT dollars. If you want to take out denominations of 100 NT dollars, I would suggest you use the ATMs of Bank of Taiwan or Cathay United Bank.

大部分臺灣的銀行的ATM只提供一千元面額。如果您想要領一百元面額的，我會建議您用臺銀或國泰世華的ATM。

♦ You can withdraw money or make a deposit or transfer money through the ATM. In addition, you can also pay your bills such as tuition, telephone bill, insurance premium, and credit card bill through the ATM.

您可以用ATM存提款、轉帳。而且，您可以用ATM來繳費，像是學費、電話費、保險費和信用卡費。

♦ You can check your balance or change your PIN number via the ATM. Most ATMs also allow their credit cardholders to take out a cash advance against the balance of a credit card.

您可以用ATM查餘額或是更改您的密碼。大部分的ATM都讓信用卡卡友預借現金。

♦ The handling fee for an inter-bank transfer is fifteen NT dollars per transaction and the handling fee for an inter-bank withdrawal is five NT dollars per transaction.

每筆跨行轉帳的手續費是新臺幣十五元而跨行提款的手續費是每筆五元。

♦ If you use our ATM to transfer money to a non-designated account or a non-registered account, the daily transfer amount limit is only up to thirty thousand dollars a day.

如果您用ATM轉帳到「非約定帳戶」的話，每日最多只能轉三萬元。

♦ You can open an electronic certificate of deposit at an ATM.

您可以在ATM開電子存單。

自動櫃員機通路
ATM Channel

Customer : Hello, may I ask you where your bank's ATMs are mostly located?

客　　戶：嗨，我可以問您們的自動櫃員機大都設在哪裡？

Bank teller : Certainly. **Our bank's ATMs can be found in many places such as Taipei MRT stations or convenience stores.**

行　　員：當然可以。**我們銀行的ATM可以在很多地方找到，像是臺北捷運站或是便利商店。**

Customer : Really? That's so convenient for me. I often take the MRT and go to a convenience store to buy stuff.

客　　戶：真的？對我來說還滿便利的。我常搭捷運和到便利商店買東西。

Bank teller : You know, **ATMs are quite abundant in Taiwan. You can find ATMs in convenience stores, like 7-11 or Family Mart.** For example, Chinatrust has set up their bank's ATMs in more than 4,000 7-11 convenience stores around Taiwan. Taishin Bank, on the other hand, has set up ATMs in more than 2,000 Family Mart convenience stores. In Hi-Life convenience stores, you can find the ATMs set up by Bank Sinopac, Cathay United Bank, or Union Bank of Taiwan. In addition to installing ATMs in convenience stores, Cathay United Bank also sets up ATMs at Taipei MRT stations. Union Bank of Taiwan, on the other hand, places their ATMs at Kaohsiung Rapid Transit stations. Furthermore, Union Bank of Taiwan also sets up their bank's ATMs at Carrefour hypermarkets. Plus, Taipei Fubon Bank chooses Taiwan High Speed Rail as their bank's ATM channel. It is said that Taipei Fubon Bank also plans to set up their ATMs at Taiwan Mobile stores and MOMO shops in the future.

行　　　員：您曉得的，**在臺灣ATM滿街都是。您可以在便利商店，如7-11或全家發現ATM**。舉例來說，中國信託在全臺的四千多家統一超商裝設ATM。另一方面，台新銀行在超過二千多家的全家放置ATM。在萊爾富，您可以發現永豐銀行、國泰世華或聯邦銀行的ATM。除了在便利商店設置ATM外，國泰世華也在臺北捷運站設置ATM。另一方面，聯邦銀行則在高雄捷運站放他們的ATM。此外，聯邦銀行也在家樂福放他們的ATM。此外，台北富邦也選擇臺灣高鐵作為他們的ATM通路。據說台北富邦也計畫將在臺灣大哥大的門市和MOMO百貨設ATM。

Customer : Wow. It seems that banks in Taiwan put much emphasis on ATM channels.

客　　　戶：哇。似乎在臺灣的銀行非常注重ATM通路。

Bank teller : Yes. **Since it is rather costly to set up a new bank branch or a mini-branch, most banks choose to set up ATMs instead. This way, it is less costly for banks.** Besides, banks might earn some service fees from ATMs because you will be charged five NT dollars per withdrawal while using another bank's ATM to make a withdrawal.

行　　　員：是的。**因為新設一間新分行或簡易型分行的成本很高，大部分銀行轉而選擇設置ATM。這樣的話，對銀行來說成本比較低廉。**

況且，銀行可能從ATM賺一些手續費，因為當您使用別家銀行的ATM來提款時，銀行會跟您收五塊手續費。

Customer ： So, banks can earn a lot of money from ATMs, right?

客　　戶：所以說，銀行能從ATM賺很多的錢，對吧？

Bank teller ： Not really. Actually, most ATMs don't bring banks any profit but cost banks more money. The reason is simple. Banks have to bear the cost of renting ATMs, hiring security companies to **restock** ATMs with banknotes and fixing and maintaining ATMs. **Only when a lot of people use their ATMs can banks make a profit; otherwise, banks may suffer a loss.** For example, Taipei Fubon Bank has once placed their ATMs in McDonald's restaurants in Taiwan. However, this decision turned out to be a big failure, so Taipei Fubon later cancelled the plan and pulled out their bank's ATMs from McDonald's restaurants because Fubon found out customers seldom used the ATMs at McDonald's and it became costly to maintain those ATMs in McDonald's.

行　　員：這倒也不是。事實上，多數的ATM並不能為銀行帶來什麼收益，反而花銀行更多的錢。原因很簡單。銀行必須承擔租用ATM、僱用保全公司來補鈔並負擔維修保養ATM的成本費用。**唯有當很多人都使用ATM時，銀行才能獲利。否則，銀行可能賠本。**舉例來說，台北富邦曾經在臺灣的麥當勞裝設ATM，然而，這個決定證明是個大失敗，故台北富邦後來取消此計畫並且把麥當勞的ATM給撤掉了，因為富邦發現客戶很少使用在麥當勞內的ATM而且麥當勞的ATM的保養成本也很高。

Customer ： By the way, I heard Standard Chartered International Commercial Bank has also started to place their ATMs outside their banks. For example, Standard Chartered International Commercial Bank has set up their ATMs in Miramar cinemas and Mos Burger restaurants in Taipei. On top of this, Standard Chartered International Commercial Bank also takes a part in placing their ATMs in Taipei Songshan Airport.

客　　戶：對了，我聽說渣打國際商銀也開始在銀行之外的地方裝設ATM。例如說，渣打銀行已在臺北市的美麗華戲院和摩斯漢堡設自動櫃員機。此外，渣打也在松山機場那邊放置他們的ATM。

Bank teller : Yes. That's right. You know so much. But I have heard other banks are not happy with Standard Chartered International Commercial Bank when it has installed its ATMs in Taipei Songshan Airport. Many banks want to set up their ATMs in Taipei Songshan Airport but they cannot. Taipei Songshan Airport has long been taken over by Bank of Taiwan, Mega Bank and Chunghwa Post as their ATM channel. However, Standard Chartered International Commercial Bank figured out a way by making a deal with Family Mart in Taipei Songshan Airport and succeeded in placing their ATM in Taipei Songshan Airport. Of course, this method is not welcomed by other banks.

行　　員：是的，您說的沒錯。您懂好多啊。但我也聽說其他銀行不是很高興渣打銀行在松山機場設ATM。很多銀行都想要在松山機場設置自己的ATM，但他們沒有辦法。松山機場的ATM通路長期被臺銀、兆豐銀和郵局壟斷。然而，渣打銀行想辦法藉由和在松山機場內部的全家便利商店合作，而成功在松山機場放置他們的ATM。當然，這種手段不被其他銀行所接受。

Customer : I see. Judging from what you told me, it seems the airport is a hot spot for banks to set up their ATMs.

客　　戶：我明白了。根據您告訴我的，似乎機場是銀行設置ATM的熱門地點。

Bank teller : Yes. **Because many foreigners will come and go to the airport, it is a great opportunity for banks to promote their banks' brand and reputation.** Besides, a great number of people will use the ATMs in the airport, so banks can earn a lot of service fees from the ATMs in the airport. Therefore, the airport has become a great place for ATMs.

行　　員：是的。**因為很多外國人會經過機場，對銀行來說是個向外國人推銷他們銀行品牌和名聲的絕佳機會。**更何況，不少人都會使用機場的ATM，這樣銀行就可以從機場的ATM賺很多手續費。因此，機場變成自動櫃員機的絕佳設置點。

Customer : Now I understand. Thank you.

客　　戶：現在我了解了。謝謝。

補充單字

♦ abundant [ə`bʌndənt] *adj.* 充滿的

♦ channel [`tʃænḷ] *n.* 通路

♦ mini-branch [mɪnɪ `bræntʃ] *n.* 簡易型分行

♦ restock [rɪ`stɑk] *vt.* 補（鈔）（＝refill）

實用金句

◆ Our bank's ATMs can be found in many places such as Taipei MRT stations or convenience stores.

我們銀行的ATM可以在很多地方找到，像是臺北捷運站或是便利商店。

◆ ATMs are quite abundant in Taiwan. You can find ATMs in convenience stores, like 7-11 or Family Mart.

在臺灣ATM滿街都是。您可以在便利商店，如7-11或全家發現ATM。

◆ Since it is rather costly to set up a new bank branch or a mini-branch, most banks choose to set up ATMs instead. This way, it is less costly for banks.

因為開一間新分行或簡易型分行的成本很高，大部分銀行轉而選擇設置ATM。這樣的話，對銀行來說成本比較低廉。

◆ Only when a lot of people use their ATMs can banks make a profit; otherwise, banks may suffer a loss.

唯有當很多人都使用自動櫃員機時，銀行才能獲利。否則，銀行可能賠本。

◆ Because many foreigners will come and go to the airport, it is a great opportunity for banks to promote their banks' brand and reputation.

因為很多外國人會經過機場，對銀行來說是個向外國人推銷他們銀行品牌和名聲的絕佳機會。

網路ATM
Web ATM

Customer : Hello, I would like to make an inter-bank transfer today.

客　　戶：您好，我今天想要辦理跨行轉帳。

Bank teller : Sir, have you heard of "Internet ATM"? I suggest you transfer money between banks through the Internet ATM. This way, you can also acquire some virtual coins. May I introduce the Internet ATM to you?

行　　員：先生，您有聽過「網路ATM」嗎？我會建議您透過網路ATM來跨行轉帳。這樣的話，您還可以多賺到虛擬的晶幣。我可以向您介紹一下網路ATM嗎？

Customer : OK. I would like to know. Please tell me about it.

客　　戶：好啊。我想了解一下。請告訴我。

Bank teller : An Internet ATM is also called a web ATM, an online ATM, or even an e-ATM. A web ATM is just like a physical ATM. It enables you to transfer funds from your account to the third party account through your chip and PIN ATM card. What is more, you can also pay your bills such as tuition, telephone bill, insurance premium, and credit card bill through the web ATM. **Plus, you can also pay your tax, including Land Value Tax, House Tax, as well as Vehicle License Tax through the web ATM. Of course, you can**

also check your balance through the web ATM.

行　　員：網路ATM也叫作Web ATM、線上ATM或e-ATM。網路ATM就像**實體的**ATM一樣。它讓您透過晶片金融卡從您的帳戶轉帳給別人。另外，您也可以用網路ATM來繳費，如學費、電話費、保險費、信用卡費。**此外，您也可以用網路ATM來繳稅，包括地價稅、房屋稅和汽車牌照稅。當然您也可以透過網路ATM來查詢餘額。**

Customer：Wow. It sounds great. How do I use a web ATM?

客　　戶：聽起來真棒。我如何使用網路ATM？

Bank teller：First, you have to have a computer which can let you surf the Internet. Next, you must have a chip card reader to let you insert your chip and PIN ATM card into. You can buy a chip card reader at a lot of places such as convenience stores or online shops. Then you have to download the related program provided by the bank and install the program into your computer. Then you go to the official web ATM website and insert your chipped ATM card into the card reader to use it.

行　　員：首先，您必須有臺可以上網的電腦。接下來，您必須要有晶片卡讀卡機讓您把晶片金融卡插在讀卡機中。您可以在很多地方買到晶片卡讀卡機，像是便利商店或是網路商店。接著您必須下載銀行提供的相關程式並安裝在您的電腦上。然後，您連到官方的網路ATM網站再把您的晶片金融卡插入讀卡機來使用。

Customer：It sounds really easy.

客　　戶：這聽起來很簡單。

Bank teller：Yes, it is easy. Besides, you don't have to take the risk of going out to use a real ATM because it was reported that some people were robbed when using ATMs. In addition, **if it is hard for you to find**

a real ATM in your neighborhood, using a web ATM is a good choice for you. You can use the web ATM anytime and anywhere.

行　　員：是的，這很簡單。況且，您不必冒著出門使用實體ATM的風險因為據說有些人在用ATM時遭到搶劫。此外，如果您碰到難以在附近找到實體ATM的時候，使用網路ATM對您來說會是好的選擇。您可以在任何時間、任何地點來使用它。

Customer : Wow. It is the right service for me. But is there any downside you want to share with me?

客　　戶：哇。這對我來是個合適的服務。但有沒有任何缺點要跟我分享？

Bank teller : Well. **A web ATM does not allow you to withdraw or deposit money as a real ATM because it does not contain a vault.** In addition, you cannot change your PIN number through a web ATM. You must go to find a physical ATM to change your PIN number.

行　　員：好吧。**網路ATM不允許您像在實體ATM一樣可以提、存款，因為它沒有金庫。**此外，您也不能透過網路ATM來變更晶片密碼。您必須到實體的ATM來變更您的晶片密碼。

Customer : I see. Is there a transaction limit for transferring funds via the web ATM?

客　　戶：我明白了。使用網路ATM有沒有轉帳的限額？

Bank teller : **If you use our web ATM to transfer money to a designated account or a registered account, the transfer amount limit is up to two million NT dollars per transaction and the daily transfer amount limit is up to a total of three million NT dollars a day through our web ATM.** On the other hand, **if you use our web ATM to transfer money to a non-designated account or a non-**

registered account, the daily transfer amount limit is up to one hundred thousand dollars a day through our web ATM. But you have to notice that the daily transfer amount limit contains both physical ATMs as well as web ATMs. That is, if you have used the web ATM to transfer 30,000 NT dollars to a non-designated account, then you cannot transfer any money via a physical ATM again in the same day.

行　　員： 如果您使用網路ATM來轉帳到「約定帳戶」的話，每筆轉帳限額是二百萬而每日轉帳限額一共是三百萬。另一方面，如果您使用網路ATM轉帳到非約定帳戶的話，每日轉帳限額是十萬元。但您必須注意每日轉帳限額包含實體和網路ATM。也就是說，如果您使用網路ATM已轉了三萬元到非約轉帳戶，那您就不能在同一天再用實體ATM轉任何錢了。

Customer： OK. I see. Do you have other words to say?

客　　戶： 好，我明白了。您還有其他的話要說嗎？

Bank teller： Yes, I forgot to tell you. **Most banks provide a lot of rewards such as lucky draw or** deducted **remittance charges to encourage customers to use a web ATM to make their transactions.**

行　　員： 是的，我忘記跟您說，大部分的銀行有提供客戶很多優惠，像是抽獎活動或是轉帳手續費減免來鼓勵客人使用網路ATM來辦交易。

Customer： That's great. I definitely will use the web ATM.

客　　戶： 眞好。我一定會使用網路ATM。

補充單字

♦ physical [`fɪzɪkəl] *adj.* 實體的

♦ deduct [dɪ`dʌkt] *v.* 扣除

實用金句

♦ Plus, you can also pay your tax, including Land Value Tax, House Tax, as well as Vehicle License Tax through the web ATM. Of course, you can also check your balance through the web ATM.

此外，您也可以用網路ATM來繳稅，包括地價稅、房屋稅和汽車牌照稅。當然您也可以透過網路ATM來查詢餘額。

♦ If it is hard for you to find a real ATM in your neighborhood, using a web ATM is a good choice for you. You can use it anytime and anywhere.

如果您碰到難以在附近找到實體ATM的時候，使用網路ATM對您來說會是個好選擇。您可以在任何時間、任何地點來使用它。

♦ A web ATM does not allow you to withdraw or deposit money as a real ATM because it does not contain a vault.

網路ATM不允許您像在實體ATM一樣可以提、存款，因爲它沒有金庫。

♦ If you use our web ATM to transfer money to a designated account or a registered account, the transfer amount limit is up to two million NT dollars per transaction and the daily transfer amount limit is up to a total of three million NT dollars a day through our web ATM.

如果您使用網路ATM來轉帳到「約定帳戶」的話，每筆轉帳限額是二百萬而每日轉帳限額一共是三百萬。

♦ If you use our web ATM to transfer money to a non-designated account or a non-registered account, the daily transfer amount limit is up to one hundred thousand dollars a day through our web ATM.

如果您使用網路ATM轉帳到非約定帳戶的話，每日轉帳限額是十萬元。

♦ Most banks provide a lot of rewards such as lucky draw or deducted remittance charges to encourage customers to use a web ATM to make their transactions.

大部分的銀行有提供客戶很多優惠，像是抽獎活動或是轉帳手續費減免來鼓勵客人使用網路ATM來辦交易。

網路銀行
Online Banking

Bank teller : Hello, what can I do for you today?

行　　員：您好，我可以爲您辦什麼嗎？

Customer : Well, **I would like to sign up for personal** online banking. Can you introduce your bank's personal online banking to me?

客　　戶：嗯，**我想要申辦個人**網路銀行。您可以爲我介紹貴行的個人網路銀行嗎？

Bank teller : Of course. Online banking is also called Internet banking or web banking or e-banking. Simply put, what Internet banking means you can use the computer to conduct your banking on the online platform provided by the bank.

行　　員：當然可以。網路銀行也叫作網銀、線上銀行或e網銀。簡單說，網銀就是您可以使用電腦在銀行提供的線上平臺辦理銀行業務。

Customer : So far I understand.

客　　戶：目前我都了解。

Bank teller : **Our personal Internet banking makes you get your online banking done anytime and anywhere. You can check on your accounts, transfer funds, pay all types of bills, or place an order to buy mutual funds via online banking.** In addition, you can use personal Internet banking to transfer money between your linked bank accounts on either a one-time or recurring basis. You can also view current balance information and review available transactions. There are a great number of functions on our Internet Banking.

行　　　員：**我們的個人網路銀行讓您可以隨時、隨地就把您的銀行業務線上就辦好。您可以透過網銀檢視您的帳戶、轉帳、繳費或是下單買共同基金。**另外，您可以用網銀在相關帳戶之間轉帳，不論是一次性的或是周期性的都可。您也可以檢視現在的餘額或是看交易明細。我們的網銀有很多的功能。

Customer : Wow, can you tell me more specifically about the services provided by Internet banking?

客　　　戶：哇，您可以再詳細點告訴我網銀提供的服務嗎？

Bank teller : Yes. Basically, our personal Internet banking can be divided into six categories: (1) banking services (2) securities services (3) credit card services (4) mutual funds services (5) insurance services (6) personal services. Let me explain. First, **online "banking services" enable you to view your accounts, check your loan, view your recent transactions on your account, check your online or physical CDs, check the inward remittance, check checks for collection, make registered / non-registered account transfers, make scheduled funds transfers, pay taxes and bills, open an online CD or cancel your online CD before maturity, buy or sell foreign currency, report the loss of your credit card / ATM card / passbook, and view the foreign exchange rates or the interest rates.** As for "securities services", if you buy or sell stocks, you will be interested because it allows you to place an order online.

行　　員：可以。基本上，我們的個人網路銀行業務有六大塊。(1)銀行服
　　　　　務。(2)證券服務。(3)信用卡服務。(4)共同基金服務。(5)保險服
　　　　　務。(6)個人服務區。讓我說明一下。首先，**網銀的銀行服務讓您
　　　　　能檢視帳戶、查詢借款、檢視您最近帳戶的交易明細、查詢電子
　　　　　存單或實體存單、查詢匯入匯款、查詢託收支票、約定或非約定
　　　　　轉帳、預約轉帳、繳稅和繳費、開立電子存單或中途解約、買賣
　　　　　外幣、掛失您的信用卡、金融卡和存摺以及查看外幣匯率或是利
　　　　　率。** 至於證券服務，如果您有在買賣股票，您將會感興趣，因為
　　　　　它能讓您網路下單。

Customer : Oh, I don't buy stocks.

客　　戶：喔，我不買股票。

Bank teller : OK. So I will jump to the next category: "credit card services".
**If you have our bank's credit card, you can use our Inter-
net banking to check your monthly statement, activate your
credit card, apply for an e-statement, apply for a** cash advance
**against your credit card, check your credit line, check your
accumulated reward points, redeem your reward points, and
conduct a credit cardholder behavior analysis.** Even if you don't
have our bank account, you still can apply for Internet banking for
"credit card services". Of course, the premise is, you must have our
bank's credit card.

行　　員：好。那我跳到下一個區塊：「信用卡服務」。**如果您有辦我們的
　　　　　卡，您可以用網銀來查看每月對帳單、開卡、申請電子對帳單、
　　　　　辦** 預借現金 **、查詢信用額度、查看累積紅利點數、兌換紅利點數
　　　　　和做信用卡消費行為分析。** 即使您沒有我們的銀行戶頭，您還是
　　　　　可以申辦我們網銀的信用卡服務。當然前提是，您要是我們的卡

友。

Customer : Good. I also have your bank's credit card. If I sign up for your Internet banking, I can use online banking to check my credit card's statement. That is really convenient for me.

客　　戶：真好。我也有辦您們的卡。如果我申請網銀的話，我可以使用網銀來檢視我的信用卡的消費明細。對我來說很方便。

Bank teller : **If you often buy mutual funds, you can also use our Internet banking for "mutual funds services", which allow you to check your investment portfolio, redeem your mutual funds, subscribe to mutual funds and check the** net asset value (NAV) **of the mutual funds you have subscribed to.** Next, **you can also use Internet banking for "insurance services" to check your insurance policies or pay your insurance premium.** Last but not least, **you can also take advantage of Internet banking for "personal services" to set up alerts, nickname your accounts, reset your username and password, update your personal information such as your correspondence address or telephone number, and deactivate the function of non-registered account transfer, the function of international withdrawal, as well as the purchase function of the debit card.**

行　　員：如您常買共同基金，您還可以用網銀的「基金服務」，它使您能檢視您的基金投資組合、贖回您的基金和申購基金並且檢視您申購基金的淨值。再來，您也可使用網銀的「保險服務」來查詢您的保單或是繳保費。最後卻也同樣重要的是，您可以利用網銀的個人服務區來設定個人提醒通知、帳戶別名設定、重設使用者代號和密碼、更新個人資料，像是您的聯絡地址或電話號碼和取消

非約轉功能、國際提領功能和消費扣款功能。

Customer : Wow, I don't know Internet banking has provided so many services.

客　　戶：哇，我不知道網路銀行提供這麼多服務功能。

Bank teller : That's OK. Now you know. Do you want to sign up for our Internet banking now?

行　　員：沒關係，現在您知道了。您要現在申辦網銀嗎？

Customer : Of course. I already brought my ID card as well as my original specimen seal with me. But before I apply for Internet banking, I would like to know the risks of Internet banking.

客　　戶：當然。我已經帶我的身分證和原留印鑑來了。但在申辦網銀之前，我想要知道網路銀行的風險。

Bank teller : Don't worry. Our Internet banking gives you the flexibility to undertake your banking at a time that best suits you, so we use secure and trusted information technology that assures your finances in the best possible care. All communication between your browser and our secure Internet banking sites is encrypted to make sure confidentiality of transactions performed on our website. However, you must also be careful when using Internet banking.

行　　員：別擔心。因為我們的網銀提供您辦線上銀行業務最適合您時間的彈性，所以我們都使用安全和可靠的資訊技術來確認您的財產有得到妥善的照顧。在瀏覽器和我們安全的網銀之間的傳輸都有加密以確保在我們網站上的線上交易機密性。然而，您在用網路銀行時還是要小心。

Customer : What should I notice when I use your Internet banking?

客　　戶：當我使用您們銀行的網銀時，我要注意些什麼？

Bank teller : First, you should know that if you key in the wrong password up to three times, your online banking account will be locked. If that happens, you will need to go to any one of our branches in person with your two forms of ID to reactivate your online banking account. What's more, you should avoid using a public computer for financial transactions in public places such as Internet cafes, public libraries, hotels and so on. You should not leave your computer unattended when connected to our Internet banking website. Always make sure you log out of the website after you finish your Internet banking transactions. Of course, don't disclose your username or password to the third party. Our bank will not display your personal information in e-mails nor ask you to confirm any personal information by replying e-mails. **Do not use passwords which can easily be identified as belonging to you such as your birthday or simple combinations.** Do not write your passwords down or store them in your personal computer. Do not use the same password on all your online access accounts with our bank and other banks. Otherwise, if one of your Internet banking is cracked by hackers, they can use the same password to crack your other banks' online banking accounts. You should also change password frequently and make it different from the last one you used. Plus, if there are suspicious transactions that indicate someone else has been using your online banking account, please contact us as soon as possible. I also suggest you have an updated anti-virus protection program as well as a current anti-spyware protection program in your computer to protect your computer from catching a virus. All in all, you cannot be too careful when you use our online banking. If you take the above-mentioned precautions, I believe you can take an active role in reducing the chance of being a victim of online account scams and identity theft.

行　　員：首先，您應知道如果您密碼輸入錯誤達到三次的話，您的網銀帳戶就會被鎖起來。如果這種事發生的話，您需要本人帶雙證件親自來任一分行重新開啓您的網銀帳戶。再來，您應該避免在公共場所，如網咖、圖書館、旅館等地方使用公用電腦來辦理金融交易。當您連線到我們網路銀行的網站時，您不應離開您的電腦。永遠確定您辦完網路銀行交易後，一定要登出。當然，也不要對別人透露您的使用者代號或密碼。我們銀行不會在電子郵件中顯示您的個人資料，也不會要求您回覆電子郵件確認任何的個人資料。**不要使用懶人密碼，像是您的生日或簡單的密碼。**不要把您的密碼寫下來或是放在您個人電腦的檔案中。不要用同一個密碼來登入我們和其他銀行的網銀。這樣的話，萬一您其中一個網銀被駭客入侵破解的話，他們就可以用相同的密碼來破解您在其他銀行的網路銀行帳戶。您也應該常常更換您的密碼，使密碼和上次使用的不同。還有，如果有不尋常的交易紀錄顯示有別人使用您的網銀帳戶的話，記得要儘快聯絡我們。我也建議您要在您的電腦上裝最新的防毒軟體和防木馬軟體來守護您的電腦免於中毒。總之，當您用網銀時，小心爲上策。如果您做到了以上的措拖，我相信您可以減少成爲網路銀行詐騙或身分被盜用的受害者的機率。

Customer : Thank you. By the way, I am also a business owner. Does your bank also provide Internet banking for business?

客　　戶：謝謝您。對了，我也是公司的老闆。您們有提供企業用的網路銀

行嗎？

Bank teller : Yes. We have our corporate Internet banking. Our corporate Internet banking is a one stop shop for all your online banking needs. **You can use our B2B online banking to view your bank account details, account balance, download e-statements, transfer fund between accounts, make all your tax payments and pay salaries as a bulk payment to all your employees.** The B2B Internet banking user is provided with account balances and transaction history of all activities on the accounts. Information on transaction history can be downloaded in different formats, such as Excel. You can use our B2B to effect payments to suppliers or employees. There is an option to make bulk fund transfers by uploading the data in file format rather than keying in individually. And our corporate online banking also enables you to view real-time exchange rates offered by the bank. Our B2B online banking provides utility for submitting requests for opening or amending LC to our customers in addition to requesting for a check book, bill collection, registering for roadside assistance, inquiry of foreign currency forward, paying utility bills, opening time deposit, or terminating CDs before maturity. Well…after I said so much, are you interested in applying for our B2B internet banking now?

行　　員 : 是的。我們有企業網路銀行。我們的企業網路銀行提供您線上辦理銀行業務一次到位的服務。**您可以使用我們的企業網銀來檢視帳戶明細、帳戶餘額、下載電子對帳單、轉帳、繳稅和批次付款來發薪水給員工。**企業網路銀行提供使用者帳戶餘額和帳戶交易歷史明細。交易歷史明細可以用不同的格式下載，如Excel檔。您可以用我們的企業網銀來付款給供應商或是員工。在做批次轉帳

時，您不用逐項輸入而可以選擇藉由上傳檔案資料而完成。而且我們的企業網路銀行也能使您能檢視即時的外匯匯率。除了申請支票本、票據託收、登記道路救援、查詢即期外匯、繳水電費、開定存存單或是定存中途解約之外，我們的企業網銀也提供您開立或修改信用狀的請求功能。嗯，在我講了這麼多之後，您現在想辦我們的企業網路銀行了嗎？

Customer : Of course. I will definitely consider registering for your bank's on-line banking for business. And I want to ask you a question. Does your Internet banking have an English version? Because one of my American friends is also interested in applying for personal online banking. But most Taiwanese banks don't have an English version for their Internet banking.

客　　戶：當然。我一定會考慮申辦您們的企業網銀的。並且我想問一下。您們的網銀有英文版嗎？因為我有一個美國朋友也有意申辦網路銀行。但臺灣大部分的銀行都沒有提供英文版的網路銀行。

Bank teller : Oh. I am sorry. Our bank does not have an English version of our online banking website, but I know Standard Chartered Bank offers an English version of their online banking. Maybe your friend can go to Standard Chartered Bank to apply for their online banking.

行　　員：喔，我很抱歉。我們沒有英文版的網銀網站，但我知道渣打銀行有推出英文版的網銀。也許您的朋友可以去渣打銀行申請他們的網銀。

補充單字

◆ online banking [`onlaɪn `bæŋkɪŋ] **n.** 網路銀行；網銀

◆ cash advance [kæʃ əd`væns] **n.** 預借現金

◆ net asset value (NAV) [nɛt `æsɛt `væljʊ] **n.** 淨值

◆ bulk payment [bʌlk `pemənt] **n.** 批次轉帳（= bulk fund transfer）

實用金句

◆ I would like to sign up for personal Online Banking.

我想要申辦網路銀行。

◆ Our personal Internet banking makes you get your online banking done anytime and anywhere. You can check on your accounts, transfer funds, pay all types of bills, or place an order to buy mutual funds via online banking.

我們的個人網路銀行讓您可以隨時、隨地就把您的銀行業務線上就辦好。

您可以透過網銀檢視您的帳戶、轉帳、繳費或是下單買共同基金。

◆ Online "banking services" enable you to view your accounts, check your loan, view your recent transactions on your account, check your online or physical CDs, check the inward remittance, check checks for collection, make registered / non-registered account transfers, make scheduled funds transfers, pay taxes and bills, open an online CD or cancel your online CD before maturity, buy or sell foreign currency, report the loss of your credit card / ATM card / passbook, and view the foreign exchange rates or the interest rates.

網路銀行服務讓您能檢視帳戶、查詢借款、檢視您最近帳戶的交易明細、

查詢電子存單或實體存單、查詢匯入匯款、查詢託收支票、約定或非約定

轉帳、預約轉帳、繳稅和繳費、開立電子存單或中途解約、買賣外幣、掛失您的信用卡、金融卡和存摺以及查看外幣匯率或是利率。

♦ If you have our bank's credit card, you can use our Internet banking to check your monthly statement, activate your credit card, apply for an e-statement, apply for a cash advance against your credit card, check your credit line, check your accumulated reward points, redeem your reward points, and conduct a credit cardholder behavior analysis.

如果您有辦我們的卡，您可以用網銀來查看每月對帳單、開卡、申請電子對帳單、辦預借現金、查詢信用額度、查看累積紅利點數、兌換紅利點數和做信用卡消費行為分析。

♦ If you often buy mutual funds, you also can use our Internet banking for "mutual funds services", which allow you to check your investment portfolio, redeem your mutual funds, subscribe to mutual funds and check the net asset value (NAV) of the mutual funds you have subscribed to.

如您常買共同基金，您還可以用網銀的「基金服務」，它使您能檢視您的基金投資組合、贖回您的基金和申購基金並且檢視您申購基金的淨值。

♦ You can also use Internet banking for "insurance services" to check your insurance policies or pay your insurance premium.

您也可使用網銀的「保險服務」來查詢您的保單或是繳保費。

♦ You can also take advantage of Internet banking for personal services to set up alerts, nickname your accounts, reset your username and password, update your personal information, such as your correspondence address or telephone number, and deactivate the function of non-registered account transfer, the function of international withdrawal as well as the purchase function of the debit card.

您可以利用網銀的個人服務區來設定個人提醒通知、帳戶別名設定、重設使用者代號和密碼、更新個人資料，像是您的聯絡地址或電話號碼和取消非約轉功能、國際提領功能和消費扣款功能。

◆ Do not use passwords which can easily be identified as belonging to you, such as your birthday or simple combinations.

不要使用懶人密碼，像是您的生日或簡單的密碼。

◆ You can use our B2B online banking to view your bank account details, account balance, download e-statements, transfer fund between accounts, make all your tax payments and pay salaries as a bulk payment to all your employees.

您可以使用我們的企業網銀來檢視帳戶明細、帳戶餘額、下載電子對帳單、轉帳、繳費和批次付款來發薪水給員工。

電話銀行
Telephone Banking

Customer : Hello, **I want to** register for telephone banking but in fact I don't know much about this service. Can you introduce it to me?

客　　戶 : 嗨，**我想要**申辦電話銀行，但我實際上對這服務知道甚少，您可以跟我介紹嗎？

Bank teller : Of course. Telephone banking is a banking service offered by a lot of banks in Taiwan. With phone banking, you can conduct your banking by phone. Needless to say, you need to use the keypad on a touch-tone telephone to perform banking functions. In other words, you push the keypad on a touch-tone phone to enter an automated system and obtain information on your bank accounts. Once you enter phone banking service, you only have to follow the prompts to go to the extended menu to conduct your banking.

行　　員 : 當然。電話銀行是臺灣很多銀行提供的銀行服務。有了電話銀行，您可以用電話來辦銀行業務。不用說，您需要使用電話上的按鍵來辦銀行業務。換句話說，您要按電話上的按鍵來進入自動化系統並且得到您銀行帳戶的資訊。一旦您進入電話銀行服務，您只要按照提示進入延伸選單來處理您的銀行業務。

Customer : What kind of services does telephone banking offer?

客　　戶 : 電話銀行提供什麼樣的服務內容呢？

Bank teller : **You can use our phone banking to hear your real-time balance, check your latest transaction records, transfer money between accounts, pay your bill, report the loss of your credit card / ATM card / passbook, and hear the foreign exchange rates or the interest rates.**

行　　員：您可以用我們的電話銀行來聽您的最新餘額、查詢您最新的交易明細、轉帳、繳費、掛失您的信用卡、金融卡、存摺，還有聽匯率或利率。

Customer : Wow. I don't know phone banking offers so many services.

客　　戶：哇，我不知道電話銀行有這麼多服務。

Bank teller : Yes, phone banking can save you a lot of time. You don't have to spend a lot of time and energy going to a bank to perform these transactions. **Wherever you are, as long as you have a telephone, you can use telephone banking at any time you want. Besides, phone banking is free to use.**

行　　員：是的。電話銀行可以節省您很多時間。您不必花很多時間和精力跑到銀行來辦業務。不論您在哪裡，只要您有一支電話您就可以隨時用電話銀行。況且，使用電話銀行不收費喔。

Customer : Good. You just mentioned I could use phone banking to make a transfer. Can I transfer to any account?

客　　戶：真好。您剛剛提到我可以用電話銀行來做轉帳。我可以轉到任何帳戶嗎？

Bank teller : Well, **if you use phone banking to make a transfer, you can only transfer money to a registered account number or a linked account number.**

行　　員：這個嘛。如果您用電話銀行來轉帳，您只能轉帳到約定帳號。

Customer : Does it cost anything to access phone banking?

客　　戶：用電話銀行的話您們會收什麼費用嗎？

Bank teller : Our bank does not charge you a service fee to access phone banking.

行　　員：我們銀行不會跟您收使用電話銀行的手續費。

Customer : OK. I want to apply for phone banking now.

客　　戶：好的。我想要現在就申辦電話銀行。

Bank teller : Please give me your national ID card as well as your original specimen seal and fill out the application form.

行　　員：請給我您的國民身分證和原留印章並寫申請表。

Customer : No problem.

客　　戶：沒問題。

Bank teller : Here is your password envelop, which contains the default telephone voice password. **Please dial this number to our phone banking system to change the password.** Do not use passwords which can easily be identified as belonging to you such as your birthday or one two three four.

行　　員：這是您的密碼函，裡面有包括您的預設語音密碼。**請打這支號碼進入我們的電話銀行系統來變更密碼。** 不要使用過於簡單的密碼，像是您的生日或一二三四。

Customer : Thank you very much.

客　　戶：真謝謝您。

Bank teller : Here is the booklet for you. It outlines all the phone banking services. If you have any problem, please take reference to this booklet. By the way, why don't you apply for Internet banking or mobile banking? Now few people want to apply for phone banking because most people like "what you see is what you get."

行　　員：這是給您的小冊子。上面列舉了所有電話銀行的服務。如果您有任何問題，請參閱這個小冊子。順便一提，您何不申辦網路銀行或是行動銀行？現在很少人想要申辦電話銀行，因為大多數人喜歡「即見即所得」。

Customer : To tell you the truth, I don't know how to use a computer or a smart phone.

客　　戶：老實說，我不會用電腦或是智慧型手機。

Bank teller : OK. Now I understand why. Maybe one day after you learn how to use a computer, you can also register for our personal online banking.

行　　員：好吧。現在我知道原因了。也許有天您學會使用電腦後，您可以來申辦我們的個人網銀。

Customer : Maybe.

客　　戶：也許吧。

補充單字

♦ register for [`rɛdʒɪstə· fɔr] *v.* 申辦（= sign up for）

♦ telephone banking [`tɛlə‚fon `bæŋkɪŋ] *n.* 電話銀行

♦ keypad [`ki‚pæd] *n.* 按鍵

實用金句

♦ I want to register for telephone banking.

　我想要申辦電話銀行。

♦ You can use our phone banking to hear your real-time balance, check your latest transaction records, transfer money between accounts, pay your bill, report the loss of your credit card / ATM card/ passbook, and hear the foreign exchange rates or the interest rates.

您可以用我們的電話銀行來聽您的最新餘額、查詢您最新的交易明細、轉帳、繳費、掛失您的信用卡、金融卡、存摺,還有聽匯率或利率。

◆ Wherever you are, as long as you have a telephone, you can use telephone banking at any time you want. Besides, phone banking is free to use.

不論您在哪裡,只要您有一支電話您就可以隨時用電話銀行。況且,使用電話銀行不收費喔。

◆ If you use phone banking to make a transfer, you can only transfer money to a registered account number or a linked account number.

如果您用電話銀行來轉帳,您只能轉帳到約定帳號。

◆ Please dial this number to our phone banking system to change the password.

請打這支號碼進入我們的電話銀行系統來變更密碼。

行動銀行
Mobile Banking

Bank teller : Hello, what can I do for you today?

行　　員：您好，我今天可以為您做什麼？

Customer : Well, I am interested in knowing mobile banking. Can you introduce your mobile banking to me?

客　　戶：嗯，我想了解行動銀行。您可以為我介紹你們的行動銀行嗎？

Bank teller : Of course. **Mobile banking is just like Internet banking. Simply put, what mobile banking means is, you use your smart phone to conduct your banking on the online platform provided by the bank.**

行　　員：當然可以。**行動銀行就像網路銀行一樣。簡單說，行動銀行就是您用智慧型手機在銀行提供的網路平臺來辦銀行業務。**

Customer : I know this.

客　　戶：我知道這個。

Bank teller : **Our mobile banking enables you to get your online banking done anytime and anywhere. You can check on your accounts, transfer funds, pay all types of bills, or even place an order to buy mutual funds. You can also view current balance information and review your bank account transactions.** There are a great number of functions on mobile banking.

行　　員：**我們的行動銀行能讓您隨時隨地線上辦好銀行業務。您可以查詢帳戶、轉帳、繳費或甚至是下單買基金。您也可以檢視餘額資訊、帳戶交易紀錄。**行動銀行提供很多功能。

Customer：Wow. Can you tell me more specifically about the services provided by mobile banking?

客　　戶：哇。您可以更具體一點告訴我行動銀行提供的服務嗎？

Bank teller：Of course. You can use our mobile banking to view your accounts, check your recent transactions on your account, transfer funds between accounts, make registered account transfers, pay taxes and bills, convert or exchange foreign currency, and view the foreign exchange rates or the interest rates of our bank.

行　　員：當然。您可以用我們的行動銀行來檢視帳戶、查詢您帳戶最近的交易明細、轉帳、辦理約定帳戶轉帳、繳稅和繳費、做外匯結購結售，以及查詢我們銀行的外匯匯率或是利率。

Customer：OK. Does your mobile banking provide any practical service for your credit cardholder?

客　　戶：好，那您們的行動銀行有為卡友提供任何實用的服務嗎？

Bank teller：Sure. **If you have our bank's credit card, you can use our mobile banking to check your monthly statement, check your accumulated reward points and redeem your reward points.**

行　　員：當然有。**如果您是我們的卡友，您可以用行動銀行來查詢每月對帳單、累積的紅利點數和兌換紅利點數。**

Customer：Great. Through mobile banking, I can check my credit card's monthly statement. That is really convenient for me.

客　　戶：太好了。透過行動銀行，我可以查詢我每月的刷卡明細。這對我來說真是太方便了。

Bank teller : If you often buy mutual funds, you can also use our mobile banking for "mutual funds services", which allow you to check your investment portfolio, redeem your mutual funds, subscribe to mutual funds, and check the net asset value (NAV) of the mutual funds you have subscribed to. Furthermore, you can also use mobile banking for "insurance services" to check your insurance policies you have bought over the bank counter.

行　　員 : 如果您常買共同基金，您可以用行動銀行的「基金服務」來查詢您的投資組合、贖回基金或申購基金並查詢您申購的基金的淨值。另外，您也可以用行動銀行的「保險服務」來查詢您在銀行臨櫃買的保單。

Customer : Wow. I don't know mobile banking has provided so many services.

客　　戶 : 哇，我都不曉得行動銀行有提供這麼多的服務。

Bank teller : I am not finished yet. **You can also search for our nearest bank branch through our mobile banking.** For example, while you are walking on the Tianmu West Road and want to find the nearest bank branch in your area, you can use our mobile banking and you will find the nearest branch is Tianmu Branch. What's more, you can check how many people are waiting in line for the bank counter service through our mobile banking.

行　　員 : 我還沒說完呢。**您也可以透過行動銀行來搜尋離您最近的分行。**舉例來說，當您在逛天母西路，想要找離您最近的分行的時候，您用行動銀行就可以找到離您最近的分行是天母分行。再來，您也可以透過行動銀行來查詢目前還有幾位臨櫃待辦人數。

Customer : Wow, mobile banking can do that. I've never known that.

客　　戶 : 哇，行動銀行可以辦到這點！我都不知道。

Bank teller : Yes. As for the interests you can get from the different types of time deposit, you can also use our mobile banking to do a trial calculation to help your understand which program of CDs best benefits you.

行　　　員：是的。至於不同定存的利息，您也可以使用行動銀行做試算來幫您了解哪種定存方案對您最有利。

Customer : It is great! But I have to express concerns about hackers gaining access to my phones and exposing my personal financial information.

客　　　戶：真棒！但我擔心駭客會侵入我的手機和曝光我的個人財務資訊。

Bank teller : Yes, security is a big issue. And you are right. Using mobile banking is potentially riskier because smart phone users connect to all kinds of networks. On the other hand, smart phones are just little computers, inevitably facing the same threat that exists online. Therefore, I would suggest you install anti-virus software available for Android or iPhone to keep your smart phones safe from Internet threats. You should also lock your smart phone when it is not in use and be sure to put your smart phone in a safe location. **You should never disclose your account information, including but not limited to account numbers, passwords, or personal information.** And you should also use reliable apps and only download mobile apps from reputable sources because apps are exposed to all kinds of viruses. I also recommend that you regularly check your bank accounts and credit card statements to make sure that all transactions are legitimate and indeed conducted by yourself.

行　　　員：是的，安全性是一個大問題。而且您說對了。用行動銀行是比較有潛在性的風險，因為智慧手機使用者會連到各式各樣的網站。

另一方面,智慧手機就是一種小型電腦,因而不可避免面臨網路上同樣的威脅。因此我會建議您裝Android或iPhone手機適用的防毒軟體來使您手機免於網路的威脅。當您不用時,您也應把智慧手機上鎖,確定把智慧手機放在安全的地方。**您應永不透露您帳戶的資訊,包括但不限於帳號、密碼、或是個人資料。**您也應使用可信賴的App並只從可信賴的來源下載手機App因為App容易遭病毒感染。我也建議您定期查詢您的帳戶和信用卡交易明細,以確保所有的交易都是正常且確實是您本人所辦的。

Customer : Thank you for the tips. I am really concerned about the security of mobile banking. According to the New York Times, Citibank customers that used an iPad app issued by Citibank to pay their bills were charged twice! Thus, in my opinion, although mobile banking brings us many benefits and convenience, at the same time it also causes some security problems for us.

客　　戶 : 謝謝您的小祕訣。我真的很關心行動銀行的安全性。根據《紐約時報》,花旗銀行的客戶使用花旗銀行發行的iPad的App來繳費時,被重覆扣款兩次。因此,我認為,雖然行動銀行為我們帶來很多福利和便利,但同時也造成安全性的問題。

Bank teller : You are probably right. Mobile banking has its pros and cons, but I think most importantly of all, **mobile banking apps provide a ton of people with easy access to their bank accounts.** It is reported about one of every five Americans in the U.S. are using their mobile phones to conduct their banking now. You cannot deny that some security problems of mobile banking occurred because its users failed to treat their smart phones like tiny little computers. Those ignorant users failed to install anti-virus software on their smart phones and with no consideration for their phones' security. You should be careful about the security of using mobile banking.

行　　員：您可能說對了。行動銀行有它的優缺點。但我認為最重要的是，**行動銀行的app為很多人提供一個使用銀行帳戶的簡便管道**。據說現在每五個美國人就有一個用行動銀行來辦銀行業務。您無法否認因為有使用者未能把他們的智慧手機當作小型電腦來看，導致行動銀行有一些安全性問題。那些沒警覺的使用者未在智慧手機裝防毒軟體而且不顧手機的安全性。您對行動銀行的安全性不能輕忽。

Customer : By the way, I know China has promoted mobile banking much earlier than Taiwan. Many China's banks have had mobile banking long time ago.

客　　戶：對了，我知道中國大陸推行動銀行已比臺灣還久了。很多大陸的銀行很早之前就已經有行動銀行了。

Bank teller : Actually, Taiwan has initiated mobile banking earlier than China but at that time few people are willing to use mobile banking due to its security and some technical problems. However, since smart phones such as iPhone or Android smart phones, hit the market and have become greatly popular, banks in Taiwan start to initiate mobile banking again to the public. Mobile banking is now regarded as a critically significant channel by most banks in Taiwan. That is why so many banks in Taiwan have developed their own mobile banking now. Some banks even enable their customers to use an iPad to use mobile banking in addition to using a smart phone.

行　　員：事實上，臺灣比大陸還要早推出行動銀行，但是在那時候很少人願意用行動銀行，原因是它的安全性和一些技術上的問題。然

而，自從智慧手機，像是iPhone或是Android手機上市並且大受歡迎後，臺灣的銀行才開始再推行動銀行給大眾。臺灣的大部分銀行都把行動銀行看作一個很重要的通路。這就是爲什麼現今很多在臺銀行都已開發他們的行動銀行服務。除了用智慧手機外，有些銀行甚至讓他們客戶用iPad來使用行動銀行。

Customer : OK. I see. One more question. If I use your mobile banking to transfer money, does your bank provide any security?

客　　戶：好，我明白了。再一個問題。如果我用您們的行動銀行來轉帳，您們有提供什麼安全措施嗎？

Bank teller : Of course. Our bank provides OTP（dynamic password） for our clients when you use mobile banking to make any vital transaction such as transferring funds between accounts or converting foreign currency. This way, not only do you not have to memorize another password but it also enhances the security of performing transactions via mobile banking.

行　　員：當然有。當您用行動銀行來辦任何重大的交易，如轉帳或是兌換外幣時，我們的行動銀行有提供動態密碼給客戶。這樣的話，您不但不用再多記一個密碼，而且也提高了行動銀行辦交易的安全性。

Customer : OK, I get it.

客　　戶：好，我懂了。

Bank teller : By the way, in addition to "mobile banking", banks in Taiwan will initiate and promote "mobile payment" as another important business. **Mobile payment** will also become an important buying and selling system in the future. After all, online shopping channels have been gradually replacing the brick-and-mortar channels.

行　　　員：順便一提，除了「行動銀行」之外，在臺灣的銀行也將要引進並推動「行動支付」作為另一個重要的業務。行動支付在未來會變成重要的買賣系統。畢竟，網購通路已逐漸取代實體的通路。

Customer：Thank you for your explanation.

客　　　戶：謝謝您的說明。

補充單字

♦ mobile banking [`mobɪl `bæŋkɪŋ] **n.** 行動銀行

♦ disclose [dɪs`kloz] **v.** 揭露

♦ mobile payment [`mobɪl `pemənt] **n.** 行動支付

實用金句

♦ Mobile banking is just like Internet banking. Simply put, what mobile banking means is, you use your smart phone to conduct your banking on the online platform provided by the bank.

行動銀行就像網路銀行一樣。簡單說，行動銀行就是您用智慧型手機在銀行提供的網路平臺來辦銀行業務。

♦ Our mobile banking enables you to get your online banking done anytime and anywhere. You can check on your accounts, transfer funds, pay all types of bills, or even place an order to buy mutual funds. You can also view current balance information and review your bank account transactions.

我們的行動銀行能讓您隨時隨地線上辦好銀行業務。您可以查詢帳戶、轉帳、繳費或甚至是下單買基金。您也可以檢視餘額資訊、帳戶交易紀錄。

◆ If you have our bank's credit card, you can use our mobile banking to check your monthly statement, check your accumulated reward points, and redeem your reward points.

如果您是我們的卡友，您可以用行動銀行來查詢每月對帳單、累積的紅利點數和兌換紅利點數。

◆ You can also search for our nearest bank branch through our mobile banking.

您也可以透過行動銀行來搜尋離您最近的分行。

◆ You should never disclose your account information, including but not limited to account numbers, passwords, or personal information.

您應永不透露您帳戶的資訊，包括但不限於帳號、密碼、或是個人資料。

◆ Mobile banking apps provide a ton of people with easy access to their bank accounts.

行動銀行的app為很多人提供一個使用銀行帳戶的簡便管道。

動態密碼產生器
OTP Token

Bank teller : What can I do for you today?

行　　員：我今天能為您辦什麼呢？

Customer : I want to ask you a question. If I want to transfer money to a non-designated account number via online banking, is there a way for me to make this transaction?

客　　戶：我想要問一下。如果我透過網銀轉帳到非約轉帳號，有辦法做到嗎？

Bank teller : Actually, there is. Have you heard OTP?

行　　員：事實上，有辦法。您有聽過OTP嗎？

Customer : No. I have never heard of that.

客　　戶：沒有，我從來沒有聽過。

Bank teller : **OTP means One-Time Password, or dynamic password.** Fundamentally, OTP is a security feature that sends a randomly generated six-digit OTP to your cellphone.

行　　員：**OTP就是動態密碼的意思**。基本上，OTP是一個傳送隨機產生的六位數動態密碼到您手機的一種安全機制。

Customer : Is OTP safe for customers?

客　　戶：OTP對客戶來說安全嗎？

Bank teller : Yes. Since OTP is not a fixed password, but a randomly generated password. It is difficult for hackers to predict. On the other hand, you don't have to memorize a long password. You only need to key in the password exactly as OTP shows to you.

行　　員：是的。因為OTP不是固定密碼，而是隨機產生的密碼。對駭客來說很難預測。另一方面，您不必去背冗長的密碼。您只要確實輸入OTP顯示給您看的密碼。

Customer : Can you tell me more about the benefits of OTP?

客　　戶：您可以跟我多講些OTP的優點嗎？

Bank teller : No problem. **OTP also improves the security of online banking by providing additional password authentication. In addition to your username and password, you will need to key in OTP when conducting log-in and making funds transfer via online banking.** For example, **if you want to transfer your money from your account to a non-registered third party account, OTP is required to complete this transaction. Generally speaking, on-line banking forbids you to transfer your money to a non-registered third party account number unless you go to the bank in person to register the account number in advance. But with the help of OTP, you can make a funds transfer to a non-registered third party account number anytime.**

行　　員：沒問題。**OTP藉由提供額外的密碼驗證也改善了網銀的安全性。除了您的使用者代號和密碼外，當您要登入網銀並用網銀轉帳時，您還需要輸入OTP。例如說，如果您要從您的戶頭轉帳到非約定帳戶時，您就需要OTP來完成這次交易。一般來說，網路銀行禁止匯錢至非約轉帳戶，除非您本人先到銀行辦理約定帳號。**

但有了OTP的幫助，您可以隨時做非約定轉帳。

Customer : Oh. I see. So, if an unauthorized person gets to know my user ID and log-in password to my online banking, he will still not be able to steal my money in my account because the OTP authentication requirement will prevent him from doing so, right?

客　　戶：喔。我明白了。所以說，如果有一個未經授權的人得知我的使用者代號和登入密碼來登入我的網銀，他就無法偷走我帳戶的錢因為要經過OTP驗證授權而得以阻止他這樣做，對吧？

Bank teller : Yes. One-Time Password (OTP) is actually an added security measure to protect your online bank account from being misused by the bad guy.

行　　員：是的，動態密碼（OTP）實際上是一種多加的安全機制，用以保護您網路銀行帳戶免受壞人濫用。

Customer : Thank you. I see. How do I receive my OTP?

客　　戶：謝謝您。我明白了。我如何收到OTP？

Bank teller : A One-Time Password is generated via the hardware token or SMS, which acts as an additional layer of authentication to prevent online banking fraud. The OTP will be valid for one minute from the time of generation and after one minute, the OTP will expire.

行　　員：動態密碼是透過「動態密碼產生器」或是「手機簡訊」所產生的，用來作爲額外的認證機制以防止網銀詐騙。動態密碼在產生後的有效時間爲一分鐘，過了一分鐘後，OTP就會失效。

Customer : So you mean there are two types of OTP. The one is through the hardware token and the other is through SMS.

客　　戶：所以您是說有兩種OTP。一種是透過密碼產生器，另一種是透過手機簡訊。

Bank teller : That's right. On the one hand, SMS-OTP is a one-time password delivered to the cell phone or the smart phone of our Internet banking customers. For this option, the customer's cellphone number must be registered with the bank in advance. On the other hand, **Token-OTP is a one-time password that is issued from an OTP token. However, you must go to the bank and purchase an OTP token first and it is not expensive. An OTP token is about 300 to 600 NT dollars.**

行　　員 ：沒錯。另一方面，簡訊OTP是一種傳送到網銀客戶的手機或智慧型手機上的動態密碼。就這個選項來說，這客戶的手機號碼必須事先向銀行登錄。另一方面，**動態密碼產生器的OTP則是從動態密碼產生器產生的動態密碼。不過，您必須先到銀行買動態密碼產生器。但這不貴，一個動態密碼產生器大約新臺幣三百到六百元左右。**

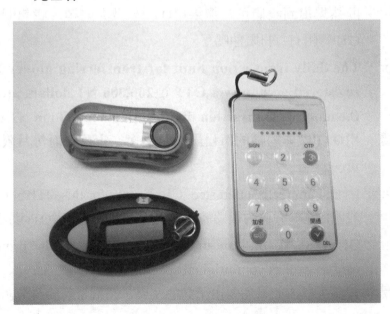

Customer : How do I use OTP?

客　　　戶：我怎麼用OTP呢？

Bank teller : **When you make outbound funds transfer via online banking or mobile banking, you will be required to key in an authorization code, which is sent to your registered cellphone number via an SMS message. You will be required to key in the OTP to complete the transaction.**

行　　　員：當您透過網銀或行動銀行轉帳出去的時候，您會被要求輸入一組認證碼，這組認證碼是會藉由手機簡訊傳到您註冊的手機門號。然後您需要輸入這組動態密碼來完成交易。

Customer : Since you mentioned that we could use OTP to transfer money to a non-registered account or a non-designated account on Internet banking, I want to ask you a question: "Is there a daily transaction limit for transferring money through OTP?"

客　　　戶：既然您提到我們可在網銀用OTP來做非約轉，我想問您：透過OTP轉帳有每日限額嗎？

Bank teller : **The daily transaction limit for transferring money to a non-registered account via OTP is 200,000 NT dollars at most and the monthly transaction limit is up to one million NT dollars.**

行　　　員：用**OTP**做非約轉的每日限額是最多二十萬，而每月限額是一百萬。

Customer : I see. I am really interested. Can I apply for this OTP now?

客　　　戶：我明白了。我真的很感興趣。我可以現在就申辦OTP嗎？

Bank teller : Of course. If you want to apply for the OTP, please bring your ID card as well as your original specimen seal to the service counter.

行　　　員：當然可以，如果您要申請動態密碼，請攜帶您的身分證和原留印

鑑到服務臺辦理。

Customer ： OK. Thanks.

客　　　戶：好的，謝謝。

補充單字

◆ One-Time Password (OTP) [wʌn taɪm `pæs.wɝd] **n.** 動態密碼；一次性密碼

◆ dynamic password [daɪ`næmɪk `pæs.wɝd] **n.** 動態密碼

◆ generate [`dʒɛnə.ret] **v.** 產生

◆ OTP token [o ti pi `tokən] **n.** 動態密碼產生器；認證密碼鎖

實用金句

◆ OTP means One-Time Password, or dynamic password.

OTP就是動態密碼的意思。

◆ OTP also improves the security of online banking by providing additional password authentication. In addition to your username and password, you will need to key in OTP when conducting log-in and making funds transfer via online banking.

OTP藉由提供額外的密碼驗證也改善了網銀的安全性。除了您的使用者代號和密碼外，當您要登入網銀並用網銀轉帳時，您還需要輸入OTP。

◆ If you want to transfer your money from your account to a non-registered third party account, OTP is required to complete this transaction.

如果您要從您的戶頭轉帳到非約定帳戶時，您就需要OTP來完成這次交易。

◆ Generally speaking, online banking forbids you to transfer your money to a non-registered third party account number unless you go to the bank in person to register the account number in advance. But with the help of OTP, you can make a funds transfer to a non-registered third party account number anytime.

一般來說，網路銀行禁止匯錢至非約轉帳戶，除非您本人先到銀行辦理約定帳號。但有了OTP的幫助，您可以隨時做非約定轉帳。

◆ Token-OTP is a one-time password that is issued from an OTP token. However, you must go to the bank and purchase an OTP token first and it is not expensive. An OTP token is about 300 to 600 NT dollars.

動態密碼產生器的OTP則是從動態密碼產生器產生的動態密碼。不過，您必須先到銀行買動態密碼產生器。但這不貴，一個密碼產生器大約新臺幣三百到六百元左右。

◆ When you make outbound funds transfer via online banking or mobile banking, you will be required to key in an authorization code, which is sent to your registered mobile number via an SMS message. You will be required to key in the OTP to complete the transaction.

當您透過網銀或行動銀行轉帳出去的時候，您會被要求輸入一組認證碼，這組認證碼是會藉由手機簡訊傳到您註冊的手機號碼。然後您需要輸入這組動態密碼來完成交易。

◆ The daily transaction limit for transferring money to a non-registered account via OTP is 200,000 NT dollars at most and the monthly transaction limit is up to one million NT dollars.

用OTP做非約轉的每日限額是最多二十萬，而每月限額是一百萬。

VISA金融卡
VISA Debit Card

Bank teller : Hello. How are you today?

行　　　員：嗨，您今天好嗎？

Customer : I am fine. I would like to know about a **VISA debit card**. Does your bank provide this type of card?

客　　　戶：還不錯。我想了解一下VISA金融卡。您們銀行有發行這種卡嗎？

Bank teller : Yes. We have this type of card. May I spend a few minutes introducing the VISA debit card to you?

行　　　員：我們有這種卡。我可以花幾分鐘跟您介紹一下VISA金融卡嗎？

Customer : OK.

客　　　戶：好。

Bank teller : A VISA debit card is different from a credit card. On the one hand, you can use a credit card to make a purchase first and pay your credit card bill after. That is to say, a credit card allows you to make purchases on credit. This way, even if you don't have any cash in your bank account, you can still buy something you want as long as your spending is not over your credit line. On the other hand, **a VISA debit card does not allow you to spend the money you don't have. You can only swipe your Visa debit card to spend as much money as you have in your bank account. In** other words, **when you use a VISA debit card to make a purchase, the expending will be debited from your bank account. If you don't have any money in your bank account, you cannot use your VISA debit card because it does not allow** overdraft. What's more, **there is no annual fee to use your VISA debit card.**

行　　員：VISA金融卡不同於信用卡。一方面，您可以刷信用卡來先消費後付款。換句話說，信用卡能讓您賒帳。這樣的話，即使您銀行戶頭沒有半毛錢，只要您沒有超過刷卡額度，您仍然可以買東西。另一方面，**VISA金融卡不允許您花您沒有的錢。您只能刷卡花您在戶頭裡的錢。也就是說，當您用VISA金融卡消費時，這筆消費會從您的帳戶扣款。如果您在銀行帳戶裡沒有半毛錢了，您就無法刷VISA金融卡，因為它不允許**透支。此外，**VISA金融卡沒有年費的問題。**

Customer　: OK. Where can I use a VISA debit card?

客　　戶：好，我在哪些地方可使用VISA金融卡呢？

Bank teller : You can use a VISA debit card to purchase in participating merchants, just like using a VISA credit card. **Some banks also allow their VISA debit cardholders to purchase online but you have to inquire your card issuer to make sure because not every bank allows its users to use its VISA debit card to shop online.** I know the VISA debit card issued by Chinatrust or Taishin Bank can be used to purchase online. Our bank's has also launched a new type VISA debit card which combines the feature of an EasyCard. You can use this VISA debit card with the feature of EasyCard to take the MRT. And let me tell you more advantages of a VISA debit card. With the VISA debit card, you are covered with VISA's Zero Liability, which protects you from fraudulent unauthorized transactions. Thus, you can use your VISA debit card with no risk of loss and your VISA debit card is covered against proven fraud that you did not cause.

行　　員：您可以在特約商店刷VISA金融卡，就像使用VISA信用卡一樣。**有些銀行讓VISA金融卡持卡人線上刷卡，但您得詢問您的發卡銀行來確認一下，因為不是每家銀行都允許持卡人用VISA金融卡線上刷卡。**我知道中國信託還是台新銀行發行的VISA金融卡可用來線上消費。我們銀行還發行了一種新的具有悠遊卡功能的VISA金融卡。您可以用這張有悠遊卡功能的VISA金融卡來搭捷運。讓我跟您講VISA金融卡的更多優點。如果您有VISA金融卡，則享有失卡零風險的保障。這樣就會保護您免於盜刷。因此，您可以使用VISA金融卡而免於承擔任何風險，並且只要證實不是您造成的盜刷，您就不必負責任。

Customer : OK, it sounds great. But I already have an ATM card. What is the difference?

客　　戶：好的，聽起來很好。但我已經有一張金融卡。有什麼不同？

Bank teller : Good question. A VISA debit card is actually an ATM card plus a debit card that lets you shop cash-free. Generally speaking, an ATM card does not allow you to swipe your card to make a purchase. The ATM card is for you to withdraw money from an ATM. But you can use a VISA debit card to make a purchase. **When you swipe your VISA debit card to make a purchase, the withdrawal is taken directly from your bank account.** All POS transactions on your card are signature based. So all you need to do next is simply sign the receipt. You don't have to key in your PIN number to authorize the transaction. **With a VISA debit card, you can shop almost anywhere in the world wherever you see the VISA symbol. And it is quick and secure.**

行　　員：好問題，VISA金融卡實際上是一種金融卡結合讓您購物免帶現金的簽帳卡。一般來說，一張金融卡不允許您刷卡消費。金融卡是讓您從ATM提款用的。但您可以用VISA金融卡來消費。**當您刷VISA金融卡消費時，會從您的銀行戶頭直接扣款。**所有您卡片在銷售點終端的交易都是以簽名為主。所以您要做的下一步只是在收據上簽名，您不必輸入密碼來授權此交易。**有了VISA金融卡，您幾乎可以在世界各地每一個看得見VISA標誌的地方消費。而且快又安全。**

Customer : Let me summarize what you just said. When I use a VISA debit card to make purchases, the amount is deducted directly from my bank account. And with a VISA debit card, I don't have to carry cash, right?

客　　戶：讓我總結您剛才所講的。當我使用VISA金融卡來刷卡購物時，金額是直接從我的帳戶扣款。有了VISA金融卡，我不必帶現金出門，對吧？

Bank teller : That is right. In most places, you can use a VISA debit card to make a purchase. VISA debit cards are accepted in around 27 million outlets and 160 countries worldwide. This way, you don't have to carry cash, and you know, the social security is not safe anymore. Carrying cash is a dangerous thing because you may be robbed.

行　　員：沒錯。在大部分的地方，您可以使用VISA金融卡來購物。VISA

金融卡可被大約二千七百萬個通路和全球一百六十個國家所接受。這樣一來，您就不必帶現金了。而且您知道的，社會治安已不再安全了。帶現金可能有風險因為您可能會被搶。

Customer : Yes, it is sometimes dangerous and inconvenient to carry a lot of cash. Occasionally, I have to fumble for coins to pay.

客　　戶：是的，帶很多現金有時既危險又不便。偶爾我還必須翻口袋找零錢來付款。

Bank teller : And **if you have signed up for Internet banking, you can check your updated balance and transaction records of your VISA debit card through Internet banking.** The transaction records detail your purchases, including merchant name, date, and amount. Thus, it can help you manage your money and see where you spend your money. What's better, a VISA debit card has a great benefit. Do you want to know?

行　　員：**如果您已申請網銀的話，您可以用網銀查詢您VISA金融卡最新的可用餘額和交易明細。**刷卡明細上詳載您的消費紀錄，包括商家店名、日期和金額。因此，它可以幫您管理您的錢並查看您把錢都花到哪裡去了。更好的是，VISA金融卡有很多優惠。您想要了解嗎？

Customer : Yes, I am interested. Please tell me.

客　　戶：是的，我想了解。請跟我說。

Bank teller : Our VISA debit cards offer rewards. In other words, you get rewarded for all of your purchases such as paying bills, buying daily groceries, or shopping online. **If you desire to amass as many bonus points as possible, the secret is to use your VISA debit card as often as possible.**

行　　　員：我們的VISA金融卡提供紅利點數。換句話說，您可以刷卡來獲得紅利點數，像是繳費、買日常用品或是網購。**如果您想要獲得更多的紅利點數，祕訣就在於您儘可能常用VISA金融卡來消費。**

Customer：Now I understand. I would like to apply for a VISA debit card now.

客　　　戶：現在我懂了。我想要現在就申辦VISA金融卡。

Bank teller：No problem. Please fill out the form. Thank you.

行　　　員：沒問題。請現在就填這張申請表。謝謝。

補充單字

◆ VISA debit card [`vizə `debɪt kɑrd] *n.* VISA金融卡

◆ overdraft [`ovəˏdræft] *n.* 透支

◆ participating merchant [pɑr`tɪsəˏpetɪŋ `mɝtʃənt] *n.* 特約商店

◆ bonus point [`bonəs pɔɪnt] *n.* 紅利點數

實用金句

◆ A VISA debit card does not allow you to spend the money you don't have. You can only swipe your VISA debit card to spend as much money as you have in your bank account.

VISA金融卡不允許您花您沒有的錢。您只能刷卡花您在戶頭裡的錢。

◆ When you use a VISA debit card to make a purchase, the expending will be debited from your bank account. If you don't have any money in your bank account, you cannot use your VISA debit card because it does not allow overdraft.

當您用VISA金融卡消費時，這筆消費會從您的帳戶扣款。如果您在銀行帳戶裡沒有半毛錢了，您就無法刷VISA金融卡，因爲它不允許透支。

◆ There is no annual fee to use your VISA debit card.

VISA金融卡沒有年費的問題。

◆ Some banks also allow their VISA debit cardholders to purchase online but you have to inquire your card issuer to make sure because not every bank allows its users to use its VISA debit card to shop online.

有些銀行讓VISA金融卡持卡人線上刷卡,但您得詢問您的發卡銀行來確認一下,因為不是每家銀行都允許持卡人用VISA金融卡線上刷卡。

◆ When you swipe your VISA debit card to make a purchase, the withdrawal is taken directly from your bank account.

當您刷VISA金融卡消費時,會從您的銀行戶頭直接扣款。

◆ With a VISA debit card, you can shop almost anywhere in the world wherever you see the VISA symbol. And it is quick and secure.

有了VISA金融卡,您幾乎可以在世界各地每一個看得見VISA標誌的地方購物。而且快又安全。

◆ If you have signed up for Internet banking, you can check your updated balance and transaction records of your VISA debit card through Internet banking.

如果您已申請網銀的話,您可以用網銀查詢您VISA金融卡最新的可用餘額和交易明細。

◆ If you desire to amass as many bonus points as possible, the secret is to use your VISA debit card as often as possible.

如果您想要獲得更多的紅利點數,祕訣就在於您儘可能常用VISA金融卡來消費。

晶片金融卡
Chip-and-PIN ATM Card

Customer : Hello, **I would like to replace my magnetic stripe ATM card with the chip ATM card.**

客　　戶：嗨，**我想要把我的磁條金融卡換成晶片金融卡。**

Bank teller : Yes, our bank is replacing a magnetic stripe card with a new ATM card that uses chip technology. Besides the magnetic stripe on your old ATM card, your new card is embedded with a microprocessor chip, which is more secure. This new ATM card is called the chip-and-PIN ATM card. In fact, a chip card is another common term for a smart card or an integrated circuit (IC) card. Just like a computer, the chip can store data and perform processing functions. The chip-and-PIN ATM card provides an enhanced level of protection against fraud. The information stored in the chip cannot be accessed by the unauthorized third party, thus making it virtually impossible to copy or tamper with it.

行　　員：好的，我們銀行正在進行把磁條卡換發成一種用晶片技術的新的金融卡。除了在您舊金融卡上的磁條上之外，您的新卡還多加了一種微晶片，並更加安全。這種新的金融卡就叫作晶片金融卡。事實上，晶片卡是智慧卡的另一種通用的名稱。就如電腦一樣，晶片也可以儲存資料和處理資料。晶片金融卡提供一個防盜用的

高性能防護。存在晶片的資訊無法被未授權的第三方使用，因而無法拷貝或是竄改。

Customer : What will happen to the existing magnetic stripe on an ATM card?

客　　戶：那還在金融卡上的磁條以後會有什麼變動嗎？

Bank teller : The magnetic stripe will remain on your chip ATM cards, so that the cards can continue to be used in some foreign countries such as the United States or China, which are still using traditional magnetic stripe cards.

行　　員：磁條會繼續留在晶片金融卡上，如此這些卡可以繼續用於國外，如美國或是中國大陸，因為這些國家還是用傳統的磁條卡。

Customer : Why did all the banks in Taiwan start to adopt chip-and-PIN cards? Why didn't they continue using magnetic stripe cards?

客　　戶：為什麼所有臺灣的銀行都採用晶片金融卡？為什麼不繼續用磁條卡？

Bank teller : OK. You are really curious. Let me tell you. An ATM scam broke out in October, 2003. A scam gang installed the card skimmers on the doors to ATM lobbies to skim the cards to obtain cardholders' information along with installing hidden cameras to record card users' PIN number. The gang then used the information to clone the cards. After cloning the magnetic stripe cards, the scam gang members used the duplicate cards to fraudulently withdraw money from several banks' ATMs, even including Bank of Taiwan. Since magnetic stripe cards are easy to clone by copying the magnetic stripes, the Ministry of Finance ordered that the magnetic cards in circulation at that time be converted into chip-and-PIN cards as soon as possible. On the other hand, the banks in Taiwan also started to review their security and risk control systems because of this ATM card fraud. For example, the card-swipe entry system on doors to ATM lobbies was canceled after this serious incident. Most important of all, from then on, the banks in Taiwan were forced to replace magnetic stripe cards with chip-and-PIN cards and to upgrade the automated teller machines to be able to accept chip-and-PIN cards. As a consequence, Taiwan has become one of the most advanced areas that introduced and started to use chip-and-PIN cards in the financial systems. Even the United States is still using magnetic stripe cards now. In 2006, all the banks in Taiwan had canceled the inter-bank transactions of traditional magnetic stripe cards. That is, you can only use your magnetic stripe card at your own bank's ATMs and cannot perform any inter-bank transaction even at your bank's ATMs. If you use the ATMs which do not belong to your account opening bank, you cannot make any transaction with a magnetic stripe card. And **in 2010, all the banks' ATMs have stopped accepting magnetic stripe cards. Only chip-and-PIN ATM cards can be accepted by the ATMs in Taiwan.**

行　　員：好，您還真好奇，讓我告訴您，在2003年十月時有自動櫃員機盜領事件爆發。盜刷集團在ATM區的大門裝設側錄機來側錄卡片以獲取持卡人的資料並架設針孔攝影機來錄下持卡人按的密碼。這集團之後用到手的資訊來偽造金融卡，在複製磁條卡後，盜刷集團用這複製的卡在多家銀行的ATM盜領，包括臺灣銀行。既然磁條卡很容易藉由拷貝磁條來複製，財政部下令那時在流通的磁條卡要儘速轉換成晶片卡。另一方面，臺灣各家銀行也因這次ATM盜領事件開始檢視他們的安全機制和風險管理系統。例如說，在

進ATM區的入口的刷卡處在這次嚴重的案件後已廢掉。最重要的是，從那時起，臺灣的銀行不得不把磁條卡換成晶片卡並升級自動櫃員機以便接受晶片卡。因此，臺灣已變成推行晶片卡最先進的金融區域之一。即使是美國現在也仍然使用磁條卡。在2006年所有在臺銀行都已廢掉傳統的磁條卡跨行交易功能。也就是說，您只能在自己發卡銀行的自動櫃員機來使用磁條卡，而且不能用您發卡行的ATM辦任何跨行交易。如果您把磁條卡用在別家銀行的ATM上，您完全無法辦任何交易。**在2010年，所有銀行的ATM都停止受理磁條卡的交易，唯有晶片金融卡能被臺灣的自動櫃員機接受。**

Customer : Wow. You have explained the history so well.

客　　戶：哇，您把這段往事講解得很詳盡耶。

Bank teller : Simply put, originally the banks in Taiwan were not willing to replace magnetic stripe cards with chip-and-PIN cards on account of its huge costs. But after the ATM scam, this incident forced the banks in Taiwan to turn to using chip-and-PIN ATM cards for their high security. Although China also wanted to imitate Taiwan and started to replace magnetic stripe cards with chip-and-PIN cards, China failed. So China is stilling using magnetic stripe cards up to now. That is why when you go to Mainland China, you still have to use magnetic stripe on your ATM card. By the way, **when you use ATMs in China or the U.S., you need to enter your four-digit password for your magnetic stripe card to conduct transactions at local ATMs.** However, **when you use ATMs in Taiwan, you need to punch in your six-to-twelve digit PIN number to conduct transactions at local ATMs.**

行　　員：簡單說，由於高成本的考量，原本臺灣各家銀行不太願意把磁條卡更換成晶片卡。但經過這次ATM盜領案後，這起案件迫使臺灣各家銀行轉而擁抱具有高度安全性的晶片卡。雖然中國大陸也想模仿臺灣來開始以晶片卡來置換磁條卡，但失敗了，所以中國大陸仍然使用磁條卡至今。這也就是為何您去大陸時，還是會用到金融卡上的磁條。對了，**當您在大陸或是美國時，您在當地的ATM還是需要輸入您四位數的磁條卡密碼來辦交易。然而，當您在臺灣用ATM時，您要輸入您的六到十二位的晶片密碼來辦**交易。

Customer : I see. **In some foreign countries such as America or China, they still use traditional magnetic stripe cards instead of chip-and-PIN ATM cards.**

客　　戶：我明白了。在國外，如美國或中國大陸，他們仍然使用傳統的磁條卡而非晶片金融卡。

Bank teller : Yes, you get it. By the way, **if you have entered the wrong PIN number three times in a row, your chip-and-PIN ATM card will be locked.** And you will be unable to use your ATM card to make any transaction in automated banking services.

行　　員：沒錯，您說對了。對了，**如果您連續輸入密碼三次都錯的話，您的晶片金融卡會被鎖卡。**而您就無法用金融卡在自動化銀行設備辦任何交易了。

Customer : Well, I thought if I have entered the wrong PIN numbers four times in a row, my card will be retained by the ATM.

客　　戶：喔，我以為我輸入密碼連續錯四次才會被ATM吃卡。

Bank teller : That was true. **If you use a magnetic stripe card and you enter the wrong password for four times in a row, your card will be**

swallowed by the ATM. But it is not the case of a chip-and-PIN card.

行　　員：這以前是真的，如果您是用磁條卡並輸入密碼連續四次都錯誤的話，您的卡會被ATM機器吃卡。但晶片金融卡不是這樣。

Customer : I see. Thanks.

客　　戶：我明白了。謝謝。

補充單字

◆ magnetic stripe card [mæg`nɛtɪk straɪp kɑrd] *n.* 磁條卡

◆ skim [`skɪm] *v.* 側錄

◆ conduct [kən`dʌkt] *v.* 辦理（業務）

實用金句

◆ I would like to replace my magnetic stripe ATM card with the chip ATM card.

我想要把我的磁條金融卡換成晶片金融卡。

◆ In 2010, all the banks' ATMs have stopped accepting magnetic stripe cards. Only chip-and-PIN ATM cards can be accepted by the ATMs in Taiwan.

在2010年，所有銀行的ATM都停止受理磁條卡的交易，唯有晶片金融卡能被臺灣的自動櫃員機接受。

◆ When you use ATMs in China or the U.S., you need to enter your four-digit password for your magnetic stripe card to conduct transactions at local ATMs.

當您在大陸或是美國時，您在當地的ATM還是需要輸入您四位數的磁條卡密碼來辦交易。

♦ When you use ATMs in Taiwan, you need to punch in your six-to-twelve digit PIN number to conduct transactions at local ATMs.

當您在臺灣用ATM時，您要輸入您的六到十二位的晶片密碼來辦交易。

♦ In some foreign countries such as America or China, they still use traditional magnetic stripe cards instead of chip-and-PIN ATM cards.

在國外，如美國或中國大陸，他們仍然使用傳統的磁條卡而非晶片金融卡。

♦ If you have entered the wrong PIN number three times in a row, your chip-and-PIN ATM card will be locked.

如果您連續輸入密碼三次都錯的話，您的晶片金融卡會被鎖卡。

♦ If you use a magnetic stripe card and you enter the wrong password for four times in a row, your card will be swallowed by the ATM. But it is not the case of a chip-and-PIN card.

如果您是用磁條卡並輸入密碼連續四次都錯誤的話，您的卡會被ATM機器吃卡。但晶片金融卡不是這樣。

金融卡的共用帳號
Two Account Numbers in One Card

Bank teller : Hello, what can I do for you, Sir?

行　　員：先生您好，我可以為您做什麼嗎？

Customer : I would like to **integrate** two different bank account numbers into a one single ATM card. Can your bank do that?

客　　戶：我想要整合兩個不同銀行帳號到一張金融卡上。您們銀行可以做到嗎？

Bank teller : Yes, we can do that.

行　　員：是的，我們可以做到。

Customer : Really? Because I just asked Taipei Fubon Commercial Bank, they told me that their bank was unable to make it.

客　　戶：真的嗎？因為我剛問了台北富邦，他們跟我說他們沒有辦法。

Bank teller : Yes, it involves some technical problems to be solved. **As far as I know, a lot of banks,** including but not limited to Chang Hwa Commercial Bank, Land Bank of Taiwan, Bank Sinopac, E. Sun Bank, Taishin International Bank, Chinatrust Commercial Bank, and Hua Nan Commercial Bank **do provide the service of integrating two different bank account numbers into one bank card so that you don't have to apply for two ATM cards for two bank accounts. Just one ATM card will do.**

行　　員：是的，這涉及了技術性問題。**就我所知，很多家銀行**，包括但不僅限彰化銀行、土銀、永豐銀、玉山銀行和台新、中國信託以及華南銀行**都可以把兩組不同銀行的帳號整合到一張金融卡上**，這樣您就不必為兩個戶頭申請兩張金融卡，只要用一張就好了。

Customer：Thank for your information. I want to integrate two different bank account numbers into a single bank card because I have a broker-age account and a personal demand savings account but I feel that carrying two ATM cards is really inconvenient for me. Thus, I want to just carry one ATM card including two different account numbers. This way, **when I insert my bank card into an ATM, the ATM will show both my bank account numbers to let me choose which one I will use.**

客　　戶：謝謝您的資訊。我想要把兩組不同的銀行帳號整合到一張金融卡是因為我有一個證券戶和活儲戶，但我覺得帶兩張金融卡太不方便了。因此我想只帶一張就包含了兩組帳號的金融卡。這樣一來，當我把卡片插到提款機中，提款機會顯示出我兩組帳號讓我選擇我要用哪一組。

Bank teller：Yes, many people don't know about this. But our bank does provide this service. The way is to set up one account number as the primary account number and set the other account number as your subsidiary account number. **You can add up to seven subsidiary account numbers in a single chip-and-PIN ATM card.** For example, if you have one account with Tianmu branch, another account with Beitou branch, and the other account with Shipai branch, you can set up your account in Tianmu branch as your primary account number and set up your accounts with Beitou as well as Shipai branches as your subsidiary account numbers in your ATM card. This way, you don't need to apply for three ATM cards for these three accounts but only one ATM card.

行　　　員：是的，很多人都不知道這點。但是我們銀行有提供這種服務。方法是先把一組帳號設成主帳號，另一組帳號設成子帳號。**您可以增加最多七組的子帳號並寫到一張晶片金融卡裡。**例如說，您在天母分行有戶頭，在北投分行也有戶頭，還有一戶頭開在石牌。您可以在提款卡上把天母分行的帳號設成主帳號，把北投和石牌分行的帳號設成子帳號。這樣一來，您就不必為三個帳戶申請三張金融卡而只要用一張就好。

Customer : Thank you. This is exactly what I want.

客　　　戶：謝謝您。這正是我想要的。

Bank teller : So **if you really want to link your primary account with other bank accounts in a single ATM card today, do you have your ID card, your health IC card, or driver's license plus your original specimen seal with you?**

行　　　員：所以如果您今天真的想要把您的主帳戶與其他帳戶連結在一張金融卡上，您有帶身分證和您的健保卡或是駕照以及原留印鑑嗎？

Customer : Yes, here you are.

客　　　戶：有，給您。

Bank teller : **OK, I will process it for you now.**

行　　　員：**好的，我立即為您辦理。**

補充單字

◆ integrate [`ɪntə͵gret] *v.* 整合

◆ brokerage account [`brokərɪdʒ ə`kaunt] *n.* 證券帳戶

◆ subsidiary account [səb`sɪdɪ,ɛrɪ ə`kaunt] **n.** 子帳戶

實用金句

◆ As far as I know, a lot of banks do provide the service of integrating two different bank account numbers into one bank card so that you don't have to apply for two ATM cards for two bank accounts. Just one ATM card will do.

就我所知，很多家銀行都可以把兩組不同銀行的帳號整合到一張金融卡上，這樣您就不必為兩個戶頭申請兩張金融卡，只要用一張就好了。

◆ When I insert my bank card into an ATM, the ATM will show both my bank account numbers to let me choose which one I will use.

當我把卡片插到提款機中，提款機會顯示出我兩組帳號讓我選擇我要用哪一組。

◆ You can add up to seven subsidiary account numbers in a single chip-and-PIN ATM card.

您可以增加最多七組的子帳號並寫到一張金融卡裡。

◆ If you really want to link your primary account with other bank accounts in a single ATM card today, do you have your ID card, your health IC card, or driver's license plus your original specimen seal with you?

如果您今天真的想要把您的主帳戶與其他帳戶連結在同一張卡上，您有帶身分證和您的健保卡或是駕照以及原留印鑑嗎？

◆ OK, I will process it for you now.

好的，我立即為您辦理。

金融卡國際提領功能
International Withdrawal Function

Customer : Hello, I would like to ask whether my ATM card can be used to withdraw money from the ATMs in foreign countries.

客　　戶：嗨，我想要問我的金融卡可以在國外的ATM提款嗎？

Bank teller : Well. It depends. Let me tell you how to judge whether an ATM card is able to withdraw money overseas. First, you have to take a look at the back of your ATM card to see if you can find the logos of MasterCard, Maestro, Cirrus, VISA, PLUS, Smart Pay or UnionPay.

行　　員：這個要視情況而定。讓我告訴您怎麼辨別一張金融卡是否可以在國外領錢。首先，您必須看一下卡片的背後看是否您可以發現MasterCard、Maestro、Cirrus、VISA、PLUS、Smart Pay或是銀聯標誌。

Customer : Yes, I have found out the logo of PLUS. What does it mean?

客　　戶：是的，我發現PLUS的標誌，這是什麼意思？

Bank teller : Well, PLUS belongs to VISA. You also should know **PLUS is one of the world's largest global ATM networks, offering cash withdrawal from ATMs in local currency in more than 200 countries.** Therefore, **if you find out the logo of PLUS at the back of your bank card, you should search for the ATMs which contains the logo of PLUS and you can use your VISA PLUS ATM card to withdraw local currency from the ATMs overseas.** Since PLUS is a financial mechanism of VISA, all VISA debit cards carry the logo of PLUS. You will never find the logo of PLUS in a MasterCard ATM card.

行　　員：嗯，PLUS屬於VISA。您應該知道**PLUS是世界上最大的全球ATM網絡之一，提供超過二百個國家的當地貨幣提款**。因此，**如果您在金融卡背面發現PLUS的標誌的話，您應該找有PLUS標誌的ATM，您就可以拿含PLUS的VISA金融卡在國外的ATM領當地貨幣**。既然PLUS是VISA的財金機制，所有的VISA金融卡都含有PLUS的標誌。您不會在萬事達卡的金融卡發現PLUS的標誌。

Customer : So what if my ATM card is not issued by VISA, but by Master-Card? Can I still make a withdrawal from the ATMs overseas?

客　　戶：如果我的金融卡不是由VISA發行，而是萬事達的話怎麼辦？我仍然可以在國外的ATM提款嗎？

Bank teller : Of course. MasterCard has invented its own global network of withdrawing cash all around the world, which is called Cirrus. **As long as your ATM card carries the logo of Cirrus, you can withdraw money from the ATMs which also carry the logo of**

Cirrus. A lot of ATMs accept both PLUS and Cirrus. To sum up, as long as your ATM card and the ATM overseas have the same symbol, you will be able to withdraw money from the local ATM in foreign countries.

行　　員：當然可以。萬事達有發明自己的全球提款網絡，叫作Cirrus。**只要您的金融卡含有Cirrus的標誌，您可以在有Cirrus標誌的提款機領錢。**很多提款機都接受PLUS和Cirrus。總結來說，只要您的金融卡和海外的自動櫃員機都有一樣的標誌的話，您就可以在國外的ATM提款。

Customer：How much can I withdraw from a local ATM carrying the logo of PLUS or Cirrus in each transaction while I am overseas?

客　　戶：當我人在海外時，我在當地有PLUS或Cirrus標誌的提款機每次可以領多少錢？

Bank teller：You can withdraw up to the equivalent value of twenty thousand NT dollars per transaction.

行　　員：您每次最多可領到等值新臺幣兩萬元的金額。

Customer：Thank you for your information. Can you tell me more?

客　　戶：謝謝您的資訊，您可以多講一些嗎？

Bank teller：No problem. Have you heard of Mondex? Mondex is a type of payment card and is owned by MasterCard. To be more exact, Mondex is a stored-value card or an e-purse. If you still don't understand, **Mondex is like EasyCard which we use to take the MRT. You have to deposit your money into Mondex first, and then you can use Mondex as using iCash issued by 7-11 convenience stores.** In 2001, a lot of banks issued their combo cards with Mondex. However, the participating merchants with Mondex were few and few people ever used Mondex in their Combo card, the banks in Taiwan then decided to stop cooperating with MasterCard. In a sense, Mondex is **eliminated** from Taiwan. One of the reasons why Mondex is not popular in Taiwan is, if you use Mondex to make a purchase, you have to punch in your four-digit password to **authorize** the purchase, which is really troublesome for most Taiwanese. EasyCard, on the other hand, doesn't need the cardholders to punch any password. All you need to do is let EasyCard be sensored by the card reader. You don't have to key in any additional PIN numbers. Therefore, Mondex is not the cup of tea of Taiwanese and has disappeared from Taiwan.

行　員：沒問題。您有聽過Mondex嗎？Mondex是一種具有消費扣款的卡片並屬於萬事達。講更精確點，Mondex是一種儲值卡或電子錢包。如果您還是不懂的話，**Mondex就像我們搭捷運用的悠遊卡一樣。您必須把錢存進Mondex，然後您就可以像使用統一超商發行的iCash一樣來使用**。在2001年，很多銀行都發行結合Mondex的金融信用卡。不過，Mondex的特約商店太少了，並且很少人有用他們金融信用卡上的Mondex，臺灣的各家銀行就決定中止和萬事達的合作。就某種意義而言，Mondex在臺灣被淘汰了。Mondex在臺灣未能普及的因素之一是您要用Mondex來購物時，您還要按入四位數的密碼來授權此交易，這對大多數的臺灣人來說很麻煩。另一方面，悠遊卡就不需使用者按任何密碼，只要讓讀卡機感應悠遊卡就好。您不必輸入任何額外的密碼。因此，Mondex不符合臺灣人的習慣並已從臺灣消失了。

Customer ：OK. I see that. I also heard of Maestro. Can you tell me about it?

客　戶：好的，我知道了。我也聽說過Maestro。可以跟我講一下嗎？

Bank teller : Of course. **Maestro, in a sense, is just like a VISA debit card but the difference lies in the fact that Maestro is designed by MasterCard while a VISA debit card is issued by VISA.** To sum it up, there are basically two types of debit cards issued by most banks, namely, a VISA debit card and a Maestro debit card. What's more, the difference between a VISA debit card and a Maestro debit card is, a Maestro debit card asks for a four-digit password while making a purchase but it is not the case of a VISA debit card. So you can say a Maestro debit card is safer and more secure than a VISA debit card. If your VISA debit card is stolen by a bad guy, he can use your card to go on a shopping spree without your authorization. However, most Taiwanese regard keying in their PIN number as troublesome, so Maestro debit cards are not well accepted in Taiwan.

行　　　員：當然可以。**Maestro就某種意義而言就像VISA金融卡一樣。但不同點在於Maestro是由萬事達所設計，而VISA金融卡是由VISA所發行。**總結來說，大多數的銀行發行兩種簽帳卡，也就是VISA金融卡和Maestro卡。此外，VISA金融卡和Maestro卡的不同之處在於，在購物時，Maestro的簽帳卡要求輸入四位數密碼，但VISA金融卡不用。所以您可以說Maestro簽帳卡比VISA金融卡更加地安全有保障。如果您的VISA金融卡被壞人偷走，他可以用您的卡片來瘋狂購物而不需您的授權。然而，大部分臺灣人認爲還要輸入密碼相當麻煩，所以Maestro簽帳卡在臺灣就沒有被廣爲接受。

Customer : So what you mean is, Maestro is also a kind of debit card, right?

客　　　戶：所以您說的是，Maestro也是一種簽帳卡，對吧？

Bank teller : Yes, it is correct. You can use a Maestro debit card to spend as much money as you have in your bank account. You can go to any merchant with the logo of Maestro to use a Maestro debit card to make a purchase. But, I might add, you cannot swipe your Maestro debit card to make a purchase in a merchant only with the logo of MasterCard although Maestro also belongs to MasterCard.

行　　員：是的，沒錯。您可以用Maestro簽帳卡來花費您銀行戶頭裡有的錢。您可以去任何一家Maestro的特約商家來刷Maestro簽帳卡消費。但我要補充一下，雖然Maestro也屬於萬事達，您無法在只有MasterCard標誌的特約商家刷Maestro的簽帳卡。

Customer : OK. I see. But I find Maestro is seldom seen.

客　　戶：好，我了解了。但我覺得Maestro很少看到耶。

Bank teller : That's right. People in Taiwan don't accept Maestro debit cards because the participating merchants with Maestro are few and you have to take the trouble to key in your PIN number while using a Maestro debit card to make a purchase. Therefore, Maestro, in a sense, has disappeared in Taiwan.

行　　員：沒錯。在臺灣的民眾不接受Maestro簽帳卡因為Maestro的特約商店太少了，而您還要費功夫輸入密碼才能使用Maestro卡來消費。因此，Maestro也在某種意義而言從臺灣消失了。

Customer : OK. Thank you. Now I understand.

客　　戶：好，謝謝，我懂了。

Bank teller : You are welcome. Now let me talk about Smart Pay. Generally speaking, now the chip-and-PIN ATM card issued by banks in Taiwan all contain Smart Pay. **In a word, a Smart Pay ATM card is like a VISA debit card or a Maestro debit card. The difference is, when you use a Smart Pay debit card to make a purchase,**

you must key in your six-to-twelve-digit PIN number to ensure the purchase. However, Smart Pay's channels are only limited in Taiwan and Hokkaido so far.

行　　員：不客氣。現在讓我談談Smart Pay。一般來說，臺灣各家銀行所發行的晶片金融卡都具有Smart Pay的功能。**簡言之，Smart Pay的金融卡就像VISA金融卡或是Maestro卡一樣。不同點在於，當您用Smart Pay金融卡消費時，您必須輸入六到十二位數的晶片密碼來確認此消費。**然而，SmartPay的通路目前只限於臺灣和北海道。

Customer : I see. It seems that Smart Pay is made in Taiwan and it has not been widely accepted around the world like VISA or MasterCard.

客　　戶：我懂了，似乎Smart Pay是臺灣自製的，所以還未像VISA或是萬事達一樣在世界各國廣泛地被接受。

Bank teller : Yes. And last but not least, let me talk about UnionPay. UnionPay is invented by China. UnionPay cards can be divided into two categories: a UnionPay credit card and a UnionPay debit card. Overall, UnionPay cards can be used in more than one hundred countries and regions globally. Some of UnionPay credit cards cooperate with American Express, MasterCard, or VISA, and they can be used outside China. In a way, you can say UnionPay cards are indifferent from VISA cards. However, China does not want to be controlled by other countries or VISA or MasterCard, so China initiated UnionPay to be its own credit cards and debit cards to fight against other international card issuers.

行　　員：是的，最後來談也很重要的銀聯。銀聯是由中國大陸所創。銀聯卡可以分為兩種。銀聯信用卡和銀聯簽帳卡。銀聯卡可以在全球超過一百個國家和區域使用。有些銀聯卡和美國運通、萬事達或

是VISA合作，並可以在中國大陸境外使用。這樣一來，您可以說銀聯卡和VISA卡沒有不同。不過，中國大陸不想被其他國家、VISA或萬事達控制，所以中國大陸推動自己的銀聯卡來成為自家的信用卡和簽帳卡來對抗國際發卡組織。

Customer : I see. It figures. So can a UnionPay card be used in Taiwan?

客　　戶：我明白了。講得很清楚。所以銀聯卡可以在臺灣使用嗎？

Bank teller : Yes. **You can use a UnionPay card in Taiwan now as long as you find out the ATMs containing the logo of UnionPay.**

行　　員：是的。在臺灣只要您看到含有銀聯標誌的ATM，您就可以使用銀聯卡。

Customer : Thank you so much.

客　　戶：非常謝謝您。

Bank teller : It is my pleasure.

行　　員：不客氣。

補充單字

♦ eliminate [ɪˋlɪməˌnet] *v.* 除去

♦ authorize [ˋɔθəˌraɪz] *v.* 授權；放行

實用金句

♦ PLUS is one of the world's largest global ATM networks, offering cash withdrawal from ATMs in local currency in more than 200 countries.

PLUS是世界上最大的全球ATM網絡之一，提供超過二百個國家的當地貨幣提款。

♦ If you find out the logo of PLUS at the back of your bank card, you should search for the ATMs which contains the logo of PLUS and you can use your VISA PLUS ATM card to withdraw local currency from the ATMs overseas.

如果您在金融卡背面發現PLUS的標誌的話，您應該找有PLUS標誌的ATM，您就可以拿含PLUS的金融卡在國外的ATM領當地貨幣。

◆ As long as your ATM card carries the logo of Cirrus, you can withdraw money from the ATMs which also carry the logo of Cirrus.

只要您的金融卡含有Cirrus的標誌，您可以在有Cirrus標誌的提款機領錢。

◆ Mondex is like EasyCard which we use to take the MRT. You have to deposit your money into Mondex first, and then you can use Mondex as using iCash issued by 7-11 convenience stores.

Mondex就像我們搭捷運用的悠遊卡一樣。您必須把錢存進Mondex，然後您就可以像使用統一超商發行的iCash一樣來使用。

◆ Maestro, in a sense, is just like a VISA debit card but the difference lies in the fact that Maestro is designed by MasterCard while a VISA debit card is issued by VISA.

Maestro就某種意義而言就像VISA金融卡一樣。但不同點在於Maestro是由萬事達所設計，而VISA金融卡是由VISA所發行。

◆ In a word, a Smart Pay ATM card is like a VISA debit card or a Maestro debit card. The difference is, when you use a Smart Pay debit card to make a purchase, you must key in your six-to-twelve-digit PIN number to ensure the purchase.

簡言之，Smart Pay的金融卡就像VISA金融卡或是Maestro卡一樣。不同點在於，當您用Smart Pay金融卡消費時，您必須輸入六到十二位數的晶片密碼來確定此消費。

◆ You can use a UnionPay card in Taiwan now as long as you find out the ATMs containing the logo of UnionPay.

在臺灣只要您看到有銀聯標誌的ATM，您就可以使用銀聯卡。

無卡存款
Depositing Without a Card

Customer : I would like to make a deposit.

客　　戶：我要存款。

Bank teller : How much would you like to deposit into your account?

行　　員：您想存多少到您的戶頭？

Customer : No, not into my own account, but I want to deposit 20,000 NT dollars into my boss's account.

客　　戶：不，不是要存到我自己的戶頭，我是要存二萬元到我老闆的帳戶。

Bank teller : Really? Just 20,000 NT dollars, right? Sir, **I suggest you use an ATM at our bank to make the deposit. This way, it is fast and convenient for you.**

行　　員：是喔？才二萬元，對吧？先生，**我建議您使用在我們銀行的自動櫃員機來存款。這樣對您來說快又便利。**

Customer : But I have never used an ATM to make a deposit. I am not familiar with machines.

客　　戶：但我從來沒有用過自動櫃員機來存款。我對機器不熟。

Bank teller : That is OK. I can teach you. Please come with me and let me show you how to use an ATM to make a deposit.

行　　員：沒關係。我可以教您。請跟我來讓我示範給您看如何用自動櫃員

機存款。

Customer : Fine. I will go with you.

客　　戶：好吧，我跟您走。

Bank teller : Do you have your ATM card with you, Sir?

行　　員：先生，您有沒有帶金融卡啊？

Customer : Oh, I am sorry. I forgot to bring my ATM card with me.

客　　戶：喔，很抱歉。我忘記帶金融卡了。

Bank teller : That is OK. **Our bank provides a service of "depositing without an ATM card", which allows our customers to use an ATM to make a deposit even without inserting an ATM card into the ATM.** All you need to do is punch in your account number and the amount you want to deposit.

行　　員：沒關係，**我們銀行提供「無卡存款」，讓客戶可以用自動櫃員機存款而不用插金融卡到自動櫃員機中。**您只要輸入您要存入的帳號和金額。

Customer : Oh. I see. So even if I don't have a passbook or an ATM card, as long as I remember the account number, I can make a deposit through an ATM, right?

客　　戶：喔，我明白了。即使我沒有存摺或金融卡，只要我知道帳號，我就可以用自動櫃員機存款，對吧？

Bank teller : Exactly. **What's better, you don't have to rush to the bank before the cut-off hour anymore. You can make a deposit through an ATM anytime you want, even on national holidays or on weekends.**

行　　員：一點都沒錯。更好的是，您不必趕在營業時間結束之前到銀行。即使在國定假日或週末，您可以隨時用自動櫃員機辦理存款。

Customer : It sounds great. Can you tell me more?

客　　　戶：聽起來很棒。可以跟我講更多嗎？

Bank teller : Of course. When you make a deposit through an ATM, you can deposit fifty banknotes per transaction. Some banks allow their customers to deposit 100 or 150 banknotes every time through ATMs. Different banks and ATMs have different rules.

行　　　員：當然，當您透過自動櫃員機存款，您可以每次存五十張鈔票。有些銀行讓客戶用ATM每次存一百到一百五十張鈔票。不同的銀行和自動櫃員機有不同的規則。

Customer : What do I have to notice when I make deposit through an ATM?

客　　　戶：我用自動櫃員機存款時，要注意些什麼？

Bank teller : **You have to notice that before you use an ATM to make a deposit, you should flat your banknotes and then you should not let other materials to be mixed into the deposit slot, like a rubber band.** If you mix a rubber band or other materials into the deposit slot, you banknotes will be jammed in the ATM. If that happens, it will become complicated to deal with. And by the way, new banknotes are easy to stick together.

行　　　員：**用ATM存款時，您要注意應該把您的鈔票整平，不要讓其他雜物，像是橡皮筋混入存款鈔口內。**如果您混入橡皮筋或是其他雜物入到存款鈔口內，您的鈔票就會卡在ATM裡。萬一發生這種情況，事情就變得難處理了。順便一提，新鈔容易黏鈔。

Customer : OK. I see. You mentioned that I don't have to have a bank card to deposit. I want to ask you whether I can use an ATM card to deposit or not.

客　　　戶：好，我明白了。您剛提到我不必有金融卡就可以存款。我想問您

是否可用金融卡存款？

Bank teller : Yes, **you can make a deposit with an ATM card. This way, you don't have to key in the account number. The ATM will show your account number by itself.** You know, some banks even don't allow its customers to make a deposit through an ATM without an ATM card such as Cathay United Bank, Chinatrust, and E. Sun Bank. Therefore, it is called "depositing with an ATM card." Some banks such as Bank Sinopac or Taishin Bank, allow their customers to make a deposit through an ATM without a bank card. Thus, it is called "depositing without an ATM card." I would suggest you inquire your original account opening bank about this matter. Different banks have different rules.

行　　　員：可以。**您可以用金融卡來存款。這樣您就不必輸入帳號。自動櫃員機會自動顯示出您的帳號。**您懂的，有些銀行不允許客戶用自動櫃員機來無卡存款，如國泰世華、中國信託和玉山銀行。因此，這稱為「有卡存款」。有些銀行，如永豐銀行或台新銀行，讓客戶不必用金融卡就可用自動櫃員機存款，因此這稱為「無卡存款」。我會建議您詢問原來的開戶行。不同的銀行有不同的規定。

Customer : Does this service have any limitations?

客　　　戶：這項服務有任何限制嗎？

Bank teller : Well, yes. You can deposit as much as you want over the counter. However, according to the regulations of the Financial Supervisory Commission (FSC), you can only deposit thirty thousand NT dollars at most into an ATM without an ATM card per day. If you want to make a deposit into your own account number through an ATM with an ATM card, there is no limitation for you. However, if you try to make a deposit into someone else' account number through an ATM with an ATM card, you can only deposit thirty thousand NT dollars at most a day.

行　　員：嗯，有的。臨櫃存款的話，您要存多少就存多少。不過，根據金管會的規定，無卡ATM存款一天最多只能存三萬元。如果您透過自動櫃員機用金融卡來存到自己帳戶的話，則沒有限制。不過，如果您透過自動櫃員機用金融卡把錢存到別人帳戶的話，您一天最多只能存三萬元。

Customer : I see. But this regulation puts too many limits on bank customers. What if I want to pay my credit card bill or my house loan through an ATM? If my credit card bill is over 30,000 NT dollars, can't I use an ATM to pay the bill?

客　　戶：我明白了。但這項規定對銀行客戶限制太多。如果我要透過自動櫃員機繳信用卡款或是房貸怎麼辦？如果我的信用卡帳單超過三萬元，我就不能用自動櫃員機來繳費了嗎？

Bank teller : In the case of paying credit card bill or loan, banks do allow their customers to use ATMs to make a deposit or transfer without the limitation of 30,000 NT dollars a day.

行　　員：在繳付信用卡費或貸款的情形下，銀行允許客戶不在一天只能存或轉三萬元的限制內。

Customer : OK. I see. Still, I think the government should not put too many limits on bank customers. I wonder if the government is trying to fulfill a cashless society.

客　　戶：好的，我明白了。不過我希望政府不要把太多限制加諸在銀行客戶上。我想知道政府是否想要創造一個無現金社會。

Bank teller : Well, that I don't know. But I know the Financial Supervisory Commission sets up this rule because too many fraudsters have used ATMs to commit a fraud.

行　　員：喔，我不知道這個。但我知道金管會設這個規定因為有太多的詐欺犯用自動櫃員機來詐騙。

Customer : OK. I understand. Thank you very much.

客　　戶：好的，我了解了。非常謝謝您。

補充單字

◆ insert [ɪn`sɝt] *v.* 插入（卡片）

◆ original account opening bank [əˋrɪdʒənḷ əˋkaunt ˋopənɪŋ bæŋk] *n.* 原開戶行

實用金句

◆ I suggest you use an ATM at our bank to make the deposit. This way, it is fast and convenient for you.

我建議您使用在我們銀行的自動櫃員機來存款。這樣對您來說快又便利。

◆ Our bank provides a service of "depositing without an ATM card", which allows our customers to use an ATM to make a deposit even without inserting an ATM card into the ATM.

我們銀行提供「無卡存款」，讓客戶可以用自動櫃員機存款而不用插金融卡到自動櫃員機中。

◆ What's better, you don't have to rush to the bank before the cut-off hour any-more. You can make a deposit through an ATM anytime you want, even on national holidays or on weekends.

更好的是，您不必趕在營業時間結束之前到銀行。即使在國定假日或週末，您可以隨時用自動櫃員機辦理存款。

◆ You have to notice that before you use an ATM to make a deposit, you should flat your banknotes and then you should not let other materials to be mixed into the deposit slot, like a rubber band.

用ATM存款時，您要注意應該把您的鈔票整平，不要讓其他雜物，像是橡皮筋混入存款鈔口內。

◆ You can make a deposit with an ATM card. This way, you don't have to key in the account number. The ATM will show your account number by itself.

您可以用金融卡來存款。這樣您就不必輸入帳號。自動櫃員機會自動顯示出您的帳號。

電子錢包
Electronic Purse

Bank teller : What can I do for you today?

行　　　員：我今天可以為您做什麼嗎？

Customer : I would like to apply for gift cards because I read the newspaper that your bank has initiated this kind of card.

客　　　戶：我想要辦禮物卡因為我在報紙上讀到您們銀行有發行這種卡。

Bank teller : Yes, you are right. **Our bank has initiated a type of stored-value electronic purse card, which is called "gift cards."** That means, this kind of card does not need you to open a bank account to own it. You can just buy a gift card from the bank and you can give it as a gift to another person. In other words, a gift card is not a registered card like an ATM card linked to your bank account.

行　　　員：是的，您說對了。**我們銀行有推這種電子錢包儲值卡，稱作「禮物卡」。**這是說，這種卡不需要您去銀行開戶才可以擁有。您可以直接從銀行買一張禮物卡並把它當禮物送給別人。換句話說，禮物卡不是像連結您銀行帳戶的金融卡一樣的記名卡。

Customer : So what you mean that I don't have to open an account to possess gift cards. I can buy as many gift cards as I want, right?

客　　　戶：所以您是說，我不必開戶就可以拿到禮物卡。我可以愛買多少張禮物卡就買多少張，對嗎？

Bank teller : Precisely. Gift cards are unregistered cards. That is, you can even give your gift cards to your friends or family members. That is why this type of stored-value electronic purse card is called a "gift card". A gift card is actually an electronic purse which is more convenient than checks for smaller transactions. Because a gift card functions independently of a bank account, it would give gift card users both greater privacy and freedom. The gift card can even make you control your budget because a user can spend only the amount on the card. You don't have to be worried about overdraft and you may fall into debt. Of course, on the other hand, **if you want to register the gift card, it is also OK. You can go to any bank branch with your ID card to apply for the registration.** The advantage of registering your gift card is, when you lose your gift card, you can report it lost to the bank and ask the bank to replace it.

行　　員 : 沒錯。禮物卡是不記名卡。也就是說，您甚至可以把禮物卡送給親朋好友。這就是為什麼這種電子錢包儲值卡叫作「禮物卡」。禮物卡實際上是一種在小額付款上比支票更方便的一種電子錢包。因為禮物卡獨立於銀行帳戶之外，它給禮物卡持卡人更大的隱私和自由。禮物卡甚至可以讓您控制預算，因為禮物卡只讓使用者花儲值在卡片裡的金額。您不必擔心透支而負債。當然，另一方面，**如果您想要把卡片記名，也是可以的。您可以帶您的身分證去任何一家分行申辦記名手續。**記名的好處是當您遺失您的禮物卡，您可以向銀行掛失並請銀行補發。

Customer : How do I use gift cards?

客　　戶 : 我怎麼使用禮物卡呢？

Bank teller : That is simple. **Different from a credit card, a gift card is a stored-value card.** You must first transfer value to the gift card by depositing or transferring money into the card via ATMs. And then you can use the gift card to make a purchase at merchants. Funds are debited directly from the gift card account. When the value on your gift card is spent, you can load new funds through our ATMs to add value to the card. By the same token, if you want to check the balance in your gift card, you can use our bank's ATMs to check it out.

行　　員 : 這很簡單。**不同於信用卡，禮物卡是儲值卡。**您必須先透過ATM把錢存入禮物卡中來加值。然後您就可以在商家消費。消費從您的禮物卡帳戶直接扣款。當您用掉禮物卡的儲值時，您可以透過ATM把新的錢加值到禮物卡中。同樣地，如果您想查詢禮物卡的可用餘額，您可以用銀行的ATM來查詢。

Customer : Yes, I get it. Simply put, a gift card is just like an EasyCard or iCash. You must put money into the card account first and then you can swipe your card to make a purchase.

客　　戶 : 是的，我了解了。簡單說，禮物卡就像悠遊卡或是iCash一樣。您必須先在卡裡儲值才能刷卡消費。

Bank teller : Yes, you are really smart. Not a few corporations have developed and issued their own e-purse or stored-value cards because they can acquire money in advance from the consumers, which gives the corporations a lot of benefits. For example, the corporations can deposit the money they get in advance into their bank accounts and earn interests. Also, they can use the money to invest in stocks or mutual funds and may get a huge return. In addition, the corporations also can analyze the prepaid card users' consuming habits by storing and analyzing the huge information from the e-purses issued by them.

行　　員：是的。您真聰明。不少企業都推出他們自家的電子錢包或儲值卡因為他們可以先從客戶那裡取得資金，這就會為公司帶來很多好處。舉例來說，公司可以把這些先取來的錢存到銀行來賺利息。此外，他們也可以把這筆錢用來投資股票或基金來得到豐厚的收益。此外，企業也可以藉著儲存及分析所發行的電子錢包裡的龐大資訊，來解讀預付款卡友的消費習慣。

Customer : I see. Can you tell me any drawback of the gift card?

客　　戶：我明白了。您可以跟我講一下禮物卡的缺點嗎？

Bank teller : OK. First of all, because of the regulations of the authorities concerned, the amount you can deposit is only 10,000 NT dollars at most. Next, **if you don't want to use the gift card anymore and you want to redeem your value in your gift card, you must pay the redemption fee for 100 NT dollars.** And if you happen to lose your gift card and you need the bank to replace it, you must pay 50 NT dollars. Last, **if your gift card is lost or stolen, the bank will not return the balance in your gift card to you.**

行　　員：好的，首先，因為相關主管機關的規定，您最多只能儲值一萬元。再來，**如果您不要使用禮物卡並想要贖回卡片內的儲值的話，您必須付贖回手續費用一百元。** 如果您不巧遺失禮物卡並要銀行補發的話，您還要付五十元。最後，**不論卡片是遺失或是被偷，銀行都不會把禮物卡內的餘額補還給您。**

Customer : In addition to your bank, where can I apply for a gift card?

客　　戶：除了您們銀行，我還可以在哪裡申請禮物卡？

Bank teller : To tell the truth, because a gift card does not need to be registered, too many gift cards are used in frauds. A lot of people reported it to the police that they transferred money to a gift card's account, but they didn't receive the goods. Since a gift card is a non-registered card, it is difficult for the police to track down the fraudster. Besides, since the EasyCard not only makes the users to take the MRT or buses but also allows the users to make a smaller purchase at a lot of merchants, the gift card lost its attraction and most banks stopped issuing the gift cards. Originally, E. Sun Bank, Taiwan Cooperative Bank and Bank Sinopac had all issued the gift card before.

行　　員：老實說，因為禮物卡不需要記名，所以有太多禮物卡被用在詐騙上。很多人向銀行報案說當他們把錢匯到禮物卡的帳戶後，他們沒有收到貨品。既然禮物卡是不記名卡，警方要追緝詐騙犯也有困難。況且，自從悠遊卡不只讓使用者搭捷運或公車，也開放使用者在很多商家小額消費後，禮物卡就失掉它的吸引力而大多數銀行也停止發行禮物卡了。本來玉山銀行、合作金庫和永豐銀行都有發行這種禮物卡。

Customer : I see. Thank you.

客　　戶：我明白了，謝謝。

補充單字

◆ electronic purse [ɪlɛk`trɑnɪk pɝs] *n.* 電子錢包

◆ register [rɛdʒɪstɚ] *v.* 記名

266

實用金句

♦ Our bank has initiated a type of stored-value electronic purse card, which is called "gift cards."

我們銀行有推這種電子錢包儲值卡，稱作「禮物卡」。

♦ If you want to register the gift card, it is also OK. You can go to any bank branch with your ID card to apply for the registration.

如果您想要把卡片記名，也是可以的。您可以帶您的身分證去任何一家分行申辦記名手續。

♦ Different from a credit card, a gift card is a stored-value card.

不同於信用卡，禮物卡是儲值卡。

♦ If you don't want to use the gift card anymore and you want to redeem your value in your gift card, you must pay the redemption fee for 100 NT dollars.

如果您不要使用禮物卡並想要贖回卡片內的儲值的話，您必須付贖回手續費用一百元。

♦ If your gift card is lost or stolen, the bank will not return the balance in your gift card to you.

不論卡片是遺失或是被偷，銀行都不會把禮物卡內的餘額補還給您。

信用卡
Credit Card

Bank teller : Sir, do you often go shopping in the Pacific SOGO Department Store?

行　　員：先生，您常常到SOGO百貨公司購物嗎？

Customer : Yes. Why did you ask this question?

客　　戶：對啊，為什麼問這個？

Bank teller : Well, our bank has launched the Cathay United-Pacific SOGO co-branded Card. You can enjoy a lot of benefits from using this co-branded card to shop in the Pacific SOGO Department Store. **This co-branded card provides you with a wide array of benefits, including an exclusive 4% shopping rebate and a 500 NT dollar Cash Voucher on first purchase by new cardholders.**

行　　員：嗯，我們銀行有推出國泰世華SOGO聯名卡。您可以用這張聯名卡在SOGO百貨購物並享有很多的優惠。**這張聯名卡提供你很多的優惠，像是消費獨享百分之四的現金回饋，還有新卡戶首次刷卡消費可獲得五百元的現金禮券。**

Customer : Why does the bank teller always try to promote a credit card to me? I just had been to Taishin Bank. The bank teller there also tried to make me apply for the Shin Kong Mitsukoshi co-branded card.

客　　戶：為什麼銀行櫃員老是要向我推銷信用卡呢？我剛去台新銀行，銀行櫃員也是要我辦一張新光三越聯名卡。

Bank teller : Well. You know, most banks are pushing consumer banking now and marketing credit cards is very important for most banks in Taiwan. But this Pacific SOGO co-branded card is really useful. It is equipped with EasyCard and MasterCard PayPass features. In addition, this co-branded card can be used at Pacific SOGO department stores in Taiwan and mainland China.

行　　員：呃，您懂的，現在大部分銀行都在主打消金，而對大部分臺灣的銀行來說推銷信用卡相當重要。但這張太平洋SOGO百貨聯名卡真的很實用。它結合了悠遊卡和萬事達的感應式刷卡功能。此外，這張聯名卡可以在臺灣和大陸的SOGO百貨使用。

Customer : Whatever you say. I don't like credit cards, so don't promote credit cards to me.

客　　戶：我不管您說什麼。我不喜歡信用卡，所以不要向我推卡。

Bank teller : Why is that? Credit cards not only make it easier for you to shop but also provide a variety of benefits for cardholders. As long as you make use of your credit card responsibly and pay off your balance in full and on time every month, you may as well use a credit card to make a purchase instead of using cash. You may earn some cash back by using a credit card to make a purchase. With a credit card, you can buy now and pay later. Does it sound great?

行　　員：為什麼呢？信用卡不但讓您購物更簡單也提供很多優惠給卡友。只要您有責任感地刷卡並每月準時付清卡費，您不妨就用信用卡而不要用現金來消費。您可以從刷卡得到現金回饋。有了信用卡，您可以先買再付款。聽起來有沒有很棒啊？

Customer : I don't think so. Many people fall into debt because of revolving credit interest. And most Taiwanese in credit card debt are confused at how they managed to get into such deep debt. To put it bluntly, credit cards mostly carry interest rates above 10% even with high rates up to 20%. It is easy for people to become credit card slaves because of this high interest rate. We both know that these interest charges add up really fast and in no time people just fall into debt.

客　　戶：我不這樣認爲。很多人因爲循環利息而負債。大部分欠卡債的臺灣人對他們如何陷入如此深的債務感到困惑不解。講白點，信用卡的利率大都超過百分之十，甚至還高達百分之二十。因爲這樣的高利率，民衆很容易變成卡奴。我們都知道利息累積得很快，而民衆在短時間就陷入債務中了。

Bank teller : As I said before, **it is important for you to pay off your balance each month in full and on time, so you won't get into a revolving debt.** In addition, you should be wise when you take out credit card cash advances because cash advances not only bear higher interest rates, but also require you to pay a cash advance fee. **If you cannot control your spending with a credit card, you should consider cutting up your cards or even canceling your credit cards.** But if you are not willing to cancel your credit card, I would suggest you have your credit limits lowered to a mild measure. There are pros and cons concerning credit cards. You cannot just stop driving just because of car accidents happening.

行　　員：就像我先前講過的，**每月準時繳清全額卡費非常重要，這樣您才不會欠循環利息。**另外，您在動用信用卡預借現金時應放聰明點，因爲預借現金的利息很高，而且還會要求您付預借現金的手

續費。如果您無法控制您的信用卡花費，您應考慮剪卡或甚至註銷信用卡。但如果您不願註銷信用卡，我會建議您減低您的刷卡額度。信用卡有它的優缺點。您不會因為有車禍發生就停止開車吧。

Customer : I got your point. I know credit cards have different ranks such as **classic cards**, titanium cards, commercial cards, signature cards, infinite cards, and world cards.

客　　戶：我懂您的意思。我知道信用卡有不同卡別，像是普卡、鈦金卡、商務卡、御璽卡、無限卡和世界卡。

Bank teller : Yes. If you are rich, you can apply for a higher ranking card such as a signature card or an infinite card because high-ranking cards provide more benefits for their cardholders. If you don't earn much money, I would suggest you apply for a classic card because a classic card carries low or no annual fees.

行　　員：對，如果您很有錢，您可以辦比較高階的卡別，像是御璽卡或無限卡，因為高階的卡別提供客戶更多的優惠。如果您賺得沒那麼多，我會建議您辦普卡，因為普卡的年費較低或是免年費。

Customer : Oh. Is there an age limit for applying for a credit card?

客　　戶：喔，辦信用卡有年齡限制嗎？

Bank teller : Yes, if you want to apply for just a classic card, you must be 20 years of age or older. But if you want to apply for a platinum or titanium card, you need to be more than 24 years old.

行　　員：有的。如果您只想辦普卡，您需要年滿二十歲以上。但如果您想辦白金卡或鈦金卡，您需要年滿二十四歲。

Customer : Is there an income limit for applying for a credit card?

客　　戶：辦信用卡有無收入限制呢？

Bank teller : Yes. There are income limits for applying for different credit cards. For example, if your annual income is more than 400,000 NT dollars, you are qualified to apply for a platinum card. But if you would like to apply for a world card, your annual income must reach at least two million NT dollars.

行　　員：有的。辦不同的卡別有不同的限制。舉例來說，如果您的年收入四十萬以上，您有資格申辦白金卡。但如果您想辦一張世界卡的話，您的年收入至少要兩百萬以上。

Customer : If I apply for a credit card, how much can I charge the credit card every month?

客　　戶：如果我辦一張信用卡，我每個月可以用這張信用卡刷多少錢呢？

Bank teller : On approval of an application, a credit line is determined based on measures such as income, current levels of debt and capacity to repay. Although the total balance of spending does not need to be paid off entirely each month, a minimum payment is required and interest will be charged on the outstanding balance.

行　　員：在核卡過後，刷卡額度取決於收入、負債比和還款能力。雖然花費的總額不必每月都繳清，但需要繳付最低金額並且也會收取未償付餘額的利息。

Customer : If I want to apply for a credit card, what should I provide the bank with?

客　　戶：如果我想辦信用卡，我要提供銀行什麼樣的資料？

Bank teller : You should give the bank the filled out application form, a copy of your national ID card, and your proof of income.

行　　員：您應該把填好的申請書、國民身分證的影本和您的財力證明交給銀行。

Customer　: OK, thanks. And can my daughter also apply for a supplementary card?

客　　戶：好的，謝謝。那我的女兒也可以辦一張附卡嗎？

Bank teller : Yes, she can apply for a supplementary card if she is more than fifteen years old.

行　　員：如果她年滿十五歲的話，她就可以申辦附卡。

Customer　: Thanks. One more question. I have a friend. He is a foreigner and he does not have a credit card in Taiwan. Is it difficult for him to apply for a credit card in Taiwan?

客　　戶：謝謝。再問一個問題。我有個朋友，他是外國人，而他在臺灣沒有信用卡。在臺灣申辦一張信用卡對他來說很難嗎？

Bank teller : Yes, it is difficult for a foreigner to apply for a credit card in Taiwan because foreigners are high-risk customers. After all, they might swipe their credit card to make a lot of purchases, then leave their debt and flee to their own country. Thus, **our bank's policy is, if a foreigner wants to apply for a credit card, he must not have a high-risk job and his annual salary must be up to one and a half million NT dollars. In addition, the foreigner also needs a Taiwanese surety, whose annual salary must also be more than one and a half million NT dollars.** Therefore, it is not easy to fulfill the requirements.

行　　員：因為外國人是高風險的客戶，所以外國人在臺灣辦卡是非常困難的。畢竟，他們可能刷卡消費很多次，卻放著卡債不管，跑回他們自己的國家。所以**我們銀行的規定是，如果外國人要辦卡，他必須不是從事高風險的工作，而且年收入達到新臺幣一百五十萬以上。另外，他還要一個臺灣人替他做保證人，對方的年收入也**

要至少新臺幣一百五十萬元以上。因此，滿足這樣的條件並不容易。

Customer : Thanks. Now I understand.
客　　　戶：謝謝。我現在了解了。

補充單字

◆ credit card slave [ˋkrɛdɪt kɑrd slev] *n.* 卡奴

◆ classic card [ˋklæsɪk kɑrd] *n.* 普卡

◆ surety [ˋʃʊrtɪ] *n.* 連帶保證人

實用金句

◆ This co-branded card provides you with a wide array of benefits, including an exclusive 4% shopping rebate and a 500 NT dollar Cash Voucher on first purchase by new cardholders.

這張聯名卡提供你很多的優惠，像是消費獨享百分之四的現金回饋，還有新卡戶首次刷卡消費可獲得五百元的現金禮券。

◆ It is important for you to pay off your balance each month in full and on time, so you won't get into a revolving debt.

每月準時繳清全額卡費非常重要，這樣您才不會欠循環利息。

◆ If you cannot control your spending with a credit card, you should consider cutting up your cards or even canceling your credit cards.

如果您無法控制您的信用卡花費，您應考慮剪卡或甚至註銷信用卡。

◆ Our bank's policy is, if a foreigner wants to apply for a credit card, he must not have a high-risk job and his annual salary must be up to one and a half million NT dollars. In addition, the foreigner also needs a Taiwanese surety, whose annual salary must also be more than one and a half million NT dollars.

我們銀行的規定是，如果外國人要辦卡，他必須不是從事高風險的工作，而且年收入達到新臺幣一百五十萬以上。另外，他還要一個臺灣人替他做保證人，對方的年收入也要至少新臺幣一百五十萬元以上。

悠遊聯名卡
Co-branded EasyCard

Bank teller : Hello, Sir, do you often take the MRT?

行　　員 : 先生您好，您常搭捷運嗎？

Customer : Yes, why did you ask me the question?

客　　戶 : 是的，爲什麼問這個？

Bank teller : Well. Our bank has promoted a new credit card, which is called a **co-branded EasyCard**. Have you heard of that?

行　　員 : 嗯，我們銀行有推出新的信用卡。叫作「悠遊聯名卡」。您有聽過嗎？

Customer : No. I have never heard of it. Can you tell me about it?

客　　戶 : 沒有。我從未聽過。您可以跟我講一下嗎？

Bank teller : Sure. You know the EasyCard, right? When you take the MRT, you will use an EasyCard to pay your fares. You can also use the card on buses in Taipei. Moreover, you can also use your EasyCard to purchase goods whose price is less than 1,000 NT dollars per transaction at convenience stores, such as 7-11. Simply put, the EasyCard has become a multi-purpose stored-value card, which enables its user to take the MRT or bus or Taiwan High Speed Rail and to make a smaller purchase at its merchants around Taiwan. What's more, you can also apply for a registered EasyCard. This way, if you lost your EasyCard, you can report it lost and have it replaced. Now let me talk about a co-branded EasyCard. The co-branded EasyCard is jointly issued by a few banks in cooperation with the EasyCard Corporation. **In a word, the co-branded EasyCard is a type of credit card but it possesses the functions of an EasyCard.**

行　　員：好的。您知道悠遊卡對吧。當您搭捷運時，您用悠遊卡來付車票。您也可以用這張卡在臺北搭公車。此外，您也可以用您的悠遊聯名卡在便利商店，如7-11，來單次小額消費一千元以下的商品。簡單說，悠遊卡已經變成多功能的儲值卡，讓使用者能搭捷運、公車或高鐵並在臺灣各地的合作商家做小額消費。此外，您也可以申請記名悠遊卡。這樣如果您遺失您的悠遊卡的話，您可以掛失和補發。現在讓我談談悠遊聯名卡吧。悠遊聯名卡是由悠遊卡公司連同一些銀行一起發行的。**簡單講，悠遊聯名卡是一種綁有悠遊卡功能的信用卡。**

Customer　：I get it. A co-branded EasyCard is the combination of a credit card and an EasyCard.

客　　戶：我懂了。悠遊聯名卡是信用卡和悠遊卡的合體。

Bank teller　：Exactly. But **the co-branded EasyCard has more features than an EasyCard. It has the auto-loading function. When your co-branded EasyCard's balance falls below 100 NT dollars, it will then automatically add 500 NT dollars to your card.** This way, you don't have to be worried that you might forget to add value to your EasyCard from time to time. If you want your co-branded EasyCard to have the feature of auto loading, you can go to a MRT station to activate the auto-loading function in your card. Of course, you still have to pay 500 NT dollars later. The auto-loaded value will be shown on your next month's credit card statement.

行　　員：沒錯。但悠遊聯名卡比悠遊卡有更多的功能。它具有自動加值的功能。當您的悠遊聯名卡的餘額少於一百元時，就會自動加值五百元到您的卡片。這樣您就不必時常擔心您可能忘記加值悠遊卡了。如果您想要擁有悠遊聯名卡的自動加值功能，您可以去捷運站啟用卡片的自動加值功能。當然，您之後還是要付那五百元。加值費用會列在您的下個月的信用卡帳單上。

Customer：Could you tell me any shortcoming of a co-branded EasyCard?

客　　戶：您可以跟我講一下悠遊聯名卡的缺點嗎？

Bank teller：Yes. First, **if you activate the auto-loading function in your EasyCard, you cannot cancel it.** What's done cannot be undone.

行　　員：可以。首先，**如果您啟用悠遊卡的自動加值功能，您就無法取消了。**覆水難收。

Customer：Last time I went to another bank and a bank teller also told me to apply for their bank's co-branded EasyCard. It seems that co-branded EasyCards are very popular now.

客　　戶：上次我去另一家銀行，行員也是跟我講辦他們的悠遊聯名卡。似乎悠遊聯名卡現在很夯。

Bank teller：Sure. A lot of banks issue co-branded EasyCards now. As far as I know, Chinatrust, Cathay United Bank, E. Sun Bank, First Bank, and Mega Bank all issue co-branded EasyCards and provide their customers with a variety of rewards. Our bank's co-branded EasyCard allows you to redeem points for a huge selection of rewards. Plus, our co-branded EasyCard even offers overseas travel and medical insurance, as well as flight inconvenience insurance.

What's better, this card has no annual fee **for the first year and if you spend over 3000 NT dollars per annum or you use this card to purchase up to six times per annum, the annual fee will be waived next year.**

行　　員：是啊。很多銀行都推出悠遊聯名卡。就我所知，中國信託、國泰世華、玉山銀行、第一銀行、兆豐銀行都有推出悠遊聯名卡並給他們的客戶很多回饋。我們銀行的悠遊聯名卡讓您可以從很多回饋中來兌換紅利點數。此外，我們的悠遊聯名卡甚至提供海外旅行醫療保險和航班不便險。**更好的是，這張卡首年免年費，如果您每年消費都超過三千元或是刷卡滿六次以上的話，次年也免年費。**

Customer：So I still have to use this co-branded credit card to make a purchase to be qualified for no annual fee.

客　　戶：所以我必須刷悠遊聯名卡消費才能符合免費的資格。

Bank teller：Yes, but if you really care about the annual fee. I will recommend our bank's combo card to you. Our bank's combo card is a no annual fee credit card if you hold our bank's account. In addition, this combo card also includes Visa PayWave technology.

行　　員：是的，但如果您真的很介意年費的問題的話，我會推薦我們銀行的金融信用卡。如果您在我們銀行有開戶的話，我們的金融信用卡沒有年費的問題，而且這張金融信用卡還有VISA的感應式刷卡技術。

Customer：I still want to apply for a co-branded EasyCard. What do I need to apply for a co-branded EasyCard?

客　　戶：我還是想要辦悠遊聯名卡。我需要什麼文件來辦悠遊聯名卡呢？

Bank teller：**You need to give me a copy of your ID card, the filled out ap-**

plication form, and your proof of income.

行　　員：您要給我您的身分證影本、填好的申請書和您的財力證明。

Customer：What? I don't have a job currently.

客　　戶：什麼？我現在沒有工作耶。

Bank teller：In this case, I am sorry to tell you that you cannot apply for the co-branded EasyCard because you need to present your proof of income.

行　　員：這樣的話，我很遺憾地跟您說，您無法辦悠遊聯名卡，因為您需要提供您的財力證明。

Customer：But I don't have a job now.

客　　戶：但我現在沒工作。

Bank teller：So you cannot apply for this card. Period.

行　　員：所以您無法辦這張卡，就這樣。

Customer：Wait a moment. I am the son of a well-known entrepreneur. Although I don't have a job now, I have a lot of money in my bank account. I possess several certificates of deposit now. Can I present my CDs as proof of income?

客　　戶：等一下。我是一個知名大企業家的兒子。雖然我現在沒有工作，但我在銀行戶頭有很多錢。我現在有很多定存單。我可以出示我的定存單作財力證明嗎？

Bank teller：Of course you can. You should have told me sooner. Now go home and bring your CDs as soon as possible. I will wait for you.

行　　員：當然可以。早點說嘛。現在趕快回家並把您的定存單帶來。我等您。

Customer：Wait! I have other questions for you. Who can apply for your bank's co-branded EasyCard?

客　　戶：等一下，我還有其他的問題要問呢。什麼樣的人可以辦您們銀行的悠遊聯名卡？

Bank teller : To apply, you must be twenty years of age or older, be a Taiwanese resident, have a good credit history, and be able to make regular repayments.

行　　員：要辦卡，您需年滿二十歲以上，是臺灣在地人士，有良好的信用紀錄和能按時還款。

Customer : How will I know the status of my application of the co-branded EasyCard?

客　　戶：我怎麼知道我的悠遊聯名卡的辦卡進度呢？

Bank teller : You can call our credit card center or check it out via Internet banking.

行　　員：您可以打到我們的信用卡中心或是透過網銀來查詢。

Customer : After I apply for your co-branded EasyCard, when will I receive my credit card?

客　　戶：在我申辦了悠遊聯名卡後，我何時可以領到我的卡？

Bank teller : Once you have completed and submitted your application and if you are eligible for a credit card, your co-branded EasyCard will be delivered to you within two weeks from the date all the necessary papers are received.

行　　員：一旦您提交申請完成並核卡有過的話，您的悠遊聯名卡會在所有必要的文件都收齊後的兩週內寄給您。

Customer : OK. By the way, what is a "**balance transfer**"? I often read the term in a newspaper.

客　　戶：好。順便一提，什麼是「餘額代償」？我常在報紙上讀到。

Bank teller : A balance transfer is when you request a balance owing on other bank-issued credit card to be transferred to our bank's credit card, like a co-branded credit card. This enables you to manage your finances in one spot.

行　　　員：餘額代償就是說，當您提出要把別家銀行發行的信用卡的卡債轉移到我們銀行的信用卡，如悠遊聯名卡上。這樣可以讓您能在一處上就管理好您的財務。

Customer：Can I make a bill payment from my co-branded EasyCard?

客　　　戶：我可以用我的悠遊聯名卡來繳費嗎？

Bank teller：Sure. You can apply for a direct debit to make a bill payment from your credit card. A direct debit is an automated payment which comes from your credit card.

行　　　員：當然可以。您可以申辦自動扣繳來從您的信用卡扣款繳費。自動扣繳就是從您的信用卡來自動付款。

Customer：How do I dispute a transaction listed on my credit card statement?

客　　　戶：如果我的信用卡對帳單有爭議帳款的話怎麼辦？

Bank teller：If you find there is an unauthorized transaction shown on your statement, call our credit card center and tell our representatives about the details of the transaction. Our customer representatives will start a dispute investigation and you should note that this process may take several weeks to resolve.

行　　　員：如果您發現有未授權的交易顯示在您的對帳單上的話，請聯絡客服中心並告知我們人員關於交易的細節。我們客服人員會開始一個爭議調查，您應當注意這個過程可能會花數個星期才會解決。

Customer：How much can I withdraw in a cash advance?

客　　　戶：動用預借現金的話，額度是多少？

Bank teller：Your cash advance limit is one-tenth of your credit limit. In others words, your cash advance limit depends on your credit line. If your credit limit is fifty thousand NT dollars, your available cash advance limit will be five thousand NT dollars.

行　　員：您的預借現金額度是您信用額度的十分之一。換句話說，您的預借現金額度取決於您的信用額度。假設您的信用額度是五萬元的話，您的可動用預借現金額度就是五千元。

Customer：How do I increase or decrease my co-branded EasyCard limit?

客　　戶：我如何調高或調降我的悠遊聯名卡的刷卡額度呢？

Bank teller：If your current credit card limit is no longer appropriate for your needs, you can apply for a credit limit increase or request a decrease by calling our credit card center.

行　　員：如果您目前的信用額度不符合您的需求的話，您可以打到信用卡客服中心來申請調高或是要求調降您的信用卡額度。

Customer：What happens after I have reported my co-branded EasyCard as lost or stolen?

客　　戶：我在掛失我的信用卡後，後續會怎麼樣呢？

Bank teller：A temporary card will be sent to you by your card issuer for use while you are overseas.

行　　員：如您人在國外，發卡組織會把一張暫時的替代卡寄給您用。

Customer：Thank you. Now I understand.

客　　戶：謝謝。現在我了解了。

補充單字

◆ co-branded EasyCard [ko`brændɪd `izɪkɑrd] ***n.*** 悠遊聯名卡

◆ annual fee [`ænjuəl fi] ***n.*** 年費

◆ proof of income [pruf ɑv `ɪn͵kʌm] ***n.*** 財力證明

♦ balance transfer [`bæləns træns`fɝ] *n.* 餘額代償

實用金句

♦ In a word, the co-branded EasyCard is a type of credit card but it possesses the functions of an EasyCard.

簡單講，悠遊聯名卡是一種綁有悠遊卡功能的信用卡。

♦ The co-branded EasyCard has more features than an EasyCard. It has the auto-loading function. When your co-branded EasyCard's balance falls below 100 NT dollars, it will then automatically add 500 NT dollars to your card.

悠遊聯名卡比悠遊卡有更多的功能。它具有自動加值的功能。當您的悠遊聯名卡的餘額少於一百元時，就會自動加值五百元到您的卡片。

♦ If you activate the auto-loading function in your EasyCard, you cannot cancel it.

如果您啓用悠遊卡的自動加值功能，您就無法取消了。

♦ What's better, this card has no annual fee for the first year and if you spend over 3000 NT dollars per annum or you use this card to purchase up to six times per annum, the annual fee will be waived next year.

更好的是，這張卡首年免年費，如果您每年消費都超過三千元或是刷卡滿六次以上的話，次年也免年費。

♦ You need to give me a copy of your ID card, the filled out application form, and your proof of income.

您要給我您的身分證影本、填好的申請書和您的財力證明。

感應式信用卡
Contactless Credit Cards

Customer : Hello, I would like to apply for a credit card. Do you have any rec-ommendation?

客　　戶：嗨，我想要辦卡。您可以跟我推薦嗎？

Bank teller : Yes, **I will recommend our newly-issued combo card. It inte-grates a credit card and an ATM card into one card, so this type of card is called a combo card.** Plus, you can choose your combo card to be issued by VISA or MasterCard. What's better, if you choose VISA, it carries the feature of the VISA PayWave. If you choose MasterCard, it has the feature of the MasterCard Pay-Pass.

行　　員：好的，**我推薦您我們新推出的金融信用卡。它整合信用卡和金融卡而合而為一，所以這種卡片叫作金融信用卡。**另外，您能選擇您的金融信用卡是VISA卡或是萬事達發行的。更好的是，如果您選VISA卡的話，它有VISA PayWave的功能。如果您選萬事達，它有萬事達的PayPass功能。

Customer : Sorry. I don't understand what you said. What is the VISA Pay-Wave? And what is the MasterCard PayPass?

客　　戶：抱歉，我不懂您說的。什麼是VISA PayWave？什麼又是萬事達PayPass？

Bank teller : The VISA PayWave and the MasterCard PayPass are actually the same thing that adopts tap and pay technology. Take VISA PayWave for example. If you have never used the VISA PayWave, prepare to be blown away. Let me explain. **VISA PayWave is the latest contactless payment feature, allowing the cardholders to pay for purchases under 3000 NT dollars without swiping, signing, or entering a PIN number at any** participating merchants. In fact, VISA PayWay now has been widely used in credit cards. A lot of banks have added VISA PayWave technology to their unembossed VISA credit cards.

行　　員 : VISA PayWave和萬事達PayPass實際說來是同樣的功能，採用感應式技術。舉VISA PayWave為例，如果您從未使用VISA PayWave，準備好驚喜吧。讓我解釋一下。**VISA PayWave是最新的感應式付款功能，讓持卡者在任何的**特約商店**消費新臺幣三千元以下的金額，不必刷卡、簽名或是輸入密碼。**事實上，VISA PayWave現在已廣泛被用在信用卡上。很多銀行都有把VISA PayWave技術加到無凸字VISA信用卡上。

Customer : So what you mean is, I no longer have to swipe my credit card and sign my name. All I need to do is just wave my card past the portal point and my payment is made automatically.

客　　戶 : 所以您說的是，我不必再刷卡和簽名。我要做的只是把信用卡感應一下刷卡機而我的交易就自動完成了。

Bank teller : Precisely. You are smart. When you use the VISA PayWave, all you have to do is tap or hover your combo card above the terminal and the transaction is processed. When you use the VISA PayWave, you are actually saving a lot of time. Of course, after the transaction is made, you will still receive a receipt for your pur-chase transaction. But you won't be using your signature or a pass-word to verify the sale. What's more, you may also want to know the VISA PayWave credit card can be integrated into your smart phone, thus making it become a portable payment device. You know, mobile payment will become very hot in the near future.

行　　員：沒錯。您真聰明。當您用VISA PayWave，您只要拿您的金融信用卡碰觸或是拂過一下終端機而交易就處理好了。當您使用VISA PayWave，您真的替自己省下很多時間。當然，在交易完成後，您還是會收到您的消費明細。但不必再簽名或輸入密碼來確認交易。更棒的是，您可能也想知道VISA PayWave感應式信用卡也可以整合到您的智慧型手機上，讓它變成一個行動支付的載具。您曉得的，行動支付在不久的將來將會變得很夯。

Customer : Wow. It sounds great. But what if the merchant doesn't accept the VISA PayWave?

客　　戶：哇！聽起來真棒。但如果商家不接受VISA PayWave怎麼辦？

Bank teller : In this case, you can still use your card in the old fashioned way such as swiping, or dipping your card in the terminal to complete the sale as long as VISA is accepted.

行　　員：在這樣的情況之下，只要VISA能被接受的話，您還是可以使用傳統的方法，像是刷卡或把您的卡插入終端機來完成交易。

Customer : How do I use a contactless card?

客　　戶：我如何使用感應式信用卡呢？

Bank teller : When you see "PLEASE TAP A CARD" on the screen of the card reader, you only have to hold your VISA PayWave card just a few centimeters away from the card reader terminal for your card to be accepted. After one or two seconds, the screen of the card reader will show "TRANSACTION COMPLETED". Then you can remove your card. The cashier will hand you your invoice and credit card receipt. Of course, don't forget one point. That is, **if your purchase is less than 3000 NT dollars, you don't need to sign your name. But if the purchase is over 3000 NT dollars, you'll need to sign your name to verify the transaction.**

行　　員：當您在讀卡機看到「請碰觸卡片」時，您只要把您的VISA Pay-Wave感應卡放在離讀卡終端機幾公分的距離讓卡片刷過。在一、兩秒後，讀卡機的螢幕會顯示「交易完成」，然後您就可以把卡片拿走。收銀員會給您發票和信用卡簽單。當然，不要忘記一點，就是**如果您的消費在三千元以下，您才不用簽名，但如果消費超過三千元以上的話，您還是要簽名以核實交易。**

Customer : Earlier on you also mentioned the MasterCard PayPass. Is it also the same thing with the VISA PayWave?

客　　戶：您剛還提到萬事達的PayPass，它跟VISA PayWave是同性質東西嗎？

Bank teller : Yes. MasterCard PayPass is just like the VISA PayWave. But you cannot use the PayPass feature in a VISA participating merchant. You have to find a shop that carries the PayPass logo to use the PayPass card.

行　　員：是的，萬事達PayPass就像VISA PayWave一樣。但您不能在一家VISA特約商店用PayPass的功能，您必須找有PayPass標誌的商家才可以用PayPass的卡。

Customer : But what if my combo card is stolen or lost and then used with PayWave technology to make fraudulent purchases without needing a PIN or a signature?

客　　　戶：但如果我的金融信用卡被偷或是遺失，且因爲不用密碼或是簽名而遭用PayWave功能來盜刷該怎麼辦？

Bank teller：Don't worry. **As long as you can verify that those transactions are fraudulent and you notify our bank immediately concerning the details of the fraud, you will not have to pay for the** fraudulent transactions.

行　　　員：別擔心，只要您能證明這些交易是盜刷且您有立刻通知銀行關於盜刷的細節，您就不必爲盜刷付半毛錢。

Customer：Could I make accidental payments if my combo card is too close to a card reader?

客　　　戶：如果我的金融信用卡離讀卡機太近的話，我可能會不小心刷到卡嗎？

Bank teller：This won't happen because in order for your payment to go through, the merchant needs to enter the amount being charged for your purchase in the first place. Then, the cardholder also needs to hold his card a few centimeters away from the card reader so that the purchase can be completed. This means the cardholder can't accidentally be charged for something he didn't buy only by being too close to a PayWave terminal with his combo card.

行　　　員：這種事不會發生，因爲要讓您的消費完成的話，商家必須先輸入您要交易的金額。然後，持卡者需要把他的卡離讀卡機幾公分遠的地方，交易才會完成。因此這意味著持卡人不會只因爲拿著金融信用卡靠PayWave終端機太近了，而遭意外扣款買下沒有消費的東西。

Customer：OK. But I also want you to tell me an important thing. Is it safe?

客　　戶：好，但我還想您告訴我一件重要的事：它安全嗎？

Bank teller : Of course, it is very safe. A combo card is also a smart card. Smart cards are the latest innovation in credit card security. Using a PayWave or PayPass combo card is a safe way to shop because you don't have to hand over your credit card to the cashier at the counter. It is always safe for you to have your card with you. And if your contactless combo card is lost, just report it lost to your card issuer immediately. Oh, I have one more advantage to add. If you hold a **contactless credit card** with the feature of PayWave or PayPass, you can swipe your card in the airplane even your card is a pre-printed or unembossed card, because most planes have wireless credit card processors now and often have their blacklists updated.

行　　員：當然，它非常安全。金融信用卡也是智慧卡。智慧卡是信用卡安全性最先進的卡。因為您不必把卡片交給櫃檯的結帳人員，用PayWave或是PayPass的金融信用卡是安全的購物方式。卡片不離身總是較安全的。如果您的感應式金融信用卡遺失的話，只要立即向發卡銀行掛失。喔，我還要一個優點要跟您說，即使您的卡是無凸字信用卡，您也可以在飛機上刷有PayWave或PayPass的感應式信用卡，因為大部分的飛機都有無線刷卡機並常更新黑名單。

Customer : Thank you so much.

客　　戶：非常謝謝您。

補充單字

◆ participating merchant [pɑr`tɪsə͵petɪŋ `mɝ·tʃənt] **n.** 特約商店

♦ fraudulent transaction [`frɔdʒələnt træn`zækʃən] **n.** 盜刷交易

♦ contactless credit card [`kɑntækt͵lɪs `krɛdɪt kɑrd] **n.** 感應式信用卡

實用金句

♦ I will recommend our newly-issued combo card. It integrates a credit card and an ATM card into one card, so this type of card is called a combo card.

我推薦您我們新推出的金融信用卡。它整合信用卡和金融卡而合而爲一，所以這種卡片叫作金融信用卡。

♦ VISA PayWave is the latest contactless payment feature, allowing the card-holders to pay for purchases under 3000 NT dollars without swiping, signing, or entering a PIN number at any participating merchants.

VISA PayWave是最新的感應式付款功能，讓持卡者在任何的特約商店消費新臺幣三千元以下的金額，不必刷卡、簽名或是輸入密碼。

♦ If your purchase is less than 3000 NT dollars, you don't need to sign your name. But if the purchase is over 3000 NT dollars, you'll need to sign your name to verify the transaction.

如果您的消費在三千元以下，您才不用簽名，但如果消費超過三千元以上的話，您還是要簽名以核實交易。

♦ As long as you can verify that those transactions are fraudulent and you notify our bank immediately concerning the details of the fraud, you will not have to pay for the fraudulent transactions.

只要您能證明這些交易是盜刷且您有立刻通知銀行關於盜刷的細節，您就不必爲盜刷付半毛錢。

無凸字信用卡
Unembossed Credit Card

Bank teller : What can I do for you today?

行　　員：今天我可以爲您做什麼？

Customer : Well, I would like to apply for a credit card.

客　　戶：嗯，我想要辦張信用卡。

Bank teller : No problem. What kind of credit card do you like?

行　　員：沒問題。您想要辦什麼卡？

Customer : Because of my job, I have to often travel overseas a lot. So, I would like to apply for a kind of credit card that offers a lot of benefits for business travelers.

客　　戶：因爲我工作的緣故，我常需要出國，所以我想要申辦一種爲商務客提供很多優惠的信用卡。

Bank teller : OK. Let me introduce our Business MasterCard to you. **By using this card, you can earn one mile per 30 NT dollars on all purchases to redeem for airline tickets of your choice, and you can also earn up to five miles per 30 NT dollars at partner hotels and restaurants.** You can use your air miles for shopping vouchers, accommodation and entertainment, or donations to charity. It is all up to you. What's better, this card lets you enjoy no mileage cap. **There is no limit to the number of miles you can earn with** our bank's business card. On top of this, you can get a welcome bonus of 3,000 extra points with your first purchase.

行　　員：好的，讓我介紹我們的萬事達商務卡給您。**刷這張卡的話，就可以每次消費刷滿三十元新臺幣就送一哩來兌換您選擇的機票，也可以在特約旅店和餐廳刷滿三十元就送五哩。**您也可以用您的航空哩程來兌換購物禮券、住宿和娛樂或是捐給慈善機構。全都由您決定。更好的是，這張卡沒有哩程數兌換上限。**您刷這張商務卡得到的哩程數是沒有限制的。**而且，您首刷這張卡還可以得到迎新的紅利點數三千點。

Customer : Wait a minute. How do I know how many air miles I have earned?

客　　戶：等一下。我怎麼知道我賺了多少航空哩程數？

Bank teller : **All your air miles collected on this card will be recorded on your monthly credit card statement.**

行　　員：您卡上所有累積的航空哩程數都會在您每月的信用卡對帳單上記載。

Customer : OK. Please go on.

客　　戶：好的，請繼續說。

Bank teller : **If you often go to see a movie, this card is definitely for you because this card lets you buy one movie ticket and get the other ticket free on any day of the week. You can get up to two complimentary tickets a month.**

行　　員：如果您常看電影，這張卡正適合您。因為它讓您在一週內任何一天買電影票買一送一。您每月最多可以換兩張免費電影票。

Customer : That's good. I do like watching a movie. It's a real treat for movie lovers.

客　　戶：這很棒。我是喜歡看電影。這對愛看電影的人來說真是好康。

Bank teller : You can also get complimentary airport limousine departure transfers and complimentary access to airport lounges in key cities around the world. You may as well take a moment to relax in luxury and enjoy a gourmet meal, widescreen TVs plus hot DVDs, and beverage services in the premium lounges.

行　　員：您也可以得到免費的機場接送專車在世界各大城市的機場貴賓休息室的使用權。您不妨在貴賓休息室放鬆休息一下，享受美食、寬螢幕電視再加上熱門的DVD和飲料服務。

Customer : How do I need to do to enjoy this privilege?

客　　戶：我要怎麼做才能享有這些優惠？

Bank teller : **You only have to present this business card and boarding pass to enjoy all.**

行　　員：**您只要出示這張商務卡和登機證就可以享有。**

Customer : Great!

客　　戶：好極了。

Bank teller : What's more, you can get a complete waiver of 2% on fuel surcharge every time you refuel.

行　　員：而且，您每次加油時，還可以得到減免百分之二加油費的優惠。

Customer : Yes!

客　　戶：好啊！

Bank teller : Plus, this card can let you and your loved ones automatically benefit from an extensive travel coverage plan, so no matter which country you go to, you and your loved one will be covered. In addition, you also enjoy complimentary travel and accident insurance coverage of up to 30 million NT dollars for yourself as well as up to one million NT dollars for your spouse and child when you charge your air tickets to your business card. All you have to do is book you and your family's airfare with your business card to get this annual multi-trip policy.

行　　　員：再來，這張卡讓您和您愛的人自動享有完善的旅遊保險方案，不論您去哪一國家，您和您喜歡的人都會獲得保障。此外，當您刷這張商務卡來購買機票時，您還享有免費的旅平險，您個人的最高保額到三千萬，而您的配偶和小孩最高保額到一百萬。您只要用這張商旅卡替您及家人訂機票，您就可以享有每年的多重旅遊保障。

Customer : Great. I am always concerned about the insurance issue. This card is really good.

客　　　戶：好極了，我總是很擔心保險的問題。這張卡真棒。

Bank teller : **You can also earn up to 1% cash back credits on all purchases. Your cash back credits accumulate automatically and appear on your monthly credit card statement.** You won't need to keep track of points in mind.

行　　　員：**您還可以在所有的購物上享有百分之一的現金回饋。您的現金回饋會自動累積並顯示在您每月的信用卡對帳單上。**您不必自己記錄點數。

Customer : Great. This business card sounds so perfect. But what are the drawbacks of this card? Can you tell me?

客　　　戶：好，這張卡聽起來完美極了。那這張卡有什麼缺點？您可以告訴我嗎？

Bank teller : Well. It is an unembossed credit card. Unlike an embossed credit card with raised numbers, the unembossed card possesses a smooth and flat surface. Unembossed credit cards lack the raised numbers, letters, and symbols required for a card imprint, so you cannot use an unembossed credit card to shop at the stores that require a manual imprint at the point of sale.

行　　員：嗯，這是一張無凸字信用卡。不同於有凸字卡號的凸字信用卡，無凸字信用卡有著光滑的平面。無凸字信用卡缺乏凸字卡號、英文字母和標誌來作卡片拓印，所以您無法在需要手動拓印的商家用無凸字信用卡刷卡。

Customer : So what is your point?

客　　戶：您的重點是？

Bank teller : Because an unembossed credit card or debit card needs connection authorization to complete the transaction, you cannot use an unembossed credit card or debit card in an airplane. For the reason of flight security, the airplane forbids connection authorization and only uses a manual imprint at the point of sale.

行　　員：因為無凸字信用卡或是簽帳卡需要連線授權來完成交易，您無法在飛機上使用無凸字信用卡或是簽帳卡。因為飛安的問題，飛機上禁止連線授權而只能用手動拓印的方式。

Customer : OK, thank you. In this case, I have to think twice before I apply for this business card.

客　　戶：好，謝謝您。這樣的話，我在申辦這張商旅卡之前可能要想清楚了。

補充單字

◆ business card [`bɪznɪs kɑrd] **n.** 商務卡

◆ boarding pass [`bordɪŋ pæs] **n.** 登機證

◆ accumulate [ə`kjumjə‚let] **v.** 累積（紅利點數）

◆ unembossed credit card [‚ʌnɪm`bɔsd `krɛdɪt kɑrd] **n.** 無凸字信用卡

◻實用金句◻

- By using this card, you can earn one mile per 30 NT dollars on all purchases to redeem for airline tickets of your choice, and you can also earn up to five miles per 30 NT dollars at partner hotels and restaurants.

  刷這張卡的話，就可以每次消費刷滿三十元新臺幣就送一哩來兌換您選擇的機票，也可以在特約旅店和餐廳刷滿三十元就送五哩。

- There is no limit to the number of miles you can earn with our bank's business card.

  我們的商務卡沒有哩程數兌換上限。

- All your air miles collected on this card will be recorded on your monthly credit card statement.

  您卡上所有累積的航空哩程數都會在您每月的信用卡對帳單上記載。

- If you often go to see a movie, this card is definitely for you because this card lets you buy one movie ticket and get the other ticket free on any day of the week. You can get up to two complimentary tickets a month.

  如果您常看電影，這張卡正適合您。因為它讓您在一週的任何一天買電影票買一送一。您每月最多可以換兩張免費電影票。

- You only have to present this business card and boarding pass to enjoy all.

  您只要出示這張商務卡和登機證就可以享有。

- You can also earn up to 1% cash back credits on all purchases. Your cash back credits accumulate automatically and appear on your monthly credit card statement.

  您還可以在所有的購物上享有百分之一的現金回饋。您的現金回饋會自動累積並顯示在您每月的信用卡對帳單上。

保　險
Insurance

Bank teller : Hello, Sir. Do you always commute to the office by scooter?

行　　員：先生您好，您常騎機車上班嗎？

Customer : Yes. Why do you ask me the question?

客　　戶：對呀，您為什麼問這個？

Bank teller : Because I want to tell you that **you can buy a compulsory motorcycle liability insurance policy over the bank counter.** Plus, if you buy the compulsory motorcycle liability insurance policy from the bank, we will give you a special handbag as a gift.

行　　員：因為我想跟您說，**您可以在銀行櫃檯購買機車強制險**。還有，如果您在銀行買機車強制險，我們還會送您特別的手提袋。

Customer : Do you give any discount?

客　　戶：有打折嗎？

Bank teller : Sorry, **because the bank is the indirect channel, we don't offer any discount.** If you want to get a discount, you can directly go to a property and casualty insurance corporation to buy the compulsory motorcycle liability insurance policy because the property and casualty insurance corporation is the direct channel.

行　　員：抱歉。**因為銀行是間接通路，所以我們沒有任何折扣**。如果您想要有折扣，您可以直接去產險公司買機車強制險，因為產險公司

是直接通路。

Customer : Oh, I see. By the way, I have heard that now people can buy compulsory automobile / motorcycle liability insurance policies through 7-11 ibon vending machines at more than four thousand 7-11 convenience stores nationwide. It is reported that 7-11 also plans to cooperate with other insurance companies and sell more insurance policies, such as fire insurance or travel accident insurance in the future.

客　　戶：喔，我懂了。對了，我聽說現在民眾可以在全國超過四千多家的統一超商透過ibon買汽機車強制險。據報導說，統一超商也計畫未來和其他的保險公司合作來賣更多的保單，像是火險或是旅平險。

Bank teller : Yes, I know. In Taiwan, the insurance companies have cooperated with the convenience stores for several years. For example, **the convenience stores in Taiwan can collect insurance premium for the insurance companies. People can pay their insurance premium at convenience stores.** Of course, some people will still buy insurance policies from their insurance agents because they want someone they can trust to provide service for them. For example, if they have questions concerning the insurance policy, they can call their agents to have their questions answered. But if you buy an insurance policy via ibon vending machines, you don't have any insurance agent or bank teller to provide basic service for you.

行　　員：是，我知道。在臺灣，保險公司已和便利商店合作多年了。例如說，**在臺灣的便利商店可以替保險公司代收保費，民眾可以在便利商店繳保費。** 當然，有些人還是會跟保險業務員買保險，因為

他們想要可以信任的人來爲他們服務。例如說，他們對保單有問題時，他們可以打電話給他們的業務員解決問題。但如果你透過ibon買保單，你沒有任何的業務員或是銀行櫃員來爲你提供基本的服務。

Customer : Yes, I think you are right.

客　　戶：是的，我認爲你是對的。

Bank teller : We also sell deposit insurance policies over the bank counter, but the **Financial Supervisory Commission (FSC)** **forbids bank tellers to sell deposit insurance policies over the counter.** However, you can still buy a deposit insurance policy from **financial consultants** at the bank. Are you interested in deposit insurance? You may want to know the tax exemption of the insurance payment is up to thirty million NT dollars.

行　　員：我們也在銀行賣儲蓄險保單，但金管會**禁止銀行櫃員臨櫃賣儲蓄險保單**。然而你還是可以跟銀行理專買儲蓄險保單。你對儲蓄險有興趣嗎？您可能想知道保險給付三千萬元以下免稅喔。

Customer : No, thanks.

客　　戶：謝謝，不用。

補充單字

◆ compulsory liability insurance [kəm`pʌlsərɪ ˌlaɪə`bɪlətɪ ɪn`ʃʊrəns] **n.** 強制責任險

◆ travel accident insurance [`trævl̩ `æksədənt ɪn`ʃʊrəns] **n.** 旅平險

◆ Financial Supervisory Commission (FSC) [faɪ`nænʃəl ˌsupɚ`vaɪzərɪ kə`mɪʃən] **n.** 金管會

♦ financial consultant [faɪˋnænʃəl kənˋsʌltn̩t] *n.* 理專

實用金句

♦ You can buy a compulsory motorcycle liability insurance policy over the bank counter.

您可以在銀行櫃檯購買機車強制險。

♦ Because the bank is the indirect channel, we don't offer any discount.

因為銀行是間接通路，所以我們沒有任何折扣。

♦ The convenience stores in Taiwan can collect insurance premium for the insurance companies. People can pay their insurance premium at convenience stores.

在臺灣的便利商店可以替保險公司代收保費，民眾可以在便利商店繳保費。

♦ The Financial Supervisory Commission (FSC) forbids bank tellers to sell deposit insurance policies over the counter.

金管會禁止銀行櫃員臨櫃賣儲蓄險保單。

代收代付
Bill Collection and Payment

Bank teller : How are you? What can I do for you?

行　　員：您好嗎？我可以為您辦什麼嗎？

Customer : I want to ask whether I can pay the utility bills at your bank or not.

客　　戶：我想要問我是否可以在您們銀行繳水電費的帳單。

Bank teller : Yes, you can. **Our bank collects the water bill, electric bill, gas bill, telephone bill, labor insurance premium, health insurance premium, national annuity insurance premium, you name it.** Generally speaking, **commercial banks collect all kinds of bills but different banks might collect different bills.** You only have to bring your payment slip and money to our bank and take a number ticket to wait until your number is called by a teller.

行　　員：是的，您可以。**我們銀行有代收水費、電費、瓦斯費、電話費、勞保費、健保費、國民年金等您想得到的費用。**一般說來，商業銀行會代收很多帳單，但不同銀行可能代收不同帳單。您只要把繳費單和錢帶來我們銀行並抽張號碼牌等待行員叫號即可。

Customer : Good. I know not every bank has the service of bill collection and payment.

客　　戶：好。我知道不是每間銀行都有代收代付的服務。

Bank teller : Yes, you are telling me.

行　　員：是的，我知道。

Customer : Oh, by the way, if I pay my utility bill here, does your bank charge me for any handling fee?

客　　戶：喔，對了，如果我在這裡繳水電費，您們銀行會跟我收手續費嗎？

Bank teller : Don't worry. There is no service fee.

行　　員：別擔心，不收手續費。

Customer : That is great.

客　　戶：真棒。

Bank teller : But I have to remind you that **if your bill is overdue, you cannot pay the bill over the bank counter.** You should pay your bills by the due date, or it will become much more troublesome for you to pay your bills. Once you have missed the deadline of your bills, you will have to take the trouble to go to the payment center or its corporation headquarters to pay your bills, which is really time-consuming for most people. **Most banks will refuse to collect utility bills, such as electric, telephone and water bills after their due date.**

行　　員：但我要提醒您如果您的帳單過期，您就無法在銀行櫃檯繳費了。您應該在到期前就繳費，不然您要繳費會比較麻煩。一旦您錯過了繳費截止期，您必須要費工夫到該家公司或其繳費中心親自繳付，這對大數多人來說很花時間。大部分銀行在帳單逾期後，會拒收水電費帳單，像是電費、電話費和水費。

Customer : OK, I see.

客　　戶：好，我明白了。

Bank teller : In addition to paying your utility bills at the bank, you can also pay the utility bill at any 7-11 or Family Mart convenience store in Taiwan. The cashier at the register will scan the bill, stamp an official seal on your copy, and give your receipt back to you. But you have to notice that you can only pay up to 20,000 NT dollars via a convenience store. The same rule also applies to your credit card bill.

行　　員：除了在銀行繳付水電費外，您也可以在全臺的統一超商或是全家便利商店繳費。收銀機的收銀員會掃描您的帳單、在上面蓋上收費章並把收據給您。但您要注意您在便利商店最多只能繳付二萬元的費用。這規定也適用您的信用卡帳單。

Customer : Wow, I don't know it before. If I can pay the utility bills at convenience stores, it will be very convenient for me. You know, I don't have to rush to the bank before 3:30 p.m. and I can pay my bill on weekends.

客　　戶：哇，我以前都不知道這個。如果我能在便利商店繳水電費，對我來說非常方便。您知道的，我不必趕著在三點半之前來銀行，並且我可以在週末繳費。

Bank teller : And let me share a more convenient way with you. That is, **you can pay your utility bills through** automatic debit **as well.** Of course, you have to fill out the application form of direct debit authorization and after that your account will be automatically debited for your utility charge monthly. This way, you don't have to pay your bill at a bank counter or a convenience store. Don't forget that you must make sure you have sufficient funds in your bank account at least one working day prior to the date of the automatic debiting.

行　　員：讓我分享一個更便利的方法。就是您也可以透過自動扣款來付您

的**水電費**。當然，您必須要填寫授權自動扣繳的申請書，之後您的水電費就會每月從您的帳戶自動扣款。這樣您就不必到銀行或是便利商店繳費了。別忘了，您要在自動扣款的前一個工作天就要確定好您在銀行帳戶有足夠的錢供扣款。

Customer：Now I understand. Thank you very much.

客　　戶：現在我了解了，非常謝謝您。

補充單字

♦ collect [kə`lɛkt] **v.** 代收（水電費）；託收（支票）；領取（金融卡）

♦ insurance premium [ɪn`ʃurəns `primɪəm] **n.** 保費

♦ overdue [`ovɚ`dju] **adj.** 逾期的

♦ automatic debit [͵ɔtə`mætɪk `dɛbɪt] **n.** 自動扣繳

實用金句

♦ Our bank collects the water bill, electric bill, gas bill, telephone bill, labor insurance premium, health insurance premium, national annuity insurance premium, you name it.

我們銀行有代收水費、電費、瓦斯費、電話費、勞保費、健保費、國民年金等您想得到的費用。

♦ Commercial banks collect all kinds of bills but different banks might collect different bills.

商業銀行會代收很多帳單，但不同銀行可能代收不同帳單。

♦ If your bill is overdue, you cannot pay the bill over the bank counter.

如果您的帳單過期，您就無法在銀行櫃檯繳費了。

♦ Most banks will refuse to collect utility bills, such as electric, telephone and water bills after their due date.

大部分銀行在帳單逾期後，會拒收水電費帳單，像是電費、電話費和水費。

♦ You can pay your utility bills through automatic debit as well.

您也可以透過自動扣款來付您的水電費。

支　票
Check

Customer : Hello, I received a call from your bank. You said you have an important thing to tell me.

客　　戶：您好，我剛接到一通您們銀行的電話。您說您有重要的事要告訴我。

Bank teller : Yes. Sir, I have bad news to tell you. **Because you have not deposited enough funds in your checking account, your check has bounced.**

行　　員：是的。先生，我有一件壞消息要跟您說。**因為您沒有在您的支存戶頭存進足夠的錢，您的支票跳票了。**

Customer : What?

客　　戶：什麼？

Bank teller : When your friend came to a bank to cash the check you have cut to him, he found that he could not cash your check.

行　　員：當您的朋友來銀行兌現您開出的票時，他發現他無法兌現這張支票。

Customer : Really? I must have forgotten to put enough money into my checking account.

客　　戶：真的嗎？我一定是忘記把足夠的錢存進我的支存戶了。

Bank teller : You should honor your credit. It is not easy to open a checking account in Taiwan. When you try to open an account in Taiwan, local banks in Taiwan will first make inquiry with the Bills Clearing House as to your credit history and standing to make sure you are not a dishonored account holder. **If you have dishonored your checks for three times within one year, you will be classified into a dishonored account holder.** Your name will officially appear on the Refusal of Deal List. You will not be allowed to apply for a checking account with any banks in Taiwan because of your bad record.

行　　員：您應珍惜您的信用。在臺灣開支存戶很不容易。當您在臺灣開立支存戶時，臺灣在地的銀行會先向票據交換所查詢您的信用歷史及名聲來確保您不是拒絕往來戶。**如果您在一年內跳票三次，您將會被列為拒絕往來戶。**您的名字會正式被列為拒絕往來的名單上。而因您的不良紀錄，您將不允許在臺灣的任何銀行開立支存戶。

Customer : I see. Thanks. And I received a check the other day, can I cash this check over the bank counter?

客　　戶：我明白了。謝謝。我前幾天有收到一張支票。我可以臨櫃兌現這張票嗎？

Bank teller : Have you put your signature on this check?

行　　員：您在支票上簽過名了嗎？

Customer : Yes, **I have endorsed this check.** Here you are.

客　　戶：是的，**我已在這張票上背書了。**給您。

Bank teller : Let me see it. Oh, I am sorry, **it is a crossed check so that you cannot cash this check directly. You must first deposit this check into your bank account.**

行　　員：讓我看一下。喔，我很抱歉，**這是張劃線支票，所以您無法直接**
　　　　　兌現。您必須先把這張票存到您的銀行戶頭。

Customer : So what you said is, I need to first deposit this check into my account. Then, I can withdraw the money from my bank account,
right?

客　　戶：所以您指的是，我必須先把這張票存入我的戶頭。然而我才能從
　　　　　戶頭領出這筆錢，對嗎？

Bank teller : Exactly.

行　　員：沒錯。

Customer : How about this one? I have another check. This check is not a
crossed checked. Can I directly cash this check here?

客　　戶：那這張票怎麼樣？我還有另一張支票。這張支票不是劃線支票。
　　　　　我可以在這裡直接兌現嗎？

Bank teller : Let me see it...Well, the answer is still NO. First, this check has
not matured yet. Secondly, this check is not issued by our branch.
Although this check is indeed made by our bank, it is not issued by
our branch. If this check is not issued by our branch, you cannot
cash it directly. After the check matures, you can either go to the
original branch that issued this check to cash the check there or deposit the check into your bank account in our branch.

行　　員：讓我看一下。……嗯，答案還是不行。首先，這張票還沒有到
　　　　　期。再來，這張票不是由我們分行開的。雖然這張票是由我們銀
　　　　　行所發出，但不是我們分行開出的票。如果這張票不是我們分行
　　　　　開的票，您無法直接在我們分行兌現。在這張票到期後，您可以
　　　　　去開出這張票的原分行兌現或是在我們分行把這張票存到戶頭。

Customer : Oh, I see. So do I have to wait for the check to mature? Can't I deposit the check into my account now?

客　　戶：喔，我明白了。所以我一定要等到這張票到期嗎？我不能先把這張支票存到我的帳戶嗎？

Bank teller : Yes, you can. Our branch can accept the endorsed check for collection. After this check matures, the bank will credit your bank account with the amount. Then, you can withdraw the money from your bank account, but **the bank will charge you for the post-dated check collection fee.** If this check is the Taipei local check, the collection fee is five NT dollars. If this check is a non-local check, the collection fee is ten NT dollars.

行　　員：是的，您可以。這張已背書過的支票我們分行可以先幫您做託收。在票到期後，銀行將會把款項匯入您的帳戶。然後，您可以從戶頭把這筆錢領出來，但是**銀行會跟您收**遠期支票**託收手續費**。如果這是臺北本阜的支票的話，託收手續費是五元。如果是外阜票的話，託收手續費是十元。

Customer : OK, I see. By the way, I would like to know if a checking account will bear any interest?

客　　戶：好的，我懂了。順便一提，我想知道支存戶有無計息？

Bank teller : No interest will be payable on a checking account.

行　　員：支存戶不計息喔。

Customer : I see. Thanks.

客　　戶：我明白了。謝謝。

Bank teller : It is my pleasure.

行　　員：不客氣。

補充單字

- bounce [baʊns] *v.* （支票的）跳票
- dishonor [dɪs`ɑnɚ] *v.* 退（票）；拒付（支票）
- dishonored account [dɪs`ɑnɚd ə`kaʊnt] *n.* 拒絕往來戶
- crossed check [krɔst tʃɛk] *n.* 劃線支票；平行線支票
- post-dated check [`post`detɪd tʃɛk] *n.* 遠期支票；尚未到期的支票

實用金句

- Because you have not deposited enough funds in your checking account, your check has bounced.

  因為您沒有在您的支存戶頭存進足夠的錢，您的支票跳票了。

- If you have dishonored your checks for three times within one year, you will be classified into a dishonored account holder.

  如果您在一年內跳票三次，您將會被列為拒絕往來戶。

- I have endorsed this check.

  我已在這張票上背書了

- It is a crossed check so that you cannot cash this check directly. You must first deposit this check into your bank account.

  這是張劃線支票，所以您無法直接兌現。您必須先把這張票存到您的銀行戶頭。

- The bank will charge you for the post-dated check collection fee.

  銀行會跟您收遠期支票託收手續費。

租銀行保管箱
Renting a Safe Deposit Box

Bank teller : Hello, what can I do for you?

行　　員：您好，我可以為您做什麼嗎？

Customer : Does your bank have **safe deposit box** for customers to rent? Can I rent a safe deposit box here?

客　　戶：您們銀行有出租保管箱嗎？我可以在這裡租個保管箱嗎？

Bank teller : Yes, we have this service, but I have to remind you that **not every bank branch provides the safe deposit box service. If you want to know which branch has this service, I suggest you go to our website to check it out.**

行　　員：是的，我們有這項業務，但我得提醒您不是每家分行都有提供出租保管箱的業務。如果您想知道哪家分行有這業務，我建議您到我們的網站去看一下。

Customer : Good. I want to put my personal stuff in a safer place.

客　　戶：很好。我想要把我的私人物品放在一個安全的地方。

Bank teller : May I ask you what kind of stuff you want to put in a safe deposit box? **You can put securities, important papers, gold, jewelry, and so on in a safe deposit box, but you are not allowed to put dangerous stuff, contraband, combustibles, or things easy to decay.**

行　　　員：我可以問一下您要放什麼物品在保管箱嗎？**您可以放**有價證券、重要文件、黃金、珠寶等在保管箱內，但您不能放危險物品、違禁品、易燃物或是容易腐爛的東西。

Customer：No problem. I just want to put some gold in a safe deposit box.

客　　　戶：沒問題。我只是想要把一些黃金放在保管箱內而已。

Bank teller：In this case, it's OK.

行　　　員：這樣的話，是可以的。

Customer：What size does your bank provide?

客　　　戶：您們銀行有提供什麼規格的？

Bank teller：We have many different sizes for you to choose. **Different safe deposit boxes charge differently.** We have three different box sizes that we can rent to you. The yearly rental fee depends on the size of the safe deposit box. Here is the form. Please take a look at it.

行　　　員：我們有很多不同的規格讓您挑。**不同規格的保管箱收費也不同。**我們有三種不同的規格可以承租給您。每年的租金視保管箱的規格而定。這是表格，請看一下。

Type（類型）	size（公分）			本行收費標準 standard	
	長 length	寬 width	高 height	1 year rent 一年期租金	security deposit 保證金
small（小）	56	11	12	1,100	550
medium（中）	56	25	12	1,900	950
large（大）	56	25	25	3,000	1,500

Customer：I would like to choose a medium-sized box. The rent fee is 1,900

NT dollars and the **security deposit** is 950 NT dollars per year, right?

客　　戶：我想要選一個中型的箱子。每年租金一千九百元加上保證金九百五十元，是嗎？

Bank teller：Yes. The total is 2,850 NT dollars. How long do you want to rent it?

行　　員：是的。總費用是兩千八百五十元。您想租多久？

Customer：I want to rent it for one year.

客　　戶：我想要租一年。

Bank teller：Please pass me your two forms of ID. Two forms of ID mean your primary identification and secondary identification. The primary identification is your national ID card, and the secondary identification can be your health IC card or driver's license. You also need to fill out the application form for renting a safe deposit box.

行　　員：請給我您的雙證件。雙證件是指您的主要證件和第二證件。主要證件是您的國民身分證，而第二證件是您的健保卡或駕照。您還需要填租保管箱的申請表。

Customer：No problem…I have filled out the form. Here you are.

客　　戶：沒問題。我已填好單子了。給您。

Bank teller：**You have to pay two-term rental fees and a one-term security deposit to the bank in advance.**

行　　員：**您還要先付兩期的租金和一期的保證金。**

Customer：What do you mean by "one-term"? How long is it?

客　　戶：您說的「一期」是什麼意思？一期是多久？

Bank teller：One term means six months, or half a year.

行　　員：一期就是六個月，或半年。

Customer : OK, I get it. So I have to pay one year rental fees and six-month security deposit to the bank in advance.

客　　戶：好，我明白了。所以我必須先付一年的租金和六個月的保證金給銀行。

Bank teller : Yes, please give me 2,850 NT dollars in cash. Or, do you want the bank to deduct it from your bank account?

行　　員：是的，請給我兩千八百五十元的現金。或是您想要銀行從您的銀行戶頭直接扣款？

Customer : I want to pay in cash. Here you are.

客　　戶：我想要付現。給您。

Bank teller : OK, here is your key. **Every safe deposit box has two keys for two locks. The first key is for the renter and the other key is kept by the bank. However, the second key kept by the bank must be sealed by the renter and a bank teller together to ensure the safety of your box.**

行　　員：好，這是您的鑰匙。**每個保管箱都有兩把鑰匙用來開兩把鎖。第一把鑰匙是給租箱人的，另一把是由銀行保管。不過，第二把銀行保管的鑰匙必須由租箱人和行員共同加封來確保您保管箱的安全。**

Customer : OK. If I need to open my safe deposit box, what do I need to do?

客　　戶：好，如果我要開保管箱時，我需要怎麼做？

Bank teller : You have to bring your original specimen seal as well as the key and you need to fill out the box opening record card. After a bank teller verifies your personal seal, he will accompany you to use the other key to open the box with you. But after that, the bank teller will leave. Whether you want to deposit other valuable stuff or take out your belongings is not the bank's business. After your rental contract matures, you must return your key to the bank. Plus, you are forbidden to copy the key to the safe deposit box.

行　　員：您必須帶您的原留印鑑和鑰匙來，還要填寫開箱紀錄卡。在行員驗完章後，他會陪同您用第二把鑰匙來會同您開箱。但開箱之後，行員會離開。不論您是否要存別的貴重物品或是取出內容物就與銀行無關了。在您的租約到期後，您必須把鑰匙還給銀行。另外，承租人不得自行複製保管箱的鑰匙。

Customer : What if I lost the key?

客　　戶：如果我遺失鑰匙的話呢？

Bank teller : If you lose your key, you must report to the bank immediately and the bank will charge you 600 NT dollars for replacing the key. Therefore, please keep your key safe.

行　　員：如果您遺失鑰匙的話，您必須立即告知銀行而銀行補發鑰匙會跟您收六百元手續費。因此，請妥善保管您的鑰匙。

Customer : Thanks. Oh, one more thing. After the lease term matures, will the bank return the security deposit to me?

客　　戶：謝謝。喔，還有一件事。如果租約到期的話，銀行會還我保證金嗎？

Bank teller : Of course. **The bank will return you the security deposit without any interest after you terminate the lease and show the bank the original security deposit receipt.** And after your lease matures, you have to go to bank to terminate the contract, take out your belongings and return the key; otherwise, the bank will charge you for an overdue rent fee along with a penalty fee.

行　　員：當然會。**在您辦理退租、向銀行出示原來的保證金收據之後，銀**

行會無息退還您保證金。在您的租約到期之後，您必須去銀行辦理退租，把您的物品帶走和歸還鑰匙。不然的話，銀行會跟您收逾期租金費用和罰金。

Customer ：I see. Thank you very much.

客　　戶：我明白了。非常謝謝您。

補充單字

◆ safe deposit box [sef dɪˋpɑzɪt bɑks] **n.** 保管箱

◆ securities [sɪˋkjurətɪz] **n.** 有價證券

◆ contraband [ˋkɑntrəˌbænd] **n.** 違禁品

◆ combustible [kəmˋbʌstəbl̩] **n.** 易燃物

◆ security deposit [sɪˋkjurətɪ dɪˋpɑzɪt] **n.** （租用保管箱的）保證金

實用金句

◆ Not every bank branch provides the safe deposit box service. If you want to know which branch has this service, I suggest you go to our website to check it out.

不是每家分行都有提供出租保管箱的業務。如果您想知道哪家分行有這業務，我建議您到我們的網站去看一下。

◆ You can put securities, important papers, gold, jewelry, and so on in a safe deposit box, but you are not allowed to put dangerous stuff, contraband, combustibles, or things easy to decay.

您可以放有價證券、重要文件、黃金、珠寶等在保管箱內，但您不能放危險物品、違禁品、易燃物或是容易腐爛的東西。

♦ Different safe deposit boxes charge differently.

不同規格的保管箱收費也不同。

♦ You have to pay two-term rental fees and a one-term security deposit to the bank in advance.

您還要先付兩期的租金和一期的保證金。

♦ Every safe deposit box has two keys for two locks. The first key is for the renter and the other key is kept by the bank. However, the second key kept by the bank must be sealed by the renter and a bank teller together to ensure the safety of your box.

每個保管箱都有兩把鑰匙用來開兩把鎖。第一把鑰匙是給租箱人的,另一把是由銀行保管。不過,第二把銀行保管的鑰匙必須由租箱人和行員共同加封來確保您保管箱的安全。

♦ The bank will return you the security deposit without any interest after you terminate the lease and show the bank the original security deposit receipt.

在您辦理退租、向銀行出示原來的保證金收據之後,銀行會無息退還您保證金。

銀行營業時間
Banking Hours

Customer : Hello, I would like to make a transfer now.

客　　戶：您好，我現在想要匯款。

Bank teller : Sorry, **it is 3:45 p.m., and it is already past cut-off time.** So, I am sorry that I cannot help you anymore. Please come earlier next time.

行　　員：抱歉，**現在是下午三點四十五分了，已經過了交易截止時間。所以，我很抱歉，我無法幫上忙。下次請早點來。**

Customer : What? Is it already cut-off time? But the cut-off time of Chinatrust is 5:00 p.m.. You should suggest to your general manager that your bank's opening hours should be extended to 5:00 p.m. instead of 3:30 p.m.. Did you get it?

客　　戶：什麼？已經是截止時間了？但是中國信託的截止時間是下午五點。您應該建議您們總經理您們的營業時間應延長到下午五點而不是三點半。您懂我的意思嗎？

Bank teller : Well, I believe different banks have different rules.

行　　員：這個嘛，我相信不同的銀行有不同的規定。

Customer : Stop arguing with me. Let me tell you, except Chinatrust, Taishin Bank's cut-off time is also 5:00 p.m.. Far Eastern International Bank also follows suit, so its opening hours are also from 9:00 a.m.

to 5:00 p.m.. On top of this, Union Bank of Taiwan starts at 8:30 a.m. and closes at 5:00 p.m.. **Cathay United Bank's Business Department and flagship branches used to extend their cut-off time to 7:00 p.m..**

客　　戶：不要和我辯了。讓我告訴您，除了中國信託，台新銀行的截止時間也是到下午五點。遠東銀行也已跟進，所以它的營業時間是從早上九點到下午五點。除此之外，聯邦銀行早上八點三十就開門，到下午五點打烊。**國泰世華的營業部和旗艦分行以前曾延長營業時間到晚上七點。**

Bank teller : I understand. It seems that you know a lot about banks. Do you also work at a bank now?

行　　員：我了解。您似乎懂很多銀行的事。您現在也在銀行工作嗎？

Customer : No, I know a lot about banks because I am interested in banks.

客　　戶：不，我知道很多銀行的事是因為我對銀行有興趣。

Bank teller : Wow, you are a banking expert. Can you tell me more about the opening hours of other banks?

行　　員：哇，您是個銀行專家。您可以告訴我更多其他銀行的營業時間嗎？

Customer : Yes, I can. Do you know some bank branches are also open on weekends or on national holidays?

客　　戶：好的，我可以。您知道有些銀行的分行在週末或是國定假日也營業嗎？

Bank teller : No, I don't know. Please tell me about it.

行　　員：不，我不知道。請跟我說。

Customer : OK. Two branches of E. Sun Bank, Shihlin Branch and Yong-an Branch, used to open from 9:00 a.m. to 1:30 p.m. on Saturday.

Standard Chartered International Commercial Bank's Tianmu Branch is also open at 11:00 a.m. to 4:00 p.m. on weekends. Furthermore, Standard Chartered International Commercial Bank's No.88 Branch is open from 9:00 a.m. to 9:30 p.m. on working days and open from 11:00 a.m. to 9:30 p.m. on weekends. Plus, it is also open from 12:00 p.m. to 5:00 p.m. on national holidays. On the other hand, Taipei Fubon Bank's Taipei 101 Branch is also open from 11:00 a.m. to 7:00 p.m. on weekends.

客　　戶：好，玉山銀行的兩個分行，士林分行和永安分行以前的營業時間在週六的早上九點到下午一點半。渣打國際商銀的天母分行在週末的早上十一點到下午四點也營業。此外，渣打的八八分行的平時營業時間是上午九點到晚上九點半，週末的營業時間是早上十一點到晚上九點半。此外，在國定假日時，它也在中午十二點開門，到下午五點打烊。另一方面，台北富邦的101分行也在週末的上午十一點到晚上七點營業。

Bank teller : I see. I think Taipei Fubon Bank's Taipei 101 Branch's opening hours follows Taipei 101. This way, when potential customers go to Taipei 101 for shopping, they may also enter into Taipei Fubon Bank to check it out.

行　　員：我了解了。我想台北富邦的101分行的營業時間跟臺北101一樣。這樣當潛在客戶去臺北101血拼時，他們也有可能進入台北富邦銀行去看一看。

Customer : Yes, it makes sense. **Now government-controled banks (national banks) also let two branches extend its opening hours to 5:00 p.m..** Take Mega Bank's Cheng-Chung Branch for example, Cheng-Chung Branch is open at 9:00 a.m. and close at 5:00 p.m..

So as you can see, more and more banks in Taiwan start to extend its opening hours.

客　　戶：是的，這說得通。**現在公股銀行（官方銀行）也讓兩家分行的營業時間延長到下午五點。**舉兆豐銀行的城中分行為例，城中分行是早上九點打烊，下午五點打烊。所以如您如見，在臺灣愈來愈多的銀行開始延長營業時間了。

Bank teller : Well, you made your point. However, you must also admit some banks also cancel its policy of extending opening hours. For instance, Chinatrust originally closed at 7:00 p.m. but it found out after 5:00 p.m., only a few people came to bank branches, so it changed its cut-off time to 5:00 p.m.. Cosmos Bank's some of its branches also used to close at 5:00 p.m. but it has changed back to 3:30 p.m. now. Therefore, I don't think all the banks benefit from its extended opening hours because it will cost banks more such as human cost and utility bills. **You cannot deny that most banks in Taiwan still close at 3:30 p.m..**

行　　員：嗯，您說的是有些道理。不過，您也必須承認有些銀行也取消了延長營業時間的政策。舉例來說，中國信託以前營業時間到晚上七點，但它發現在下午五點之後，很少人到分行，所以它變更截止時間到下午五點。萬泰銀行的部分分行以前也是營業到下午五點，但它現在已改回下午三點半了。因此，我不認為所有的銀行都從延長營業時間受益，因為會增加銀行成本，像是人力成本和水電費。**您無法否認臺灣的大多數銀行營業時間仍至下午三點半為止。**

Customer : Well, I think what you said is also right. I am glad talking with you.

客　　戶：嗯，我想您說得也對。很高興和您談話。

補充單字

◆ cut-off time [kʌt ɔf taɪm] *n.* （辦理交易的）截止時間

◆ flagship branch [`flæɡ͵ʃɪp bræntʃ] *n.* 旗艦分行

實用金句

◆ It is 3:45 p.m, and it is already past cut-off time.

現在是下午三點四十五分了，已經過了交易截止時間。

◆ Cathay United Bank's Business Department and flagship branches used to extend their cut-off time to 7:00 p.m..

國泰世華的營業部和旗艦分行以前曾延長營業時間到晚上七點。

◆ Now government-controled banks (national banks) also let two branches extend its opening hours to 5:00 p.m..

現在公股銀行（官方銀行）也讓兩家分行的營業時間延長到下午五點。

◆ You cannot deny that most banks in Taiwan still close at 3:30 p.m..

您無法否認臺灣的大多數銀行營業時間仍至下午三點半為止。

附　錄

附錄一：銀行合併簡史

90年12月	《寶島銀行》更名為《日盛銀行》。 Baodao Bank changed its name into Jih Sun International Bank.
91年2月	《台新銀行》合併《大安銀行》。 Taishin International Bank merged Dan-an Bank
91年7月	《匯通銀行》更名為《國泰銀行》。 United National Bank changed its name into Cathay Commercial Bank.
91年10月	《亞太銀行》更名為《復華銀行》。 Asia Pacific Bank changed its name to Fuhwa Commercial Bank.
92年10月	《世華銀行》合併《國泰銀行》更名為《國泰世華銀行》。 United World Chinese Bank merged Cathay Commercial Bank and changed its name into Cathay United Bank.
92年12月	《中國信託》合併《萬通銀行》。 Chinatrust merged Grand Commercial Bank.
93年4月	《泛亞銀行》更名為《寶華銀行》。 Pan Asia Bank changed its name into Bowa Bank.
94年1月	《臺北銀行》合併《富邦銀行》並更名為《台北富邦》。 Taipei Bank merged Fubon Bank and changed its name to Taipei Fubon Commercial Bank.
94年3月	《聯邦銀行》合併《中興銀行》。 Union Bank of Taiwan merged Chung Shing Bank
94年11月	《陽信銀行》合併《高新商業銀行》。 Kao-Shin Commercial Bank is merged by Sunny Bank.

94年12月	《誠泰銀行》合併《台灣新光銀行》，並更名為《台灣新光銀行》。 Macoto Bank merged Taiwan Shin Kong Commercial Bank and changed its name into Taiwan Shin Kong Commercial Bank.
95年5月	《中國農民銀行》併入《合作金庫銀行》。 The Farmers Bank of China is merged into Taiwan Cooperative Bank.
95年8月	《交通銀行》與《中國國際商銀》合併，並更名為《兆豐國際商業銀行》。 The International Commercial Bank of China merged Chiao Tung Bank and changed its name into Mega Commercial Bank.
95年11月	《建華銀行》合併《臺北國際商業銀行》，並更名為《永豐銀行》。 Bank SinoPac merged International Bank of Taipei and changed its name into Bank SinoPac.
96年1月	《第七商業銀行》併入《國泰世華銀行》。 Lucky Bank is merged into Cathay United Bank.
96年6月	《渣打銀行》與《新竹國際商業銀行》合併更名為《渣打國際商業銀行》。 Standard Chartered Bank merged Hsinchu International Bank and changed its name to Standard Chartered International Bank.
96年7月	《中央信託局》併入《臺灣銀行》。 Central Trust of China is merged into Bank of Taiwan.
96年9月	《復華商業銀行》更名為《元大商業銀行》。 Fuhwa Commercial Bank changed its name to Yuanta Commercial Bank.

96年12月	《花旗（臺灣）商業銀行》接管《華僑商業銀行》。 **Bank of Overseas Chinese is taken over by Citibank.**
97年3月	《匯豐銀行》接管《中華商業銀行》。 **HSBC took over The Chinese Bank.**
97年5月	《星展銀行》接管《寶華商業銀行》。 **DBS took over Bowa Bank.**
98年1月	《稻江商業銀行》更名為《大台北商業銀行》。 **First Capital Commercial Bank changed its name to Bank Taipei.**
99年2月	《元大商業銀行》承受《慶豐商業銀行》18家分行資產、負債及營業。 **18 branches of Chinfon Bank are taken over by Yuanta Commercial Bank.**
99年4月	《遠東國際商業銀行》承受《慶豐商業銀行》19家分行資產、負債及營業。 **Far Eastern International Bank took over 19 branches of Chinfon Bank.**
102年10月	因被台北富邦以「名稱混淆」控告，《大台北銀行》在敗訴後更名為《瑞興商業銀行》。 **Bank of Taipei changed its Chinese name.**
104年1月	《萬泰銀行》因被併入開發金控而更名為《凱基銀行》。 **Cosmos Bank changed its name into KGI Bank.**

附錄二：常用銀行代號

004	臺灣銀行	101	瑞興銀行
005	土地銀行	102	華泰銀行
006	合庫商銀	103	臺灣新光商銀
007	第一銀行	104	台北五信
008	華南銀行	106	台北九信
009	彰化銀行	108	陽信銀行
011	上海銀行	118	板信銀行
012	台北富邦	119	淡水一信
013	國泰世華	120	淡水信合社
016	高雄銀行	147	三信銀行
017	兆豐商銀	700	中華郵政
018	農業金庫	803	聯邦銀行
021	花旗（臺灣）銀行	805	遠東銀行
022	美國銀行	806	元大銀行
025	首都銀行	807	永豐銀行
039	澳盛銀行	808	玉山銀行
040	中華開發	809	凱基銀行
050	臺灣企銀	810	星展（臺灣）銀行
052	渣打商銀	812	台新銀行
053	台中商銀	814	大眾銀行

054	京城商銀	**815**	日盛銀行
072	德意志銀行	**816**	安泰銀行
081	匯豐（臺灣）銀行	**822**	中國信託

附錄三：各銀行延長營業時間一覽表

中國信託	所有分行 週一到週五 09:00～17:00
台新銀行	所有分行 週一到週五 09:00～17:00
聯邦銀行	所有分行 週一到週五 08:30～17:00 部分分行 週六 09:00～13:00
聯邦銀行	微風簡易型分行：週一至週日11:00～20:30
日盛銀行	所有分行 週一至週五 09:00～16:00
元大銀行	士林／大同／南京東路／館前／永和分行 週一到週五 09:00～17:00
新光銀行	敦南分行 週一到週五 09:00～20:00
萬泰銀行	部分分行 週一到週五 09:00～17:00（已取消延時，現改回3:30）
玉山銀行	永安分行和士林分行 週六 09:00～13:30（已取消延時）
遠東銀行	所有分行 週一到週五 09:00～17:00
台北富邦	臺北101分行 週一至週五 9:00～19:00 臺北101分行 週六及週日 11:00～19:00
國泰世華	總行營業部和三家「旗艦分行」（建國分行、篤行分行、四維分行）週一到週五 09:00～19:00（已取消延時）
渣打銀行	八八分行 週一至週五 9:00～21:30 週末 11:00～21:30 八八分行 國定假日 12:00～17:00
渣打銀行	天母分行 週一至週五 9:00～15:30 週末 11:00～16:00
臺灣銀行	桃園機場分行 出境 5:30～21:20；入境 全天24小時

臺灣銀行	小港機場分行 出境 5:30～17:00 入境 週一到週五 9:00～24:00；例假日 12:00～24:00
臺灣銀行	館前分行 / 三民分行 週一至週五 09:00～17:00
土地銀行	忠孝分行 / 中港分行 週一至週五 09:00～17:00
合作金庫	西門分行 / 台中分行 週一至週五 09:00～17:00
兆豐商銀	城中分行 / 北台中分行 週一至週五 09:00～17:00
第一銀行	光復分行 / 基隆分行 週一至週五 09:00～17:00
華南銀行	忠孝東路分行 / 北高雄分行 週一至週五 09:00～17:00
彰化銀行	光隆分行 / 建興分行 週一至週五 09:00～17:00
臺灣企銀	南京東路分行 / 西屯分行 週一至週五 09:00～17:00

附錄四：臺灣金融機構統計（分行數）

銀行名稱	分行數	銀行名稱	分行數
合作金庫	271	台新銀行	98
第一銀行	189	聯邦銀行	89
華南銀行	185	元大銀行	87
彰化銀行	184	渣打銀行	86
國泰世華	164	台中銀行	79
臺灣銀行	163	上海銀行	68
土地銀行	151	大眾銀行	66
中國信託	146	板信銀行	63
玉山銀行	135	京城銀行	63
永豐銀行	128	花旗銀行	59
台北富邦	124	遠東銀行	55
臺灣企銀	124	安泰銀行	52
兆豐銀行	107	凱基銀行	48
新光銀行	104	星展銀行	42
陽信銀行	100	HSBC	41

附錄五：外匯英文補強祕笈

公式① The exchange rate (now) is ＋A幣別＋ against / to / for / per ＋ B幣別.

（現在的匯率是A幣別兌B幣別。）

例：The exchange rate now is 30.2 New Taiwan dollars against one US dollar.

＝ The exchange rate now is 30.2 New Taiwan dollars to one US dollar.

＝ The exchange rate now is 30.2 New Taiwan dollars for one US dollar.

＝ The exchange rate now is 30.2 New Taiwan dollars per US dollar.

＝ One US dollar to 30.2 New Taiwan dollars.

（現在的匯率是30.2元新臺幣兌1美元。）

=>注意，上面的30點2的「點」在英文發音念作point。如果覺得這句話太長而背不起來的話，其實也可以直接說： One US dollar to thirty point two New Taiwan dollars.

公式② One ＋外幣 ＋ makes ＋ 多少金額 ＋ NT dollars.

（某一元的外幣可以兌換成～新臺幣。）

例：One US dollar makes 30.2 New Taiwan dollars.

＝ The exchange rate is 30.2 New Taiwan dollars to one US dollar.

（現在的匯率是30.2元新臺幣兌1美元。）

One euro makes thirty-six NT dollars.

（1歐元可兌換成36元新臺幣。）

公式③ 各種匯率的正確表示法。

即期買進匯率：spot buying rate	現鈔買進匯率：cash buying rate
即期賣出匯率：spot selling rate	現鈔賣出匯率：cash selling rate

=>當然，如果要特別指出是the buying / buy rate（買進價）或是the selling / sell rate（賣出價）的話，可以在rate前面加上buying / buy或selling / sell，例：The buying rate is thirty point two New Taiwan dollars to one US dollar now.（買進價現在是30.2元新臺幣兌1美元。）

如果還要強調這是「現鈔買進匯率」，可以這樣講The cash buying rate。注意，坊間其他的金融英語書籍都把「現鈔買進匯率」錯誤地譯成the buying rate for notes，其實是the cash buying rate才是「現鈔買進匯率」的道地講法。如果是「即期買進匯率」則可以說成the spot buying rate。當然我們知道「即期匯率」（the spot rate）本身就是銀行專有名詞，一般客人也聽不懂。因此另外一個比較好懂的說法就是non-cash rate（非現鈔匯率；即期匯率）。因為不是現鈔匯率的話，那就一定是即期匯率，所以用non-cash rate也可以表示「即期匯率」。如果要跟外國人說明「即期匯率是在銀行戶頭做買賣」可以這樣說For the non-cash rates, you buy or sell foreign currency on your foreign exchange account.

公式④　You can change / convert + A幣別+ into / to + B幣別.
　　　　（您可將A幣別換成B幣別。）

例：You can change 100 British pounds into 5,500 New Taiwan dollars.
　　= You can convert 100 British pounds to 5,500 New Taiwan dollars.
　　　　（您的一百英鎊可以兌換五千五百元新臺幣。）

公式⑤　There is a +手續費金額 + fee added on charge.
　　　　= The service fee / the service charge is +手續費金額.
　　　　（要收多少元的手續費。）

例：There is a one hundred New Taiwan dollars fee added on charge.
　　= The service charge is one hundred New Taiwan dollars.

（要收一百元的手續費。）

公式⑥　I want to exchange / change ＋ 金額.
　　　　（我要換多少錢。）

例：I want to exchange five hundred Euros.
　　（我要兌換五百元歐元。）

=>上面的change和exchange的不同點在於，change是「換掉」而exchange是「交換」，但在口語上，因為exchange發音比較麻煩，用change表示「兌換」外幣也可以。

公式⑦　Our bank only exchanges ＋ 幣別 / 現鈔.
　　　　（我們銀行只能兌換…。）

例：Our bank only exchanges US dollars and Euros.
　　（我們銀行只能兌換美金和歐元。）

　　Our bank only exchanges banknotes. We don't accept foreign coins.
　　（我們銀行只能兌換鈔票，不接受硬幣。）

公式⑧　匯率變動和敲價的表現法。

如果要提醒銀行現在給外國人看的匯率時常變動時，可以說The exchange rates are merely for information purposes only. Foreign exchange rates are subject to change at a moment's notice.

然後，行員要提醒外國人只有當正式敲價時，匯率才會確定時，可以這樣說：
Rates can only be guaranteed at the time the purchase or sale is conducted.

附錄六：銀行代碼記憶方法

004	臺灣銀行	臺灣銀行一直For (four) you. （臺銀總是「為你」設想。）
005	土地銀行	「無」(5) 土地，就「無」家產。
006	合庫商銀	六(6)「合」彩
007	第一銀行	007是英國特務第一高手。
009	彰化銀行	從臺北去彰化要很「久」(9)
013	國泰世華	一閃(13)一閃(13)亮晶晶
017	兆豐商銀	背號17號的林來「瘋」（豐）
054	京城商銀	『五四』運動
808	玉山銀行	爸爸(88) 爬玉山
809	萬泰銀行	保齡球 (809)
812	台新銀行	爸厲害(812)
822	中國信託	822＝爸愛愛（兒女）

附錄七：臺灣各銀行VIP門檻

臺灣銀行	VIP：300萬元；150萬元可請理專以投資往來狀況以個案申請。
土地銀行	AAA級優惠貴賓戶：3000萬元以上 AA級優惠貴賓戶：1000萬元～3000萬元 A級優惠貴賓戶：300萬元～1000萬元
華南銀行	皇冠會員：鑽石會員持有「VISA無限卡」升等為皇冠會員。 鑽石會員：採『邀請制』，門檻不定，大約為1500萬以上。 VIP：300萬，或是100萬元以上經評估有潛力之客戶。
第一銀行	VIP：300萬以上。
合作金庫	白金貴賓戶：1000萬以上 一般貴賓戶：300～1000萬 潛力貴賓戶：300萬以下，但經主管放行認可
臺灣企銀	VIP：200萬
國泰世華	私人銀行（法人／企金戶）：5000萬 鑽石VIP：3000萬以上（私人銀行） 白金VIP：300～1000萬 黃金VIP：300萬
台北富邦	白金理財VIP：150萬元
新光銀行	VIP：150萬
花旗銀行	私人銀行（Private Banking）：3000萬以上 Citigold：300萬元
澳盛銀行	Signature優先理財帳戶：300萬

渣打銀行	優先理財Priority Banking：300萬元 創智理財Preferred Banking：100萬元
匯豐銀行	私人銀行：100萬美元（約3000萬） 卓越理財Premier：300萬元 運籌理財Advance：50萬～300萬
華泰銀行	VIP：300萬元
上海銀行	第一類VIP：300萬 第二類VIP：100萬～300萬
大眾銀行	VIP：100萬元
玉山銀行	VIP：100萬
安泰銀行	尊寵理財會員：800萬元以上 尊榮理財會員：300萬元～800萬元 尊貴理財會員：100萬元～300萬元
日盛銀行	VIP：100萬
聯邦銀行	VIP：200萬元
永豐銀行	豐御理財客戶：1500萬元以上 豐盈理財客戶：300萬元～1500萬 豐收理財客戶：100萬元～300萬元
遠東銀行	VIP：200萬
萬泰銀行	VIP貴賓客戶：300萬元以上 VTP優質客戶：100萬元～300萬元
星展銀行	豐盛理財VIP：400萬元以上〔I級〕 豐盛理財VIP：200萬元以上～400萬元〔II級〕

台新銀行	金鑽會員：3000萬以上（私人銀行） 千萬會員：1000～3000萬 尊爵會員：300～1000萬 富裕會員：100～300萬
中國信託	傳富家：3000萬以上（私人銀行） 鼎富家：1500萬元～3000萬 首富家：300萬元～1500萬元 創富家：50萬元～300萬元

以上資料僅供參考，實際資料請依據各銀行的揭露資訊。

附錄八：文法大補帖

文法① 要說The bank或A bank？

什麼時候用the還是用a？如果抓不到語感，我建議可以用that來試驗。既然the是指「特定的」人事物的代名詞，所以和that一樣，當你在talk in English或寫作時，不確定可不可以放the時，可以先代入that來實驗一下。如果念起來語感不對，就不是用the，而是用a。

例：假如一個銀行員想向主管報告說，剛剛有一個有錢人來開戶。

　　她說的是，A rich man just opened ＿＿＿＿＿ bank account.

　　空格中應該放a還是the？可以先放that來試試語感。

　　＝ A rich man just opened that bank account.

　　中文就是「有一個有錢人剛剛來銀行開了那個帳戶。」

念起來有沒有覺得怪怪的？因為中文講「那個」時，代表說話者和聽話者都知道「那一個」是哪一個。問題是，銀行員報告時，銀行主管根本不知道有沒有人來開戶，也不知道開戶的人是誰，直到行員向他報告時，他才知道有一個有錢人來開戶。因此用that不合理，所以當然也不用the，這時就要用a，正確的句子是：

A rich man just opened a bank account.

判斷的重點在於，「對方（聽者）知道我在說哪一個東西嗎？」若對方不知道，是你第一次提到，就說a或an，不能直接用the。不過俗語說得好，凡規則必有例外。有些生活中常說的「機構名稱」，特別是在指「金融機構」時，老美習慣上都要用 the這個冠詞，如the bank, the post office和the Internet。

例：Joseph just went to the bank.

　　（剛剛約瑟去了銀行。）

上面即使聽者不知道是哪一家銀行，還是說the bank而不是a bank。因此中文翻譯時，不要翻成「剛剛約翰去了那間銀行。」因為雖然the bank前面有the，但在這裡只是習慣加上the，而非指「特定的」銀行。

筆者認為也不必死背，因為the bank或the post office都有很強的「功能性」的隱含意思在，例如銀行就是提供金融服務，如存提款、轉帳的場所，而郵局就是寄信、寄掛號、寄包裹等的場所，即使聽者第一次聽到the bank，也知道bank的「功用」就是處理金融交易的地方，心裡早已知曉bank的屬性和功用，因此前面就不用加a，而固定和the這個表示限定的、特定的冠詞來搭配。

文法② 在行動銀行上轉帳要用on或in？

在網路上找資料，當中的「在」網路上、上網要用on the Internet或是in the Internet？「在」行動銀行轉帳，要用on the Internet banking app或是in the Internet banking app？在手機上玩遊戲，要用in the cellphone或是on the cellphone？或是在電腦上看了一個銀行廣宣的影片，要用in the computer或on the computer？

筆者在這裡提供個人獨創的英文文法邏輯：就是介系詞要用什麼？不妨可以用「平台」這個觀念來想，在網路或手機上辦金融交易。「網路」、「電腦」、「電視」、「手機」等可以看作是一個「平台」，在這平台上提供各式各樣的金融資訊或金融交易的處理，透過這個「平台」我們可以看銀行廣告的影片、查匯率、或和線上客服溝通等。既然是「平台」，而我們「在平台上」就要用on（在～之上）而不是in（在～裡面）。

因此要說I transfer funds on the Internet banking app.

例：I subscribed to the fund on Fubon e-banking app.

（我在富邦行動銀行上申購了一檔基金。）

I saw a bank commercial on TV.

（我在電視上看了一個銀行廣告。）

I checked my balance on Bank of Taiwan app.

（我在臺灣銀行的app查詢了我的餘額。）

I transferred my money to my wife on the Internet.

（我在網路上轉帳給我妻子。）

I checked the foreign exchange rate on my smart phone.

（我在智慧手機上查了一下外匯匯率。）

其實用中文來思考也是差不多，我們說「上網」或「掛在線上」而不說「在網路裡」。

我整理成下面公式：「表示平台」相關的媒介，如TV或手機，要用on。

on TV / on the computer

on the Internet / on the site / online

on the smartphone / on the cell phone

on the iPad / on the iPhone / on the Android phone。

iPhone是手機的一種，所以也是用on。而平板iPad也是一種「平台」，所以也是用on，基本上，有「螢幕」的3C產品，作為「平台之用來處理銀行交易、查看資料等」，都是用on。

例：I taught my friend how to take a screenshot on his Android device.

（我教我朋友如何在安卓裝置上截取螢幕畫面。）

另外，在網路上看影片的那些網站，也是「平台」的概念，所以也用on。

像是I watched an awesome movie on YouTube / Tudou.

就如同不管是用哪一種手機，蘋果、三星、華為、小米、華碩或是hTC都是用on，所以不管是在「哪種網站」也都是用on。而像最近很紅的app（手機應用程式），也是一種「平台」的概念，因為你可以在這個app平台上玩遊戲或是看影片、聊天、打電話等。

例：I sent my girlfriend a message on Facebook.

（我在臉書上傳了一則訊息給我女朋友。）

My classmate sent me a message on Twitter.

（我的同學在推特上傳了一則訊息給我。）

I paid for the beer on Line Pay in the convenient store.

（我在超商用Line Pay付款買了一個啤酒。）

My boss gave me an assignment on Line.

（我主管在Line上交辦了我一個工作。）

I watched a movie on the YouTube app.

（我在YouTube的手機應用程式上看了一部電影。）

另外，看電視看哪一個頻道也說on。例如：

I saw TVBS news on the channel 55.

（我在55頻道看TVBS新聞。）

I saw an interesting program on the Fox News (Channel).

（我在福斯新聞頻道上看了一個有趣的節目。）

I saw a documentary about lions on Discovery Channel.

（我在探索頻道上看了一則獅子的紀錄片。）

國家圖書館出版品預行編目資料

即選即用銀行英語會話／楊曜檜著. －－二
版.－－臺北市：五南圖書出版股份有限公
司, 2022.09
　面；　公分
ISBN 978-626-343-114-0（平裝附光碟片）

1.CST：英語　2.CST：銀行業　3.CST：會話

805.188　　　　　　　　　　111011564

1AG3

即選即用銀行英語會話

作　　　者 ― 楊曜檜(313.7)

發 行 人 ― 楊榮川

總 經 理 ― 楊士清

總 編 輯 ― 楊秀麗

副總編輯 ― 黃文瓊

責任編輯 ― 吳雨潔、黃懷萱

封面設計 ― 吳佳臻

出 版 者 ― 五南圖書出版股份有限公司

地　　　址：106台北市大安區和平東路二段339號4樓

電　　　話：(02)2705-5066　　傳　　真：(02)2706-6100

網　　　址：https://www.wunan.com.tw

電子郵件：wunan@wunan.com.tw

劃撥帳號：01068953

戶　　　名：五南圖書出版股份有限公司

法律顧問　林勝安律師事務所　林勝安律師

出版日期　2014年6月初版一刷
　　　　　2021年4月初版七刷
　　　　　2022年9月二版一刷

定　　　價　新臺幣530元